FORBIDDEN

A ROMANCE ANTHOLOGY

ABIGAIL DAVIES   YOLANDA OLSON

MICHELLE BROWN   C.L. MATTHEWS

J. M. WALKER   C.M. RADCLIFF

ALEXANDRA SILVA

ENFORCE HER

AUTHOR NOTE

This novella is a complete standalone, however, if you've read the **_Burned Duet_**, you would have met Jax briefly!

I hope you enjoy!

Abi xo

BLURB

My entire life was mapped out from the moment I took my first breath. For years I'd been shaped into the perfect enforcer for the motorcycle club.

We ran the state and controlled everything coming in and out. But the judge in town threatened that.
Bribes never failed...not even with him.

He was trying to make an example out of us, but he'd made a mistake. He'd shown one of his cards, a fatal flaw in his plan.

His daughter. Innocent.
Forbidden.
The opposite of my chosen taste.
But that didn't matter when it came to protecting the men who were my family.

The task was simple: use her to get to him. But I hadn't expected her touch to ignite a roaring fire inside of me.

I'd lived by a set of rules my entire life, but the most important one was to protect my family. No matter the cost.

CHAPTER ONE

HAISLEY

My stomach rolled and my nerves consumed every inch of my body with each step I took down the long hallway. The floors were marble, the walls a perfect white with portraits of my dad and his latest trophy wife, and the air had a biting cold to it. It was meant to be a home—our home—but it felt more like a museum than anything else.

I'd lived in this mansion since before I could remember. The older I got, the more my bedroom was moved farther and farther away from the main hub of the mansion, and now I was in the last room at the end of the hallway of the east wing. I actually preferred it like that. It meant no one would disturb me, at least, not often anyway.

Rules were followed in this house to a T, and not one person disobeyed them, least of all me. I'd once rebelled as a teen, but after taking a belt buckle to my back and receiving thirteen harsh lashings as punishment, I never did it again. I'd learned my lesson the first time, and bore the scars to prove it. Not that anyone had ever seen them —I'd never allowed anyone to get that close.

I halted at the top of the left stairwell and stared down into the grand foyer and the crystal chandelier polished to within an inch of its life. From the outside looking in, this mansion was the epitome of wealth. People were jealous of the mansion and immaculate gardens surrounding it from all sides. If only they knew it was more like a prison than a home—a prison my dad had created. He sent criminals to prison every day of his life as a judge, and I was sure it was why he ran our home the way he did—he brought his work home with him.

"Haisley? Is that you?" a soft voice muttered, a second later, heels clicking on the floor rang out as Sophia—wife number six—drifted out of the main dining room and to the bottom of the stairs. Her long red hair was curled to perfection, and her face was a masterpiece of makeup. It was only 8 am, and she was dressed as if she was about to attend a major event.

"Morning," I greeted. She was the best wife out of all of them. She didn't push me, didn't demand things of me. She just got on with her life with my dad, and left me to my own devices. I couldn't say the same for the other wives though.

Wife number three had been the worst. She'd been the wife married to my dad when I'd rebelled, and she'd taken great pleasure in my punishment, then tried to deal her own along with it by making me clean the mansion from top to bottom. She should have known she didn't have a say when it came to this house. That had been the final straw in her and my dad's marriage though, thank God. He lived by the saying "Do as I say; not as I do." There was no way he was going to let her gain any control in the house, so she'd been divorced and given a settlement, then three months later wife number four had appeared. She'd been better than the previous, but there was something dark and eerie about her and the way she barely spoke a word.

Sophia smiled up at me and pushed some hair behind her ear. "Your dad will be down any minute. We should head in and take our seats." Her words seemed normal, but I knew the hidden meaning behind them: Let's adhere to his demands so we can both go on with our day outside the house until we have to do the same thing again at dinner time.

I nodded in response and made my way down the stairs. My black jeans stretched over my legs as I took each step, and my T-shirt rode up and revealed a slither of my stomach. I yanked at it and cursed my stupid chest for growing yet again. I hadn't developed until I'd turned fifteen, but even then, it had been slow going. Now I was about to turn nineteen and they were *still* growing. I needed them to stop asap, because all my favorite T-shirts were starting to not fit.

Sophia smiled once again when I got to the bottom of the stairs, clasped her hands in front of her, then led us into the dining room. I'd been eating meals in there every day of my life, and my spot at the table hadn't changed in all those years. My dad at the head, his wife—whichever one it was at the time—on his right, and me on his left.

We both took our seats and waited patiently for my dad to come down, but after ten minutes and no other sounds in the house apart from the cook in the kitchen, he still hadn't appeared. My stomach grumbled as the time ticked by, and my leg bounced up and down underneath the table. I had my first class of the day at 10 am, and I couldn't be late for it. I'd only started college a month ago, and unlike most of the other students, I didn't live on campus—I wasn't allowed to live on campus.

"I'm sure he won't be much longer," Sophia said as I kept my gaze on the clock on the far wall. It was now nearing 8:30 am and my nerves were overtaking me for another reason. I couldn't be late, I hated being late and entering the classroom when everyone was already there. I'd be the center of attention, something I'd trained my entire life not to be.

Finally, quick footsteps neared, and then the white dining room door swung open. Dad appeared, all five foot seven of him. He may not have been the tallest man, but his presence was larger than anyone else's I'd ever met. He commanded a room when he was in it, and my body's instinct was to sit up straighter and pay attention to him.

"Good morning, William," Sophia greeted, already pouring him some fresh orange juice.

"Morning," he grunted back as he pulled out his seat. "Tell Maria I'm ready for my breakfast."

Sophia didn't reply, instead just scuttled off into the kitchen and appeared a minute later with Maria who was holding Dad's usual breakfast: two slices of bacon, a poached egg, and a slice of toast unbuttered. He'd eaten the same thing for years, just like I had. My plate was placed in front of me after Sophia's grapefruit, and I stared down at my scrambled eggs and toast, wondering why I also ate the same thing every morning. I hadn't changed it—I'd never thought to change it—but for some reason, I felt the urge to ask for something different.

"Maria?" Dad's head whipped around at the sound of my voice, and his dark-blue eyed gaze met mine. I'd spoken at the table, and I shouldn't have. Shit. What was I thinking? I should have just gone with the flow like I always did and asked Maria for something different for tomorrow once he'd left. "It doesn't matter," I whispered, picking up my fork and digging it into my eggs.

"Manners," Dad barked at me, and the single word was all I needed to know he wasn't happy with me, not that the look he'd given me hadn't already confirmed it too.

"Sorry," I murmured, keeping my gaze connected with my plate of food and nothing else. The air in the room seemed to cool even more than it already was, and I shivered. I should have put my jacket on, but I knew it wouldn't be acceptable at the dining table.

Silence ensued as we all ate, and as soon as Dad had finished, he pushed his chair back, stood, and walked out of the room without a single word said. Sophia leaned back in her chair and blew out a breath, and I felt exactly the same, but I knew better than to let my emotions come to the forefront. I had to keep them locked up inside, just like I always did.

I scooped up my last forkful of eggs, said, "I'll see you later," to Sophia, and exited the room. I ambled over to the cloakroom and grabbed my jacket and school bag, then walked out of the house, just in time to see Dad driving down the pebbled driveway and toward the main road. It would take him all of a minute to drive down there, but would take me ten to walk, and I didn't have the extra time this morning. So I pulled both straps of my backpack over my shoulders and sprinted. My breaths became heavier as I pumped my legs faster, and by the time I got to the end, I had to slow down to a walk so I could inhale a full breath.

Time was ticking by and I was making a plan for if I was late. I just wouldn't be able to go into the class; it was that simple. I'd have to miss it. There was no other choice because—

Tires squealed behind me, the smell of burning rubber singed my nostrils, and I spun around, my eyes wide. My heart now pumped a crazy beat in my chest for another reason: danger.

The side door of the van whipped open and three men jumped out, their faces covered with black masks while dark clothes adorned their bodies. I knew what was happening before they'd made the three steps to me, and deep down I knew I should have tried to run. I may not have been able to get away, but at least I would have tried. But something told me to keep my feet planted to the floor. Something told me to let them do whatever they were going to do. Something told me not to fight back.

So as hands grabbed me and a piece of cloth was pushed over my mouth and nose, I couldn't help but be thankful that I wouldn't be showing up late for my class. I wouldn't be showing up at all.

CHAPTER TWO

JAX

"She's normally left by now," Prospect said, keeping his eyes on the road to Judge Roopers house. He wasn't wrong, she normally had exited the house to go to college, but she never left before *he* did. His car was still sitting in his elaborate driveway according to the surveillance cameras our IT guy, Tech, had hacked. Which meant we hadn't missed her. We had to bide our time and be patient.

"He's getting in his car," I grunted, keeping my gaze fixated on the tablet. The four of us: me, Prospect, Tech, and Speed—had been sitting here for the last three hours, waiting for the right moment to complete our mission. I turned to stare out of the small window on the back of the van and watched his car zoom past us. The black metal gleamed in the early morning sunlight, and the sports engine roared and echoed around the upmarket neighborhood. It was only moments later that I spotted the girl sprinting down the driveway. She was running late, that much was clear, so she'd be even less on guard than she usually was. Not that she was very particular about keeping an eye on what was happening around her. I'd been following her for nearly two weeks, and not once had she taken a look around her environment to see who was about. She either didn't care, or didn't think she had to.

"Now," I ground out to Speed, our driver. He'd gotten his name because he'd been a professional bike racer as a teen and young adult. He never drove at the speed limit. He was a speed junkie, so was the perfect person to be our getaway driver.

He slammed his foot down and sped toward the girl as me, Prospect, and Tech got ready. We pulled the balaclavas over our faces and crouched near the sliding door. I threw my arm out as Speed squealed to a stop, then yanked the door open.

Tech and Prospect were out first, and I followed them. We each knew what our jobs were, and we were prepared to fight. She spun around, her eyes wide, but didn't make a move to run. If I really thought about it, I would have realized it wasn't the normal reaction you'd have when three men were running toward you, but I was caught up in the moment, intent on completing my mission and taking her for ransom.

Tech grabbed her and Prospect slammed the rag over her face. It only took seconds for her to go down and her body to go limp. I caught her, threw her over my shoulder, then jumped into the back of the van. It had all taken around eleven seconds until we were back on the road to the clubhouse with the answer to our problem.

Our VP, Torch, had been arrested on trumped up charges, and word from the higher ups in the police force had come down that they were intent on nailing him, even if it meant adding more charges, simply to show us who was boss around here—their words, not mine. We were one percenters. We lived by our own rules. Rules they didn't understand. They thought they could keep us in line, but they had no idea the extent we would go to in order to protect the family we had created in the MC.

I pulled my balaclava off my face and blew out a breath. The girl was sprawled out on the floor of the van, her light-brown hair covering half of her face. Her chest moved on each breath, and the rainbow on her T-shirt stretched with each upbeat. Who the hell wore a rainbow on a T-shirt?

"She's pretty," Prospect commented.

My nostrils flared as I slowly turned my head to face him. Speed was racing us back to the clubhouse, so we wouldn't be out in the open much longer. "She ain't for you, Prospect." He held his hands up in surrender and opened his mouth, but I didn't give him the chance to say anything. "You keep your damn hands off. She's our prisoner until we get what we need. Got it?"

"Got it," three voices replied. I may have been the enforcer of this club, but I was also the son of the President. They knew I'd take over one day which meant I was shown more respect. But it wasn't just because of that. I'd earned it over the years. I'd been around the club from the moment I took my first breath. I'd been a marine and still come home to the club to pick up right where I left off. I'd finished my prospecting term by the time I was seventeen, and had been officially patched in at eighteen. The club was my life—my everything. And I wasn't going to let these trumped up charges ruin some of what we had built.

She was the answer to everything. She was our get out of jail free card.

———

HAISLEY

My mouth was dry. Drier than it had ever been. I needed water STAT. I moved my head side to side then slowly opened my eyes. Darkness surrounded me. Grogginess weighed my body down. I was stiff in places I hadn't known I could be, but that wasn't the worst of it, it was the pins and needles in my hands that made me wince. I jerked my wrists to get rid of the feeling, but they wouldn't move. They wouldn't—

"Wouldn't do that if I was you," a gruff voice said, and a second later, a bright light flashed. I slammed my eyes closed and groaned as my eyeballs burned. "Oops, probably should have warned you about that." He laughed, the kind of laugh that had the hairs on the back of my neck standing on end.

"Where—" I cleared my throat and tried to gather some saliva to be able to talk, but reality was, I needed water. "Where am I?" Slowly, I opened my eyes back up, taking everything in around me. The air smelled musty, no windows as far as I could see in front of me and to the sides. Was this a basement? Was I tied to a...chair?

"It doesn't matter where you are," the deep voice said. He stepped forward, and I dipped my head back to take him all in. His dark hair was combed back and the sides shaved. Several tattoos ran from his scalp, over his neck, and down underneath the neckline of his T-shirt. But it was the leather vest that caught my attention. I knew who people like him were, and it had my pulse racing and my fight or flight instinct kicking in. "You're not gonna get anywhere doing that," he said, smirking down at me. The kind of smirk that had me wanting to fling an insult at him.

I jerked my wrists and legs once again, but it was no use. I was stuck on this stupid chair with no way to get out. It was something straight out of a gangster movie, and I was in the thick of it. What the hell was happening? Was I dreaming? Was all this a bad nightmare?

The guy crouched in front of me, and the musty smell of the basement was replaced with his musky cologne. "Do as you're told. Don't kick up a fuss, and you'll be out of here before you know it." I blinked and opened my mouth, but his hand whipped out. His fingers gripped the left side of my face and his thumb the right side, making it impossible to talk. "I didn't say you could talk, Haisley." He raised a brow, daring me to say something, but I knew when to keep my mouth shut. I'd been training for this my entire life, he just hadn't realized it yet.

"Good girl," he praised, and I was locked in a stare off with him. I wasn't sure if it was the lighting down here, or my imagination, but I could have sworn his eyes were so light they were almost white. He sneered, and I understood the words he'd spoken were the complete opposite to what he was actually saying. He tensed his hand on my face as one final warning, then let go. But he didn't move away. He stayed right in front of me, not moving a single inch. He was a predator, ready to pounce on his prey, I just wasn't sure whether that was me. And I wasn't sure why I liked the thought either.

CHAPTER THREE

JAX

"How did it go?" Dad asked from the head of the table. Ryder had been President of the Satan's Angels for nearly forty years. His dad had started this club way back when, and Dad had taken it over when he'd died taking three bullets to the chest on a run. Things had been more openly violent back then. Nowadays though, it was mostly about the game playing. Who could one up each other without anyone losing their lives, but it didn't mean there weren't casualties between wars with rival clubs. Right now we were in a peaceful stage of our club's life, but I had no illusion it would last much longer. There was always someone who had beef with you. It was just a matter of time before it showed up on your doorstep.

"Good. We got the package, now all we need is to send the message." I leaned back in my seat on the right side of the main table in the meeting room. Twelve head members of the club sat around it with me, and all other patched members around the sides of the room. The only people not inside were the prospects.

"Tech, ready the message and get it sent," Dad demanded.

It had only been ten hours since we'd taken Haisley hostage from outside her own house. And although her dad wouldn't have been worried enough to call the police, I had no doubt he was wondering where she was. She kept to a strict timetable and was home every day by 5 pm. Which meant she was now two hours past her home time. I'd known twelve year old girls have less of a curfew than she did. She was almost nineteen, in college, and yet she didn't act like it.

"On it," Tech replied, already typing away at his laptop. "We need a video of her to show she's still alive."

"Already done," I gritted out, sliding a memory card across the table to him. I was the one who had come up with this entire plan, and yet they were acting like I hadn't. It pissed me the hell off, but I knew we were all under stress. Torch had been gone for over a week now, and there was a huge hole left in his absence.

"Any other club business we need to discuss?" Dad asked, swiping his hand down his face. He was stressed out. Bags under his eyes. His hair sticking up in all directions. Torch wasn't only his Vice President, but his best friend. They'd fought in the marines together. They'd come up in the club together. Every part of their lives was intertwined. And it included their wives. My mom and Torch's wife had been sisters. Sisters who were closer than any two people ever were. Right up until the point my mom died from bone cancer. It had been ten years. Ten years since she'd walked the halls of this clubhouse, but her presence was felt every single day.

"Think that's it," I murmured. No one else was willing to say what Torch normally would. They didn't want to step on anyone's toes, but now wasn't the time to act like a bunch of goddamn pussies. We needed to get on with our mission and get Torch out as soon as we could. We needed to be on guard, more so than ever.

Dad banged the gavel down. "Meeting adjourned." Chairs scraped against the floor and the room emptied out within seconds. We'd all been on edge since Torch had been arrested, and now, finally, we had a small light shining at the end of a pitch-black tunnel. Prospect was already lining bottles of beers and spirits on the bar top in the main room, knowing we needed them. Tonight we would prepare for what was ahead. We'd gone into the plan with our eyes open, but we all knew it could take a turn for the worse and land us in hot fuckin' water.

It was a risk I was willing to take though. A risk we were all taking.

———

HAISLEY

I'd fallen asleep at some point. I wasn't sure whether it was still day or night thanks to the lack of natural light, but they've kept the main light on. It may have been to disorientate me, or to keep me awake. Either way, I was used to sleeping with the light on, so as soon as I felt tired, I'd slept for a little while.

It wasn't the pounding music from above me that woke me up though, but the icky feeling of being watched and the footsteps in the basement. I peeked one eye open, trying to take in what was around me, and that was when the murmuring started.

A guy paced in front of me, from one wall to the next.

He ran his hands through his hair and kept them there, I wondered if the way he was yanking was causing him pain. He seemed distressed, more distressed than I was and *I* was the one tied to a chair in the middle of this damp, dingy basement.

"Hi?" I whispered, figuring I had nothing to lose. They hadn't put anything in my mouth to stop me from talking, so I may as well use what I could.

He paused in his pacing, his back going ramrod straight, and slowly, oh so slowly, he turned his head to face me. He looked similar to the guy with the cologne from earlier, but smaller, thinner, and more haunted. He blinked at me and dropped his hands from his head. "Hi," he said back, his gruff voice small.

I wasn't sure what I should have said. I hadn't expected him to reply to me, but my instincts were kicking in. "Are you okay?" It should have been something he said to me, but I felt compelled to ask. My gut told me to be me; not a version of me they expected. I'd always tried to help the people around me, no matter what situation I or they were in.

"I can't sleep," he murmured, and his eyes widened at his confession. Maybe he hadn't expected to answer me either.

"Why?" It was a simple question, but I knew the answer was never easy. People couldn't sleep for various reasons, but with the tension in his body and his frantic movements, I had no doubt his was haunting. There was a darkness to him, but more than that, a bleeding pain for everyone to see. It may not have been physical, but his expression spoke a thousand words.

"I can hear them." I swallowed at his words and jerked as he lunged forward but stopped a foot away from me. "Every time I close my eyes, I hear their screams." He slammed his hands over his ears and shook his head side to side, almost as if he was trying to get rid of them. "The bullets, the explosions, I can't stop hearing them." A lump built in my throat at his words, and I wanted nothing more than to help him. I wanted to help one of the people who were keeping me captive, the irony wasn't lost on me, but...he was in pain. The kind of pain not many of us ever experienced.

"Why were they screaming?" I asked, keeping my voice low and calm, but my heart was beating so hard I was afraid it would escape my chest.

He lowered his hands and stared down at me. "We were at base camp and they attacked us." *Base camp.* That meant he was in the army, right? "We'd been patrolling the local villages all day and had come back to get food and sleep. And then they started their strike." He pulled in a deep breath. "We weren't prepared. We hadn't known they were so close." Tears streamed down his cheeks, and I knew he was back there. He wasn't in this basement with me anymore, he was reliving what had happened. How many times had he done that? How many times had he played it over and over in his head?

It had been nearly six years since my dad had taken a belt to my back, and I remembered it like it had happened yesterday.

"What's your name?" I asked, trying to distract him. It had always worked for me. Pretend like it wasn't happening and then deal with it a little at a time when you were in the right frame of mind.

"Al." He tilted his head at me as I winced from the rope binding my wrists together. My shoulders ached so bad, but I didn't want to complain. I was still alive, and I'd

22

been given some water since I'd woken up the first time. "You hurting?" he asked, and gone was the pain from his eyes, and in its place a clear determination.

"A little," I whispered. I didn't complain, I never complained. "I'll be fine," I continued.

"I hate this," he gritted out, then darted behind me. Goosebumps prickled over my skin at how quick he moved, but a second later, the rope was gone, and my arms were free. I groaned from the sensation and moved my hands into my lap, rubbing at my wrists. Red marks encased the soft skin, but I couldn't focus on that right now.

"Thank you."

"Welcome." He huffed out a breath then scraping echoed around the room. I jerked at the noise and raised my brows when he reappeared in front of me, this time with a crate which he placed a couple of feet away and sat on top of. "It wasn't my idea to do this to you." His gaze darted around the room. "We won't hurt you. We just... we need you to help the MC."

I frowned. "How can I help?" I chuckled at the absurdity of it. "I'm a college student, a—"

"The daughter of the judge our VP will be presented to in a couple of days," Al interrupted. I didn't need him to expand on it, because I'd read between the lines. I was bait. I was the thing they were holding to get my dad to do what they wanted him to. It was on the tip of my tongue to tell them using me was useless. My dad only cared about one thing: his job. Oh, and of course his arm candy to keep up appearances. But if I told them that, I wouldn't be of any use to them. And there was no telling what they would do then. So I kept my mouth shut.

"Al?" a voice called followed by the squeak of a door.

The music got louder and then footsteps pounded on the stairs to the left. The door slammed shut, the music quieted, and the atmosphere in the room changed. "You down here?"

"Yeah," Al responded, not looking away from me, but I couldn't keep my gaze off the man sauntering down the wooden, creaky stairs. It was the same man from earlier— the one with the white eyes.

"You shouldn't be down here, lil' bro," the man ground out as he made it to the bottom of the stairs. His gaze flicked over me and back again, then down to my lap. "You untied her? Fuck sake, Al."

"What?" Al turned in his seat to face him. "She looked like she was in pain, Jax."

"Jesus Christ." The guy ran his hand through his hair, and I tilted my head to the side. His name suited him. "Go back upstairs. If Dad finds out you've been down here he'll flip his top."

"I'm not a fuckin' kid," Al whipped back, but he stood and made his way over to Jax. "You treat me like I'm a damn basket case."

"We don't—"

"You do." He shoulder barged Jax, but Jax didn't move an inch from the force. "I hate you," Al murmured, walking past him and up the stairs. I wasn't sure if I was meant to see the reaction on Jax's face, so I turned away, giving him privacy.

The air in the room swirled and my breaths came faster the longer the silence ensued. My skin burned from his gaze and I pushed my shoulders back, preparing for whatever he would do next. I knew he was watching me, seeing what my next move would be. But I didn't have a move planned. Maybe they thought I was desperate to go home, but if I was honest, I was kind of relieved to be out of the house and have a valid reason other than to go to college.

His footsteps echoed across the room as he moved closer, and I didn't want to admit I was excited to smell his cologne again. He was keeping me captive and yet I was drawn to him. Drawn to his eyes. Which was why I couldn't stop myself from looking up at him.

Our stare met, and I swallowed from the intensity. He was trying to keep his emotions locked down, but whatever just happened had affected him more than he probably liked to admit.

"I won't do anything," I whispered, and my voice brought him out of his trance.

"Shut the fuck up," he gritted out. He grabbed my wrists, his grip hard and unyielding, then picked the discarded rope up off the floor next to me.

I pulled in a breath, wanting to say more, but I knew it wouldn't do me any good. I was here for a reason, a purpose, for them to get what they wanted. Then they'd let me go. If I believed what Al said, then no harm would come to me, but I couldn't help wonder if it was the truth.

"I hope you get what you need," I murmured, and winced as he wrapped the rope around each of my wrists, tying several knots. He ignored me, not gracing me with an answer, so I continued, "I'm sure you think this will work but—"

"I told you to shut the fuck up," Jax growled, and my brow raised. He tied a final knot and let go of my wrists. "Do as you're fuckin' told." His gaze met mine, and I nodded to let him know I understood. I'd been doing as I was told my entire life, so this wouldn't be hard for me to do. He placed his hand around my jaw, keeping my face in place, and moved closer to me. His breath fanned across my skin and I shivered from the sensation. "And don't talk to my brother again." He squeezed his fingers and my eyes fluttered closed. There was no doubt he had strength and power. "You hear me?"

My eyes sprung open and I whispered, "I hear you."

He stared for several more seconds, his impossibly light eyes searching mine for some kind of answer. Once he'd seen what he needed to, he let me go, forcing my head back a little, then sauntered away from me. The door opened, music became louder, and then it shut, the scraping of the lock deafening.

I was alone again. Just like I always was.

CHAPTER FOUR

JAX

The clubhouse was so quiet you could hear a pin drop. The only time it was ever like this was after we had a blow out party the night before. Usually, I would have slept in until after lunch and then rolled out of bed and gone and tinkered with my bike for a while. But there was something about this particular morning that had me on edge. A heaviness in the pit of my stomach that caused me to roll out of bed at 7 am and go get some food out of the kitchen.

But it wasn't food for me. It was food for *her*.

I shouldn't have given a flying fuck if the girl hadn't eaten since yesterday morning when I'd sent one of the guys to take her some breakfast. But I did. Fuck. I *did* care if she'd eaten. I didn't want to do anything but the bare minimum. She was here to fulfill a purpose, to do the job we needed her to. The plan wasn't to hurt—it was never to hurt her—just to keep her until her dad had done what we'd demanded.

Which was why I'd stayed away from her yesterday. I didn't want to see her, not after catching Al down there talking to her. He'd undone her ropes which meant *I* was the one that had to redo them. I was the bad guy. Not him. Not anyone else in the MC. Only me. And I felt like a bastard for it. So instead of facing it head on, I'd left it to the prospects and Al to make sure she was watered and fed.

But now I was here, sneaking around before anyone else was up to bring her something to eat. I'd tried to keep myself occupied yesterday with cleaning my bike then taking apart the engine on one I was trying to fix up. I'd even gone over to Asher's tattoo shop to kill a couple of hours. But still, I hadn't been able to stop thinking about the girl we'd taken.

Fuck. She was just a girl.

I shook the thoughts from my head and unlocked the door to the basement. All I had to do was take the food in, let her eat, then leave again. That would be all she'd need today apart from a prospect giving her water.

My stomach rolled as I stepped through the door and closed it behind me. I had no goddamn idea what was going on, and I didn't want to either. I had a job to do. A mission to complete. That was all there was to it. I couldn't waste time thinking about the way my body and mind were reacting at the thought of seeing her. She was a meek girl, the total opposite to Reign from the strip club we owned.

Reign was my favorite stripper; the one I went to exclusively when I needed to get balls deep in some pussy. She was tall, thin, and had dark-brown hair so shiny you could practically use it as a goddamn mirror. Where Reign was alluring, Haisley was petite and... weird. But fuck me, I couldn't stop thinking about her weird. The way she'd reacted to us—to me. Fuck. I needed to stop.

I ground my teeth together as I slowly moved down the stairs. I didn't know what I expected when I got down there, but it wasn't her curled up on a bed in the corner. What in the actual fuck was going on? Who had untied her? And who had brought a mattress down here for her? That wasn't the fuckin' plan. We weren't a goddamn hotel.

"Get up," I barked, pushing the toe of my steel-toe boot into her thigh. She was still wearing the same clothes she had been two days ago when we'd taken her. I swore that fuckin' rainbow on her T-shirt was haunting me.

"Sorry. Sorry," she blurted out and darted into a sitting position. Her T-shirt was askew, showing a sliver of the pale skin on her stomach. Another difference she had from Reign. Reign never went anywhere without her tan. Haisley rubbed at her eyes and I had to contain my grin at how her hair was sticking up on one side. She looked cute and—no, fuck. She didn't look cute. "I'm awake. I'm...ah, crap. I forgot I was still here." Her shoulders drooped and she inhaled a deep breath. It wasn't out of fright that she did that though, more like...relief? I tilted my head and looked at her, really fuckin' looked at her. Not once had she screamed for us to let her go. Not once had she fought us to not keep her here.

I frowned. Why wasn't she fighting? Why wasn't she desperate to leave?

"Jax?" she whispered, and my name coming out of her mouth had my pulse racing. I didn't like it. I hated how it sounded—how it made me feel.

"Don't call me that," I ground out, dropping the tray of food on the floor next to her. The toasted bread bounced and teetered on the edge, but eventually stayed in place.

"I...isn't that your name?" She was confused, and rightly so. What *did* I expect her to call me? I had no goddamn idea, but I couldn't bear hearing my name with her voice. It was soft...*too* soft. It reminded me of my mom.

I jerked back, my entire body feeling like it was on fire. "I brought you some food. Eat it and shut up." I spun around, not waiting to see if she would say anything else. I had to get away from her. I had to get out of here. And there was only one place which would get my mind off of her: *Pink Feather*, the strip joint. Reign would take my mind off of this—off her. She knew what I liked. She was simple. Effortless. *Easy.* The total opposite of Haisley.

HAISLEY

It hadn't taken me long to eat the two slices of toast and banana that Jax brought me this morning. Mere minutes. And then I had the rest of the day to do...nothing. Boredom was the enemy. An enemy I never thought I'd have. I'd always kept my mind occupied on school work or painting in my mom's old studio. That was probably the only thing I missed about being at the mansion.

I remembered times me and my mom would spend entire days in there, painting and laughing. She'd open the balcony doors and we'd eat sandwiches and drink iced tea. It was a happier time, one which was so faint of a memory I had to concentrate really hard to remember. It was the only wife my dad hadn't divorced, but he'd still lost her, just like with every woman who came after her. He never stepped foot in her studio, so I'd claimed it as my own. My little slice of heaven.

Huffing out a breath, I sat on the edge of the old mattress. Al had gotten permission from the President of the club to untie me and give me a bed yesterday, so at least I could stretch out and be comfortable. But the problem was, with me being able to walk around the entire basement, it also meant no one was coming inside either.

I was lonely. More lonely than I had ever been.

I'd found a stone on the floor at some stage in the day —or was it night—and scraped it over the walls, trying to use it as chalk to draw a sun. But it barely made a mark, no matter how hard I tried. I was about to give up and try to get some sleep, then the sound of the lock on the basement door pulling aside sounded out. I jumped up, eager to see who it was. I wouldn't deny that I was hoping it would be Jax again, but anyone was better than no one at this stage.

A few stairs creaked under the person's weight, then Al's face appeared. He placed his finger over his lips which were pulled up into a huge grin, and waved his hand toward me. "Quick, they're all out and the prospect has fallen asleep."

I hesitated, gnawing on my bottom lip. Was he telling me to come out of the basement? "I...what are you doing?"

"Giving you some fresh air." His gaze darted to the pot they'd given me in the corner. "And the opportunity to use a proper bathroom."

My eyes widened at the thought of not having to crouch over the pot. But was it safe to leave here? I had no idea, but I couldn't miss the chance to get out of these four walls, even if it was only for a little while. I darted forward, but had to make sure this wasn't a prank he was pulling on me. "Really?"

"Yes, really." Al grabbed my hand and pulled me up the stairs. "Come on, let's go watch the stars and pee in real toilets!"

I laughed at his words, feeling more carefree than I ever had before. The darkness was still there in his eyes, the pain still a weight on his shoulders, but he was trying to ignore it. Trying to replace it with something else, and I was all for helping him with that. He may have been part of this entire plan, but I knew if he could, he'd set me free. I understood what they were doing, I really did. It just sucked it had to be me stuck down there all alone.

We moved through the basement door and into a hallway; the air was much clearer up here than down in the basement. Although there was a tinge of oil and leather too, a smell I'd never experienced but found comforting.

"You can use the bathroom in my room," Al said, leading me down the hallway and to one of the middle doors. He pushed it open, revealed a room complete with basic furniture and a huge bed in the middle. He pointed to a door in the room, and waited near the main door while I rushed forward.

It only took a minute to do my business and to wash my hands, though I kept my gaze off the mirror above the sink. I didn't want to see my face. I didn't want to be reminded of the life they'd snatched me from. I wanted to live in the moment, even if that moment was one I wasn't meant to be enjoying.

"Where to now?" I asked, pulling my lips up into a smile at Al.

"Come on." He grabbed hold of my wrist this time

and led me through the building. One room had loads of sofas and a pool table, another had a seating area and kitchen, and finally, he took me up a set of side stairs, to a lone door. He turned back, flashed me a wink, then opened the door, revealing the night sky.

Had I been in the basement all day? Had that many hours passed by since Jax had brought my breakfast to me? My stomach rumbled at the thought, and I clutched it, hoping Al didn't hear.

"I come up here all the time," Al murmured. He moved to the middle of the roof and my mouth dropped open at the view. You could see the entire city from up here, but more importantly, the stars shone so bright you could make out the constellations.

"Wow," I whispered, in awe of the beauty surrounding me.

"I know, right?" Al sat down on one of the makeshift chairs—another crate—and patted the one next to him. "Come sit and watch."

My legs burned as I moved over to him, and I winced. My body needed more food and water than they were providing, but I didn't want to moan about it. It wouldn't be long before I was out of here—I hoped. Or did I hope? I wasn't sure what I felt any more.

"It's beautiful," I told Al, staring up at the sky. The wind whipped across my face, and I closed my eyes at the sensation. It had been days since I felt it whispering across my skin, and yet I thought I missed that more than anything else.

We sat there, side by side, watching the stars in silence. We didn't need words to fill the time. We didn't need anything else. We just needed the quiet and the night sky. I'd never felt so at peace, so when the roar of motorbikes rang through the air, getting closer to where we were, my heart lept in my chest.

"Fuck," Al spat, shooting up and knocking the crate over. He pulled something out of his front jean pocket and it lit up the area we stood in. His cell. He had a cell. And I hadn't thought once about where mine was. "They're back already." He stared at me in horror. "We've been out here three hours."

Had that much time really gone by? It felt like minutes, seconds even. Not hours.

"Can you sneak me back in so you don't get into trouble?"

Al shook his head. "No, they'll all be in the main part of the building and that's the only way in from the roof." He started to pace. "Shit. Fuck. Shit."

"It's okay," I murmured, holding my hands up. "We can work—"

"It's not okay!" he roared, and for the first time since I'd been here, I was genuinely scared. His eyes shuttered, showing no emotion. "Dad warned me about what would happen if I crossed boundaries." He muttered something else, but I couldn't understand him. I couldn't decipher what he was saying.

"Al," I whispered, backing away from him. He was stuck inside his own head, trapped, a prisoner in his own mind. "It's okay. Let's just go back inside and—"

"It's your fault!" he shouted, lunging for me. He grabbed my wrists much like he had earlier, only this time his grip was so much harder. He pinched my skin, causing my pulse to throb where he was holding me.

"Please, Al, you're hurting me." He didn't answer me, instead he just yanked me over to the door, swung it open, and practically ran down the stairs. My leg caught on a protruding nail and scraped through my jeans and skin. I howled at the stinging pain, but still he didn't acknowledge me. He kept on going, through the main part of the clubhouse and into the room with the sofas and pool table. Men were gathered in crowds and I tried to keep my mouth closed and my eyes on anything but them, but I was panicking. "Al, let go. Ow. Stop."

He finally halted and turned to face me. His pupils were so large I couldn't even see the color to his eyes any longer. I didn't know what he was going to do, what he was going to say, but a voice demanded, "Let her go." I'd never heard the voice before, but I knew as soon as it spoke that this was the authority here. This was the president, and as I turned to face the sound, I saw the patch on the front of his vest, and his unyielding face.

"She needs to be dealt with," Al ground out, and my head spun. How had he gone from nice and gentle to this in the matter of moments? This wasn't the Al who had been coming to talk to me. This wasn't the Al who had dragged a mattress into the basement and untied me from the chair. This was a completely new Al. An Al I didn't know. An Al I should have known was there.

These weren't gentle men. These weren't men who you wanted to spend your time with. And yet, I'd let myself believe I was safe here.

I wasn't safe here.

I'd never been safe here.

I'd lulled myself into a false sense of security.

"Go get Jax," the new voice told someone, and they rushed out of the room. "Come on, Son, let her go and we can go have a drink. Maybe even go on a ride."

"Can't," Al croaked out, his grip getting even tighter. "I made a mistake. I have to fix it."

"You don't," another voice said, and I recognized this one. *Jax.* "Let her go, bro. Come on. It's all good. I was going to take her out of there for an hour today anyway." Jax's gaze flicked to mine, and his light eyes tried to tell me something. It wasn't just the lighting in the basement, his eyes were really that light. A cross between a light-gray and ice blue. They were mesmerizing, and right now were drumming something into me I didn't understand.

I winced again at the grip Al had on me and moved my leg up and down, trying to see where the screw had caught me. Blood dripped over my jeans and I wobbled. I wasn't good with blood. I hadn't been since the day my dad had ripped my skin open with the belt buckle.

"Whoa." Jax darted forward, his hands grasping onto my hips and keeping me upright. His front met my back so I leaned all of my weight into him, needing something to keep me upright. "Stay with me, Hais," he whispered in my ear, and all I could do was nod in response. "I got her now, bro." Jax's voice was louder, clearly not talking to me. "I'll take her back down there."

Al shook his head. "I'll do it."

"Nah," Jax said, his tone easy. "You've had her for long enough. About time you took a break, huh?"

Al stared at me, but he wasn't really looking. He was seeing through me. "I..." I waited with bated breath, hopeful Jax had managed to talk him down, and as soon as his hands let go of my wrists, I rushed behind Jax to put him between me and Al. I gripped onto his leather vest and a growl vibrated from him, but I didn't let go.

His arm maneuvered behind him and he wrapped it around me, keeping me peeled to his back as he side-stepped us out of Al's view. The President's voice rang out and I heard him mention going on a ride, but anything after that was useless to my ears because I was too focused on getting away from the situation.

We moved out of the room, and as soon as we were in the hallway, Jax moved me to his side but kept his arm around my waist. He pulled open the third door on the left, walked us inside, then shut the door behind us. The click of a light switching on sounded out, and I turned to face Jax. His head was pressed against the wooden door, his shoulders slumped.

"I'm sorry," I whispered, staring down at my wrists. The faded marks from the rope had all but disappeared thanks to Al's grip, but in their place was bruising coming to the surface almost immediately.

"There's a blanket on the end of the bed. Use that and sleep on the sofa." His voice was rough and raw. "I'll lock you in. Don't answer the door to anyone." He lifted his head off the door, slowly turned to face me, and asked, "Got it?"

"I...I got it."

"Good." His gaze drifted over my body and to my leg. "First aid kit is in my bedside table. Don't try and escape. We got dogs guarding outside and they'll rip you to shreds." My eyes widened at his words, and my hand fluttered to my throat. Were there really dogs out there that did that to people? Or was he just trying to scare me? Either way, it worked. "I'll be back." He unlocked the door, yanked it open, then left without another word, leaving me in this room, all alone once again.

CHAPTER FIVE

HAISLEY

Sleep came better than it ever had. It wasn't a particularly comfortable sofa, and the blanket was thin, but it was being in this room that calmed me. There was something about it that allowed me to let my guard down, even after everything that had happened with Al. Maybe it was because it was Jax's room. Or maybe it was because it was a change to the dark, damp basement I'd been kept in up until now.

I'd patched up the cut on my leg the best I could without taking my jeans off, but if I was honest, I didn't have the first clue how to do it. I'd never been in a situation where there wasn't someone there I couldn't rely on to help me figure it out. If it wasn't the staff at school and college, then it was Maria, the cook, or Pat, the house-keeper. For the first time in my life, I was truly on my own, having to fend for myself.

There was a power to having no one to rely on, and I wanted more of it. I wanted more independence—to live my life the way I wanted and not the way I'd been commanded to. But I knew as soon as I was let go from here, I wouldn't have it. I may have been kept here against my will, but my home was also a prison.

The creak of the door opening had me staying deathly still. I listened intently as someone locked the door then moved around the room. They were trying to be quiet, but they weren't very good at it. It was weird all of a sudden having access to the time and knowing it had been four hours since Jax had locked me in here. It seemed longer somehow.

The person moved closer to me, and the unmistakable scent of Jax's cologne drifted over me. I swallowed, keeping my eyes closed, and tried not to move as he lifted the blanket. "Fuck," he murmured, and a second later, his hand grasped my shoulder gently and shook. "Haisley? You awake?"

Did I answer him? Or did I pretend to be asleep? The choice was taken away from me when his finger poked at the measly dressing I'd tied around my jeans. "Ow. That hurts." My eyes sprung open, my gaze meeting his immediately. Why the heck would he do that?

"Thought you were awake."

I narrowed my eyes at him. "No, you didn't."

He smirked, the same smirk he'd given me days ago, only this time I didn't want it to disappear. "I did. You were holding your breath." He raised a brow. "If you were sleeping, you'd be, you know, *breathing*."

He was right, but that didn't mean I was going to tell him that. "Whatever."

His expression turned serious, more like the Jax I'd seen more of. "You haven't cleaned your cut properly. It'll get infected." I bit down on my bottom lip, not wanting to answer him. It wasn't like I could tell him the truth. He'd judge me, just like everyone judged him and the leather he wore.

"I'll be fine."

"That right?" He crouched next to me, his face so close to mine I could feel each of his breaths. "What did you cut it on?"

I turned my head to look away from him as I murmured, "A nail, I think."

"Then we definitely need to treat it properly. No one has cleaned up there in years." He stood, but I didn't turn to see what he was doing, not until the creak of another door opened and more light basked into the room. A moment later, the telltale sign of running water sounded out, and my stomach rolled. Was he about to let me wash? Because God knows I stunk. "Go get in the shower and I'll clean your cut up."

I sat up slowly, trying to work out why he was acting like this, and couldn't help blurting, "Why?"

He paused in front of a closet, a towel in his hand. "Why what?"

"Why are you helping me?" I stood too, not wanting to be at a height disadvantage, but he still towered over me. I was small, taking after my mom, but in that moment I wished I was at least six feet and not five feet dead on. "You have no reason to help me. Just throw me back down the basement and be done with me." I crossed my arms over my chest, feeling my blood boil. I'd only ever been angry a few times in my life, the kind of anger that encompassed every fiber of your being. And right now, I was angry with him. Angry at the situation I was in. Angry at the whole damn world.

He prowled toward me. The temperature in the room soared. Every hair on my body stood on end, warning me of the danger he was. "I'm only gonna say this once, Haisley. Get. Your. Ass. In. The. Goddamn. Shower. Now." Part of me wanted to refuse, to fight back for once, but the bigger part of me knew I wasn't going to disobey him. My shoulders drooped and I looked down at my feet as I shuffled forward. I didn't need to say anything for him to know I was going to do as I was told, he could see it —feel it.

I took the towel from his outstretched hand as I walked past and shut the bathroom door behind me. Steam filled the room, and the mirror fogged up, refusing to let me look at myself. I dropped my dirty clothes on the white tiled floor, then stepped into the shower, moaning as the water washed over every inch of my skin. It was a welcome relief, one I hadn't known I'd needed.

I just stood there for a minute, basking in the warmth surrounding me, then finally washed my hair and skin with what was on the shelf beside me. And it was as the scent of the bodywash hit my nostrils I realized it wasn't cologne I could smell on Jax, but this. So I lathered it up, using more than was probably necessary, then rinsed it off.

A knock ricocheted through the bathroom, followed up with, "Hurry up!"

"Coming!" I shouted back then switched the shower off. I wrapped the towel around my chest, and just as I was about to exit the bathroom, spotted a toothbrush on the side of the sink. It was still in its wrapper, so I wondered if Jax had put this out for me. Why would he have done that? None of this made any sense. He'd kept me in his basement for two and a half days, but now he was letting me shower *and* brush my teeth?

I shrugged, figuring there was no point in me turning

down the offer, then loaded toothpaste onto the bristles and sighed as the minty freshness took over my mouth. I didn't think I'd ever felt as clean as I had when I finally opened the bathroom door to a waiting Jax.

He sat on the edge of his bed, staring down at the first aid kit in his hands, then slowly looked up at me. His light eyes had darkened a shade, and his pupils dilated. "Come and sit down so I can clean the cut," his rough voice demanded. There was an edge to it I hadn't heard before. An edge that told me to do as he said and not talk back.

"Okay." I swallowed and took three steps toward him. "I...I don't have clean clothes—"

"You can wear this," he said, handing me a T-shirt. "I'll make sure your clothes are washed and dried overnight."

"I...thank you." I gripped the T-shirt in one hand and the towel wrapped around my body with the other.

Jax placed the first aid kit on the bedside table and slowly moved his hand toward me. His fingertips whispered over my skin as he pushed the edge of my towel aside, showing my thigh and the cut. "Shouldn't need stitches," he murmured, but I wasn't sure if he was talking to me, or himself. He turned and grabbed some gauze, poured something onto it, then pressed it against the cut.

"Holy shit," I breathed out. It stung, worse than the actual nail scraping my skin had.

"Sorry," Jax whispered, and my eyes widened at the solo word. Was he apologizing? It seemed so...unlike him.

"It's...fine." I looked away, preferring not to watch him.

It only took a minute or so for him to pat my leg and announce, "You're done."

"Thank you." I stood and pushed my leg out a little to

see the large Band-Aid he'd applied, causing my wet hair to move aside and over my shoulder.

"What the fuck is that?" His thunderous voice had me standing up straight and twirling on the spot. I backed away a step at the expression on his face and his flared nostrils. "Haisley." He stood slowly, like a tiger preparing to lunge at its next meal. "What the fuck is that on your back?"

"Huh?" I backed away another step. "Nothing. Just some old—"

He laughed, full on laughed at me. But it wasn't funny in the slightest, he was being condescending, and I hated it. "Nah, sugar. I don't think it is nothing." He planted his hands on his hips. "Turn the hell around and let me see."

"I..." I pulled the towel tighter around me. "No," I whispered. It came out more like a question than an answer.

"Yes," he growled, taking a step toward me. "You either turn around and let me see or I'll tie you to my fuckin' bed so you don't have a choice." He raised his brow. "Either way, Hais, you're gonna show me." It was the way he said Hais which had me lowering my guard. No one had ever given me a nickname, yet it slipped so freely from his lips, as if he'd been saying it all of his life.

"I don't want you to," I confessed. "I've...no one has ever seen them."

He shrugged. "Guess I'll be the first then, huh?"

I stared at him, really stared at him, and tried to figure out if I could trust him. He'd taken me from outside my home, kept me locked in a basement, only fed me the essentials, and now he wanted to see my scars? The one thing in this world that was mine, and only mine.

But did it really matter if he saw them? In the grand scheme of things, it wasn't like he could do anything about it. Wasn't like he cared to. So instead of over-thinking it, I turned around and dropped my towel to the floor.

He wanted to see them, so I'd show him the entirety. I'd let him view the pain etched into my skin, but that was as far as it would go. Once he'd had his fill, I'd get dressed and demand to go back to the basement. At least there I was alone. At least there it was peaceful. At least there, I wouldn't get—

"Who did this to you?" he asked, his voice low but rough. His fingertip trailed over the marred skin, and I shivered from the contact. He continued all the way down to the middle of my back then back up again. If you looked really carefully, you could make out the belt buckle shape as well as the strap.

"Does it matter?" I asked. I wasn't willing to tell him how or why I got them. He wanted to see them, but it didn't mean I had to tell him the story behind the marks. He wasn't owed an explanation.

"Not really," he growled, and his hand grasped my naked waist. "Still makes me want to kill whoever did it." His front met my back, the rough material of his clothes drifting across my skin.

"Why?" I asked. With my back to him I felt empow-ered, like I could say anything I wanted to. "I'm just a thing to get you want you want. I'm not a person, not to you."

His hand flattened on my stomach, his fingers span-ning so wide he almost touched my— "Never said that, sugar." His lips met my ear, each of his breaths fanning across the sensitive skin of my neck. "I'm just tryin' to do what is right. Don't mean I fuckin' enjoy it." He paused and placed a gentle kiss under my ear. "But this...you naked in my room?" He whistled, yanked me farther back, and pressed his erection into my back. "This I damn well enjoy."

"What are you doing?" I choked out. My skin flashed cold then hot, and I squeezed my legs together, trying to ease the ache between them.

"You want me to stop?" he asked, following it up with another kiss to my neck. I wasn't sure what to say, so I stayed silent. "You only gotta say the word, and I will." I believed him. Believed each and every one of his words. But the truth was, he made me feel alive. He made electricity shoot through my veins. He made me feel...sexy.

"I don't want you to stop," I managed to get out, and as soon as I'd spoken the words, his hand lowered on my stomach. I was fascinated watching as his long fingers dipped between my legs, but it was the way he flicked my clit with his thumb while simultaneously pushing a finger inside me that had me losing my balance. But he was there, ready to steady me. He banded his arm across my stomach and up to my chest then tweaked one of my nipples.

"Oh God."

"Just me, sugar." His tongue slicked across my neck then a moment later he spun me around, bringing me face to face with him. He didn't give me the chance to react, he simply picked me up and threw me down on the bed like I weighed nothing.

I'd never been with anyone like him. Never experienced a man so...rough yet refined. He was the epitome of biker, and damn if I didn't want everything he had to offer right then. He stood at the side of the bed, staring down at me while slowly pulling his T-shirt over his head. His abs were so defined I wondered if he spent hours in the gym like the athletes at school.

"Like what you see?" he asked, and I nodded, not scared to be honest. He was perfection with his tensed muscles and tattooed art work, but it was the marine tattoo on his bicep that caught my attention.

"What's that?" I asked, pointing at it. He glanced down, shrugged, then shucked his jeans off, revealing the rest of his body to me. It was a distraction, one I had no choice but to accept. He was huge, bigger than I'd ever seen before, not that I'd seen many...cocks. My one and only time had been with one of the staff's sons who had come home for summer break last year. And his had *not* looked like that.

"You ready?"

"Huh?" I stared up at him, wondering what he was doing as he crouched down. He gripped onto my thighs, pulled me to the edge of the bed, and buried his face between my legs. "Oh....ohhh." My eyes widened then slammed closed as he sucked on my clit, and I couldn't stop my knee-jerk reaction to push my fingers through his hair.

He pulled his face away, looked up at me, and growled, "That's it, Hais. Yank on it." He ran his tongue over his lips. "Show me how much you want me to suck this pussy dry."

His dirty words were turning me on even more, so I pushed his face back down, needing more of him right there. He pushed a finger inside me, licking me like a man who'd never get the opportunity to ever again. My back bowed off the bed, tingling started down low, and I shouted out, "I'm close, Jax. So damn close."

He grunted in response, pulled his finger out, and grasped onto my ass cheeks, digging his fingers in so hard I was sure he'd leave bruises. But this time they were bruises I wanted. This time they spoke of something good.

Jax pulled my entire clit into his mouth, sucked on it, then let it go, scraping his teeth gently across it, and that was all I needed to explode. I went off like an elaborate firework display, huge, impactful, and loud. I thought he'd stop once my orgasm started, but he continued, eeking it out for as long as he could. Then finally, *finally*, he stopped and crawled on top of me. "That was the best damn thing I think I've ever seen."

I opened my eyes, feeling the burn on my cheeks from the blush now covering what I was guessing was most of my body. I wasn't sure what I'd expected to see on his face, but it definitely wasn't the genuine smile I witnessed.

"We can stop there," he murmured, pushing some hair out of my face. "Or I can fuck you." He shrugged. "Totally up to you, sugar."

Slowly, I lifted my hand and placed it on his cheek. He was already so close to being inside me. I'd let him see parts of me no one else ever had, so there was no way I was going to fall at this last hurdle. "Fuck me," I whispered. "Fuck me so I can still feel you next week."

His nostrils flared at my words and he stared down at me. His gaze didn't move off mine, searching for the truth, but he wouldn't find any deceit in my eyes. I'd be gone soon so I'd take a glimpse of him while I could, because I had no doubt once I was gone, he wouldn't look back. I'd just be another memory to him, like he would be for me.

Jax leaned down, pressing a soft kiss to my lips, and I

returned it. It was so gentle and loving, a complete contra-
diction to how he was treating my body. "You sure?"

"Surer than anything," I assured him, and at my
response, he thrust inside me, widening my walls. I wasn't
sure I'd ever be the same after this, but I didn't want to be.
Jax had left his mark on me, it just didn't hurt as bad as
the others did.

CHAPTER SIX

JAX

I sat on the edge of the bed, staring at Haisley, engrossed with watching her chest move up and down with each breath she took. She looked peaceful, delicate...beautiful. There was something about her, something that drew me in and threatened to hold me captive. But I knew I had to let her go. She wasn't for me. Girls like her didn't stay with guys like me.

I'd kidnapped her.

I'd held her as a hostage.

And now this.

Now she was in my bed, naked, with only my sheet covering her. I reached out and trailed my finger over the scars on her back. The puffed up skin told me they hadn't been treated properly, and the dark pink color spoke of years of healing. They were her battle scars—marks which depicted part of her story. Just like this would become part of it too.

She groaned at my touch so I moved my hand away, intent not to wake her up yet. I hadn't been asleep, not with the prospect of her being beside me. So I'd gone and worked on my bike then taken a shower before it became light outside. The sun was just starting to rise, pushing through the gap in the blind on my window, but I needed a couple more minutes. Just a little more time to pretend this wouldn't all be over today.

Torch was due in court this afternoon, and whether the judge let him go or not, she'd be gone. I couldn't keep her, no matter how much I wanted to.

I puffed out a breath and stood, needing to get my mind off her. I'd tried yesterday by going to see Reign at *Pink Feather*, but even she couldn't do the job she was normally best at. The sway of her hips hadn't made a difference, and neither had her hands touching me. Yet seeing Hailsey in just a towel had me as hard as a goddamn rock. What the fuck was wrong with me? I was fuckin' losing it.

"Jax?" Haisley's soft voice whispered, but I didn't turn to face her. I had to collect myself and perfect my mask. I couldn't show her anything but the man she'd first met, not if I was going to let her walk away from all of this. She was the daughter of the enemy. Forbidden, and yet so goddamn alluring.

"Get dressed," I barked out and headed over to the sofa where I'd placed my cut last night. "I'm taking you back."

"Back?" Her voice was shaky, causing my stomach to drop. "Back where?"

I put my cut on, straightened it out, then turned to face her. She sat in the middle of my bed, her hair a mess, the sheet wrapped around her chest, and fuck if I didn't want to go to her. I wished I could have stayed in bed with her all day long. Touched her in places she'd never been touched. Made her scream my name over and over again.

But I couldn't.

She had a purpose, a reason she was here, and it wasn't for me. *She* wasn't meant for me.

"Yeah," I gritted out. "Back into the basement."

Her eyes widened and her shoulders drooped. "Oh." She bit down on her bottom lip, and goddammit, it made me want her even more. I adjusted my cock so she couldn't see the effect she was having on me. "Okay." Her stare met mine, her golden eyes piercing me right down to my soul. "Could I erm...get something to eat first?"

My nostrils flared and my hands clenched by my sides. She was asking for food, something nobody should be asking for in that way. I'd done that to her. I'd made her only eat once a day, and it made me feel like a dick. But there was no other way we could have done it. It wasn't like she was here for a goddamn vacation.

The sooner she was gone, the fuckin' better. She was twisting my mind, making me think things I never had before, and I didn't like it. Not one goddamn bit.

"Just get dressed," I demanded, keeping my gaze on her as she slipped out of the bed and into the bathroom. I'd washed her jeans and T-shirt overnight, and I cursed myself. I was meant to be holding her hostage, not doing her damn laundry.

I tilted my head back, looked at the ceiling, and pulled on my hair. I never should have brought her in here after last night. I should have thrown her back into the basement and been done with her. I had plenty of people around me who could have seen to her and given her the essentials. But fuck...I didn't want them to. I wanted to see her small button nose. I wanted to stare at the spattering of freckles on her nose. I wanted...her.

"Ready," her soft voice announced, and my stomach dropped.

I may have wanted her, but I'd never have her. Our worlds didn't mesh. She was the good girl, and I...I was the bad guy.

HAISLEY

I'd been a fool to think things would change. I didn't know what I thought would have happened when I'd woken up this morning in Jax's bed, but it wasn't being thrown back down into the basement. I'd built it up in my head as I'd fallen asleep next to him last night. I'd thought it meant more than it actually did.

I'd been stupid.

Did I really think because he'd fucked me that he'd treat me differently?

The honest answer was, yes. I was sure I saw something shining in his light eyes, a gentleness I hadn't seen up until that point. But I'd been wrong. So very, very wrong. Yet, I couldn't deny I still wanted him. He made me feel alive, like my existence in this world wasn't for nothing.

I brought my legs to my chest and wrapped my arms around them, staring out into the empty basement. I'd barely moved from my position for hours, and I was sure by the sounds of the music and cheering above that a party was happening, which meant it was already nighttime.

My stomach rumbled and I squeezed my eyes closed. Jax had given me something to eat this morning, but it still wasn't enough. I was used to eating at set times in the day, and now my body was rebelling against the new eating rules it had been given.

Laughing echoed through the basement door, and a second later, it opened up, filling the room with loud music and cigarette smoke. "Hey, hostage!" someone shouted, and I winced. They knew my name, but Jax and Al had been the only ones to use it. To the rest of the people here, I was just a means to an end.

But maybe that was how Jax saw me too? He'd gotten what he wanted from me then was done. He'd fucked me then thrown me away. My heart raced in my chest, my hands started to shake. Part of me didn't want to believe Jax was like that, but the evidence was stacked against him. Still, deep down, I wondered how he would have treated me had we met under different circumstances. Would he have held my hand? Bought me flowers?

"Come on, let's go!" the same voice shouted. "Hurry the fuck up!" I slowly moved my arms from around my legs and shuffled to the edge of the mattress. "Come on, you're leaving!"

Leaving? I was leaving? My stomach churned and hope sprung inside me. Had Jax changed his mind? Did he want me up there instead of down here?

I rushed forward and up the stairs to see two of the members who had been bringing me water over the last few days. The tallest one sneered at me and grasped my bicep. "Hurry the fuck up, we got a party to attend."

"A party?" I asked.

I didn't know what possessed me to ask, and I wasn't sure I'd get an answer. But when he replied, "Yep. Daddy dearest came through and let Torch out," I knew Jax hadn't changed his mind. I was leaving...to go home. My stomach dropped at the thought of having to go back to the mansion, and it was on the tip of my tongue to beg to stay. I'd be in that basement for another hundred days if it meant I didn't have to go back to the life I'd led up until now.

"But...Jax?"

The guy yanked me down the hallway and took a left, the opposite direction to where all of the music was coming from. Was Jax through there? Was he partying and celebrating while I was being taken out of here?

"What about him?" the guy grunted and shoved a door open. Wind whipped at me, causing my hair to blow in my face. It was night again, only this time the stars didn't shine as bright. They were muted, much like I was.

"Does he know what you're doing?"

He laughed, so loud it hurt my ears. "He was the one who gave the order." The stones on the ground dug into my bare feet as we walked past a line of motorbikes and toward a van. The same van that had squealed to a stop next to me and taken me off the street. The same van they'd brought me here in.

"What...where are we going?"

The second guy swung open the side door and waved his arm at it. "You're going home."

My breaths came heavy and fast at his words, but there was nothing I could say. Nothing I could do. I was going home. I was leaving all this behind.

Leaving Jax behind.

But it wasn't my choice. It was his. He could have kept me here if he wanted. He could have done anything he chose to, but he'd demanded I leave. He was sending me away, and I wasn't sure how to feel about it.

The guy holding onto my arm pushed me forward,

and my knees smacked into the edge of the van. I threw my hands out to stop me from falling completely, and tried to keep the tears at bay. I wasn't in control of my life; I'd never been in control.

Stones crunching under boots rang out in the otherwise quiet night, and I turned my head to where the sound was coming from. Concealed in the darkness was a pair of light eyes and an unreadable face. He'd come to make sure I was leaving. He wanted to make sure I was gone.

And I understood then.

He didn't care.

No one ever cared.

CHAPTER SEVEN

HAISLEY

They'd dropped me off at the edge of my street and sped away, leaving me to my own devices. My legs moved automatically toward the mansion. It was the only place I had to go, whether I wanted to be there or not. I didn't know what I expected as I made it to the end of the driveway, but it wasn't the silence that consumed me. There wasn't a car in sight, a person hanging around—nothing.

I winced as I walked down the pebbled driveway, sure someone would come running out at any second and throw their arms around me. They should have been happy I was home, safe and sound, right? I should have known better. I always had hope things would be different, but I was let down time and time again. The people surrounding me didn't care, that much was evident.

My stomach dipped as I walked up the two steps to the wide front door, and I reached my hand out to turn the knob to let myself in. But it was locked, so I had no choice but to ring the bell. I had no idea what time it was, no idea where everyone was.

The door swung open and I was greeted by the last

person I wanted to see: my dad. "Get inside," he ordered, looking behind me as if there was someone else there, or maybe he was making sure no one saw me coming home. He was on edge, that much was clear.

I walked into the main foyer, the coolness of the floor seeping into the soles of my feet. I'd forgotten how cold this mansion made me feel, and even though they'd given me my backpack, jacket, and cell when they'd dropped me off, I hadn't thought to put them on. I hadn't wanted to, not until this second.

"What the hell were you thinking?" Dad fumed, throwing his hands in the air. "Why would you let someone take you?"

I blinked, sure I'd heard him wrong, but nope, he'd actually said that. "I didn't let them take me—"

"I had to break the law to get you back!" he shouted, and his voice echoed off the empty walls, causing me to wince. His nostrils flared, his anger clear as day. But what did he expect me to say? I didn't ask for any of this to happen.

"You didn't have to do what they wanted you to," I whispered. Because he didn't. He could have called the police, or even better, forgotten about me altogether.

He rolled his eyes. "I didn't have a choice. Imagine what my colleagues would say if they found out you'd been taken and I'd done nothing about it?" He paced in front of me, his robe wafting behind him like a superhero cape, but he was so far from being a superhero it wasn't even funny. "It's all your fault. If you followed the rules and did as you were told, none of this would have happened. I could have—"

"Are you serious?" My brows raised and my head

reeled back. I couldn't believe what I was hearing from him. "You think I wanted to be kidnapped?"

"I don't know, Haisley." Dad stepped toward me, each of his movements done with purpose. "Did you? Maybe you wanted to teach me a lesson." He tilted his head to the side. "Or maybe this was all an elaborate plan you concocted."

"Really?" I laughed. "You really think I'd do that?"

"Yes," he answered immediately. Surely I was dreaming, because right now he was *blaming me* for someone taking me off the street and holding me for ransom.

"You're unbelievable," I ground out and spun around. I wasn't going to stand there and listen to him. I wasn't going to take the blame like I always did. I'd had enough. Enough of this mansion. Enough of this life. Enough of *him*.

"Where do you think you're going?" His hand wrapped around my arm, halting me in my tracks.

"No." I turned my head to face him. "You don't touch me. Never again." I glanced down at his fingers biting into my skin. "Get your damn hand off of me."

"Haisley—"

I yanked my arm from his grip and narrowed my eyes on him. "I'm going to bed." I pushed my shoulders back. "I'll see you at breakfast." He stared at me and opened his mouth, but I didn't give him the chance to say another thing. He'd said enough, told me how he felt, and that was all there was to it.

I was back in my normal life. The life I had before all of this. The life my dad controlled.

JAX

It had been two days since I'd watched Tech and Prospect drive Hailsey off the clubhouse property. I'd told myself to stay inside, to let them deal with her, but I hadn't been able to stop myself. I'd needed to see her face one last time.

Which was what I was telling myself as I sat on the seat of my bike behind a parked car on her college campus. I was just making sure she was okay, that she'd gotten home safely. That she was continuing on with her life. But it was a lie I was telling myself. A lie I couldn't keep up for much longer.

She walked down the path between two grassed areas and toward the main part of the building, her backpack over her shoulder, and a pair of skinny jeans covering her legs. But it was the way her light-brown hair moved with the wind that had my hands twitching. I'd pushed my fingers through that hair, held it in my grip as I pushed my cock inside her.

Fuck.

I adjusted myself and gritted my teeth. I hadn't been able to fuck Reign, not since Haisley had been in the clubhouse. My downstairs brain was demanding something my upstairs brain refused. But I was here, watching her, waiting for her to look around and see me.

I didn't know what I would have done if her gaze met mine. Maybe I would have rode off, or maybe I would have thrown my leg over my bike and sauntered over to her. I could have wrapped my arms around her, told her she was driving me crazy, and slammed my lips down onto hers.

But it was all a dream. A dream I'd never have come true.

She paused at the main doors, her hand on the handle, and turned her head. My stomach rolled as she glanced around. She was more aware of her surroundings, and I couldn't help but grin. I'd changed her. Changed the way she acted. I just hoped it was for the good and not the bad.

Her gaze paused on the tree twenty feet away from me. My heart raced in my chest at the prospect of her finding out I'd been following her since she'd left the clubhouse. She didn't know I'd watched the security footage of her house. She didn't know I waited for her to leave each morning to make sure she was okay. I was treading a thin line, sure to topple off at any moment.

But would it be so bad if I did? If she found out I was looking out for her? If she realized she meant more to me than I'd let on? I silently chanted, hoping she'd search a little farther, but she shook her head as if she was telling herself she was imagining things, then turned and pulled the door open.

CHAPTER EIGHT

HAISLEY

I'd been home for three days and each one felt exactly like the one before it: hazy. I hadn't had time to take a break and process everything that happened. I hadn't had the chance to talk it out with someone—anyone. Not that I would have been able to, because it was apparent the morning after I'd gotten home that my dad had told everyone I'd gone away with friends.

They should have known better. They should have known to question his explanation. But they hadn't.

And now I was here, in my mom's studio, staring at her artwork on the walls, and wishing my entire life had been different. If she hadn't died, would my days have been filled with the monotonous college classes? Would the rules in the house have been as strict? Would my dad still have had a total disregard for anyone but himself?

All it took was one moment to change the course of your life. To throw it off track and send you down a completely new path. Mom was that for Dad, and I was starting to wonder if Jax was that for me. He'd opened my eyes, shown me the way I was living wasn't the only one out there. He'd been rough and demanding, but also gentle and caring. He was everything across the board, while I was nothing.

I was Haisley. The girl who did as she was told, no matter what.

But I didn't want to be her anymore. I wanted to be the girl who dropped her towel in front of Jax. The girl who had told him to fuck her. The girl who had lived in the moment.

"Haisley Rooper," a deep voice ground out from behind me. Normally I would have spun around, apologized right away, but today...today I'd had enough of it, enough of *him*. "Haisley! I've been calling your name for five minutes."

"Leave me alone," I murmured, staring at the portrait of me on the wall. I must have only been six or seven, but I could remember it like it happened only yesterday. The smell of freshly cut grass. The sun shining across our elaborate backyard, and the tree we would sit under to have picnics.

"What did you just say?"

I lifted my hand and stroked the side of my face on the painting. "I told you to leave me alone." I turned my head, connecting my gaze with my dad's. "I don't want you in here. Get out."

"Excuse me?" His face turned a bright shade of red, a warning I should have heeded to, but I didn't care anymore. I didn't care what he did or said.

"You heard me." I faced him completely. My fingers twitched, my body's reaction to wrap my arms around myself trying to take over, but then he'd know he'd won.

He took one step inside the studio, then another, and closed the door behind him. I swallowed as the air swirled around us, the atmosphere warning of the danger I was in, but I couldn't bring myself to care. I couldn't back down, not now, not after everything I'd been through.

"I thought I'd only have to teach you how to behave once and that would be enough." His hand moved down to his belt, the clacking of metal against metal making my body jerk backward. The portrait teetered on the wall and I tried to keep it in place. "But it looks like you still don't know your damn place."

"What..." I cleared my throat, trying not to sound as scared as I felt. "What are you doing?"

His eyes lit up, a fire roaring behind them at his excitement. "Teaching you a lesson." He whipped his arm out, causing his belt to fly through the loops of his pants, and the leather cracked against the floor. It was the same exact belt. The one he wore every day. The one he'd used on me before. The one that left scars on my skin.

All of the bravado slipped free, leaving behind the same thirteen year old girl he'd first used the belt on. But this time I was bigger, I was more grown up, I was—

I threw my arms out as the belt thrashed through the air, screaming as it connected with my forearms. "Stop!"

"Know your place!" he shouted back, pulling his arm back and throwing it at me again, but this time he missed. I rushed to the side, intent on escaping the room through the balcony, but turning my back on him was a mistake—a big mistake.

The buckle made contact with my upper back and I slapped my palm onto the glass doors. The door handle was so close; all I needed was to turn the lock and get outside. But another lashing slapped against my skin, and my body started to crumple in on itself.

"Please, Dad." I turned my head, making sure my

gaze met his. "Stop, please!" I begged him—begged him to not do this again. But he didn't listen, he was in a world of his own, sweat dripping down the side of his face as he whipped the belt again and again. The leather strap met my shoulder, and then the buckle smacked me in the face, ripping my skin in the process. Wetness poured from the side of my eye and my cheek, and I threw my hands over my face, trying to protect it, because he wasn't stopping. He carried on, hitting any part of my body he could.

He was rage personified. I should have known he was capable of the anger pouring out of him. But I'd pushed it —pushed him—to this point.

"This is *my* house!" He roared, slapping the leather against my hands on my face. I slid down the door, the wetness on my shoulder causing a squeaking sound. "You live by *my* rules and respect *me*!"

He gave me one final lashing across the back of my legs and halted. His breaths were heavy, the only sound in the room apart from my crying. I didn't move my hands, didn't make a single move, not until his footsteps echoed out of the room and the door closed behind him.

He dealt his punishment and walked away. Just. Like. That. It didn't bother him, didn't matter to him, not one bit.

I sobbed, regretting the way it made my face move and the pain it caused. I swallowed, telling myself I needed to get out of here. I couldn't stay here, not now, not after what he'd done. It was time...time I left. Time I started the life I wanted to live. I was done letting him have all the control he wanted.

My hands gripped onto the wooden floor and I pushed down on them, trying to stand on shaky legs. I swayed to the side and blinked as more blood flowed over my face and my eye. My palms were covered in bright red, my legs stung, and my back screamed in pain.

The leggings I'd put on when I'd gotten home were ripped in several places, and blood spatters covered the front of my lilac T-shirt. I needed to get changed, I needed to look at the damage he'd caused, but I didn't have time.

My hand slid over the white walls of the hallway, and distant voices rang though my ears. My heart raced in my chest, my body demanding I get out as soon as I could. I stumbled at the top of the stairs and gasped as my vision came in and out.

The front door was so close. My escape only meters away.

"Haisley? What happened?"

I turned to look at Sophia and her pale face, but her eyes told me she knew what had happened. She knew my dad nearly as well as I did. I glanced back at the door, hearing heavy footsteps from behind Sophia, and I knew this was my only chance. It was time I put myself first. So I darted down the stairs, flung the door open, and sprinted out of there.

I fell several times making it up the driveway, but as soon as I was past the main gates, I could finally take a full breath. I was gone—out of his clutches, and all on my own.

Free. I was finally free.

———

JAX

I threw my leg over my bike, turned the ignition on, and felt the roaring engine vibrating under me. There was nothing like the raw power of a machine between your thighs and the open road ahead. I hadn't rode aimlessly, not since I'd come home from the marines. And right then, I needed it. I needed the air to whip under my cut, the endless road in front of me. I needed space to think. Which was why I'd decided to go out on the run this weekend, which meant I needed to tie up some loose ends at the strip club before we left.

I clipped my helmet in place, kicked the stand up, then lifted my feet to place on the footrests. I was about to pull away from outside the clubhouse when one of the prospects darted from inside and halted in front of me.

"Jax." He held his stomach, trying to take a breath, and I raised my brow at him. "Al called. He needs you to head toward Pink Feather."

"What?" My back straightened. "Why? What's happened?"

"I don't know." He placed his hands on his thighs, still trying to catch his breath. The guy needed to do some goddamn workouts. "He said he's on the main road and that you'll see him if you make your way there. Sounded urgent."

"Move the fuck out of my way then, Prospect," I fumed, fed up with watching him trying to fuckin' breathe.

"Right, sorry." He jumped to the side and I flicked my wrist and moved my hand on the accelerator, peeling out of the make shift lot toward the strip club. It was only a ten minute drive, but I made it in five. Al had been going out on more rides since the incident with Haisley, which meant I'd barely seen him. I drove around the back of the strip club but still couldn't see them. Where the fuck was he? I was starting to get antsy, not knowing what I was going to find when I finally saw him.

My cell vibrated in my pocket and I yanked it out, seeing Al's name on it. "Bro—"

"On the main road. She won't let me help her."

"What? Who won't...Al? Al?" I pulled my cell away and cursed when I realized he'd dropped the call. What the fuck was going on? I shook my head and sped out onto the main road, searching for Al's bike, then finally I spotted it, halfway between the club and the gas station.

I frowned as I saw him standing there, his hands in the air in front of him. I pulled off to the right and parked next to his bike then switched my engine off. Why the hell was he here? And why did he need—

"I promise I won't hurt you," he said, his voice calm. This was the Al I'd grown up with. The Al we all knew. All he ever wanted was to help everyone around him. "I was having an episode when I did that to you. That's not me, it's not who I am."

"Just leave me alone," a small voice replied, and my body jerked from the sound. Haisley. What was she doing — "Please," she sobbed out.

I rushed forward, coming into view, and Al turned his head to face me. "I found her wandering down the side of the road." I swallowed at his words and glanced at Haisley, feeling like my whole world was tumbling down. "She's in a bad way."

He wasn't wrong. Her face was swollen and half covered in blood, her T-shirt had patches of red, and her leggings were ripped in several places.

"Hais," I whispered, stepping forward. She held her hands up, trying to protect herself, and I knew right then and there that I couldn't walk away from her. I'd taken her without her permission. I'd started all of this. But I wouldn't regret it. I wouldn't regret touching her, feeling her, *needing* her. "What happened, sugar?"

Her stare met mine and I winced at the cuts on her face. Blood dripped from her eye and cheek. Someone had hurt her, and my gut told me it was the same person who had left the scars on her back. "Jax?" Her chest heaved on a breath. "I...please...I..."

"It's okay," I said, trying to tell myself the same thing. I moved closer to her, giving her enough space to process who was standing in front of her. "Tell me what happened."

"He...he wanted to teach me another lesson." She wrapped her arms around her waist. "But I couldn't...he can't...I won't do it anymore, Jax." She pushed her shoulders back and grimaced at the move. "I won't let him control me anymore."

"Who, Hais? Who won't you let control you?" My pulse raced, my gut already telling me who it was, but I needed to hear it come out of her mouth.

"My dad." She hiccuped a sob and folded in on herself. "I...I can't go back there. Don't make me go back there."

"I'll fuckin' kill him," Al ground out, and I agreed with the sentiment. He wouldn't get away with this, not again. But there were more important things to figure out first, like how the fuck I was gonna get her off the side of this road and by my side. I wasn't letting her go this time. I'd set her free once, yet she'd managed to fly back onto my radar.

"Not over my dead body, sugar." I stepped forward, trying to ignore the jerk of her body as I got closer. "I shouldn't have let you go in the first place." I lifted my hand and placed my palm on the side of her face that was unmarked. "Come home with me, Hais."

Tears slid down her cheeks, mixing with the blood on her face, and all I wanted was to wipe them away, to destroy the pain she was in.

"I...but you didn't want me. You made me leave—"

"Because I thought it was for the best." I pressed closer, my body centimeters from hers, but I was afraid to touch her, afraid to cause her any more agony. "Come home with me."

"With you?" she asked, tilting her head back.

"Yeah, sugar." I bent down and placed the gentlest kiss to her lips. "Be with me. Just me."

Her lashes fluttered closed and she inhaled a stuttering breath. My nerves were on edge as she stayed silent for what felt like hours when in reality was only seconds. She opened her eyes back up, stared right down into my soul, then eradicated the distance between us. "Okay."

"Okay?"

She nodded. "Yeah, okay." She looked up at me, her lips trying to lift into a smile. "No basement though?"

I shook my head. "Never the basement." I breathed deep and pressed my forehead to hers. "Only ever in my bed."

ABOUT THE AUTHOR

Abigail Davies grew up with a passion for words, storytelling, maths, and anything pink. Dreaming up characters—quite literally—and talking to them out loud is a daily occurrence for her. She finds it fascinating how a whole world can be built with words alone, and how everyone reads and interprets a story differently.

Connect with Abigail

Reader group—Abi's Aces
Newsletter
www.abigaildaviesauthor.com

facebook.com/abigaildaviesauthor

twitter.com/abigailadavies

instagram.com/abigaildaviesauthor

goodreads.com/abigaildavies

bookbub.com/authors/abigail-davies

amazon.com/author/abigaildavies

pinterest.com/abigaildaviesauthor

MORE BOOKS BY ABIGAIL

The Easton Family

Fallen Duet (Forbidden Angst)
Book 1: Free Fall
Book 2: Down Fall

Fated Duet (Student/Teacher Angst)
Book 1: Defy Fate
Book 2: Obey Fate

Bonded Duet (Age gap/Forbidden Angst)
Book 1: Torn Bond
Book 2: Tied Bond

Burned Duet (Age Gap/Forbidden Angst
Book 1: Fast Burn
Book 2: Deep Burn

LOLITA

YOLANDA OLSON

BLURB

No one ever believed that I could make something of myself.

I got kicked out of my home right before my thirteenth birthday, but I made the best of things. I found a way to keep my head above water and I've become damn good at what I do.

Not to say that my way is the best, but I will say that it's the *only* way.

A fair few have treated me kindly and with respect, and in return, I've treated them the same.

Pretty little girls can get what they want and I haven't failed to get what I want so far. It's strange in a way because I never knew how far I would go to take what I want, but I want him—no; I need him.

The way a junkie craves their next fix.

The way a hunter stalks their next prey.
It's the thrill of the chase, I suppose, and the high of getting what you want.

Someone should have warned him that pretty little girls like me aren't all just barbie dolls and bubblegum. Some of us harbor darker thoughts than the meanest of men.

I'll use what I know best to get him, though.
In the end, he'll be mine.
Just like he was always meant to be.

CHAPTER ONE

I blow another bubble and lick the sticky gum off my lips. I've been standing in front of the "help wanted" board stationed in the center of the community college campus looking for a job. I don't go to this school, nor am I old enough to attend, but I've been on my own long enough to consider myself well-versed in the adult way of life.

My eyes narrow as I scan the flyers and just when I'm about to give up hope, I see it. I take a step closer and read the somewhat professionally designed sign, a smile curving the edge of my lips.

Babysitter wanted. Four weekdays and one Saturday per month. Experience preferred, but will consider all. Please call the number below Monday through Friday between nine a.m. and five p.m.

I pull the first tag off the flyer, fold it up, and slip it into my pocket. I glance around to make sure no one is watching me as I pull the flyer down, crumple it into a ball, then toss it into the trashcan nearby.

No competition is the best kind and it seems that I'll be the first and only person to reach out. I don't mind dealing with some brats for five days a week as long as the pay is good.

And considering that I'm strapped for cash, I won't put up too much of a fuss over what they're willing to pay.

I shrug my jacket off when I get back to the shelter.

I've been homeless for about four years now and this place has always been good to me. I don't have much of anything, so no one ever tries to steal from me when I'm gone or asleep. And if they do, well, I just sit them down and have a chat about it. Sometimes, people need more than what they're willing to say and I don't mind helping where I can.

I walk over to my cot and drop my jacket onto it before I head toward the office. Miss Jean is one of my favorite people to talk to because even though she's always busy, she has time for each and every one of us.

A gentle rap on the half-open door gets her attention. She looks up at me with her warm, chocolate-brown eyes, and smiles. I grin in return and step in when she waves at me.

"Well, good morning Meryska! What can I do for you?" she asks me brightly.

The thing about Miss Jean is that she's always genuine with her emotions. She never forces a fake smile or warm sentiment for the sake of our feelings, so I know she's having a good day.

"I think I found a job," I tell her excitedly as I sit down and cross my legs underneath myself. I roll the sleeves up on my t-shirt and Miss Jean's eyes fall on my tattoos.

I got most of them done when I ended up on the street; traded some of the best tattoo artists blow jobs and some finger fucking action for them. They let me stay in their shops at night sometimes if I did a good job sucking their cocks, and I thought it was nice to have a place to stay. I got really good at it, I even learned how to grind down on their fingers when they decided that was how they wanted to be paid instead because having a roof over my head was more important to me than having my virginity.

Of course, I never said who they were. Being thirteen years old with a dick in my mouth for the first time or a fist in my pussy wasn't exactly something you tell people about. They'd end up in jail for kiddie diddling and I'd end up with nowhere to sleep for the night.

"Tell me about it," Miss Jean says, resting her hands on the table and leaning forward.

"Well, I'd love to, but I need to use your phone first," I admit sheepishly. She arches an eyebrow with a curious shine in her eyes so I reach into my pocket and pull out the number. "It's a babysitting job. I know it won't pay me enough to get my own place, but I can start saving whatever they give me."

"Oh, honey. You know that's not why I was asking," she replies softly.

"I know. I just think it's time for me to move on and try to make something of myself and I'm hoping this job will help me," I say with a shrug.

Miss Jean reaches across her desk and gives my hand a squeeze before she turns her phone toward me, then excuses herself from the room. She gives me a reassuring pat on the shoulder on her way out and I take a deep breath.

Hopefully, whoever is on the other end of this phone call won't let me down, I think as I glance down at the tearaway then begin to dial the number.

CHAPTER TWO

I'm standing in the bathroom running a brush through my hair. I've never been so nervous in my goddamn life before, but my interview is in an hour and I want to make sure that I look somewhat presentable.

I decided not to hide my tattoos because that would be hiding a part of myself that I'm kinda proud of. Not necessarily what I did, but the fact that I was able to survive at such a young age by doing it.

After I finish dabbing some gloss on my lips, I pucker them, then give myself a critical once over before I decide that it's the best I can do considering the circumstances I live in.

As good as it gets, I think as cheerfully as I can. I head back out into the main room then grab my jacket from my bed. On the way toward the door, I stop by Miss Jean's office and peek in.

"You look very nice, Meryska," she says with an approving nod. "Good luck, honey. Remember, if you need references, you give them my phone number."

"Thanks, Miss Jean," I reply gratefully.

She's taken down the phone number of the family I'll be interviewing with, and if they call, she won't say the shelter name. She's really smart like that sometimes. I fish around in my pocket quickly then pull out the loose change I have, counting it to make sure that I have enough for the bus ride over and back again.

With a nervous smile, I give her a little wave as I make my way out of the shelter and head toward the bus stop down the street.

Half an hour and ten stops later, I find myself standing on the front stoop of one of the fancier houses in town. It does absolutely nothing to ease my nerves, but I've come this far and I have to at least try.

Here goes nothing.

I smooth back my hair, take a deep breath, and raise my hand to knock on the door. I begin to chew the inside of my mouth nervously. It's a bad habit that I picked up from when the tattoo guys would finger fuck me. It kept me from making any sounds that would get all of us in trouble and it rears it's head when my heart rate picks up a little.

I can hear some kids running around inside and it brings a smile to my face because I'd like to think that if I had a normal childhood, that could have been me and my brothers.

I raise my fist again, but before I have the chance to knock, the door opens and one of the most beautiful women I've ever seen in my life smiles so brightly at me, that I'm worried I'll be blinded if I don't look away.

"Meryska?" she asks curiously.

I nod and extend a hand which she takes firmly, initiating a shake and I can feel myself blush. It's not because of how pretty she is, it's because of how nice she's being to someone she doesn't know.

I'm not used to that.

"I'm Calista Gastrell; it's a pleasure to meet you. Come on in, once I get the children wrangled, I'll grab my husband and we can sit down and have a chat, okay?"

I nod again as I step into their home and immediately feel like the piece of trash that I know I am. The ceilings are high, the foyer is as big as the main room in the shelter, and there are blatantly expensive paintings hanging along the walls as far as the eye can see. I want to tell her that there's been a mistake and that I can't take the job after all, but pride stops me.

I may be nothing more than trash to most including myself, but I know I can be better and I'm damn determined now.

Mrs. Gastrell ushers me into the living room, which is bigger than the foyer if that's possible, and tells me to take a seat while she gets her house in order. It almost sounds like something someone says when they know they're going to die, but I brush it off and perch myself on the very edge of one of the opulent couches. I blow out a breath as my leg begins to shake nervously and I try to convince myself that this is the break I need to get things going on the right path for a change.

Twenty minutes later, I'm ready to give up and sneak out of the fancy house on Fancy Lane, when I hear Mrs. Gastrell's heels echoing down the hall again. I clear my throat and clasp my hands on my lap. If I look like a scared little girl, that's exactly how I'll be treated and I know that I'm not.

Intimidated and scared are two completely different things.

"Sorry to keep you waiting!" she says as she walks into the room. I turn my eyes toward her and smile, taking her in again. Mrs. G. is about five foot six, has pretty sandalwood colored hair, and big brown eyes. She's very striking with her severe chin and sharp nose, and when she smiles, the corners of her eyes crinkle.

But when my eyes wander over to the man that enters behind her, I immediately have to fight the urge to start chewing the inside of my mouth again. My heart begins to beat erratically in my ears and I can almost just make out the sound of the blood rushing to my face.

If Mrs. G. is the most beautiful woman I've ever seen, then the man I'm assuming is Mr. G. has got to be the most stunning man in the entire world. He's taller than her; about six foot one, has sackcloth-colored black hair that sits messily and neatly all at the same time on top of his head, and his eyes—they're sleepy, hazel blue, and seductive even when as dormant as they are.

Holy shit.

I do my best not to stare, because not only is it unbecoming, but because he isn't mine.

"Meryska, this is my husband, Everett. Honey, this is Meryska—she's here for the babysitting job," she explains after introducing us to each other. He nods at me with a tired look on his face as he sits down next to his wife opposite me, and I clear my throat again. Hopefully, I'll find a way to break through the iceberg that's sitting between us and shake something loose.

Scared is when you're worried about things known and unknown—intimidated is sitting across from a couple that looks like the Gastrell's in their fancy fucking house.

"We're going to ask you some questions, and you answer them as honestly as you can, okay?" Mrs. G.

begins as she sits back against the cushions and rests a hand on her husband's leg. "There's no right or wrong answer."

"Shoot," I say as enthusiastically as I can, fully aware of the way her husband's stare is holding me down in place like Atlas carrying the weight of the world on his shoulders. She seems impervious to it, though. *Must be years of practice,* I think dryly as I do my best to avoid his eyes.

"How old are you?" she asks, the smile never faltering.

"I'm seventeen."

"And have you babysat before?"

"Officially? No, but I do have younger brothers that my mom would leave me to watch when we were younger. And if I can keep those two in line, I'm sure I can deal with anything," I say with an eye roll.

Mrs. G. chuckles.

Mr. G. sits in stony silence.

"Our children are ten and eight—the oldest is our daughter, Anna Leigh, and our son's name is Maynard," she says as she leans forward. I raise an eyebrow at her son's name and she rolls her eyes, "Family name."

I chuckle and her smile widens into a friendly grin.

I cut my eyes quickly toward Mr. G. who's still staring at me like he's trying to see right through me to the center of my soul and I decide it's best to shrug off my jacket to help. If he thinks I'm hiding something from them, showing them who I really am, bare skin and all, should help the matter some.

"Oh my!" Mrs. G. exclaims when she sees all of the designs that almost completely cover my arms. I never did get a chance to get my sleeves finished cause the guys moved and I never knew where to find them next.

Besides, I've grown up since then and I don't know if they'd still trade me some diddling for ink.

"Hope these won't be a problem," I say nervously.

"Not at all!" she exclaims quickly, "I'm just a little shocked that you're only seventeen with all of that work already. Do they have any meaning?"

Just that I need a place to sleep.

"Not really," I lie with a shrug as I look down at my arms. "I guess you could chalk it up to being a bored kid."

Mr. G. clears his throat and I look up at him expectantly, but he just continues to stare at me with his damn Medusa eyes and offers nothing in the way of words.

"Everett doesn't talk much if you can't tell," Mrs. G. offers dryly.

I smile at her because it's obvious that she's trying her best to not let his silence unnerve me.

"Well, do you have any references? One is fine if that's all you have," she says getting to her feet. I nod as I reach for my jacket and pull Miss Jean's phone number out of my pocket. I hand it to her and notice how clean and manicured her nails are as opposed to my dirty chipped ones. She doesn't seem to notice and if she does, she doesn't show it.

"I'll be right back," she promises with a warm smile.

Great. Left in silence with someone who obviously doesn't want me around.

I let out a sigh as I sit back on the couch and cross a leg over my lap, trying to make the best out of an awkward situation.

CHAPTER THREE

Mr. G. keeps staring at me.

When I look up and meet his eyes, though, he turns his face away—almost as if he's trying to decide if this entire facade is a waste of his time.

It's nothing at all like when Mrs. G. was in the room and I can't help but wonder if there's something he wants to say to me. He looks a little bored with the entire thing, but I know better than to ask prodding questions—Miss Jean prepped me for this interview by giving me the dos and don'ts.

Do speak when spoken to, don't ask intrusive questions.

Those are the two that I repeated to myself on the bus ride over and the ones that I'm trying to hold on to because I feel that they're the most respectful. Plus, I didn't really listen to much else of what she said.

I hear Mrs. G.'s laughter ringing somewhere in the house and it makes me smile. It also makes me wonder how two obviously opposite personalities attracted to the point of marriage, but honestly, by now I'm willing to bet that it has to do with how beautiful they both are.

Some strange unwritten law of nature where beauty begets beauty.

"Your name is Meryska?"

I startle.

I was convinced up to this point that Mr. G. couldn't speak, though it seems now that he just chose not to.

"Yup!" I confirm as brightly as I can.

"Hm."

"What?" I ask, wrinkling my nose.

"Huh? Oh. Nothing, I've never heard it before today is all," he responds reasonably. *Right,* I think with an internal eye roll as I nod and push my hair behind my ears. Just to be able to break the gaze he has on me, I look down at my nails wondering when I'll be able to talk Miss Jean into helping me fix them up. They never bothered me before, but after seeing Mrs. G.'s I feel kind of inadequate.

"Oh," I mumble distractedly.

God, I really need to clean these damn things.

"Don't do that," he says sharply.

I look up at him in confusion waiting for him to elaborate but before he has the chance, the woman of the house walks back into the room with two little kids in tow.

"Anna Leigh, Maynard, this is Meryska and she's going to be your new babysitter."

The bus ride back was much faster than getting to Fancy House, and I felt like I could have flown the whole way back. I guess the saying is true; going back home is always faster than leaving it—or something like that, anyway.

Miss Jean waves at me from the shelter entrance way

and I break into a sprint. We hug each other as I let out a squeal of excitement and she pats my back proudly.

"I knew you'd be just fine," she states with a huge grin on her face. "When do you start?"

"I can start on Saturday," I reply happily. "I'll be raking in the dough in no time!"

"I guess we'll have to get a special supper prepared so we can all celebrate with you," she states with a wink and I groan inwardly, the grin still on my face. Miss Jean fusses over every little accomplishment we make and *always* makes sure that we're all happy for each other regardless of how small said accomplishment may be.

"It's okay," I reply with the wave of a hand, "that's not necessary."

But she smiles, shakes her head, and insists until I finally give in.

I walk away from her office feeling like a million dollars. I'm sure that the Gastrells won't pay me that much, but at this point, anything is better than nothing.

After I make it to the common room, I glance down at my hands. I bring my nails eye level and sigh. I know I won't be able to enjoy whatever special supper we get tonight with such dirty fingernails.

Maybe once they're clean, I can have Miss Jean help me paint them the same pretty red color Mrs. G. has.

CHAPTER FOUR

I feel better about things.

After we ate a really hearty meal of garlic and butter mashed potatoes, pork shoulder, and biscuits, Miss Jean took me out to buy a small bottle of dark red nail polish.

I'm pretty sure this is the same color that Mrs. G. uses, and after she helped me with my first couple, I was able to do the rest myself. Now I'm just sitting by one of the windows in the common room, blowing on my fingernails every so often, while enjoying the cool breeze that wafts in from time to time.

Thoughts of Everett Gastrell seem to follow the breeze in, invading my mind and reminding me of his stoic demeanor.

I wonder what it would take to make a man like him smile, or feel any kind of emotion. Considering they have two children, I have to believe that he's not completely dead inside.

Maybe something happened that made him the way he is now, or maybe having those kids sucked whatever life he had out of his body.

I clear my throat as another breeze comes in and tickles the flesh of my arm. The small hairs stand up as goosebumps become visible and I can feel my lips curving into a smile.

It seems that Everett is thinking about me too and this is a sign. I'm what's supposed to make him feel alive again and I won't let him down.

Today is going to be an exciting day. I made the rest of the week go by faster by keeping busy so that the time would pass by quicker than if I just sat around and did nothing.

It worked and Saturday came a lot faster than I had hoped for.

Miss Jean helped me pick out my outfit for today. It's a nice, fitted graphic t-shirt with a happy face on the front. Not the generic bullshit one, but one made of sparkles and happy thoughts—all of the things I know I can never be. She gave me a brand-new pair of blue jeans shorts to wear too, and I spent last night cleaning up my checkered canvas shoes.

I have my hair slicked back into a neat, tight ponytail and my dark red nails look clean and proper.

The Gastrells don't know where I live and I'd like to keep it that way by doing my best to be as presentable as their fancy house on Fancy Lane.

I know that I'll never truly fit in with anyone outside of the walls of the shelter, but that doesn't mean I can't put some kind of effort into it.

I watch the world go by outside the bus windows again wondering if maybe I'll finally make a lasting impression on someone besides Miss Jean.

I never cared about fitting in—I just want to be remembered.

I sigh as the bus stops and allows for passengers to get off and on, glancing at the time on the clock that sits above a bank entrance. I have thirty minutes to get there which is plenty of time. Actually, I think if the bus stays on schedule, I may get there fifteen minutes early.

Miss Jean told me that it's better to be early than late. Even though I've already made my first impression on the Gastrells, the first day on the job will be the one that lasts.

CHAPTER FIVE

"Hi!"

Anna Leigh pulls the door open after I knocked a couple of times and smiles up at me brightly and with excited eyes.

I grin down at her as I run a hand back over my hair to make sure that the short walk from the bus stop didn't knock anything out of place.

"Hey, Anna Leigh," I greet her cheerfully.

"Mama!" she hollers at the top of her lungs, "Meryska is here!"

My face reddens slightly at her enthusiasm. This is the first time in a long time that anyone has been this excited to see me and I can only hope that once I step inside the doors, that her mood will catch.

Mrs. G. makes her way toward the door and smiles when she sees me. She gently puts a hand on Anna Leigh's hair and tells her to let me in.

Once inside, I take a steadying breath and force the grin to stay on my face. If I want to keep this job and have any hope of ever leaving the shelter, I'll have to do my best to stay on everyone's good side.

"Hey, Mrs. Gastrell," I say shyly as I shrug off my jacket.

"Calista is fine," she replies holding up a hand before she reaches for my jacket. "You're almost an adult and that earns you some respect."

The tone of her voice is pleasant but I can't help that I feel a little mocked. Still, I fight against my lips wanting to falter and maintain the smile on my face.

"Everett is in his office. He's working from home today so it would be a good idea to keep these two as quiet as you can," she says as she leads the way to their opulent living room where Anna Leigh and Maynard are playing a board game. "I'll be gone for most of the day, but I'll call to check in from time to time. If you can answer the phone on the first couple of rings, that would be ideal. I hate to sound like a drill sergeant on your first day, but the fewer interruptions Everett has to deal with, the more amiable he can become," she finishes with an eye roll.

I bite my lower lip to stop myself from asking her why her husband seems to be such a miserable fuck. It's not my place to ask anything that isn't volunteered—Miss Jean hammered that one home again before I left this morning.

"There's plenty of food in the refrigerator," she continues as she motions for me to follow her into the kitchen.

My eyes dart around the room as soon as we enter because it's so big that it could be another house unto itself. It's at this moment that I regret taking this job. It makes me feel so inadequate to be in the fancy house on Fancy Lane, but I need the money so I know I just have to swallow my pride and get the job done to the best of my ability.

I place a hand on my stomach when she pulls the refrigerator door open. Everything inside is neatly placed but it still looks so overstocked that I know they've never known what it feels like to be hungry.

Miss Jean and the shelter provides for us as best as they can, most of what they can do for us comes in from community donations, but sometimes I wonder if the community forgets about us because I've gone to bed hungry more often than not.

That's part of the reason I didn't want that celebratory spread—because I know it would run through most of the food supplies we have for the rest of the month.

"The kids can have a light snack between lunch and dinner," she says, glancing at me with a warm smile. "And you feel free to help yourself to anything you'd like."

My stomach lets out a low growl of appreciation and I turn my face away, but Mrs. G. smiles, reaches into the fridge and pulls out an apple for me. I take it with a small nod and blink back the tears that are threatening to spill over my cheeks.

I never have breakfast, especially not after a couple of new single moms moved in with their small children. I can go without so they don't have to feel the hunger pains I feel sometimes.

I take a bite of the apple, wiping away the juice that runs down my chin, and nod.

Be grateful.

Take direction.

Service with a smile.

As I follow Mrs. G. back into the living room where

she retrieves her purse, kisses each of her children on their heads, then gives me a pat on the shoulder.

"You'll do just fine, Meryska. If you need anything, you can knock on Everett's door. Anna Leigh can show you where his office is if the need arises."

Do not disturb signs immediately begin going off in my head.

I won't bother Mr. G. no matter what happens. I'll prove to the Gastrells that I'm more than capable of taking care of the little family they've built.

And most of all, I'll prove to myself that I'm not the throwaway I've felt like my entire life.

CHAPTER SIX

Glancing over at the grandfather clock against the wall, I realize it's almost time for lunch. Mrs. G. has already been gone for a few hours, Anna Leigh and Maynard have been engrossed in their game of Candy Land, and no sign of Mr. G. even being in the house has happened yet.

"Ew! I hate licorice!" Maynard exclaims loudly when he ends up moving his piece toward Licorice Castle.

"I'm going to fix lunch for you guys. Anything in particular you're hungry for?" I ask as I get to my feet.

Anna Leigh shakes her head and her brother shrugs. I actually like that they've been so complacent so far—it makes for a nice, easy way to make some cash.

Once the eldest of the Gastrell children picks up the dice in her hands and begins to shake them, I shake my head and walk out of the room.

Maybe one day when I'm old enough and have finally made something of myself, I'll be able to have a family of my own and a nice little house too.

Nothing like this one because fuck knows what kind

of cash they have to be raking in to live in a neighborhood like this, but something that's cozy and all mine.

As I walk toward the kitchen I look down at the hem of my shorts and pull away a small piece of threading that I didn't realize had been coming loose until I felt it tickling my thigh.

I wish I could say I wasn't embarrassed since I know that Miss Jean bought these for me brand-new, but it still manages to add to the inadequacy I feel being here.

It'll pass, I promise myself as I step into the kitchen and glance around. As I walk over to the island and run a finger over the squeaky, clean surface, I can't help but wonder what it feels like to wake up every day in a place like this. To have the world at one's fingertips for the taking, a refrigerator full of food, and to never have to worry about what tomorrow will bring.

I pull out one of the stools and sit down, drumming my fancy, dark red fingernails along the top of the island. I have no idea what to make these children and I'm sure that unlike the ones at the shelter, a couple of peanut butter and jelly sandwiches probably won't suffice.

"What was your name again?"

I almost jump out of my skin at the sound of the voice, and glance over my shoulder with a startled expression on my face.

Everett—*Mr. G.*—is standing in the archway of the kitchen looking at me with that stoic expression in his eyes.

"Um, Meryska," I mumble as I feel my cheeks becoming hot. I don't understand how he can't remember my name, but he seems to enjoy making me squirm over something as simple as this.

"That's right," he confirms indifferently as he walks

into the room and over toward the fridge. "Not sure how I could have forgotten that," he mutters under his breath as he pulls out a glass Tupperware bowl full of what looks like leftovers.

"So, what are you doing here alone?" he continues as he walks over toward the counter, pulls back the saran wrap, then retrieves a plate from the cabinet over the sink.

"I was gonna fix the kids some lunch," I reply quietly.

"And how's that going?"

I fold my hands on the island top and lower my eyes toward my Calista-inspired nails, then take a deep breath.

Be yourself.

"Fuck if I know what to make them," I blurt out as nonchalantly as I can.

Mr. G. chuckles as he puts his fixed plate into the microwave then turns to face me.

"They eat anything if that helps."

"Including leftovers?" I ask nervously.

I can almost swear that I see a smile trying to curve up the edge of his lips, but his resolve holds strong as his eyes begin to bore into mine.

"Anna Leigh! Maynard!" he suddenly booms at the top of his lungs causing me to jump slightly.

I can hear the footsteps of his children rapidly approaching and when they enter the kitchen, I swivel in my stool to look at them. They're both staring at their father expectantly, with Anna Leigh stealing a glance at me and sticking the tip of her tongue out of the corner of her mouth. I look away and stifle a giggle—it's obvious to her that I'm on edge right now and she wants to make me feel better with her silly gesture.

"Yes, Daddy?" she asks.

"Do you think you can go easy on Miss Meryska

today and share some of this with me for lunch?" he asks, using a knuckle to tap the side of the bowl.

"Well, what is it?" Maynard asks, causing Anna Leigh to rib him with her elbow almost immediately.

"Sure!" she replies with that same enthusiasm she had when she opened the front door for me.

Thank you, I mouth to her and she smiles. I get to my feet, walk over to where Mr. G. is standing at the counter and reach up into the cabinet next to his head to pull out two smaller plates for them. He nods at me to set them down on the counter before he reaches for a clean spoon and scoops out smaller portions for the kids.

After the microwave *dings,* he retrieves his plate, then waits patiently while each of his children's plates heats up. They come over to take them from the counter with a sound, *thank you Daddy and Miss Meryska,* before they disappear back toward the living room.

"Help yourself," Mr. G. tells me as he picks up his plate and begins to walk out of the kitchen.

As I begin to fix myself a small plate, I smile. Maybe he's not so bad after all and he won't be so quick to forget me again.

CHAPTER SEVEN

Five o'clock came and went and Mrs. G. still hasn't come home yet. I'm sitting in the dining room with Mr. G. and the kids since he insisted that we all take a place at the table.

"It's almost bedtime anyway," he reminded them with a stern tone, "you have to take your showers and get ready for bed soon."

I push my food around my plate with the fork wondering how I'm going to get home. Part of the deal was that Mrs. G. would give me a ride back to the shelter, though I planned on having her drop me off just down the street.

"You aren't hungry?"

I glance up at Mr. G. and swallow hard under the weight of his eyes. They have that stern hue to them again and I almost feel like one of his children right now.

"Lunch is still sitting, I guess," I reply with a shrug as I set my fork down.

"Well, you make sure you clean your plate," he tells me with a nod as he goes back to his dinner.

I guess he thinks I'm one of his kids, after all. May as well act like one then.

I let my fork clatter onto my plate as I push my chair back and get to my feet. I pick up the glass of water I've been sipping in between bites and walk out of the dining room.

The silence in the room behind me now is as stony as the man who rules the home, but I don't care. If this is how he is on day one because Mrs. G. isn't around, then it's possible I don't need this job as much as I thought.

I carefully place my plate in the sink and the glass on the counter as I turn the water on. There wasn't much left on my plate for him to make a big deal over, so I know that the garbage disposal will take care of the rest.

I'm hoping that Mrs. G. will be home by the time I'm done so I can tell her what a dick her husband is and give her notice. That should make everyone involved in this farce happier than a pig in shit and hopefully, I'll at least get paid for my time today.

I may not be much to anyone, but I do have my damn pride and I won't be treated like a child.

As I busy myself washing my plate, fork, then glass, another plate is placed into the sink. I glance up to see Mr. G. watching me with amusement dancing in his eyes. With a sigh, I grab his plate and begin to wash it, when I'm done with that one, he places one of the kids' plates in the sink next.

And the cycle repeats itself until four dinner plates are spotless and in the dish strainer.

"Calista probably won't come home tonight," Mr. G. begins thoughtfully as I dry my hands with a small dish-towel. "Whenever she's with her mother, she tends to stay gone for a day or two."

I grit my teeth.

Had I been informed of this, I would have walked out the front door the day of my interview, but honestly I shouldn't be surprised.

It's probably what fancy, rich people do.

"Okay, well, I still need to get home," I tell him indifferently. "I know you can't leave them alone here, so I'll just call for a ride."

"Stay."

I arch an eyebrow as I cross my arms over my chest and look into Mr. G.'s eyes. He seems serious enough about it, but I'd still have to tell Miss Jean so she doesn't stay up all night worrying about me.

"I insist," he says in a quieter tone, his eyes becoming soft.

I blow out my breath as I hook my thumbs into the belt loops of my shorts and begin to chew the inside of my mouth thoughtfully.

"You can consider it overtime, Meryska," he adds with a soft chuckle and I grunt. *Does overtime come with a bib and a bottle too?*

"I have to call the lady I stay with," I tell him after giving it a little more thought. I don't understand why he's treating me like this, but I guess I should just play along. "She's expecting me to come home tonight and if I don't she'll probably call the cops."

He gestures to follow him and I do.

Through the dining room and the kitchen, past the children cleaning up the table and down a hall that I haven't wandered down before until we stop in front of a door. He reaches into his pocket, retrieves a key, and slips it into the lock, giving the door a push, then stepping back to let me in first.

"You can use the phone on my desk. I'll put the kids to bed while you make your phone call," he says.

I step into what I'm assuming his office, and when I turn around to thank him, the door is already closed with the *click* of the lock greeting my ears.

CHAPTER EIGHT

It's been an hour and Mr. G. still hasn't come back to check on me. I may not remember what it was like to tuck my brothers into bed, but I do know it doesn't take this damn long.

After I called Miss Jean to let her know I'd be back in the morning, I tried the door even though I knew it was locked. I guess I was hoping it was just a game of sorts, something for him to pass the time to become "amiable" like Mrs. G. promised he would be, but no such luck.

I'm honestly locked in the office of the most beautiful man on Earth and a dead phone line on the next try to call out for some help, which I'm assuming was his plan the whole time.

Most accused get one phone call after they've been contained—even if I have nothing to be accused of.

Perhaps he doesn't like that I didn't make the kids lunch and that he had to let them encroach on his left-overs, or perhaps he doesn't like the fact that I didn't finish my dinner. Either way, this is getting more fucked up as the minutes tick by and I'm starting to slowly slip into survival mode.

It's strange because I haven't felt danger in such a long time, though I do intend to return any favor he may try to dole out to me.

I didn't get this far by staying on the straight and narrow lines of life.

I go back to his desk and sit down, making myself comfortable in his leather chair. I begin to pull open desk drawers and rifle around to see if there's anything that will give me some kind of idea as to what he does for work, but what I find sets my teeth on edge.

There are notepads, all blank and neatly stacked without a single word, line, or scribble inked into the pages.

I furrow my brow as I sit back and think. He has to do *something* to be able to afford this place, so what the fuck is it?

I glance over at the mouse sitting on the desktop and sit up. Gripping it, I give it a shake from side to side to bring the screen to life. Mr. G. doesn't seem to be a fan of passwords so the last thing he was working on fills the screen and I begin to read.

Seventeen year old female. Tattoos on legs, chest, and arms. Pretty, sassy, willing to train before sale.

"What the fuck? " I mutter under my breath.

Click.

Creak.

Chuckle.

I bring my legs up and cross them beneath me as I swivel the chair to glance over at the door. Mr. G. is standing there with a smirk on his face, a legion of demons dancing in his eyes, and a leather belt firmly wrapped around a fist.

"Lesson one: don't poke around in other people's affairs," he says softly.

I reach up to smooth my hair back, before I swing my legs down and get to my feet. I place my hands on my hips, square my shoulders, and look Mr. G. straight in the eyes.

"Don't forget the second part of that, Everett. Never try fucking with a bitch that's already lost everything," I reply evenly.

"Good," he remarks with a nod as he begins to walk toward me. "I love it when they put up a fight."

CHAPTER NINE

Mr. G. has a hand wrapped firmly around my throat. Each time he squeezes, I can feel my eyes bulge slightly and my lungs constrict resulting in a burning sensation.

"Lesson two: fuck when you're told to," he growls as he parts my legs with his knee and trades the hand around my throat for his belt. He quickly loops it, latching it on the tightest loop he can fit it through, then pulls it—and me—back with full force.

I grunt as my fingers begin to claw at the leather around my neck, trying to gasp for air, but it's no use. Mr. G. has lost his shit this time and honestly, I think it's been too long for either of us, anyway.

He opens one of the top drawers as he uses the belt to slide me up the desk, then closes it securely around the buckle.

Once he's secured me in place, he makes his way around the front of the desk and roughly pulls my shorts off.

I keep trying to find some way to breathe but I can tell

he isn't going to let up any time soon. Especially not when he rips my panties apart, tosses one half aside, and stuffs the other half into my mouth.

"Try not to be too loud," he instructs with a smirk as he hovers above me for a moment. I've seen that look he has in his eyes before; one too many times for my liking, and I only ever stopped seeing it when I moved into the shelter.

I close my eyes tightly and continue to tug at the belt. Granted, this isn't the ideal position to be in, but having my obituary say *died of asphyxiation due to panties and a belt,* isn't the lasting impression I want to leave behind.

I want to be remembered, but not like this.

As Mr. G. slips a finger into me, I do my best to try and lock my knees together, but he's much stronger than me.

"Lesson three: if you put up a fight, you should make sure you're capable of taking down the man that has you in such a compromising position, little girl."

I use my tongue to push my panties out of my mouth and take in as deep a breath as I can. He's going to be even more pissed off that I'm not gagged anymore, but I'll be angrier if I die like this.

Once again, I try to lock my knees together in an attempt to force his finger out of me, but he just laughs and finally relents.

"I guess you want to move on then, Meryska? Is that it?" he asks as I listen to the zipper on his pants being undone, then the dull sound of them hitting the carpet.

Mr. G. steps forward, forcing himself between my legs, parting them with ease, then places the tip of his cock against my pussy.

"When was your last time, little girl?" he asks in a thick tone.

I shake my head because I honestly can't remember and I can't form words since my damn oxygen is still being cut off.

As if he's read my mind—or decided to finally show some mercy—he presses his body against mine, holding me in place, as he begins to undo the belt loops and releases it from the drawer. I let out my breath in a rush as the leather finally gives way, then grunt, when he jerks me upright.

"This," he begins holding up one of my hands in my line of sight, "makes you look like a whore. Don't ever paint your nails this color again."

I blink rapidly a few times as the world explodes around me. It's not because he hit me, it's because my body is desperately trying to take in oxygen and get the blood flowing properly again.

Mr. G. loops the belt around his fist again, jerking my head back as he shoves his thick cock into me without mercy. He begins to thrust his hips in a manic, yet controlled manner. Almost like an animal aware that it has rabies and still trying to hold on to the shred of normalcy it felt before becoming infected.

He grunts as he continues thrusting, using me as his personal fuck toy—ragged, abused, and being trained for whoever places the highest bid on me.

Mr. G. pulls out of me for a moment and begins to pump his cock until he comes against the inside of my thigh, then uses the belt to force me to turn over onto my stomach, my face against the sweaty desk, and he enters me again.

The harder he fucks me, the more I bite back tears of pain.

The deeper he goes, the more I realized how much I missed this.

CHAPTER TEN

"What are you going to do about Calista?" I ask him after he's had his fill of me. My legs are shaking, my neck is bruised and raw, but I honestly can't remember a time I felt so damn wanted.

He lets out a tired chuckle as he runs his hand back through his hair, then grins at me.

"She hasn't caught us so far, what makes you think she'll be a problem?"

"Well, it was different before, Everett," I remind him with an eye roll. "Hotel rooms across state lines because you're 'on business' are different than having me in your home and taking care of your kids."

"You've got a point there," he says thoughtfully. He thinks for a moment as I use tissue from the box on his desk to clean up my thighs, then he snaps his fingers.

Everett walks over to his desk and sits in his chair, then taps a few keys on the computer to bring it to life.

I wrinkle my nose, "You could have at least let me get you a towel before you plunked your ass down."

"You'll clean it later," he replies dismissively.

"I will?"

"Mhm. With your tongue while I fuck you again," he says with a smirk as he hits the backspace bar on the keyboard a few times and then begins typing again.

I roll my eyes.

Everett loves to make me do degrading things because it helps get him off faster. I'm starting to think that's what the problem with Calista is—she's probably way too vanilla for his real tastes, whereas I just want to be his no matter the cost to my body and soul.

I met him a couple of years back when I was on my way to the mall, feeling very grand because Miss Jean had given me a twenty dollar bill for my birthday. I thought I was on top of the world and able to buy anything my heart desired.

Of course, when I tried to take a pile of new clothes to the register and found out I was wrong, Everett swooped in to save the day. He was there alone shopping for Calista but I guess I caught his eyes.

Could have been the tears of embarrassment falling down my face, or it could have been my ass hanging out of the bottom of my too-short-skirt, but that didn't matter to me.

Especially not when he paid for everything, told me to keep the twenty for a rainy day and have lunch with him in the food court. He told me I was the most beautiful girl he had ever seen and in return, I blew him in his car before we parted ways.

We've been fucking each other ever since behind Mrs. G.'s back. But she's been suspicious of him cheating on her lately, and we had to stop for a while. I busied myself at the shelter trying to take my mind off of him by doing menial things and playing secretary for Miss Jean, hoping that one of the phone calls would miraculously be him—even though he never knew where I lived.

I guess he's been feeling lonely lately and that's why he came up with this damn scheme of me babysitting his kids when I ran into him at the mall again. It kind of felt like fate wanted us to be together because when we laid eyes on each other, it felt like it was for the first time all over again, and I knew I couldn't be without him anymore.

He turned down every potential babysitter that called and urged me to hurry up and get an interview because Calista was losing hope.

And in a way, I guess he was too.

I hate that I had to fool my way into his home, but we played our parts well and now the only thing that's left is the ever lingering problem of his wife.

Everett finally stops typing and glances over at me. I'm standing on the other side of his desk, crumpled and used tissue in hand, and he tilts his head to the side for a moment.

His eyes travel up and down my body as he takes me in again. He loves my tattoos—hell, he paid for most of them as long as I agreed to let him sit in on the sessions because he didn't want "some young punk" trying to steal me away from him. He was particularly pissed off about how I got the ones I got before I met him and he wanted to make sure that I'd never have to resort to that again.

"You really are a beautiful girl, Meryska. Maybe one day, you'll see yourself the way I see you," he says, his eyes becoming soft.

My body burns crimson from the compliment. "Yeah, well ..."

Everett chuckles as he shakes his head, then reaches

under his desk for the wastebasket, holding it out toward me.

After I've deposited the dirty tissues he places it back beneath his desk and motions for me to come sit on the arm of his chair.

"So, how's this?" he asks as he slides an arm around my waist and rests the side of his face against me.

I lean in slightly and start reading.

Female. Thirty years old. Decent looking, already trained. Fertile, three thousand dollars or best offer.

"You're going to sell her?" I ask him curiously.

Everett laughs and shakes his head, "How else do you think I make money?"

"But the kids—what will they say when she never comes back?" I press cautiously.

He gives my side a gentle slap, "Up."

I get to my feet and lean against the desk while he begins typing again. As I wait for him to show me his next grand idea, I inspect my dark, red nails and sigh. *He's right—this color does make me look like a damn whore.*

"Alright, I think that does it," he finally says as he reaches for me and pulls me onto his lap.

I raise an eyebrow as I begin to read his new listing.

Female, ten years old. Male, eight years old. Dimwitted, barely able to earn their keep, spends most of their time playing board games and complaining. Unable to care for, willing to trade for a better set.

"They aren't ours anymore, Meryska. We'll find a pair of children that will compliment our new little family and this way, we won't have to answer any of their questions," he tells me as he kisses my arm.

I shake my head.

Well, he definitely knows how to handle things, I think

with a chuckle as I give the top of his head a gentle kiss in appreciation and approval.

A man that's willing to restart his entire life over to be with the woman he really wants is someone worth holding onto.

After Everett posted the listings to the Devil's Candy website, I went about cleaning up the house.

Once everything was nice and neat, I went into Anna Leigh and Maynard's bedrooms and started packing their belongings while they slept.

I know it won't take long before someone decides to take up Everett on his offer of a trade—especially not after I convinced him to post their pictures to sweeten the temptation.

Whoever gets them will be good to them, because like he said, they're simple and are happiest playing in Candy Land and ignoring the world around them.

We'll get the perfect children that will suit us just fine until I can give him some of his very own.

Everything we deserve will happen in due time because we're smarter than everyone around us, we love each other, and nothing can stop us from being together now that there's no one left to try.

ABOUT YOLANDA OLSON

Yolanda Olson is USA Today Bestselling and award-winning author. Born and raised in Bridgeport, CT where she currently resides, she usually spends her time watching her favorite channel, Investigation Discovery. Occasionally, she takes a break to write books and test the limits of her mind. Also an avid horror movie fan, she likes to incorporate dark elements into the majority of her books.

Sign up for her newsletter here.

And keep in touch with her online here:

MORE BOOKS BY YOLANDA

Inferno (Taboo)

Scavengers

Bones

LOVELESS

C.L. MATTHEWS

BLURB

I lie to everyone my entire life.
Hiding.
Lonely.
Loveless.
Then *he* came along.
The light to reveal me, casting my shadows away.
The partner to be here for me, who never allows me to be lonely again.
The man to prove I'm worthy, promising to show me I'm not loveless after all.
My little prince.
My savior.
My happy ending.
Mine.

CHAPTER ONE

TEXAS

We all stumble at some point.

That's not a dance reference but a life one.

Whether you're rich, somewhere in-between, or like me—dirt poor and homeless—we all experience a low. It may be really shallow and pure squalor, even less than the bottom of the barrel, or just a setback that makes your life temporary feel unstable. Either way, we all stumble, misstep, or trip at some point.

That's exactly what has happened to me.

My dad, Bert Silver, a hard-ass for all intents and purposes, is an ex-Navy Commander. He lived his life serving his country and met Mom when he was stationed at Everett. They fell madly in love, but I never experienced that side of him. Not that memories trigger, at least.

Mom died when I was five. Cholangiocarcinoma. A cancer that kills you swiftly from the inside of your liver, swallowing your life wholly.

My mom was our middle ground. She loved endlessly and made sure I'd never felt alone or helpless. Dad only loved me because she did. Since forever, my dad and I butted heads. I like color. He likes formation. Music is my addiction. Reading the Washington Post is his. Flavor is a necessity, but steak and potatoes could be his singular palette for life. One is up, while the other is down. We never see eye-to-eye, but I did the best I could. The problem is, my best and his best are opposites of one another. Mine is sub-par to his idea of exceptional, which means I'll never make him truly happy.

I've known since I was fifteen that I'm into guys. It was also the first time I tried and failed to sleep with a girl. She understood and believed me when I lied about drinking too much. Patty Sinclair, the first and only girl to ever kiss and touch me. Luckily for me, we went to different schools, and I never saw her again, but I will always remember her name, the eyes that seemed to know it all, and the smile she left with.

It wasn't until today, when I'm twenty-one years of age, that I finally got caught with my pants down.

Literally.

I'd been jerking it to porn on my cell. Nothing abnormal. It's all I can do being in a small-as-fuck town with as many gay people as there are gas stations. Five. That's a total of five. There's no one I could spend time with that won't get back to my dad somehow. I live at home while going to Valley West University. Living with Dad is all I can afford, and he allows it, claims it's the only way I won't be a sad excuse to his name, especially since I didn't go into the Navy. He wants me to be a huge businessman, while I want to be happy. That's right... *happy*. Doesn't seem so taboo, does it? Well, it is. Happy means being open about my attraction to dicks. In Valley West, dicks are only allowed to be inside pussies. Guess happiness won't happen after all.

The guy on the screen pounds into another lither one. They're both athletic and built, just how I like them, but the bottom is smaller like me. There's something addicting about muscles, wide shoulders, and the sheer voracity of how a man can pound into another's ass like it's their last shag. My hand grips my shaft greedily, wishing to be the man taking it, being pushed into like no one else could possibly get the top off like me. Right as I'm about to bust a nut, my dad comes in. I'm so lost in the moment that it takes me a huge breath to grasp the fucking situation I've gotten myself into.

The horror on his face only lasts a second before he witnesses the two dudes fucking on my screen. Perfect timing too, the top exclaims, "That's right, you little cumslut. Take my seed."

"What the fuck?" Dad's voice booms, and I've finally gathered my wits to pull up my boxers. "You're a fucking faggot!"

My whole body heats in shame and fear. That vein in his forehead I rarely see pops and pulses along with my raging heart rate, and I'm scared shitless.

"Dad—"

"Don't. Just get your shit and leave, Texas. Queers aren't welcome here."

It comes out softer than I expected, almost too calm with a touch of disappointment. He slams the bathroom door as he leaves, and I clean up, shut down my porn app, and get my grab bag.

When you live in a home with a military man, you always have a *go-bag*. It's something that holds essentials. Passport. ID. Clothes. First Aid kit. Dad was huge into planning for the end of the world. He even has an underground bunker in the Sevier Mountains a half hour east of our home. It's *just in case.*

I grab the picture of my mom and me as a kid, my bottle cap collection from friends that went around the world while I stayed in this Podunk town, and my bag. It takes me five seconds to breathe and to text Prim, my best friend.

Who is a girl.

Who doesn't know I'm gay.

She's my escape. Her fruity-colored hair and passionate vegetarianism brings me peace. I'm a carnivore, but she's practically a rabbit. Somehow, it works.

Dad kicked me out. Meet at Grounders? It's not our normal day to meet, but she'll keep me from having a full mental breakdown.

Grounders is our favorite coffee shop in the center of town. It's small, family-owned, and makes the best coffee. She's more of a tea girl, but luckily, they serve both.

I leave before my dad can come back inside and decide to beat some straightness into me. I've seen it happen on the shows he watches. It wouldn't be a surprise if that ends up being the route he takes. If you witness the way he talks about gay people, you would be disgusted.

I've given him excuses over the years because he's my dad. No more.

Sure thing, jelly bean. See you in ten.

Her text has me smiling. She never second-guesses me, just goes with the flow no matter how hard it may be for her.

I grab my car keys from the dangling wood plaque Mom made and rush outside. Dad can't keep my car. It's my only home from now on until I can get a job. Plus he didn't pay for it. Why I haven't had a job since high school was my first mistake. Dad told me to focus on school, and I didn't realize I wouldn't have anything to keep me afloat if he decided to finally disown me. Poor planning on my part.

Staring at the text message, I think of Prim. Primrose Loveless. We met at Grounders one day. Her hair back then had been a bright blue, almost still blonde but not, a glowing soft turquoise shade that made her seem angelic.

I would find out later, she was, in fact, an angel.

"Earl Gray with a dash of honey, whip cream, and sprinkles!" the barista yells out the finished order.

From around the aisle, a dainty little woman hops to the counter—literally skips—for her disgusting-sounding concoction. As the lady said, there is, in fact, whip cream and sprinkles. Even from several feet away, the rainbow diabetes drink is visible. My dark heart bleeds a little here for the unicorn in front of me. She has these piggy tail buns on her head, and there are stray hairs curled to make her seem even more charming. She's vivacious, full of life, the exact opposite of my dark self.

She's wearing white skinny jeans because she's insane with rips up and down the legs, bright blue leggings underneath them, and a soft pink crop top that's a little too baggy for her small frame. It hangs off the shoulder a little, and there's a small tattoo there. Meow. *It says* meow.

It takes everything not to chuckle at her, but a slight one slips out anyhow, and her eyes collide with mine. They're an orange-y color, almost feline. She offers me a raised eyebrow, and I smile.

I have no room to talk with my pitch-black outfit, gauged ears, seafoam green hair, lip piercing, and tattooed arms.

If not for already being called a delinquent waste of

space by my dad, my ink would definitely garner the same reaction from him. It's why I didn't second-guess every line, inch, or image on my body. Not even the piercings.

After I order my shotgun coffee, which wasn't something I chose for flavor, I find myself watching her from afar. Our eyes constantly meet in silent conversation. What would it be like to be that bright and comfortable with myself?

To be free and unbothered.

To live simply for the sake of living...

We became friends that day and spend every Wednesday getting drinks to talk about nothing. It's almost meaningless conversation. It's telling a stranger why you want to die or finding peace in another human because they just listen.

She's my human.

I listen.

She talks.

We *live.*

Even if it's not romantic, it's peaceful. It's platonic and safe, and she doesn't ask for anything in return but my ears and Wednesday afternoons.

The small distance drive to Grounders goes by quickly, and as soon as my car rounds the corner, her Tesla is already visible. Yes, a fucking Tesla. It stands out like a sore thumb, making it the most noticeable vehicle in town.

Prim is environmentally aware, so no gas guzzler for her. She definitely teases me from time to time for my 2005 Nissan Altima. It's not the worst carbon footprint offender, but it isn't as green as she is.

Oh, and she's a vegetarian. *Go meatless!* Inside joke. *Sorry.*

After parking, I lock my entire life in my car and head to the front.

"Tex!" Prim's exhaustingly exuberant voice beams from outside the door. Her pink cotton candy hair is down today, flowing in loose waves to her midback. In the few years we've known each other, she's refused to cut it.

Today, she's sporting shorts and a crop top. In this miserable foggy weather? No thanks. I'll stick with my black hoodie, black jeans, and combat boots. Her clothes are as bright as her, though, and it never ceases to make me smile.

The pain from earlier is the last thing on my mind as she brings me in for a hug. She's not fazed about my random invite at all. It's such a different response than all my other friends, none of which are in Washington anymore. The difference between Prim and them is astronomical. She's colorful, and they're dull. It's a perfect contrast. Everyone needs a little brightness to challenge their dark.

"I missed you," she hums into my chest.

Her arms tighten around me, begging for me to return the hug. I'm not much for embraces or touching. Any human contact is a restriction, a straitjacket to my soul, something that brings awareness and pain. It's why affection makes me uncomfortable.

My arms wrap around her eventually, knowing it's the only way she'll detach herself from me. As we awkwardly block the door to the shop, the barista Carol gives us a disapproving look.

"You're letting in the gray, you two."

Carol has been like a mom to me without the constant love. She's sixty-seven and quicker than a whip. Her hair is graying throughout, but it's barely noticeable with her being a blonde. Almost looks like shimmering silver, or at least, that's how she corrects me when I bring it up.

We hurry in, and she starts our order without asking. It's been like this for three years. Prim and I—my salvation. These meetups, our conversation, her peppiness.

There's no one in the shop. A smile tugs free at that. It means our table will be free of rando tweens and writers who pretend to work while browsing social media. Prim rushes to it, dragging my hand along. We get seated, and I just sigh. It's all I've got to offer after my shit morning.

"Let's talk, Tex," Prim articulates.

Her eyes are digging into my head, not literally, of course. She's trying to compile what transpired. I can't tell her, not the truth or reality of what happened. She wouldn't understand. If on the slim chance she would and isn't like every other snub-nosed person in this town, where would that leave us? Would she be accepting or weirded out? Would she not want drama or damaged-friend goods?

"My dad kicked me out. Not much to say other than a big disagreement he wouldn't compromise with. I don't have a job, so my car is my new home, and I'm tired as fuck."

She has this saddened expression marring her peaceful features, bringing her eyebrows downward and her lower lip out. It's an expression that needs to go away. I want to wipe it clear from her and not allow her to feel sorry for me. It's not her fault.

Prim, unlike most, isn't meant to be sad. It's almost more devastating for her to feel your emotions than experiencing them yourself.

"Don't be upset, Prim. I'll figure it out," I calmly say, trying to reassure her. And I will figure it out, not that there's much choice. Starving isn't on the roster. Homelessness won't do. "Just need to find a job and drop out. I can make it work."

"You're not dropping out!" she hisses loudly, peering around to see if anyone is listening. No one but Carol can hear, or she would tell us to hush. "I've got the perfect place for you to work."

My ears prick at that tidbit.

"What? Where?" The eagerness in my tone can't be cramped down with hesitation. I'm pretty desperate at this point.

She smiles conspiratorially. "You're twenty-one now, Tex. You can work at Drink More, Love Less!"

I stare at her, wondering why that sounds familiar. Yes, it's her last name, but—

"Your Dad's bar?" I ask, cutting off my own thoughts, realizing she told me once about the place. I might be twenty-one, but bars aren't my thing. If I got too drunk and hit on someone, I would be better off dead.

Prim nods, a big smile encompassing her face. "And you can stay with me. I've got extra room. Or rather, we do. Dad has another two spare rooms."

My eyes bug out. A bed. A place to stay.

It all sounds nice, but she's making these big decisions without her dad's approval. She may be nineteen, but she's still under his roof. There are restrictions. Believe me, I would know.

"No, that's okay. Don't need to make your old man hate you as much as mine does me."

"Oh, stop!" she says, exasperated. "He'll be fine. Plus, we know once you get on your feet, you can get a new place."

I'm nodding even though I shouldn't. I'm not a free-loader. I work for my shit.

"Maybe *we* can get a place together when you're in a better financial place," she continues. "I've been meaning to get a job, too. Imagine us living together."

The way she said *we* has me feeling bad in more than one way. We're best friends, yes, but she likes dick.

Me too, Prim. Me fucking too.

"Your drinks," Carol interrupts us with her raspy leather-like voice. It brings comfort, always has. It's like my home away from home, especially since that home was never more than a roof over my head. "If I had enough business to hire help, Texas, you'd be the first to know."

It's in those words and the shine of her eyes that I realize she's upset about my entire situation.

"Thanks, Care." The sincerity in my voice speaks volumes, and in return, she squeezes my shoulder.

After we start drinking, Prim comes up with a plan. I gave her shit for trying to push me onto her dad and begged her to have a conversation with him before jumping the gun. She gives me enough cash to stay at the little inn on the corner and to get dinner, saying she'll approach her dad about the job and moving in.

Lettuce pray.

Get it? She's a vegetable-tarian.

No?

Just me?

CHAPTER TWO

DEVIN

Married at sixteen.

A father at seventeen.

Gay the entire goddamn time.

My mom never raised a quitter. A man who likes dick, yes. But a quitter? Never.

When Whitney got pregnant, my first and only *wanted* time with a woman, I stayed. No one has to stay. Yes, for the child, but in the relationship? Not at all. No one wants a loveless marriage. But we found love, just not in the same way. Having sex with her for twelve years after, well, that nearly killed me.

Having a secret as deep and hidden as mine isn't an easy feat. Whenever we were in bed together, I had to imagine I was plowing into an ass. I'm such a prick, though. We never had face-to-face intercourse after the first time. It took everything to push into her at all and only ever from behind as I imagined a man beneath me.

It made me feel worse each time, but upsetting her made me feel physically ill. She only wanted love. We had a great friendship, something that grew and made us bond for years.

One day though, she found out the truth. Instead of a screaming match that anyone could expect, she hugged me.

"I had a feeling for a long time, Dev. For years, it seemed to hurt you to be with me. In your eyes, there was a respect and love, but in your heart, it was shelled and cracked, faking something you weren't capable of."

Her words make me cry. For the first time since our daughter was born, I cry. She understands in a way many people in this town wouldn't.

"I-I'm sorry." I choke over the words.

She pulls me closer, tighter, holding me together. "No need. Yeah, the time is gone and spent being unhappy in a romantic sense, but it's you, Dev. You stayed for our daughter. You loved me in the only way you could. You were never mean or hateful. You tried. We had a good life."

It was in that moment I realized how much I lucked out with Whit. She didn't berate me or call me harsh names, and we promised to not tell our daughter until I was ready.

We don't exactly live in an understanding and progressive town. If anything, we're frozen in the past, only sticking to one social norm of a man and woman.

Whit and I finalized our divorce when our daughter turned thirteen. It was harder on her than us. We never spoke ill. Hell, there isn't hatred on either side. She wanted love, and so did I. We deserved to live our lives and find our happy endings.

She did a few years later.

Now, it's my turn.

I'm just not sure how to broach dating or how to tell

my nineteen-year-old daughter that I'm gay. "Hey, I'm into dicks. It's why Mom and I aren't together."

Scratch that.

No, fuck that.

I'm not ready.

Why tell her when there isn't a single dude in Valley West who's openly gay and also someone I'm into?

It's not that I haven't been with men. Just that none of them are from this town, want a relationship, and are willing to relocate. It's tedious enough to drive two hours to find them. My first time was sloppy. *Awkward and quick.*

Whit and I had been separated for a whopping fifty hours. It took five shots of Jaeger and a shit ton of courage from the guy convincing me to top him.

"You're definitely a top," he muses. He isn't what I imagine I would want. Slim, tall, but shorter than me. Almost lanky and feminine in a soft but hard edges kind of way.

"A top?" I question, not knowing the lingo. In all the years I'd been with Whit, I never watched porn or let my eyes stray. Except that one time... *Why give myself a taste when I'd be in a closet and married to someone with the wrong-for-me parts?*

"You know, you do the fucking." His smile widens with that.

My dick jumps in my pants. Yeah, he likes that idea too. It's not a stretch. The thought of getting plowed hasn't really appealed to me. But giving? Hell yes.

"I-I've never done this," I mutter, almost feeling low and fucking ashamed. I'm thirty and have never been with a man.

"Oh, honey. It's not hard... yet." He laughs and escorts

me to his room. My first time could be a lot worse, that's for sure. At least he isn't an asshole.

It took me a few minutes to stop freaking out, but he showed me how to stretch him, and we fucked. I'm a little ashamed to say it was only five minutes. But we both came, and the next few times after that with different guys over the years, I found what I liked.

"Daddy!" my daughter, Primrose, yells from in the front room. Or is it the kitchen?

I'm getting ready for tonight's shift. Being a bar owner has its advantages. I can do whatever I want, show up when I want, and still manage fine.

"In here!" I holler back, folding up the cuffs to my buttoned-up shirt sleeves. We have a fairly casual establishment. They all wear the logo tees and whatever else they want. I'm a little more old-fashioned. Buttoned-up with a shirt underneath and nice jeans with boots. It's not too fancy, but I keep a clean cut.

She opens the door and comes toward me. "I need to talk to you. It's really important."

I raise an eyebrow. Primrose always beams in one way. Whether it be her colorful attire or her radiant smiles, she's vibrant in everything. Tonight, she seems nervous—possibly even scared.

"What is it, wild child?"

She smiles at that, and the glimmer of light that leaks through her stressed gaps make me believe she's serious. My child, the one who brings my life full circle, is never this out of place in her own skin.

"Remember my friend I told you about?" she asks, her eyes a little downcast.

The thing about Prim, is that she has tons of friends. If she walked into a bar—my bar, even—everyone and their cat would be her friend. *Especially the cat. She's obsessed.* I'm allergic, so that's a no go, but she loves from afar.

"Which one?"

She pouts, and I can't help the chuckle that leaves me. With that, she's crossing her arms and narrowing her eyes. She reminds me of when she was little and would get whatever she wanted with that adorable expression. Not much has changed.

"You're friends with the entire town, sweetheart."

"I know, Dad, but jeez, you could try and think of the only person I always talk about."

"Texas?"

She nods.

"I thought you were talking about the state. I didn't realize this was a person."

She smacks my arm lightly, her glare as admonishing as a unicorn's glitter. "*Dad.*"

"*Primrose,*" I tease.

She huffs, and I love this immature side, the childish one that reminds me she'll always be my little girl.

"He got kicked out today, and I offered him a job and a spare room," she rapidly explains. It's like she ran a race with how fast she spilled the words out.

My eyes widen. This Texas is apparently a guy. My daughter has... a *guy*? *Abso-fucking-lutely not.*

"Are you two dating? Scratch that. There's no fucking way your boyfriend will stay under the same roof as my daughter."

"Daddy! Come on. He's not my boyfriend. We're *just friends.*"

"Just friends, my ass. I was a boy once, Primrose. They only want one thing."

"He's twenty-one! Not a child. He's desperate and has *no one*. Please, Daddy," she implores, using those doe eyes—the ones that are slightly glistening with emotion and hurt—that force me to almost give in.

"Fine. He can stop by tomorrow. We'll talk then."

She jumps up and down and squeals. "Thank you, Daddy!" Her arms wrap around me as she continues to celebrate. What I would do for my child.

"I've got to head out, but we'll talk tomorrow. It'll be a late night tonight. Stock order."

"See you then!" she squeaks before kissing my cheek and running off.

I swear if this dude is only trying to fuck my daughter, he's in for a rude awakening.

I'm not scared to show him the door.

CHAPTER THREE

DEVIN

The bar is already being prepped by the time I get here. We open in an hour, and the only thing I do beforehand is to make sure everything is on task for the start of the night. We already had our shipment delivered, restocked, and cleaned.

We've been waiting ages to branch out, and finally, we can afford it. People think expansion isn't as costly as it is. You can live a lush life for a tenth of the price versus starting up another location.

The new store in Vegas opens up in a few months. Dusty manages everything for now, but even my best worker can't handle it all. I'll have to fly out and help too, which will mean leaving Landon, Sandra, and Jules to run this store.

I'm blessed to be managing a store and starting a new one in another state altogether. Yes, I'm living the dream, but I want more in life. Don't we all?

After I double-check everything, the doors open, and our regulars pour in. Todd comes straight for me, knowing I'll make his Old Fashion in a jiff without question.

Sliding it back to him, I head to the tables the patrons usually are, and go back to my laptop.

Searching real estate in Vegas isn't easy. It's not cheap, and anything somewhat near the bar is gaunt and overpriced. I look into nearby cities, especially Overton and Mesquite. They're close but far enough to be cheap. They're pretty unpopulated, too, which means it won't be too hard to venture around. Nevada is an open-minded state. Being gay isn't a big deal there, and in Vegas, I could meet tons of new people and possibly even find love.

After bookmarking a few properties that appeal to me, I head toward the bar and watch Sandra and Landon pour drinks for people.

On the far side of the tabletop, I notice someone I've never seen in here before. Not in this town or my bar. His hair is dark, but with the lamp shining down on parts of it, I can tell it's a deep blue, navy possibly? Like my jeans but with black roots. It's longer, wavy, edgy and different, but it also makes him seem very young. A *hipster*. Like my daughter, he's not going with normal hair color.

Unable to help myself, I make my way to him, spotting arms full of tattoos and a lip piercing that glints in the light.

He doesn't see me yet, so I take the time to admire his sharp jaw and sad posture. He's troubled. I'm not sure how, but I can tell from his presence.

An urge swells within me to help him out. It's what makes me a good bartender, knowing the people, feeling them out, and listening to their stories. I know so many stories without asking for them.

From behind the bar, I reach for a towel, I'm finally in front of him. I wipe the area down out of habit, and he finally peers up. His piercing honey eyes connect with mine, and my heart beats a little faster. *Weird.* I'm not one for being attracted to *different* or *young* and he's definitely both. The despondence in his posture has a frown decaying inside me, unwilling to break free and scare him off.

"Another?" I ask, nodding to his drink. I'm not sure what it is, but I'll help him to whatever he needs. Maybe even just to hear him speak, to feel his pain, and to soothe whatever misery he's carting around.

"Not sure if I should. I don't drink often," he mutters, his face full of emotions that refuse to spill out.

"Need a cab then?" I offer, not wanting this kid to wander off but not wanting him to leave either. It doesn't make sense why I'm experiencing this urge to keep him here.

He doesn't seem even a little tipsy. The stiffness in his shoulders make me believe he's ready to bolt at any wrong move. His desire to leave might be more aimed at despair and the wish to be alone than it does his excuse of not drinking often. Either way, it doesn't stop the need unfurling inside my chest to help him.

"No."

It's one word, but it feels like a punch to the balls, bringing a larger pit from my stomach to my chest, weighing heavily with each beat.

"What're you having?" It's not exactly a question but rather a band-aid, a forced one. "On the house."

His eyes meet mine again, and he tongues his piercing with his fingers, almost like he doesn't understand my kindness. He pulls on it, making it indent his lip in an appealing way. My cock stirs at the motion, a burning in my insides, making me crave the taste of silver, and I long to delve into its flavor.

"Jaeger," he whispers, eyeing my mouth in a way that makes my chest tighten.

Fuck. What is it with this guy? I've never felt even a glimmer of attraction for anyone in this town, yet this stranger walks into my bar and has me wanting to use my stock room.

"Good choice."

"Fucks me up every time," he muses, but there's no smile. Just sadness. A whole lot of fucking sadness.

I grab the entire bottle and two glasses and end up pouring us both a shot.

"Jaeger's my poison," I admit when he doesn't ask me the question burning in his gaze.

He takes it, raising to his mouth. "To poison."

"To poison," I respond and throw it back. By the time I lick the edge and glance at him again, his eyes are honed in on my throat, and the lust reflecting in his eyes has me steel in my jeans. Fuck.

Unable to resist the urge, I nod toward the stock room, giving him the option to see if he's interested. His eyes follow the movement. Putting up a hand for five minutes, I turn in that direction. No one seems to have caught our silent conversation, but I tell my bartenders I'll be back.

As I make it to the room, my heart races, galloping like a fucking horse. I've never done this, not in this town, definitely not in my own bar, and sure as fuck not with someone my daughter's age.

He's drinking, though, so he has to be legal.

A knock sounds on the door five minutes later, and I open it to see him standing there with the most devilish lip bite known to man. My lips tilt in a smirk, and I'm happy to know it wasn't a one-sided attraction.

It's not like you can stare at someone and see that

they're gay, but when someone flirts, it's usually telling enough.

His hand connects with the door, and he closes and locks it. He saunters over to me with sureness. If I had an ounce of his confidence at his age, I would have been a happier man a helluva lot sooner.

Instead of letting him lead, though, I take his face and crash my mouth to his. Surprise stiffens his posture for only a moment before a small groan rips from him. My cock practically rages against my zipper, wanting an escape. When my tongue strokes his metal, my body shivers in response, making my nipples as stiff as the drink we just shared.

The silver of his piercing has me growling against his mouth. I push him against the metal door, grinding my cock into him.

It wants all he has to offer.

Feeling him solid beneath me has me desperate with a need to roar with some type of exultation. It's an impulse that should scare me, but it doesn't. He ruts against me, rocking our hips together while our lips fuck how our bodies are desperate to. Our teeth clack when we go the same way twice, and it only has the molten urgency between us growing.

"Fuck," he grunts against my lips, pulling back to run a hand through his hair. Is it soft? Why the fuck do I want to fuck him so bad and pull on it while he screams for me?

My cock twitches at that. We're in agreement.

It's been months since I've been to Olvier, the town where I go to meet men. If I'm not in this guy in the next five seconds, my cock might actually die.

I don't want to talk or ask questions. It's unsafe and

intense, scary, even, but I just want to taste, lick, and fuck this sad boy.

It's a bad combination that has me salivating. Crowding him against the door again, I sniff his throat. It's so primal of me, but I can't help it. It's an incessant compulsion burning, blistering, and begging me to mark, mark, mark.

He groans as my tongue licks a path to his ears, finding huge ass holes in them. I tongue them too, deciding all these differences in him from the normal men I've been with makes me deprived of freedom, like a caged bull.

"Fuck, fuck, fuck," he practically sings in my hair.

I bite the tendon in his neck, the one where his heart-beat throbs, beating life into him. After licking it better, I suck and suck and suck. He moans, his legs slightly giving out at the motion. There's nothing I crave more in this moment than to leave my imprint, to give him my name in the only reasonable tattoo I can offer.

Pulling back to see my hard work, I grin. It's the most pride I've felt in a long time. I take no time to remove his shirt, he allows it, just sitting back for the ride. My, my, *sad boy*. Soon, my cock will be so deep he'll scream.

Ogling his muscular body, I hum my approval. He's fit beneath his baggy black shirt. My eyes catch his light brown nipples and the little barbells through each one, and I fucking lose it. Leaning down, I flick one with my tongue and pull on the other.

"Fuck!" he groans as if in pain. Not a pain that asks me to stop, though, the kind you can only get from pleasure.

"We've got to teach you more words than that, *kid*."

"Not a kid," he grunts, touching my chin and urging it upward. "I'm a fucking man."

His words come out sharp and harsh before he bites my bottom lip and takes my mouth for his gratification. Now it's my turn to groan as he grips my raging dick in his hand. He's not soft or sweet. He knows what he wants.

"You're fucking huge," he hisses.

I take his hands, both of them, and successfully pin them above his head.

"Hope you love a good pounding, *sad boy*." Only a flicker of fear settles over his eyes before he's simpering.

"Do your worst, *bartender*."

I want to correct him and tell him I'm the mother-fucking owner, but I like the game, and I like that he sees us as equals. It's his ass that I'll be taking, though. He'll enjoy every thrust, that much I promise.

As I lean forward, my nose drags down his cheek, and I inhale his masculine scent. It's crisp like mint and linen, mixed with that musk that only a man exudes. His skin feels perfect beneath the bite of my teeth. He's rubbing into me as I taste him, and I'm unrushed for the first time tonight. Only pulling back to get to business, I release his arms that carry my fingerprints like a brand.

"Undo my pants, *kid*."

He narrows his eyes for only a moment before he's brushing his chest against mine. Instead of reaching for my pants as I've told him, he crouches and bites the flesh of my hips. I hiss, grabbing his hair as he continues his exploration. *Soft*. It's softer than I pictured, so fucking delicate in its purity. After strumming my fingers through it, my fist tightens at the back, forcing his throat to be exposed.

Purple.

Blue.

Red, red, red.

A growl emanates from me, seeing my marks on him, remembering the taste of his salty raised skin.

"Can't handle a little tease, *bartender*?"

His taunt is all it takes for me to dominate again.

He'll know exactly what I can handle, and he'll never question it again.

CHAPTER FOUR

TEXAS

What the fuck am I doing?

Who is speaking for me? *'Cause it's not me.*

My heart nearly explodes out of my chest as the bartender's deep amber eyes penetrate me as surely as his massive erection is about to.

I've never done this. No matter how many men I've watched get plowed or do the plowing, it's nothing in comparison, this I'm sure of. There's no connection, nothing but cameras, lube, and the knowledge that someone is going to be jerking off to it.

And his cock? It's huge. Porn star envy huge.

My entire body throbs with unabated yearning. All I've ever wanted was to find someone who's into dicks as much as I am and show me I'm worth every second of that returned craving.

He stares at me as if I'm his and *only ever* his. It's shaking me inside, rattling the battered cage holding my beating vessel inside. I'm not used to this kind of desire, especially reflected back to me from a man who could put

David Gandy to shame. Maybe it should scare me that he's older, more meticulous, and has his life together, but it doesn't.

You don't get to choose who finds you.

Only how you allow them to keep you.

He forces me to my feet. My teasing must've set him off, and it's the most exciting thought, knowing I attain that power over a man as strong and as beautiful as this one.

His fingers find my jaw, tilting it to the side, studying, appreciating, and landing on the hickeys I'm sure he left. It was so hot, feeling his tongue lash at me as if I've misbehaved and he had the utmost urgency to teach me a lesson. And his teeth...

I've lived in a fantasy world since I was fifteen, a world that never anticipated this bartender and his skilled mouth and hands. It couldn't possibly prepare me for every sensation zipping through me right now.

"Turn around," he demands. His voice is so low and gravelly, deep and unrestrained. It's my new favorite sound.

"I'm guessing you can't handle—" I begin to taunt before he forces me to turn around, my cheek against the metal surface of the door, and he smacks my ass *hard*. A hiss escapes, unburdening me with its loss.

"That mouth of yours," he rasps before reaching around to undo my pants, "is going to get you in a world of trouble, but don't worry. I'm an excellent teacher."

As they drop, I hear the sharp intake of his breath. Did I mention I didn't put on boxers after showering? His hands roam my ass worshipfully, and everything in me wishes to see the strained expression more than likely pinching his face as he roves over me.

"What? Nothing to say?" It's meant to come out mockingly but comes more as a plea.

He squeezes my right ass cheek, almost as if he can't resist, like he's memorizing every inch.

"Fuck," he groans painfully, his tenor raw, fileted open like my heart right now.

I crane my neck at him, hoping he doesn't notice my innate need to watch him, at this first touch, my only experience with a man. He hovers over me surely, tracing himself above my skin without touch, inking himself respectfully against my bare flesh.

My dick feels like it'll bust through the door at this rate while waiting for him to fucking touch me. I hear a rustling from him but can't see anything.

When the hot and hard flesh of him brushes the crack of my ass, I breathe in so deeply, forgetting why I'm here in the first place. Not this room, but the bar. I'd meant to escape, and I guess that's exactly what I'm doing. It's all erased when he rubs the rigid length of himself up and down, making me feel how he's about to take everything from me.

It's hot. Sweltering. I'm melting into a pool of *Texas Silver* by this man.

He grips my hips with purpose, dragging his mouth to my gauged ears. "So fucking hot," he whispers, his breath teasing my sensitive flesh. His fingers tweak my nipples, and the feel of him lowering to the ground has a chill of both anticipation and fear slicing through me.

"W-What are you—"

"Shh," he silences me, dragging a finger down the swell of my cheeks and between their crease. It's purposeful, deliberate. He's testing both our limits.

As soon as his finger slides between, teasing my hole

with the patience of a practiced man, I fist my palms. This is the first exploration of my body by anyone other than me. I can finger myself over and over, but nothing feels as intimate as this man below me.

He's wrecking me.

The touch of his lips on my right cheek has me whimpering. I'm losing it while my dick leaks against his cold door, proving the influence he has over me. If he wouldn't yell at me, I'd rut against it and force my release. But bad boys get punished, and bartender here wouldn't second guess a punishment.

The sensation of his breath hovering over my spine has me arching into him. He spreads my cheeks, and there's a stroke that ignites an explosive ardor inside every nerve ending.

"Holy shit," I rumble as his tongue probes the tight ring. He licks up and down and fondles my balls as he continues his ministrations. "*Goddammit.*"

I'm a mess. My tip leaks as he fucks me with his mouth. After I'm practically falling into a heap in response to the sensations tingling my shaft, he stops. It's silent. All that's present is the music humming from the bar and our staggered breathing.

"You're fucking perfection, *little prince.*"

Little prince? I argue in my head, not wanting to ruin the moment he's sharing with me. I'm far from royalty, and I'm not revered in any case, either.

There's a bit of shuffling before his fingers are back at my entrance, wet, cold, and probing. It's soft at first, like a featherlight caress, a whisper only shared between two lovers in the dawn of night. It's molten. Invading chills build from my toes and rise to my nipples, making them feel even harder than their normal pierced pebbles.

Then, he hits that spot, the one they show in porn, the pleasurable one, and I fucking yell.

He chuckles and bites my shoulder harshly. "That's it. Scream for me, little prince. Let it all out while I make you fall to your knees for your king."

I groan in approval as he adds a second finger and then another. The full feeling offers sweat and peace. Perspiration lines my forehead, trails my spine, and tingles every inch of me. It's perfect, so fucking good.

"Tell me you want my cock, and I'll feed it to you," he grits into my ear, commanding, brushing his muscular chest against my dampened back. He grinds into me, and I break.

"Fuck me," I demand, needing to feel him filling me up.

"That doesn't sound like you're desperate," he taunts, leaving scorching kisses across my shoulder blades. His teeth dig in, dragging, stealing heavy pants from me. I want to push back against his swollen length, to force him into me.

"Stick that monster in me, and show you're better than I've ever had," I mock.

He removes his fingers to fill my ass. It's rough and a one-shot, splitting me in two while bringing me to a sort of completion I've never experienced. He doesn't need to know I'm a virgin and haven't done this before.

Ferocity is worth the lie.

Pleasure is worth the pain.

Escape is worth the loneliness.

"What's that? Need me to remind you that my cock is the only cock you'll ever have? Is that what you want?" he barks as his hips smack me rhythmically.

The pain has already gone away along with my trepidation, and I'm practically a mess of moans and pure lust as he pistons into me. It's everything I never knew was missing in life.

"Yes," I practically whimper, putting the majority of my weight into the door.

He reaches around me and fists my length, his hand smacking the door with every sloppy draw.

The warmth of his hand has me thrusting in sync of both his fist and cock. I leak all over his palms and fingers, and he groans his approval into my neck. He towers over me, sucking on my throat and shoulders, all while keeping his pace rigid and wild.

"That's right, *little prince.* Take my cock."

His voice has my orgasm swimming through my body and out of my dick so hard that I'm seeing stars. Sweat seeps out of my skin as my release beckons.

"Yes, just like that."

We thrust together a few more times. His body slows and jerks with each one.

"Fuck. So good and tight," he hisses, sending shivers through me. "Come with me, little prince."

He barely gets the words out as he comes inside me, and mine has already painted the door. We're panting, heaving against each other in a perspiring mess, and all that I can think about is that I've never felt this harmonized in my life.

His lips meet the space between my shoulder blades, leaving the softest kiss I've ever felt. I lean against him, wanting to hold onto this moment for as long as I can.

He brings his arms across my chest, holding me like I'm his lover, like this is any other night and we're fucking because we love each other, need each other, and can't imagine a better way to lose time.

It hurts. It feels good. It's so confusing.

"Tell me, little prince. What's your name?"

I still beneath him. If I tell him, I'll be screwed. Hell, I'm not sure if I'm ready to meet Prim's dad tomorrow and ask for a job. If I have to work with this guy, it'll make everything a mess. He's too hot for me to resist, and I'm too hidden to come out.

"I'm thirsty," I whisper, evading his question.

As I turn to him, he grips my face as if he knows this ends here. His lips connect with mine, and we only part so he can get dressed and grab us drinks.

I stare at his flushed face, really taking him in now. He's got at least four inches on me with dark, nearly-black hair that's messy in a sensual way. My bartender towers me in both height and muscle, like the man in the porn from this morning.

His shoulders are wide and strong. There's a smattering of hair across his chest, and it's unbelievably sexy. My eyes roam his hips, and I bite my lip ring when I see the deep lines that lead to his already stiffening cock.

And, boy, is it a fucking cock. Huge, veiny, and ready to go again.

My chest feels warm at the sight of him and the realization that he took my virginity, gave me a semblance of peace, and cherished my body like it was his honor.

In this moment, I feel free.

I kiss him again, unable to resist a last taste for the road before he heads out. After the door clicks, I rush to get ready, not wanting to be here when he gets back and forces me to give him my name. Without my boxers, I can feel his seed ease out of me, proving he's planted in me, ingrained deep.

It's now or never, I think.

Then I do what I do best.
I run.

CHAPTER FIVE

DEVIN

"Another Jaeger good?" I ask as soon as I re-enter the stock room, holding what's left of the liter we used for our first shots. When I lift my gaze and meet nothing but booze crates and everything else that's usually in here, my stomach caves a little at the sight of the barren room.

As dank and somber as it is normally, it feels even more so now. It's as if he was never here. Nothing is out of place. The only thing that gives anything away is the used lube packet on the floor.

"Guess not," I angrily mutter.

My heart sinks for some unknown reason. It was a simple fuck, right? A quick rump without strings attached. I've done this several times out of town with different men each time.

We agreed.

The difference here is that I fucked him bare. *Bare.* I'm so fucking dumb. Tension had been high, and my dick made all the decisions, not that he mentioned it either. Regardless, we weren't cautious at all.

I'm never careless.

Not once have I gone without a condom. It's always the first thing on my mind. If not for the lube in my wallet, we wouldn't have even fucked.

Fuck. My soul aches as if this pivotal moment was meant to be more than one night. It throbs almost as much as my shaft did when he teased me. With other men, teasing never turned me on. When they baited me, it made me soft. But my sad little prince? He tore me up.

He's *still* tearing me up.

Why do I care? He's probably an out-of-towner who needed a fix, a bedmate for the night, something *fun* to tell his friends when he goes home. They don't come often. There isn't much up in Valley West, but it happens.

He didn't even tell me his name.

My little prince is enigmatic, nothing I've experienced before. Hard and soft, a perfect blend of the two, creating a harmony I didn't realize I need until now.

I sit on the wooden pallets in the farthest part of the room and just relive our moments. The shared breaths. Moans. My mouth on him. His body painted with my hands, tongue, and teeth.

Not once in all the times I've been with a man did I feel the connection my blue-haired sad boy and I shared. He had to have felt it, too. It burned too bright to ignore. It festers even now. He's only been gone for twenty minutes top, yet it feels like a wisp of memory. His scent still wafts in the room, keeping his memory perfunctory, but that's all he left. Did he have secrets, too? Ones that forced him out the door?

Would he have stayed if I told him we could meet up again? That even though we only just met and fucked I wanted it to be a permanent thing?

What's wrong with me?

I drink and drink until the bottle of Jaeger is long gone and spots line my vision. By the time I wake up, my back is sore. My neck feels like it stayed angled wrong too long, and the music from the bar is dead. Shuffling out of the room, I spot a note on the door.

Bossman,

We figured you needed the sleep. Locked up, and left the key in the lockbox outside.
See you tomorrow.

- The coolest employees ever

If my soul didn't feel so detached from my body, I would laugh. Landon, the smart ass. He had to have written the note. Sandra would've smacked me into awareness. She isn't one to let it slide when anyone drinks on the job.

This hasn't happened since Whit and I had *the* conversation. The drinking only truly happened because of the guilt of making her stay so long in a romance-less marriage. It drove me to be less of a man for a while.

Now, I'm foggy, hungover, and cotton-mouthed beyond belief. Unlocking my cell, I notice several texts from my daughter.

Dad? You okay? You said you'd be late, but it's like five in the morning.

I'm calling Sandra.

I searched the entire house, even your mini man cave in the back. Where are you?

Sandra said you got wasted. That's so unlike you. Talk to me. What's wrong?

I'm guessing you haven't woken up. I'll wait for you.

Nausea claws its way up my throat, making me heave before I race to the bathroom. I stumble through the door, getting to the sink before hurling up all the liquid in my stomach. That's all there is. *Booze.* Did I even remember to eat yesterday? It was a busy day, and duties needed fulfilling... Jesus.

Wiping my mouth, I rinse the sink and mentally chastise myself for the choices I've made in the last twenty-four hours. Then, I gargle with some water to clear the alcoholic burn frothing in my throat.

Checking the time, I see it's nine in the morning. Fuck, I'm such a bad father. Flipping the water to cold, I splash it on my face, hoping to get out of this fog of sadness and culpability. After a few deep breaths, I try collecting myself.

Prim's going to ask so many questions.

What the hell do I say?

"Hey, princess, I think I met my soul mate last night. Oh, and here's the kicker. It's a guy. *I'm gay.* Sorry I didn't tell you, but I've been in the closet my entire life. *Great conversation.*"

Yeah, this fucking sucks. No matter the turn of events, it won't bode well for me.

I drive home on autopilot, hoping to get a shower before her friend stops by. Hopefully, he isn't there already. That would be embarrassing for me and her. How do I grill the dude who may have bad intentions when I can't even admit to my daughter that I'm not into women? She's going to flip. My only wish is that she didn't really stay up the entire night. She's a worrier, never willing to back down on the ones she loves.

What a snafu.

———

Texas

I've never run from a situation faster. He wanted my name, and I fucking booked it while he went to get us a drink. Maybe it's being a closeted gay or the fact that he could tell Prim since her dad owns the place. Either way, fear took over me in an instant. There's a less than zero chance I'll forget our time together. His possessive hands are engraved on more than just my skin. How do you get a connection from one simple chance encounter? It's like fate. We met and found each other, but we both didn't end up together.

They never claimed fate wasn't cruel.

Bartender was not only my first. He left his mark in more than one way.

After staring at myself for an insanely long time in the mirror of the little inn, I jerked off several times just to ease the tension rolling off me in waves.

My body has many colors. All are beautiful and all from a man with more experience than I have. I'm such a piece of shit. He *cared*. Anyone could tell. I'm not sure why, but I cared too. Even with us barely meeting, you couldn't hide the way his eyes held me up and that nickname...

Little prince.

My body warms at the memory.

I didn't sleep at all, unable to get the memory of us together and, to top it off, how I left. It shouldn't bother me that we're strangers and had a one-night stand of sorts, but somehow, it does. This hasn't happened to me *ever*. Not a single soul in this shitty town has ever caught my attention, yet the single time I walked into that bar, lost and confused, a man as big and as powerful as him gave me a simple look and stole my soul in one night.

Now, as I head to Prim's house on zero sleep, feeling like shit, I hope I make a decent impression on her pops. I'm also praying she can't somehow tell where and how my night was spent. I've literally got hickeys and bruises all over from Bartender. He took and gave and made me want the touch of no one else but him ever again.

I'll have to come up with some story just in case she asks, a lie to somehow not get a job with him. How would that work? My being employed by my best friend's father while employed by that man? It won't work. I'll be a mess, and they'll all know something is up.

Instead of my cut-off shirts, I wear a black *Falling in Reverse* hoodie with their last tour on the back and *Everybody's on Drugs* on the front. Probably not the smartest move when I'm going to meet someone who I need to make a *good* impression on, but it's my good luck shirt.

If I show my neck at all, she would know. The only thing helping is the fact that the jacket covers most of my chest-to-neck area. Even still, there are colors everywhere. *Marks*. Tattoos from his mouth. My jeans, like usual, are ripped and skinny, and I'm topped with a beanie over my blue locks, hoping it will distract her from the hickeys under my ear where he wouldn't stop caressing, sucking, and owning.

That's what he did.

He owned every part of me last night.

Seems like he hasn't quite let me go, either.

As soon as I've arrived at Prim's, the anxiety comes rushing back. Everything depends on whether this man accepts me. My own father wouldn't, so why would this complete stranger?

Her Tesla is parked in the drive. A huge truck that looks like it's meant to be in a competition is parked next to it. I wonder if he has something to make up for with such an unnecessarily large vehicle. That's what they always say, at least.

Parking on the curbside of their house, I breathe out a shaky sigh. It's full of angst, despair, and a lot of desperation.

My mind travels to where life will lead if this plan doesn't work. I wonder how long it'll take for my dad to turn off my phone. I'll have to get a new plan. School starts soon, and I'm nowhere near being prepared. Luckily, the deadlines for financial aid happened last winter, or I'd be shit out of luck for money. Valley West doesn't have on-campus dorms like normal universities. The housing is through a nearby complex. It's way too expensive. Staying with Prim and her dad will save me.

If it happens, at least.

Their house is much bigger than Prim made it seemed. It's modern, and the bottom half of the house is layered in stones—river rocks, I think. The top almost looks tiled in slabs. Its cool gray tones and shuttered windows make it appear as the perfect house. The front door and garage one are both black, and the pillars leading to the entrance give it a grander appeal. Prim never said her dad was loaded.

As I raise my hand to knock, the door opens. Her cotton candy pink hair greets me. It's in piggy tail braids today. Her face is makeup-free, which is a nice change.

She usually goes for a glowing angelic appearance, but her fresh face shows her natural beauty and charming freckles.

"Hey," I say, my voice sleepy, almost too dragged out.

She smiles. "Hey, yourself. You look exhausted, Tex."

I chuckle at the way she scrunches her nose. "Didn't sleep."

"Me either. We'll match." She yawns, covering it as she moves to let me in. "Dad's in the shower. He'll be out soon. Coffee?"

I nod, even though my body is tingling with more nerves than my fingertips have. While she makes the coffee, I sit in an anxious stupor, waiting for something to blow up. That's how my life always works.

"What are you doing here?" I hear his gravelly voice sound out from nearby.

Jerking my head, I gape, and my heart stops.

It must be a trick. I left him last night. Am I asleep? Drunk? My eyes rake his frame. He's in a buttoned-up shirt, and his near-black hair is wet and sexy, little wisps flicking in every direction. He looks as exhausted and as sad as I feel.

His amber eyes meet mine.

Lifeless. Loveless. Pissed.

Wondering if I'm imagining things, I shake my head, which causes my hair to reveal part of my throat. A growl rumbles from my bartender.

"Oh! Daddy, looks like you've met Tex." She's holding two mugs in her hand, giving one to me and one to *him*.

It hits me that she just called him *Daddy*. Daddy? My eyes must look like fucking saucers because he offers a clipped nod, and I'm trying to hide my neck in the next breath.

"Daddy, this is Texas Silver. Tex, this is Devin Loveless. My dad."

Devin. That's my bartender's name. Not bartender... *Owner.*

I swallow. It's more like a dry sand-papery gulp, forcing a discomfort able pang and a soft hum to burst through my body simultaneously.

He hasn't stopped glaring, and his gaze is pointed at where he touched me last night. It's like he's angry but possessive. There's this greedy and envious look in his eyes that has me shifting from foot to foot. It's like he's tearing off my clothes but choking me while he does it. I can't tell if I'm terrified or aroused. *Both?* my treacherous mind offers.

"Hello," I try, failing at sounding normal. Putting my hands in my pockets, I watch as his attention roams lower, and I'm praying that he can't see the stiffness I'm hiding.

Prim smacks her dad's chest lightly, not noticing his steely expression is for me because of last night and not for reasons she's probably shuffling through.

"Don't be rude, Daddy." He hands her his cup and steps toward me. Too close. Too fucking close. T-Too... close.

She doesn't know I'm gay.

A shiver goes through me. With him so close, I'm ten times tenser than before.

"Hello, *little prince,*" he whispers low enough for only me to hear.

My dick jumps in my pants, straining against the fabric, wanting its master. His hot, heated body somehow emanates into mine, making me feel so many things I'm not allowed to feel about my best friend's dad.

"It's nice to meet you," he rumbles grumpily, loudly, wanting Prim to hear. "Primrose has said a lot about you."

"I-I, uh," I stumble over a response. "She has?"

"Daddy! Don't be embarrassing," she hisses from behind him.

He steps away from me, giving me a look that isn't decipherable. His face almost seems pained when she pulls me into her arms. She kisses my cheek, and it takes everything in me to not flinch at the sensation.

He narrows his eyes at us both, honing in on me as if I've physically hurt him. And maybe I have. He asked for my name, and running was my only answer.

Even my heart throbs from my actions, especially now. Prim never mentioned her dad is gay. Not that it would have ever came up, but she bleeds her truths and information without trying. She knows I'm not one to talk. I listen.

"How was last night, Tex? I got worried when I didn't hear from you."

Prim's words are laced with offense. She's right. I should've made sure to check-in. After all, she's saving me. Or trying to.

She pulls away, and her makeup-less face making more sense now. She stressed over me and this meeting. I'm such a dick.

Tipping her chin up, I try to convey how sorry I am. "I'm sorry, Prim. I am. I should have texted you, but I got caught up in my own issues."

Her eyes light up, and I let her go. She's so understanding and caring. I feel like utter shit for making this harder on her.

When my eyes meet Devin's, every shade of envy and discourse cover his features. Why and how did this happen? Was it fate fucking me or giving me the best outcome?

Prim leads me to a couch, gesturing me to sit. As soon as I do, she sits next to me, her skin burning mine as it's too close. Uneasiness has me wanting to move away, but what kind of friend does that?

Touch doesn't feel good to me like it does others. It makes me want to hide in my own skin, fade away from sensation. *Except Devin.* My bartender. Not once did my skin crawl, not once did he make me want to separate, not once did I feel the need to escape. His touch is different.

He sits opposite of us, holding his mug tightly. His knuckles are so white that I know he's feeling as affected as I do.

CHAPTER SIX

DEVIN

It takes every ounce of restraint to stay seated. My heels strain against the couch to keep me grounded. The way she squeezes his knee in comfort has me aching. Actual, physical, pure ache. His distress is visible when she touches him. It never occurred to me last night he didn't enjoy being touched. He sank into me, not the opposite.

It's obvious now that Primrose likes him and not as a friend. Does she not know he's into men? Into me...

Maybe he's in the closet too.

It's not surprising in this small town. How I missed ever meeting him has another sadness settling over me. Texas Silver. My little prince has a name.

When we were close just now, just barely, his bruises showing just briefly, it was insanely hard not to take him, kiss him, and fuck him into submission. Tease his cock until it hurt for not giving me his name. Stave off his orgasm until he apologized for hurting me by leaving.

I was troubled this morning, having to meet a guy who could be interested in my baby girl, not to mention losing the man I'd shared my body with carelessly, never realizing he was one in the same.

The man my daughter is into and her best friend is the same one who took my cock deep inside his body last night. My entire system flares with an animalistic hunger to kiss him senseless, to claim him, to tell her he's the one I've been looking for forever.

It would ruin everything.

For now, I'll have to allow him to live here under the guise of helping him for her. In truth, I'm only looking at my interests and how to get him under my body again. She said he was kicked out? I've got inkling I know exactly why.

Wonder if he got caught with someone in his pants. A growl escapes at the imagery, catching my little prince's attention. No, no one touched him. I can't believe he would go from one person to me. Then again, he didn't argue with me over last night. My heart snaps, crippled and beaten over an imagination I can't keep at bay.

When my eyes connect with him, it's like he knows where my mind went. His eyes almost reassure with a surreal kind of innocence, settling me immediately.

How can a conversation happen between the two of us so easily? Without words. Only amber and honey. Seamless and shameless beauty.

"So, this is a little stiff," Primrose states, making an awkward face. "We should have a conversation."

I look to Texas, seeing his posture uncomfortable and wanting nothing more than to sooth it.

"I thought about it all day and *night* last night," I enunciate the first *night*, and it almost looks like he stopped breathing in result. "He can stay."

She squeals, grabbing him in a tight hug that he doesn't return. His pain saddens me.

She pulls away. "See! This is great!"

He nods solemnly. Why is this kid so sad? Why do I want to fix him?

"You'll start work tomorrow," I add. "We can talk tonight about that. I'll have Sandra and Landon cover for me."

"I've got spin class tonight. Can we resch—"

"No, it's okay. Texas and I will be okay," I reassure her softly.

He visibly relaxes next to her, and she doesn't argue, but she seems disappointed.

"Don't worry your little head, Prim. I'll be okay," he says gently.

Her body lights up at the softness in his tone.

That's what he does, lightens his voice to be gentle for her benefit. It's apparent that he feels what she feels and maybe even catches what I feel.

He's empathetic while most people his age care less and less every year. I can't help the warmth settling in my stomach at the knowledge of my little prince caring for my daughter. It's a weird sensation that feels too close to love, but love this soon isn't possible, right?

"I'm going to go out and get some tea," she pipes up a moment later. "If you can show Tex around the house while I'm gone, that'll be great."

I smile at her, trying to show her I won't hurt him.

"Behave, Daddy."

A chuckle escapes me as inappropriate images of Texas bent over my bed infiltrate my head. Behaving is the last thing on my mind.

"I'll be good, baby girl."

Texas looks at me then with admiration. It practically knocks me off my feet. His eyes are glossy in a prideful way. It's silent communication, but I hear it loudly. *I love how you love our girl.*

She is our girl, isn't she? It dawns on me that he could take care of her with me, love her alongside me, and be what she needs when I can't be.

"Bye, Tex." She gets on her tiptoes and leaves a big kiss on his cheek then follows suit with me. "Text me your shopping list, Dad. I know you have one." She giggles when I smile at her.

"You do know your old man," I muse.

She gets her jacket and purse and heads out the door. As soon as her car door opens and closes, I'm on him. He doesn't act surprised when I grip the back of his neck and force his lips to mine. My little prince falls into me as I take all my anger and disappointment out on his mouth. He shouldn't have left, all it offered was a gaping hole inside me.

Pulling back, he stares at me in both trepidation and wonder.

"Why'd you leave?" I rasp, my voice laced with too much feeling. It's too soon. I've never felt this way. Ever.

"I-I couldn't risk Prim finding out."

"Finding out what?" I ask, already knowing the answer. I'm hiding too.

"That I'm gay," he hisses. "Fuck." He pulls off his beanie and runs a hand through his soft hair. "I've never said it out loud."

I stare at him in open shock. How not? Wouldn't his—

"Was that your first time?" I plead, not sure what for since he quite possibly gave me something treasured by most.

169

"Yes." It's one word, but I see the importance in his eyes. "I've never wanted to risk it before..." He closes his eyes, and I want to touch him, hold him, reassure him in every way I can.

My body hums when he touches my chest.

"You came from nowhere." It's a whisper, but the words eradicate the fear from my body.

Our lips meet again, this time not as frenzied. It's more relaxed, absolute, giving me a peace I didn't know was possible to have.

My phone rings, breaking us apart. Seeing it's Prim makes my heart hammer unnaturally.

"Hey, made it to Jubilees. I don't see your list."

I try controlling my breathing, but a full-blown panic comes over me as I realize my daughter doesn't know about either of us. This situation could get messy. Why isn't it easy to just come out and tell her?

"I-I'll..." I choke on my words.

Visions of her hatred clog my mind and mouth. Her mom understood easily, but when I'm with the guy Prim's in love with, will she understand then?

Not even a moment later, Texas pulls my phone from me, understanding in his features.

"Sorry, Prim. Your dad just stubbed his toe," he lies easily. He lets out a fake chuckle that doesn't meet his eyes. "We're getting along great. Your dad is quite the *talker*. I'll get it sent over. It's in his note section on his phone? 'Kay, got it."

He has this conversation with her as I attempt to control my breathing. By the time he hangs up, he's checking my notes and sending it over. The fact that he's in more control than me right now only shows he's gone through this scenario before. He's used to the panic, the reality of being caught.

"You okay?" he asks, touching my chin as he did to her.

Heat simmers in me. A new wave of pride overcomes me, and I'm kissing him again. He groans in my mouth, pushing me on my back, flat against the couch. His hands make use of my clothes, touching me where he couldn't last night, exploring where he may have been too afraid to.

He grinds into me, and my cock feels ready to slide into him again. Knowing he gave me his first time only furthers my rampant need to claim him again and again and again until my cock is the only one he'll ever crave.

"What is it about you?" I whisper against his cheek as he's kissing my throat.

He lifts a little, his sweet eyes shedding each layer of me in a single glance.

"I've been asking myself all night. I-I'm sorry I ran," he murmurs. Shame licks his features, but I understand now. It makes sense.

"I never would have outed you," I affirm, grabbing his jaw with resolution. "She doesn't even know I'm gay."

My admission has him staring at me with fear.

"She doesn't even know about you?" he questions.

It isn't an accusation, but with his discomfort, I think it's a scary revelation, as if I'm not telling her because of her reaction. It's partially that, but it's also because this town might talk about me for it. I'm already cast out by being divorced. Not that they should care or have a say. Putting Primrose in the spotlight keeps me in the closet just as much as dread.

"Until last night," I say slowly, gauging his reaction. "I didn't feel the need to."

It's honest, truthful. My sad boy. Him coming into my bar with a solemnness that fit mine changed everything. It shouldn't. Happenstance doesn't define anything, but last night, it did.

"That's why I was up all night," he whispers against my throat. "That and my rock-hard dick wanting more of *you*."

A groan leaves me like a wish, and my patience and need to be subtle snaps like a fucking rubber band. One second, he's against me, and the next, I'm flipping him on his back, taking what's mine.

"Fuck," he hisses when I find his piercing through his hoodie. I bite and tug almost too roughly, unable to stop the greediness filling my veins.

Sitting up, I undo his jeans, trailing them down his thighs. No boxers *again*. My eyes meet his, and he fucking smirks, playing with his lip ring with amusement. He's hard and ready for me. With a teasing grin of my own, I take him into my mouth in the next breath, and he's swearing unintelligibly. From his balls to his shaft and up the veiny length of him, I lick.

Tasting him.

Savoring his unique flavor.

Absorbing all he gives

All of him.

Salty. Sweet. Perfect.

Him.

My little prince.

My Texas.

My sad boy.

He makes this choked noise when I grab his balls,

massaging and tugging on them in a way that I know feels good. Sucking him all the way to the back of my throat, I groan at him leaking. It's making me ravenous.

"Oh, fuck, fuck, fuck," he bites out as I feather his tip with my tongue.

He grips my head, and I can't tell if he's trying to stop me or make me go faster, but I grip his shaft and move it up and down in tune with my mouth's pull.

"Gonna come."

The gritty way he says it nearly has me coming in my pants. I take him in another deep tug as he shoots down my throat. I'm not stopping until every drop is gone and in me. It's *mine*. Just like him.

I'm only popping off when his tang slicks my mouth. With a leisure lick across the slit of his head, I smirk.

"Jesus fucking Christ."

The sedated look on his face and how flushed he seems only makes me want to do it over and over until the memory sticks. Tucking him away, I crawl up him and steal his mouth. He doesn't hesitate to lick inside mine. My little prince is going to kill me. I know it.

As soon as I'm backing away, the sound of a car's door closing echoes. *Primrose.* I jump into action, wiping my mouth of drool and straightening my clothes.

Looking at Texas, I notice he needs to fix himself. "Bathroom. She's back."

His eyes widen, and he stands.

"It's the last door on the right."

It's not. It's my room, and that's where I want him. My bathroom. My room. And if I wanted to deny why I want him in there, I could, but it has everything to do with his scent mixing with mine and seeing him in *my space*.

Instead of waiting on bated breath, I rush outside to

help Primrose bring in the groceries, hoping my face doesn't indicate how little I showed Texas around the house and instead took pleasure in him once again.

"Need help?" I offer, wishing to seem normal.

Why am I like this? Why can't I come out and say I want that guy in my house?

"Thank you!" she chirps happily.

She's such a bright light. So happy. She's constantly smiling and wanting the best for everyone.

Let's hope Texas is cleaned up by the time I'm back inside.

CHAPTER SEVEN

TEXAS

Fate. A four-letter word. Something out of the control of all parties involved.

Happenstance. A twelve-letter word. Something that just seemed to happen.

Both have similar traits. One defines Devin and me, and the other is the bar. It just so happened to have occurred there. Maybe all this time that I was alone, lost, and unable to control my future was fate working for me. That run-in with Prim on a random sad afternoon, a domino in the race of life.

Now, me being caught and kicked out, it's all falling into place for some reason.

Maybe I'm meant to be happy.

To find love and peace in a man.

Maybe I'm not sick or broken, just lost. Lost until my bartender found me.

Last door on the right, he told me. I open the door. He wanted me to come in here, and I can see why. Devin's room is black and smoky, all full yet empty. There's something missing from the space, a disposition I understand.

He's been isolated for years. It shows in the lack of pictures on the charcoal gray walls and the way his black sheets are fitted and topped with a black comforter, showing no color or life.

Someone with a vibrant daughter reflects how my soul feels inside perfectly. I'm smiling yet still feeling somber, seeing how alone he must feel on a daily basis.

Making my way around the room, I pass his massive closet that could be its own room before spotting the bathroom. My hands meet the brass of the knob, and when it opens, the huge room inside takes my breath away. Dad and I lived a small life, less than comfortable but not bad enough to be entirely miserable. This bathroom alone is the size of my living room back at home. It has a huge shower that could fit five people, a huge tub possibly with jets, I don't know, and a double sink vanity. I've never seen anything so elegant in person.

Everything is colored black and white, cool tones, and all modern. I swear my dick jumps out at this. Didn't realize that could happen. It's probably the visual of what I just did with Devin and what I could easily see myself doing to him in this bathroom.

The thought rots soon, turning into negativity like all my thoughts tend to do.

Is this the same bathroom his wife was in? My stomach cramps. You know that feeling of melancholy, the one that comes regardless of knowing all the facts, just for the sake of your heart getting in the way? That's me. My mind. How much I allow myself to believe I don't deserve to be happy.

I'm very aware that he doesn't enjoy women. It's obvious that there are only men in his heart and mind, but knowing he could have and possibly did live here his entire marriage, raising Prim and loving her makes me very sad. Very fucking depressed, really. Did they fuck in here and in that room?

Stop, I chastise myself. It's over now. It happened before me. I didn't and don't have any claim on this man, even if everything in me says otherwise. *He's mine.*

After taking a few minutes to calm my jealous heart and fix my clothes, I creep out of the room to hear Prim and Devin having a conversation.

"He's the best, Dad. We met by chance a year ago, and he's the best thing to happen to me," she explains with awe.

My chest seizes up. Does she... have a crush on me? An icky feeling invades my senses. Fuck. Am I that naive to think we could be friends and she'd be okay with it?

"Does he feel that way too?" Devin questions.

She may not see anything in it, but I hear the green monster. Just experienced it myself.

"I don't think so, but it's okay. He'll eventually like me, right? He doesn't date, ever. What if he's waiting for me to make a move?"

Everything I worried about comes to head when she admits that. No. Nothing will change. I don't date for my own safety and peace. It's not because I'm waiting. Or maybe it wasn't, and now Devin has come along, throwing that notion out the window.

"Sweetheart," he stops her from explaining how we're best friends. "I don't think love works that way."

"What do you mean?" Her voice sounds so far off, like she's in the clouds, high on this idea of happiness that no one can take away.

"Love comes when you least expect it. Instead of searching, it finds you. It slams into you at random moments, first by hitting you in the gut and tugging at the strings inside you that hold all your feelings, and in the end, making sure you realize it's real. You cannot force love out of someone. It works against that."

"That kind of makes sense," she finally responds. "Is that how it was with you and Momma?"

I grimace, not wanting to hear it.

"No, baby. It didn't. Your mom and I had a different companionship. We loved each other so much, but we were never *in love*. Love found her when Nick came into the picture. He loved her like I couldn't. He made her feel like she was the only person in the room. They are soul mates."

"What if that's me and Tex?"

I hear him let out a long breath, and I realize I'm letting one out with him too, virtually sending him support for this next part.

"If he felt how you do, Primrose, I don't think he'd hide it. You're too beautiful and lively to avoid."

She scoffs. "You have to say that. You're my dad."

He chuckles. "I might be your dad, Prim, but I'm right. Tex wouldn't hide his feelings. I've just met the kid, and I can already tell you he'd seep love. He'd show you his sadness, the soft center of his being, and express it entirely."

She sniffles, and my heart aches. I hope she's not crying. I would feel like the biggest shit. "I-I get it." She hiccups. "I just love him."

There's shuffling, and I'm sure Devin pulls her into his arms, the same arms that make me feel safe. "I know, baby. I think he loves you too. *I do*. Just not in the way you hope."

"Thank you for listening, Daddy."

"I'll listen whenever you need. No matter how big you get, you'll always be my little girl."

Warmth and grief fill me, seeping through as it overflows with emotions I'm not used to having. He's such a good dad. If my father was even an ounce as loving as Devin, I probably never would be as empty as I am.

After swiping the shed emotion from my eyes, I interrupt them. "What's wrong?" I ask, but Devin can tell I already know. Nothing fools that man. Guess I'm found out then.

"Nothing," Prim answers, wiping her face. "Just needed a cry."

I pull her into my chest, hoping to give her all the love I can, the only love I can give. Usually, I avoid skin contact, affection, and emotional moments, but she needs this, and I can give it to her.

"Thank you for being my best friend, Prim."

She shakes with new tears, and I hold her as Devin watches. Something in his face tells me he needed this as much as she did, like there may have been a disconnect, and now it's patched up.

"Let's make those nasty rabbit sandwiches," I mutter.

Devin's eyebrow raises skeptically at me.

I laugh, tipping my head back. It feels so good to do so.

Prim punches my arm and glares at me. "It's not rabbit sandwiches, Tex. You big brat. It's vegetarian cuisine."

We all burst out in amusement at that. Prim makes these inedible sandwiches with random food she finds and puts almost an entire head of lettuce on it, ketchup, mayo, mustard, you name it, and I've even noticed her with peanut butter on there before. She always brings one when we get a late drink from Grounders. It's the most despicable thing I've witnessed.

"If you say so, Prim. I'm going to just pretend it's edible to make you smile."

She giggles, covering her face. "I can't. I've got spin class in thirty. Don't worry, though. I got you and Daddy some meat."

We both look at each other and then smile, enjoying the moment together.

CHAPTER EIGHT

DEVIN

Primrose leaves, and we eat lunch in silence. I know he heard our conversation. It was plain as day on his face.

I don't know how to move forward with this when she's in love with him. Dads are supposed to be the last person to break their child's heart, and eventually, it'll come out. Feeling the way I do and seeing him feel it too, it's bound to destroy her.

Do I keep my distance?

Is it okay to dive in with someone nearly half my age for love?

It's love. It has to be.

You can't stumble into something this brutal if it's not meant to be, right?

After about four hours, Primrose comes through the door. The sun has already set, and I'm not entirely sure how time flew by so quickly. Being lost in the mind erases it altogether.

"Hey, Dad. How did it go while I was gone?" She's in her yoga pants and a loose tank. She's flushed but smiling.

Something about working out gives me the same

peace of mind. Pushing my body to its limit has always given me a type of satisfaction that equates to success. She's like me in that sense.

"He's been in his room. I think he has a lot on his mind," I offer, not knowing whether that's true or not.

She nods and then heads toward his room. Jealousy flares to life. If I was a better man, I would tell her. If I was better at this, I would also be the one with him, comforting him.

But I'm not, and she is.

When Texas lets her in and she disappears, I ball my hands into fists. I'm not angry or annoyed with her. No, I'm angry with myself. This would have been easier if I didn't ask Whit to lie. She would have had the conversation with Primrose too, and it would have changed how I feel at this very moment.

Pulling out my cell, I call her. She's the only person I can talk to. She understands. She's forgiving, and she will know what to do.

"Dev?" her voice sounds out from the other end.

"Hey, Whit. Got a minute?"

I hear a door closing and then she's back.

"What's up?" She sounds concerned, which only makes me love her more. We were best friends for so long. It's why I trusted her to have sex with. I don't want Texas and Prim to go through that. It would kill me.

"I think I'm in love?" It comes out like a question, and I hear a small chuckle from Whit.

"Sounds like you're as unsure as I am if that's a statement or question."

I laugh derisively, hating myself at this moment. She's easy to talk to, yet this is the hardest thing I've ever discussed.

"I met someone last night."

"Last night? That must be why Rosie called sounding upset. Did you not come home?"

Whit knows me too well, almost better than I know myself. She waits for me to answer, also understanding me enough to know I need a moment.

"I didn't. Fell asleep at the bar," I explain, running a palm through my hair and tugging a little to ground myself. She must be nodding. She and Prim have that in common. They nod, forgetting they're on the phone and not in person.

"You remember when I met Nick, right?"

Her question is airy with that feeling of nostalgia and romance. She's such a romantic at heart. How she stayed so long is beyond me.

Not waiting for my answer, she continues, "We were both in Olvier for that night, me for that deposition, him because he needed an escape."

I remember this story like yesterday. She called me right after it happened, asking me what to do.

"You guys bumped into each other in the lobby of Fort Inn Plaza," I offer. "He caught you as you tripped over his bag, trying to read the map in your hand."

She giggles at my explanation. It's such a light sound coming from her. The happiness-filled noise makes me grin wider than I have in a while.

"You were in his arms, and he kissed you, said he couldn't help himself—"

She cuts me off. "Technically, he asked. Said, 'you're the prettiest woman I've ever seen. Can I kiss you?' Of course I laughed, but I could see how serious he was, and I nodded."

"You ran away." I chuckle, remembering that. "Called

me for advice. Said you've never felt this way before. He practically whisked you off your feet."

"I knew right then and there. Even though I was scared and calling you, I knew. Yeah, it was a simple kiss. Maybe even a cheesy love at first sight thing, but I felt it then. I still feel it now."

Her story, the memory of it was exactly what I needed.

"Thank you, Whit."

"You're welcome, Dev. Don't let him go. You deserve to find love, too."

The shit-eating grin won't leave my face as we hang up and I think of my little prince and his honey eyes.

It's getting late, really late.

When I open my bedroom door, I notice the lights are off everywhere besides the living room. Prim sits cuddled in blankets, watching her favorite teen drama, Riverdale. How I can remember the name? I can't tell you, but she spent hours explaining the entire plot to me and how much she loved Cheryl. I don't know who Cheryl is, but my daughter thinks she's cool.

I sneak over to the room Texas now homes and don't knock before entering. It's silent as I close the door without a sound. Turning around, I see him in the dimly lit room, laying on his back with his arm over his eyes. His ears are plugged with earbuds, and he must not hear me.

For a moment, I take advantage of the opportunity to just watch him, relaxed, on a big bed, only a lamp on to light the room. He seems less depressed like this. It's almost like my sad boy needs the quiet for peace and has a hard time finding it.

I walk toward Texas, enjoying the view of him with only jeans on. His tattoos that I never paid attention to last night are completely visible now. One day, I'll ask him what they mean. Sometimes, they mean nothing. Other times, they have stories.

Unable to help myself, I stare at his hard chest and the plains and dips of his muscles that lead to his pebbled, pierced nipples. They may be my favorite part of his body. The little black barbells make me do crazy things.

My eyes travel to the first bruise or, rather, hickey. Which is still a bruise, just the enjoyable kind. There are many littered all over his throat, chest, and his ear. I just can't see that one with his hair covering it.

He goes to move, his arms raising, when he notices me. His body jolts a little, making the bed squeak before he pulls out his music. Placing a finger to my lips, I hush him. A look of understanding crosses his face as he adjusts and sits up. I'm vaguely aware that I'm moving closer to him, reluctant to keep my distance. Sitting on the lip of the bed closest to him, I go to talk but end up opening and closing my mouth several times.

"Pussy got your tongue, *Dev*?" he taunts.

Did he somehow hear Whitney and I on the phone? I didn't see him if so. My phone didn't seem that loud. She's the only one who calls me that. Always has.

"I'll allow that snide remark because I know what it's like to feel suffocated by wanting something someone else has," I muse, watching him narrow his eyes.

I must've hit the nail on the head considering he bites the inside of his lip ring, making his lip dip inward. To be able to tug on that freely, that's what would make me pleased right now.

"Are you bisexual?" he asks without a preamble, throwing it out there like it's an easy question for anyone to answer. Sexuality is a mystery to most, even a man like me.

"No. I identify as gay," I reply slowly, enunciating every word. "Whit—the one I was on the phone with—is my ex-wife. She was also my best friend, like you and Primrose." Letting out a heavy sigh, I scratch my chin then hold it while leaning my elbow on my thigh. "I've known for a long time that I'm not into women, even when I slept with Whitney. But I trusted her to try. I'm not sure how to explain it, but I knew she'd understand my struggles somehow if I couldn't..."

My eyes shut with the cringy memories.

"Well, I was sixteen and dumb. We had sex. We'd already stopped talking after that awkward situation. Low and behold, three months later, she called to tell me she was pregnant. We got married before Primrose came. I wanted to be there for her."

It all comes out in a rush, and I see understanding through his eyes.

"We stayed together until Prim was twelve," I mutter sheepishly, feeling a huge weight leave as the words tumble free. "I tried to love her *that* way, to please her body the way she wanted..."

He grimaces at me with that, his face displeased.

"You slept with her?" It sounds more like a choke as he rubs a palm down his face, fisting the sheets a moment later.

"Not as often as I'm sure a normal couple would, but I wanted to satisfy her—to make her *happy*. It's the least I could do."

His face isn't showing happiness. It's almost upset and chagrined.

"What happened?" he whispers. It's so light I barely hear it.

"I was in Olvier with her. We were at a hotel, scouting out bars. I'd already owned mine for some time. It was more to see how I could branch out and make more. We already were fairly loaded. We lived comfortable lives, but I wanted to leave this place." I rub the back of my neck uncomfortably. "I went to the pool while she was sleeping. Left her a note that I'd be up there."

He nods, waiting for me. I don't know how to admit it, how to continue.

"And?" he prods, seeing my hesitation.

"I met a man. His name was Victor. He was from out of town, visiting for ski season. We flirted. *A lot.*"

My stomach hurts thinking of this. For all those years, I didn't watch porn. Didn't touch a man, or do anything unfaithful. Because in my heart, I knew.

"He made me harder than a rock," I admit, feeling as much shame now as I did then.

Texas leans into me, brushing his hand against my pants. "Like this?" He rubs back and forth, making me solid in a few breaths.

"Yes," I hiss then shake my head. "No, not like this." A groan rises as he grips me with possessiveness. I love this feeling, the anger in his eyes, the need to claim what's his. "Nothing feels like this."

He takes my mouth with that, rubbing my length fervently. I'm groaning and humping his hand for friction.

He wrenches back, and it's like losing all oxygen in my system. We're fire, him and I. We can't exist without oxygen, but it also absorbs all the air at the same time, siphoning our essence away. We're both panting, and if our dicks are any show of good faith, we're both horny and eager.

Instead of waiting for him, I shove into him, planting both my palms at either side of his head.

"*Nothing*," I growl. "Feels like *you* or *us*."

A smirk plays at his lips, and I fucking kiss it, marveling at this man beneath me. I'm unable to stay away for any longer. He has me twisted up. Texas moans loudly, and it occurs to me we have to keep silent. Placing a palm over his mouth, I hope for my own strength.

"Be quiet, little prince. Don't need our princess hearing how much you like to take my cock."

He closes his eyes as if in pain, and I grind into him, forcing them back open.

"Watch me as I fuck you, Texas. Because I'll be the last man to ever have you. You're *mine*. Do you understand me?" I rasp, feeling my heart catapult at my own words.

He bites my palm and forces me to remove it.

"That goes for you too, *bartender*," he growls avariciously. It's the sexiest I've heard his voice. Even with me deep inside him last night, it doesn't touch the intensity now. "This is my cock—" His palm slips under my pants and fists my solid length, and the roughness of his hand abrades my skin in a delirious way. "—and only I'm allowed to pleasure it, fuck it, and make it cum."

I groan, biting his throat to avoid being too loud. He slides his palm up and down, rubbing my precum everywhere. He's not as unpracticed as I would think.

His grip loosens and lowers as he squeezes my balls, making them tighten in response. We fuck with our mouths, our tongues thrashing as we fight for the power of domination. He's good with his tongue, and it makes me wonder if he'd suck me off well.

Rising off him, I remove his hand. "Have you ever taken a cock down your throat, little prince?"

His eyes darken, but I already know the answer.

"I'll teach you." My mouth nearly salivates with the offer. My voice sounds nearly inhuman with how predatory the words come out of my mouth.

He simpers and gets off the bed, lowering to his knees.

"Good princes take their king's cock," I explain.

"The best princes make their king weak for their prince's mouth," he argues with confidence.

"Guess it's a good thing your king likes your mouth," I hiss before he's taking off my pants.

My eyes meet his, and my heart swells. This is what I've been searching for, a little prince to please me.

CHAPTER NINE

TEXAS

How he challenges me with a look of utter ecstasy isn't something I can forget. As I lower to my knees, I see the adoration mixed with juxtaposed desperation on his face. It's unadulterated, passionate, needy. He wants this. He wants *me*.

Looking up at him through my eyelashes, I remove his pants and boxers in one go but take my sweet time dragging them down, making his impatience grow. His jaw ticks as I'm sure his dick throbs too.

After he kicks them off, he brings the tip of his engorged head to my mouth, painting me with precum. I lick the salty bead at the tip then my lips for good measure.

A low rumble is all I can hear as I lick a long trail from his head to his balls. The flavor is something I'll forever crave and the feel of him against my tongue feels as memorable as the tattoos inked across my skin.

I draw him into my mouth, only a little, testing my gag reflex. As nothing bothers me, even though I feel my jaw may split, I take more and more of his length. He pats my head reverently.

"Such a good sad boy. Relax and take more," he coos, making my body warm.

As I relax my jaw, he goes deeper. Then, he grips my hair, pulling tightly. Arching into him, I groan around his rigid length and see how his head is bowed backward. He's enjoying this. My dick swells in approval as I move for him, putting my palms on his thighs for support.

He growls and jerks me off him.

"Fuck. Slow. Go slow."

His voice is broken, and it's sexy hearing him lose control.

He places my mouth back around him, and I keep going, not decelerating. I want him to feel how I felt earlier, limbless, numb from pure pleasure, and at my mercy.

His hips pick up pace as he fucks my mouth, and when I think he'll finally blow, gifting me his salty tang, he pulls out, massaging my head for a minute while his chest rises and falls shakily. He stares down at me, a king to his prince. A ruler to his subject. A lover to his lover.

He helps me up and stares at me in wonder. "Get undressed. I'll be back."

Without another word, he puts on his bottoms and leaves. I hurry out of my pants and socks as he's gone. He's quiet, so much so that I don't hear him in the other room, only when my door barely clicks back open and closed as he comes back in only boxers. His toned stomach has scratch marks, and his thighs bear little bruises already showing from my grip on them a moment ago.

I'm sprawled out on the bed when he saunters to me, his steps purposefully, his eyes greedy, and his cock tenting his boxers. He kneels on the bed, now naked, and crawls to me with a predatory gaze. Chills sweep my frame in response.

"Why can't I stay away, little prince? Why do I want to sink inside you and never leave?"

It's rhetorical, but I need to know too.

"I'm not sure, but I want that too. Sink into me and never let me go."

He sighs almost happily. Then he's above me and trailing kisses to my nipples. Bringing a bud to his mouth, he bites, sending a sting of pleasure through me. He repeats his action with my other nipple all while slowly lowering, biting and leaving kisses along the way.

When he makes it to my hips, I have to swallow back a moan while he taunts me. I bow my hips upward, begging for some sort of friction. Devin looks up at me, and I watch in awe as he takes my entire length in his mouth in one practiced move.

My eyes roll back, pure bliss sizzling up and down my spine. His mouth makes a pop when he releases me. That's when I notice a bottle of lube. With half-lidded eyes, I watch his face lower to my ass. He forces my thighs upward. My knees bend on their own accord.

"We didn't eat dinner, little prince. I'm fucking famished," he grits out before spreading my cheeks and delving between them.

A low groan releases, and he pinches my cheek in warning. His tongue penetrates my hole, poking and probing and I writhe beneath him. Without him even touching my dick, I feel like I might explode.

I'm not sure when he lubed up his fingers, but his mouth is replaced by one then two. As he stretches me, my back curves into the air. It's not discomfort. It's pure pleasure.

After he gets a third into me, he's lubing his cock and probing my entrance.

"Try and be quiet, little prince. I know how you like to scream around my cock."

"Please," I beg, wanting the fullness he offers. "Please fuck me."

He eases in. Unlike last night, it's gentle as he lifts my legs and settles in me.

There's only one porn I've ever watched like this. Men tend to fuck from behind, not face to face, but seeing the expression of awe on his face has my dick pulsing in a way it never has never before.

His hips meet the back of my thighs, and I'm so full of him I could cry. The connection we have is a driving force. It takes away the sad and replaces it with yearning.

"Watch me as I make you mine, Texas. Squeeze my cock for me."

I tighten around him and watch his abs flex as he restrains himself. He moves and hits my prostate, and I'm unable to hold back my rapturous cry. That sets him off. One second, he's giving me slow thrusts, and then he's pistoning into me.

Thrust. Slap. Thrust.

I try moving with him, but he's chasing his own high.

"Devin," I moan. "Fuck, Devin."

His eyes stay with mine as he keeps his pace. Sweat lines his forehead, and when his mouth meets mine, he fists me and pumps my erection in tandem with his hips.

We're rutting, groaning, and working ourselves over until we both slow. His seed fills me. The warmth of it satisfies me, marking me. My cum sprays our stomachs, spurting swift and long strokes, and he keeps going until we're both out of breath and spent.

He hasn't even left my body before we hear a scream.

"Tex?"

Her high-pitched screech has me frozen. I can see her from around Devin. Her face is pale as she rubs at her eyes. She closes them and runs out just as quickly, slamming the door. It shakes the frame, or maybe that's my heart. Either way, everything feels raw and deafening.

"Fuck, fuck, fuck," Devin hisses as he exits me slowly.

The loss of him inside me leaves me feeling absolutely empty. Something about the way she looked and the lost expression on his face has me worried this will end before it really started.

He throws on his boxers and rushes out of the room. Before I know it, I'm rocking back and forth on the bed, crying uncontrollably. It was *my* groaning. It was my pleasure that did this. I'm sick and fucking ruined. I've messed everything up. For me, for her, for them.

Fuck. What have I done?

My body heaves as I start hyperventilating. Within seconds, I'm rushing to pack my shit before they can come back. I've already destroyed everything. I've fucked it all up. This is why I don't make friends. It's why I keep my distance, and it's why, in the eyes of the world, I'm straight and unavailable.

I'm so sorry, Prim... Devin... everyone. I get all my stuff in one go and leave the room. They're not in the living room, so I take that opening, grab my keys, and leave. I've got no money, no family, and now no Loveless clan.

The tears continue to fall as I get to my car and turn it on. My entire chest rips in two as my car backs away, leaving half at this house with a man who has stolen every piece of me.

CHAPTER TEN

DEVIN

My moves are frantic all the way toward my room. I throw on pants and a shirt, not checking if they're on correctly or even matching or appropriate for the cold. The only desire rushing through me is the hope to catch my daughter before she leaves. If she's anything like me, she'll storm out in an attempt to cool off. Her mom has always been the level-headed one, but Prim and I tend to go off emotions, using them as our fuel, driving us to whatever destination we rush into.

That's the thing with miscommunication and lies. They tear people apart from anonymity alone. Being dishonest with her shouldn't have happened. It's just like her loving Texas. My heart can't pick who to love either. It just happens. It's natural, and it's unexplainable.

Precautions... Usually, I take many, whether it's driving hours away or meeting at a hotel. It's for her protection. Being careless can singlehandedly be put on my shoulders. No matter my strong feelings toward my little prince, I'm an idiot for thinking we could sneak around. I should have held him down and covered his mouth. Fuck, I should have just kept my distance and not fuck her best friend, especially while she was here. What kind of father am I?

Guilt eats at me, gnawing like a tick in the woods. It's bitter, feeling that blistering pain of misguided emotions. I've got to apologize. Then, if need be, I'll move out. I'm not willing to displace her for my pleasure.

Regardless of my love for her, Texas stays. I want him. Wrong or not, he's not someone I'm willing to give up, not even if my daughter needs that of me. I'm selfish enough to tell her no. Love comes so little in life, briefly, without cause. This is the first time I'm sure I've experienced it. He may be half my age, might even be in the closet like me, but I'll do anything to keep him, even if moving to Vegas for my other bar is the only answer.

Tears leak from my eyes. I'm not sure if they're evidence of her pain, mine, or Tex's. We're all suffering now.

Whit's words repeat in my mind on replay. *Don't let him go.* He can't be a blip in my life. He's too powerful for that. Cataclysmic. He's an asteroid, bursting in through my atmosphere just to explode into a million pieces, destroying everything but him and me, making himself known forever.

After searching the entire house, the only place I forget to check is her room. I knock twice and wait for a response.

A minute of silence passes before she mutters, "Come in."

The sound of her sniffling makes me want to change everything. Be open with her. Prepare her for this. Somehow make her not fall in love with Texas.

"Hey." It's a lame thing to say when it should be sorry or anything with more depth.

Concern lines her face as sadness trails her cheeks. She's red and puffy. The regret and guilt swallowing up her features shows me she's sorry for overreacting. On my one hand, I can count how many times Primrose has had a tantrum or freak out. This is only the third. Even as a baby, she always seemed settled and calm. Sweet. My baby girl's heart is massive. It's always growing with a never-ending love for people.

"I'm sorry I freaked out." Her voice cracks as she apologizes.

Fresh tears fall, and I approach her slowly, not wanting to invade her space if she's freaked out. She doesn't flinch or falter when I sit at the edge of her bed.

"I should have told you." It's a whisper, but it brings a bite of shame, reminding me how much I've hidden. "I-I—"

"It's not my place to judge you for who you love, Dad, though it makes a lot of sense. But why him? Why the one guy that's been nothing but perfect to me?" Her tone, as heartbroken as it sounds, seems strong, not destroyed. She'll heal.

"I can't answer that for you," I rasp, my throat clogged with emotion. She's not even bothered that I'm into men. She's only hurt that I got the guy. "We met by chance last night. When I went to work. I-It happened so fast. I've never—" I pause, struggling for words. "No one has ever made me feel this way. I'd never risk hurting you like this."

With my admission, she nods, her jaw clamped shut. If I could erase this pain, eradicate the imagery of me and

Tex from her mind, I would. I would do whatever she needed.

Except let him go. If that makes me a bad father, then I'm a bad fucking father.

"It makes sense now. Why he never tried anything. Also, our conversation. You knew and were trying to protect me," she says rhetorically, filling in her own blanks. "Never wanted that visual of you, though. Could live my entire life not seeing that."

I laugh, throwing my head back at her grimace. "I'd have rather you not have learned that way either," I confirm. "I'm sorry that's how you found out about me."

"Me too," she mutters, wiping her face. Prim sits back against her headboard like she always used to, tucking her feet beneath her and covers herself with her pink comforter. "I wish you would have trusted me enough to let me in."

I choke up at that, feeling the burn of tears at the edge of my eyes. "What if you hated me?" I ask honestly, my heart hurting at the pictures I'd conjured the last seven years.

She leans forward and places a hand on my knee. "You're my dad. I'd never hate you."

The words are so open and honest that I'm breaking down. It's amazing how such a simple response can bring a man to tears, but it's the acceptance that's making me emotional. All the years spent hiding, being unhappy, and unwilling to wreck her world for my happiness all leaks out of me.

"Is Tex okay? He seemed really upset," she says.

I stare at her, remembering that I left him alone right after sleeping with him.

"I've got to go," I explain, standing up. "We can talk later?"

She nods and shoos me.

I'm not sure what I did to deserve such a perfect child, but I wouldn't trade our relationship. She's kind, considerate, and so open.

I rush out of the room, open the guest door, and find it empty. I check the bathroom next and nothing.

My heart beats too fast, and fear swims through me. He ran.

After finding my keys, I rush to put on my shoes and coat before rushing out into the cool air. It's pitch black. Clouds are hiding the moon and stars. As eerie as it is, somberness consumes me. Where would he go? We've only met. If anyone would know, it'd be Prim. I dial her, and she answers immediately.

"He's gone, isn't he?" Her tone is sad, almost guilty, but it's not her fault. It's mine.

"Do you know where he'd run if he felt cornered?"

"He doesn't have a home. Maybe he went to the cemetery? His mom is buried there."

"I'll check. Anywhere else?"

"I don't think so. He always talked about how his dad hated him and his mom was the only person who cared. If he felt helpless, maybe he went to find peace?"

"Thank you."

By the time I'm in my truck and back out of the drive, my worry has turned into dread. What if he isn't at the cemetery? How will I possibly find him? Twenty-four hours ago, my biggest worry focused on a new place in Vegas. Now it's stuck on a blue-haired prince who has stolen my heart. Why it happened so fast, so fiercely, and undeniably so, I'm not sure, but letting it slip away isn't on the agenda.

Once I hit Valley West Cemetery, I park and jump out. It's even worse here. The darkness invades every crevice, expanding everywhere. Even with a little crack in the clouds, I can only see a foot or two in front of me. My phone illuminates the ground, and I see grass, graves, and rocks strewn about. The graves here range from ancient to new, back and forth, scattered in a weird pattern. The only sounds that fill my ears are the ground beneath my feet and the slow whistle of the wind. After walking for five minutes, I'm near desperate. It doesn't help I'm not sure where her grave is or if he's even here. Graves give me chills and an odd sense of being watched. Maybe it's superstition, but the longer I'm here, the colder it feels.

As I'm about to give up, I hear someone whimpering. The noise catches me off guard, but I circle my phone, searching for the source of it. When my gaze lands on a shaking form, I creep slowly, hoping it's Tex and not some crazy rando who hangs out around dead things.

When I get closer, I can see his blue hair clearly. Rushing him, I practically fall to get to him. His gaze shoots to me, and once the shock subsides, he stares at me in wonder. His eyes are red-rimmed, and he looks beyond exhausted.

Touching his chin, I bring my mouth to his, needing to feel our connection, desperate for him to know I'm choosing him—us—whatever this is.

His lips are ice and shuddering against mine. I reach for him, pulling him into my arms, enjoying the way he fits me perfectly. He feels like ice, freezing, all alone. Why did he come out here without a jacket? His hoodie isn't enough for the biting temperatures tonight, let alone the wind and moisture in the air.

"Why would you run, little prince? You scared me." The words come out strained, showing how hurt I am.

He shakes against me as I hold him. "S-She h-hates m-me," he brokenly whispers, his teeth chattering. "My f-fault."

I kiss his head and help him up. "Let's get you warm, baby."

He shakes harder, and I'm lifting him in response. I love the way he clings to me like I'm his savior. Like I'm *his*. I am. He can have me. Every fucked-up part.

Carrying him to my truck takes longer than coming out here. Navigating without the light is miserable, but I try to watch my steps, hoping to not disturb any area. When we make it there, I open the door, and he raises himself in. After I close the door, I jump to my side and start the engine, turning the heater on. He shivers as my hands rub up and down his arms to warm him.

"Primrose doesn't hate you, Texas," I finally state.

She doesn't. If anything, she's more upset with herself for caring about us being together because you're her best friend, than us being together because we're gay.

"She just felt like she lost us both in one night."

He eyes me with an *I don't believe you* expression that has me smiling.

"I'd never lie to you."

It's true.

I'll always be open and honest.

It's my vow.

"Do you hate me now? For hurting your relation—" he starts apologizing, but I interrupt.

"Never. I'd never hate you, Texas. You didn't hurt anything, baby. If anything, you fixed it, bridging a gap I set by keeping my sexuality from her. She'll be okay. Time is all she needs."

"You called me baby twice," he murmurs softly, his face a little flushed. Whether it's from the nickname or the cold, it's a good color on him.

"That's because, in this short time, you've become everything to me," I admit. "It's fast, I know, but—"

He stops me. "I feel the same way."

We lean in at the same time, bringing our lips together. It's not erogenous, but quick and furtive.

"I love you, Texas Silver. If that makes me a mad man, then I'm a fucking lunatic."

He chuckles, capturing my jaw reverently. "I love you too, Devin Loveless. Even if your last name is a lie."

EPILOGUE

DEVIN

Loveless. An eight-letter word.

The mentality that there's no love in the heart.

What a lie *our* last name is.

Texas and Devin Loveless, two men fated for one another.

Subconsciously, I roll my ring between my thumb and forefinger, loving the weight of it. It's heavy almost, but a good kind of heavy.

When Whit and I married, it felt like a shackle, a suffocating device that hid me from the world and everything I wished for but couldn't obtain.

My little prince and I tied the knot six months ago. We flew to California and had a beach wedding. We eloped last minute, and Prim came to the celebration dinner to congratulate us both.

It's beautiful seeing my husband love my daughter as ferociously as I do. Even now, they're best friends, just more open than before. Tex and I moved to Vegas after our honeymoon, Prim decided to stay and build her own path. She still visits us. Me and Tex started helping with

Loveless so Dusty can breathe. We cut the *Drink More* portion of the title before opening and made it one word. It's already one of the biggest party spots on the strip. With how fast it's rising up, I'll be expanding across the US in no time.

"Dreading the fact that you can't run from me, bartender?" Tex muses, leaning against the door frame of our balcony, his shirtless abs flexing as he interrupts my overwhelmed mind.

I can't help but stare at his chest and the newest tattoo that matches mine, covering our hearts. *Love More not Less.* My perusal doesn't stop there, though. It's stuck on the little black piercings begging to be pleasured.

With my mouth.

He smirks, biting his lip slowly. "How can I taunt you when you look at me like that?" he asks sheepishly, his face flushing.

Even after a year, I can still make him blush.

He runs a hand through his light sandy blond hair. After the blue and black started to fade, he stripped the color and went to a baser tone that matched as close as his natural hair as he could. In a way, I miss the blue and black, but this makes his honey eyes almost seem inhuman. They're vibrant, endless, and perfect. The sun shines on us as we stare at each other, waiting for one to make a move.

Instead of answering, I rise off the lounger and stroll toward him like he's the prey. Maybe he is, or maybe he's been the hunter this entire time. Guess it's time to test that theory, huh?

"We both know you're the one stuck."

He stares at me in awe. It's something I haven't quite gotten used to.

I lick his throat, making sure to nip my favorite spot where his shoulder and neck connect, and he moans.

"Being adventurous, Mister Loveless?" he asks.

"Feeling daring, Mister Loveless?" I return with a smirk.

His smile reaches his eyes. No more is my boy sad. No, he thrives, lives, and wants to watch as the sun shines on his face.

"I'm willing to try anything with you," he whispers in my ear, making goosebumps erupt over my skin.

I pull away then grab his hand, leading us to our bedroom. Tex wanted to be trendy—hipster-like if you will—and convinced me to buy a circle rotating bed. You'd be amazed at how good the sex is when you're more than dick dizzy.

I push him onto the bed. It spins a little, and we chuckle. It's not exactly something you get used to, rather you make use of the advantages and wing it.

"I've never done this," I finally say, going to our toy drawer for lube. When I find it, my heart hammers like a caged beast wanting to break free.

"And what's that?" he questions, not reading into my posture, fear, or still frame.

I finally turn to him and feel my face and body heat. It's a mixture of excitement and nervousness. I've always topped. Even with Tex. Not once has the need or desire to switch consumed me. If anything, the fear ebbed any type of desire toward it. Now, with his tattoo-laden body open for me, I want to give that to him. He always seems in pure rapture when I'm deep in him, pushing hard and harder, and now, it's an experience that's tempting me.

"I want you to fuck me, little prince."

His eyes snap to mine, honey zeroing in on amber, like

they'll tell him whether I'm lying or not. As if he has found the answer, he rises to his feet and comes to me. The absolute yearning on his face makes my cock thicken, pushing against my board shorts. When I look at his gym shorts, his erection is noticeable, tenting, begging me.

"Say it again," he grits, his voice deep and predatory. He holds my jaw, unwilling to drop my gaze.

"I want you to fuck me," I nearly hiss as he's gripping my shaft tightly. His thumb rubs the head of my cock leisurely, teasing me.

"Get on the fucking bed," he growls. It's sexy and grumpy, almost like he's waited our entire relationship for this moment, and maybe he has.

He turns us and walks me backward until I fall to the bed. He eats me alive with his unabated hunger, roaming my skin like a metal detector, not missing a single inch.

My husband hovers me before taking the lube bottle from my hand. Then, he's kissing me. Texas is a helluva kisser. He takes and takes and takes, and when you think he's done, he takes a little bit more.

I cave into his lips, his thrall, and moan when he starts lowering my boxers. His mouth leaves mine to tease my throbbing dick the way I crave. Licking from tip to the base, all the way to my balls, making sure to suck along the way, he pleasures me.

"Fuck," I grind out as he sucks my sack in his mouth.

He pops off, trailing his tongue to the crease of my ass. As he lifts my thighs, I can't help but hiss. Tex has rimmed me several times. It's always tortuously slow as if he's savoring me. With each swipe of his tongue, I feel like I'm coming undone. When he breaches the tight ring, a loud growl escapes me. It's almost pained, desperate for more.

"Let me show you how I worship my king."

As soon as the words leave his mouth, he's deep-throating me and teasing my hole with a wet finger. He doesn't push in, only presses against it, making me buck toward him. With a loud slurping sound, he's taking my balls again, all while grabbing the lube. My prince knows how to use his mouth and hands in tandem.

I'm delirious when he finally sinks a single digit in me. There's a little pinch, but as he taunts me to the brink of orgasm, I'm too high to care. He adds a second finger and sucks me slowly at the same time. The roughness of his hand mixed with the velvet of his tongue bring me near combustion. As he senses it, he stops his cock ministrations, adds a third finger, and presses into my prostate like it's a video game.

"Fucking Christ," I groan, squeezing his hand.

"Close enough," he jokes. "Relax for me, baby."

I do, and he eases his fingers out.

"Look at me." It's a command, a frenzied one.

I do. His honey eyes are brighter than I've ever seen them.

"Watch me worship you."

And he eases into me, his cock breaching easily. It only stings until I fully relax. Once he's seated in me, the frantic thirst filling my veins has me wiggling.

"Move," I hiss, needing the friction, the heat, the plea-sure-pain.

"Can't. Going to come if I do." It's barely a breath, coming out strained.

He inhales, and I start stroking my dick, needing something. His eyes darken, watching me work myself over.

"Fuck it," he barks, and then he's moving in me. It's hard and hot. Perfect. So perfect.

"Ah, fuck," I moan, panting as I try to rub myself off.

He pulls out, bringing barrenness I'm not used to. Laying down next to me, he turns his head my way. "I want you to take, husband. Sit on my cock and top me from the bottom." His gaze flames when I take his mouth, sucking on his lip ring in the process.

Rising to my feet, I grab the bottle of lube and pour it on his dick. It's red and angry, probably so close to the edge he won't last long. Mine is pointed straight forward, angrier, needier, barely holding onto its seed. He watches me as I ghost over him, and when I line him up to my ass, his gaze finally drops, and the hiss he lets out only gets louder as I sink onto him.

"Fist my cock, little prince. Don't come until I say."

"Fuck, that's going to be hard," he complains, gripping my length in his palm, pouring lube over his hand a second later.

"Whoever comes first has to deal with Darcy," I wager, making him narrow his eyes. Darcy is our most talkative and obnoxious bartender. She works well, but she never shuts up.

"Deal. We both know who can't stand her more," he mocks, thrusting upward and forcing me to flatten my hands on his abs as chills break out over my flesh. This is where they belong, worshiping his body, bringing him rapture, and taking whatever they damn well please.

I use his muscles as leverage, rise on his swollen rod, and slam back down. This time, it's both of us who groan.

Adjusting to this new position, I test the rise and fall of my hips, using my thighs to lift. My little prince has sweat all over his chest, matching the wetness on my spine.

We move together, our synced noises flirting the edge of abandon. When he rotates as I go down, he hits my prostate, and it's game over for us both. I practically bounce on him, holding myself up with one arm and grabbing his balls with the other. His pace on my cock quickens, and he squeezes harder, making me see every fucking color.

It doesn't take long before spots blur my vision. "Come for me, little prince. Fill me up."

He detonates. I feel him jerk in me, and that sets me off. My cum splashes on him in long ropes, shooting farther and farther with each continued pump. When we're both panting and exhausted, he takes a drag through my release and brings it to my mouth.

"Suck," he croaks.

And I do, licking his fingers until he's whimpering. Lifting off of him, I bring our mouths together and make him taste our shared love.

"Now, that's how you top a bottom," he wheezes, nipping my lip.

"Correction. That's how you do a proper switch," I tease, pinching his nipple.

"I love you, my king," he promises, putting a hand over my heart and tattoo.

I repeat his action over his heart and ink, and amber meets honey. "I love you too, little prince. More, not less."

The End

ABOUT C.L. MATTHEWS

C.L. Matthews lives in lala-landia with her husband and invisible friends. She wants to riot the lack thereof authentic Mexican food in her state, but she's an introvert at heart. She enjoys tacos, Red Bull, and warm water, because she's crazy. She's an oddball, and realizes it's been mentioned before, just go with it. Her joys in life consist of writing unconventional romances, making book covers, causing havoc to her reader's hearts, and genre hopping when she needs a change of scenery. She's a special kind of weird and enjoys every moment of it.

Website: clmatthewsbooks.com

ILLICIT

C.M. RADCLIFF

BLURB

I have one job to carry out, a true test of loyalty.
My brother has one job, to make sure I follow through.
And her... she has her own agenda.
She's here for a reason and I will find out.

With the looks of an angel and the devil's soul,
She's a threat sent here to destroy us all.
In the game of love, deceit, betrayal and blood,
Who will be the one to rise above?

CHAPTER ONE

ALEKSEI

With every step she takes, her hips sway and her tits bounce, threatening to spill out of the top to her low-cut shirt. She's slim and fit, with curves accentuated by taut muscles.

She doesn't belong here. A tainted world like the one we live in doesn't deserve such beauty and grace.

I am one of the most controlled people I know yet here I am about to come in my pants like a fucking schoolboy.

I could kill her. A single shot to the head, a swift slash across her throat, sending her off to a better place.

My cock twitches in my pants.

Fuck. I need to fuck her or kill her, or maybe both.

Arnold, my boss, would be livid. Hell, I'm pissed off at myself right now. I don't do anything personal—nothing outside of work. My line of work requires that I be well controlled, emotionless, and manipulative. I'm like a chameleon; I adjust well to my surroundings and can disguise myself as whoever I need to be in that given situation.

Instilled in my mind at a young age was one imperative rule: trust no one, not even my own blood. To prove a point, my father had my mother put six feet underground. Granted, she became a liability by saying she wanted to be done and move out of the country. Their relationship was more of a business relationship than anything.

My father is a powerful man, he shaped me into the machine I am today. When Arnold's family and ours decided to make peace, the Russians became one of his ally's and my father handed me over to him. Working for Arnold, I'm one of the most valuable men in his operation. Arnold runs the empire, calling the shots and ordering the hits and most of what I do for him involves taking people out. And trust me, I'm not taking them out to dinner.

I lose track of her for a moment but after surveying the bar, I easily spot her. Watching her like a hawk until we make eye contact, I signal for her to come over. She saunters across the room with confidence and a seductive look on her face, as if she intends on seducing the seducer.

Bring it on.

"Is there something else I can get you tonight?" She purrs as she reaches the table.

Slowly stroking my chin, I eye her up and down. "There is something you could do for me, actually."

Her eyebrows rise in curiosity. "And just what might that be?"

The sound of her sultry voice and the look in her eyes make my dick jump.

"Tell me about yourself," I pause, looking at her name tag, "Lyra."

I'm going into unknown territory right now and completely off script.

A strained smile covers her lips and it throws off her whole demeanor. "I can tell you that I'm just your average girl working to get myself through college."

"I'm sure you are far from average," I retort, getting too personal. "Tell me about your *real* self"

Shifting her feet nervously, she starts fidgeting with her hair as she clears her throat.

"I can, um, assure you there's not much to tell. I hate to rush off, but I really should get back to work. If there is anything else, please let me know."

"I need to be on my way as well," I throw some money on the table.

"I haven't even brought you your bill yet," she grabs the glasses as I stand up. "I will be right back."

Standing with her back to me, I want nothing more than to bend her over the table and leave my mark on her.

Coming to stand right behind her, I put my mouth beside her ear. "Don't worry love," I assure her, "I'll be back for you and trust me, you want me to come back."

CHAPTER TWO

LYRA

What the hell just happened?

The mysterious man dressed in black disappears from the bar before I get a second look at him. He sees right through me, that much is obvious and because of that, I definitely don't want him coming back.

Rushing through the rest of my shift, I leave work as quickly as possible and race home.

Walking through the door, I don't even bother hanging up my purse or keys. Throwing all my stuff down, I take in my surroundings.

Living with my father, we always had nice things like what I have now. Living with my mother was the complete opposite. Unlike the house I grew up in, everything here was mine—I paid for everything within these walls myself. I refused to accept any help from my father, despite his financial standing with his dirty money which happened to be washed very carefully.

My apartment is my space. I make sure everything is cleaned and basically as sterile as an OR. There is no trash littering the floor, no coffee table covered in money, drugs, or weapons.

Crawling into my plush king-sized bed, I don't bother to change my clothes. Gross, I know but seeing as the sun is going to be rising soon, I need to sleep.

Sleep never comes. Every time my eyes close, I'm greeted by those crystal-clear blue eyes and that panty dropping smile. That man oozed sex and danger, two things of which my senses were well attuned to. He's the exact thing I don't want to get involved with.

Jesus, what am I saying?

This man is nobody to me and here I am thinking about if I were to get involved with him. I'm already casually sleeping with another guy, so I'm just letting the complications pile up right now.

After tossing and turning for what seems like hours, I roll out of bed. It's six o'clock in the morning. I guess there's no better time than now to have a glass of wine. Shit, I'll need to drink the whole bottle to relax at this point.

The day comes and goes faster than I expected. I managed to get roughly two hours of sleep between drinking a bottle of wine and watching shitty daytime shows. Before I know it, it's time to head back to work and pray I get through the night without any sightings of the Russian.

"So, where is that fine ass man tonight?" One of the bartenders, Damian, asks after a few hours pass by without any sign of him.

I shrug. "Probably went back to his throne in Hell.

Come on, I'll admit he was hot, but he's dangerous as fuck."

"Who knew the Devil wore Armani suits? And who cares if he is the Devil? He looks like someone who can fuck!" Damien winks.

"Oh look, there's a table! Gotta run!" I start walking away as he laughs. That stupid fuck can read me too well. I flip Damien off as I walk over to the couple that just sat down and he blows me a kiss.

As much as I love the guy, he really needs to learn to shut the fuck up sometimes. I have never been one for relationships. I have attachment issues, which has resulted in a lot of friends with benefits and one-night stands. I never brought them back to my place, though, that way I could sneak out and not have to see them again.

But...

I want the Russian man to sneak in.

I *want* to see him again.

CHAPTER THREE

ALEKSEI

I told her I'd be back for her but in reality, I shouldn't even be here. There's a hint of darkness hidden behind those hazel eyes mixed with the golden light that still shines from her. The light that shines from her eyes, although it may be subtle, should never be dimmed. My world and my demons are too dark for her.

I take a seat at the hotel bar. I'm hoping she'll be here tonight. If not, I'll watch her from afar and make my move when the time is right. Like an animal stalking its prey, I'll be waiting for the perfect moment to attack. This is a predator and prey situation and she's most definitely the prey.

I can feel her walk in before I see her. My primal and conditioned instincts collide as she walks into the room. The sound of her heels, the smell of her perfume mixed with her natural scent. My senses come alive; her presence surrounds me.

She walks behind the bar and begins talking to one of the other bartenders. Slowly bringing my glass to my lips, I watch her. I know she saw me and she's struggling to avoid my gaze. Sizing her up, I study her movements. As she contorts her hands, her weight shifts from one leg to the other. She scratches her forehead as if she really has an itch. Being taught at a young age to know different behaviors, I know she's nervous. She's practically squirming under my gaze.

I raise my glass, signaling to the bartender I need another drink. As my attention shifts back to her, she finally meets my gaze. The energy can be felt across the room, almost hearing the air sizzle. There's no longer any nervousness about her. Instead, she's sizing me up, challenging me. Rather than looking away, she maintains eye contact as she stalks toward me.

"So," she smiles. "We meet again."

"So, we do," I reply as my drink is placed in front of me.

My original bartender seems small standing beside Lyra. "Can I get you anything else?"

"I got it from here Marcy," she answers for me, neither of us breaking eye contact. "I wasn't sure you were coming back."

"I'm a man of my word," I admit. "I told you I'd be back for you".

The lust is evident in her eyes as she clenches her thighs together.

"You wanted me to come back," I bait her. "You've been waiting for me."

Raising an eyebrow, she smirks. "Is that what you think?"

Slowly, I shake my head. "That's not what I think, it's what I know. Your body betrays you; it gives me everything I need to know."

I wait for a response but instead she just stares me down.

"Run while you still can," I warn, leaning closer to her. "I'm the big bad wolf in this story and if you don't run now, you're going to get eaten alive."

Her cheeks flush as she gasps at my words. I'm much better at this game than she is.

She should run in the opposite direction and I should want her to, yet here I am, coming on to her. The last thing I should be doing is engaging with a woman like this.

"I never was good at running away from danger," she shrugs.

Marcy, the other bartender appears with a scowl on her face. "Lyra, think you could do your job and help take care of some of these customers?"

"Yes, Lyra," her name rolls off my tongue, "please don't let me keep you."

As she turns to walk away, I lean over and gently grab her elbow.

"Don't think you're getting off that easily," I tell her in a hushed voice. "We're not done here."

With that, I release her arm and resume drinking my vodka, all the while drinking her in. After a moment, she moves on to another customer.

A vibration in my pocket pulls me away from watching her. I pull out my phone and check the screen.

I sigh when I see it's my brother.

The stork has a baby to drop off.

His idiotic way of telling me we need to meet up to talk. We all speak in some sort of code if we're using text messaging or talking on the phone. You never know who might read or listen in on your conversations.

.   .   .

I go find a table to sit at and wait for Nikolai. With how reckless he drives, I'm sure it won't be long before he's here. I take a seat at a table not far from the bar, but slightly hidden in the shadows. Lyra may not see me lurking in the darkness, but she's in plain sight for me.

"Wake up dickhead," Nikolai scoffs as he sits down in the seat across from me.

"You're so classy with the way you speak to people," I scold him.

"Fuck you man. We have more pressing issues here."

"I'm listening," I stare at him, waiting.

"Arnold wants to see us. He has some kind of a mission for us," Nikolai explains, but I cut him off.

"I will wait until I get a call from him, since he is who I take orders from—not you," I correct him.

"What the fuck, Aleksei? I don't fucking work beneath you," he shakes his head in disgust. "Why don't you do all of the dirty work for yourself then from now on?

I laugh loudly. "Right, because what you do is the real dirty work."

"Yeah, it is. What you do is some sick, twisted shit that most of us can't even stomach half of the time," Nikolai glares at me.

"With that being said, don't you think it would be in your best interest to tread lightly?" I question him. "You know some of the things I'm capable of."

"All bark, no bite," he chuckles. "I'm not afraid of you. You may not have a conscious, but you wouldn't kill your brother. Now, let's get drunk. Oh wait, you don't know how to let loose like that and have fun." He jabs.

I'm barely listening to him anymore. My attention is

directed to the man who just grabbed Lyra's ass. I see red and want to rip the motherfuckers throat out.

Nikolai's eyes follow to where I'm looking.

"No way," he says in disbelief. "Some chick actually has your attention instead of business? Is hell freezing over, sir Lucifer?"

I ignore him as I go take care of this situation. The security guards grab the man and haul him out the door. No need for me to intervene. She barely seemed to care about what just happened and slid back behind the bar.

Nikolai's face lights up with his devilish grin. "Let me go grab those drinks now."

I narrow my eyes at him, knowing damn well he's going to make sure she gets the drinks for him.

Nikolai, being my younger brother, is more immature. He's not as cold and closed off as I am. Our mother spent more time with him being somewhat of a motherly figure. Me—on the other hand—I was old enough that I had already been molded into exactly what my father needed me to be. I have to give him credit, though. Nikolai does have an evil streak in him, and he can be just as ruthless. He still believes that there is some good out there to balance out all the bad, even if we are the bad.

Nikolai is testing me by singling her out. He saw how captivated I was by her and is now looking for a reaction to prove whether or not she's of any importance to me. This should be no problem at all. I have nothing that is important enough to pose as a weakness for me. Especially not this girl, whom of which I don't know personally.

CHAPTER FOUR

LYRA

The bar is so busy that I barely notice he moved to a table. He's lurking in the shadows, so I can't get a clear view of him. My body, however, can sense he is still here.

As I'm mixing some drinks, I notice another person slide up to the bar. I glance over and see a younger version of Aleksei. He can't be much younger than I am—he looks to be around the same age as me. They both have the same high cheekbones, bright eyes, and prominent jawbone. This man appears to be a hair shorter, but he has the same build. You can tell they are both solid and muscular yet lean as to not appear to be built like a bulldog.

Jess, the other bartender tonight, is swamped on her side of the bar, so it looks like I'll be fetching him his drinks.

I finish up the small talk with one of our regulars. Lucky for me, he tips very well. He'd much rather be my sugar daddy, but I'm going to keep it strictly as getting tips from him.

Walking up to the Aleksei clone, I plaster a fake ass smile onto my face. "What will you be drinking tonight?"

"You."

I glance up, taking in his appearance in the darkened room. "Nikolai?" The surprise is apparent in my voice.

"Well, good evening my sweet Lyra," he smiles, leaning onto the bar.

"What the hell are you doing here?" I ask him in a hushed voice.

"I could ask you the same thing," he narrows his eyes at me. "What the fuck?"

"I fucking work here," I tell him, breathing heavier. "And you don't belong here."

"What's your deal with my brother?" he demands.

I let out a harsh laugh. "Excuse me?"

"Don't bullshit me, Lyra. I saw the way he was looking at you. Don't fuck with him," he warns.

Laughing again, I shake my head. "And why do you say that? Because little brother has trouble sharing?"

He flashes his perfect white teeth. What the hell is it with these men? They have to have some sort of flaw. No one can have such perfect looks and be such smooth talkers without there being a catch.

"Vodka," he declares. "On the rocks."

"Oh, and you know none of that bottom of the barrel shit," he adds as I walk across the bar.

After making his drink, I bring it over to him. He takes a long, slow sip, savoring the taste. The corners of his mouth slowly curl upward and he has a very satisfied look on his face.

"You make a mean drink," he mocks.

"I'm glad to have a satisfied customer," my voice drips

with sarcasm. "Is there anything else I can get for you right now?

"Well, that depends on what is being offered," he cocks his head to the side with a smile. "I'd like nothing more than to take you home with me tonight. You look like you need some satisfaction in your life."

"While I appreciate the offer, I'm going to have to politely decline," I say, attempting to be professional. "Please feel free to let me know if there is anything else you need tonight."

"Don't be so dismissive," he insists. "*You* are what I need tonight. Be open minded about it. We could have a lot of fun together."

"I think I'm good, but thanks," I tell him, rolling my eyes. "We've already been down that road."

I turn to walk in the other direction.

"You're not good," he calls after me. "You'll feel a lot better after I've had my way with you."

I spin around, pissed off now. "Listen motherfucker," I start, but he cuts me off.

"You can call me Nikolai," he replies calmly.

"I don't give a flying fuck what your name is," I bark. "I've told you no multiple times. Do I need to cut your dick off and shove it down your throat for you to understand that I said no?"

"I would love for you to do anything with my dick," he chuckles.

"Cut the shit, Nikolai. I've had my fair share of your dick. Drink your drink and get the fuck out before I signal for my friends over there to escort you out."

"That won't be necessary," he smiles, grabbing the one glass. "I'll take a vodka straight on the rocks and I'll be out of your hair. My brothers over there waiting for me."

He grins over at his brother—who happens to be a very pissed off looking Aleksei.

I get him the drink as fast as I can. I do not want to be on the receiving end of Aleksei's anger. I know nothing of the man, but I do know that it's something I would not want to experience.

As quickly as Nikolai appeared, he's gone. I glance over toward the table and can see Aleksei talking very quietly to him. This must be some type of a joke, for them to be fucking with me like this.

Nikolai, while he was more arrogant, was not nearly as intimidating. Aleksei, on the other hand, looked like he was starving for something—or *someone*. And that something or someone was me.

Thinking of Aleksei, I replay our conversation in my head. The fucker sure was smooth and knew exactly what to say. He was very calm and controlled about it. He has the upper hand and he knows it. Maybe I should take his advice and run in the other direction.

I run, or walk, is more like it, in the other direction to go outside and smoke a cigarette. I wouldn't mind taking a couple shots as well. Thankfully, I'm off for the next two days so I can get this shit out of my head and pray to God they don't come back again.

"Do you know what cigarettes can do to your lungs?"

I jump and spin around. I was so caught up in my head I barely noticed I had company. That company just so happened to be the one occupying my mind.

I stare at him, having nothing to say.

"What's the saying?" He inquires. "Cat got your tongue?"

The cat must have taken my tongue and my brain

because I cannot form a coherent thought, let alone speak any words.

As I go to take another drag, he takes the cigarette from me.

"Excuse me, I can smoke if I—," I start, pissed off at both of these men now.

I stop mid-sentence as I realize he's not going to put it out. Instead, he takes a long, slow drag of the cigarette.

Slowly exhaling, he gives me a small smile. "I am not a regular smoker, but damn if I don't mind indulging in it every once in a while."

"If you'd like to give me mine back, I have no problem giving you one of your own," I quip.

"I'd rather smoke yours instead," he concurs.

I pull out another cigarette and turn away from him.

"I'm making you uncomfortable," he states. "Why? Is it because you can't deny the strong attraction between us?"

I choke on the smoke as I light my cigarette and laugh at the same time. "I'm not sure what you're talking about. Clearly, I'm out here minding my own business and you and your asshole brother are playing some sort of a game with me and guess what? I don't fucking play games."

"Lyra," he says softly. "I must apologize for my brother's behavior. I can assure you he won't behave like that again. He likes to do that to mess with me. It wasn't a game toward you."

Aleksei is much more serious than Nikolai is. Besides looks, there are only a few other similarities.

"Okay."

What else am I supposed to say to him? I spoke my peace and he apologized for how his brother acted. I should get back inside, but I remain in the same spot with my feet cemented to the ground.

"Now, I know you feel it. I know you want me," he whispers. "There are many things I can think of to solve this problem. However, I'd like for you to enlighten me on what you think we can do about this."

And just like that, we're back to me being a mute.

He pulls out a small business card and flips it over, writing something on the back.

"Unfortunately, I have to get going," he frowns. "Here is my phone number. What you decide to do with it is up to you. As much as I'd like to encourage you NOT to call me, I'm really hoping that you decide to."

He grabs my hand and places the card into it. Before letting go, he brings my hand up to his mouth and lightly kisses my fingers.

"Until next time, Lyra," he whispers against my skin.

And with that, he's gone, taking any common sense I had with him. He's dark and dangerous, disguised behind a calculating smile and a pretty face. I should throw the card out with my cigarette. Instead, I slide it into my pocket and head back inside, silencing the warning sirens in my head.

CHAPTER FIVE

ALEKSEI

With the day beginning to fall into night, I slip my arms into my suit for our business meeting. The meeting is being held at Arnold's mansion. Having multiple locations used for different reasons, his home is our main place of business.

My dress shoes echo on the white marble floor as I walk down the hallway through Arnold's home. I walk into the basement where the main conference room is. There are numerous doors on either side of the hallway, each containing an office; some offices hold hidden doors that lead into different torture rooms while others house Arnold's many women.

My office looks like that of a regular one with a massive oak desk occupying the room and walls lined with bookshelves. I walk passed my office and head for the door at the end of the hallway. The door opens to a massive conference room with a large oak table surrounded by plush chairs. The corner of the room contains a small bar with top shelf liquor.

When I arrive, only my brother and Arnold are seated around the vast table.

"Aleksei, we've been awaiting your arrival. Now that you're here, let us begin."

Nodding, I take a seat next to Nikolai, naturally.

He jabs me in the ribs with his elbow as I sit down. "Way to show up late, jackass. You know you're late when I'm here before you."

I throw a glare his way, not reacting to him.

Arnold clears his throat, demanding our attention. "As you can see, we have an important matter to discuss, a personal one; which is why the two of you have been brought here tonight."

Nikolai glances around, raising an eyebrow at me.

"What do you need us for?" I inquire in a neutral voice.

"Your father has become a serious liability. Over the years, as you know, he's become very paranoid and even more impulsive. He killed Rossi, whom I know you are both familiar with," Arnold cuts his eyes at Nikolai, who stares back at him, hard.

Their exchange is peculiar, but I begin to tune out Arnold, seeing as I most likely won't be needed for this mission. What Arnold doesn't know is I've been trying to find my father myself and all leads have turned cold at this point. Arnold is going to need to bring in other men to do more tracking to find him before he would need me.

"Aleksei, we will need you for this mission," Arnold states, breaking through my thoughts.

Of course, I jinxed myself.

"Your brother has managed to get ahold of him, seeing as he knows of no connection between Nikolai and I, so he was able to trace him to a secluded area in upstate New York."

Glancing over at Nikolai, I stare at him for a moment before looking back at Arnold. "Okay, so why must I be involved?"

"You know exactly what you're needed for," he smiles, "but I'll be bringing someone else in, just as a little reassurance you don't suddenly go soft on me and have a daddy moment."

Nikolai chokes on his drink beside me, letting out a strangled laugh. "Of all people, you really except Ice Cube over here to have some sentimental feelings toward that shitbag?"

"We don't need any outsiders, Arnold. It won't be a problem," I assure him.

"I don't think it will be either but that's just it, I don't know. Plus, we can't afford to have this traced back to us. You hide in the shadows so no one can put your face on anything. The woman is also unknown, with no one knowing of her ties to the Rossi family. She is very skilled in manipulation and transforming to who she must be. You both possess similar skills that others do not."

My eyes narrow ever so slightly. "A woman?"

"She fits the bill perfectly and is exactly who I need to send. Is the fact that she doesn't have a cock and set of balls going to be a problem here?" Arnold asks, cocking his head to the side.

"Surely you don't plan on shying away from this job, Aleksei," Nikolai challenges, taunting me.

Arnold shakes his head and continues, "There is no option for this mission. You will fly out first thing in the morning and you'll be debriefed on the specifics during the flight there. Your new associate."

A soft knock sounds on the large wooden door.

"Speak of the devil and he shall arrive," Nikolai chuckles. "Or should we say *she*?"

Just then, the door slowly opens, and I choke on my drink as she walks in.

Arnold rises to his feet, pulling out a chair. "Lyra, welcome. We were just discussing the mission."

Her eyes find mine, mirroring the same look of shock.

What. The. Actual. Fuck.

CHAPTER SIX

LYRA

Looks like Aleksei now knows I'm definitely not who he thought I was. I'm officially the world's biggest idiot. I should have connected the dots, but I didn't because, you know, I'm clearly an idiot.

Of course, Aleksei is one of Arnold's men. I shouldn't have expected anything differently. I was too caught up in my new life I didn't even notice the signs. His dangerous aura pointed directly to this Table of Death.

He claimed he wanted to know my darkest secrets.

He won't be finding those out, but he now knows one of them and who I actually am.

I avoid his gaze for the rest of the night. We briefly discuss what we will be doing and as soon as we finish, Aleksei storms out of the room. Who the hell pissed in his cheerios?

Nikolai approaches me. "You?" he questions.

"Aw man, you caught me."

"What the fuck are you doing here?" He questions me in a harsh, hushed voice.

"I'm sorry," I reply sweetly. "You're supposed to question me for what reason?"

"You're not supposed to be here. And you fucked my brother?" He asks with a fury in his eyes.

"I'm sure the look on his face answered your question. Not to mention, the way he ran out of the room like his ass was on fire. I'll get this out of the way and answer your questions. I'm here to help you, to make sure he doesn't slip up. Your father killed mine, so Arnold knows I have no problem putting a bullet in both of your heads." I pause, a slow smile creeping onto my face. "And yes, actually, I did fuck your brother. Last time I checked, you and I weren't together."

I didn't fuck his brother, not yet at least. I played him like a fucking fiddle and it's only a matter of time until I have him by the balls. Aleksei and Nikolai are both vital parts of my plan now and if I have to ride both dicks to get it done, I will.

"What do you say we go get a drink?" Nikolai questions after I get lost in my head. "And then you can let me remind you which brother should be balls deep in that tight pussy."

Internally rolling my eyes, I bat my eyelashes at him. "You know what Nik, that actually sounds great. Have the driver take us to the hotel I'll be at for the night and we can go to the bar there."

Fuck it. What's a free drink and a good fuck? If Aleksei wants to be a little bitch and go hide for the night, then so be it, because after tonight he's not going to be able to get away from me.

We get to the bar and I suddenly have a change of heart. I

now have every intention of getting shit faced. Ordering a bone drink martini, I get right to it. I don't hear Nikolai's order, but I've been out with him enough times to know it is most likely vodka on the rocks.

"You better slow your roll, Lyra," he tips his glass toward mine as I drain half of the glass.

Shrugging, I roll my eyes at him. "Tonight is about getting nice and ready to pray to the porcelain god."

"Keepin' it classy. I dig it, but do you think you can refrain from puking your guts out until after I've had my way with you?"

I laugh directly in his face.

"You're delusional if you think anything is happening between either of us tonight. I have one thing in mind and that is getting annihilated."

"Whatever," he mutters. "While I'm fucking another girl tonight in the room next to yours, remember, that could have been you."

If only things were that simple.

"It's cool," I shrug, smirking. "You'll hear what a good fuck sounds like when Aleksei is deep inside me."

Nikolai laughs loudly, shaking his head at me. "This is why I like you, Lyra."

Laughing along with him, the tension drops, and the topic quickly changes. We shoot the shit about mindless stuff that neither of us care about. What else are we supposed to do? Share our feelings? I may have a vagina, but I don't do that shit.

Three drinks and two shots later, I am well on my way to spending my night on the bathroom floor.

Then, of course, Nikolai has to bring up his brother and I end up with word vomit, saying shit that should stay in my head.

"What happened with you and Aleksei? The moment he saw you he looked like he was ready to draw his gun and then he was gone."

"Your guess is as good as mine. We had a good time or at least I thought we did..."

I'm lying but I have no idea what is coming out of my mouth at this point nor do I care. I'll regret this conversation in the morning.

"Lyra, Aleksei can't relate to people like you and I. Yeah, we're a part of the criminal world and families but we weren't raised the same as others. By the time I was born, my father had already trained Aleksei and brainwashed him into what he is now. My mom wanted out and didn't want me to have the same fate as Aleksei. So, I received some *"love"*, if you want to call it that. Which in the end, only had me getting beat close to death numerous times by our father and his men and our mother dead."

"The man you're describing sounds like a completely different man than the one I know," I admit, my own mind and feelings a jumbled mess.

"The only person he cares about in his life is me and even then, he's not my biggest fan. If he gets involved, you will become his weakness and you should know in our line of business that's not something you need."

"Well fan-fucking-tastic," I reply sarcastically. "It's a good thing I'm not looking for his hand in marriage. All we would do is destroy each other which wouldn't be good for either of us."

I down the rest of my drink before ordering two more shots and another drink.

"I'm glad you realize that. But, us on the other hand baby, you're a fighter, I can tell. I don't usually like when they fight back, but we could have a lot of fun. Fuck him being my brother, I can make you forget him."

Thankfully, my drinks show up. I throw back the two shots with ease and start consuming my drink much faster than I should.

Yep, I'm definitely drunk off my ass.

Nikolai's offer is starting to seem appealing. I could use a good distraction right now and I've used him for that purpose quite a few times already.

"I'm going to the bathroom. Don't leave. Should I get you a bottle, you've been nursing your drink for a while pussy," I taunt.

"Maybe because I'd like to remember *your pussy* in the morning."

I get up from my seat in the most ungraceful manner. The room is definitely spinning. Turning around, I run directly into a hard, warm body.

Aleksei. Just my luck.

My drunken mind forces the words *Fuck you* out and I stumble away toward the bathroom.

"I'll be back for you motherfucker. And if you're lucky, I'll kill you rather than turn you into a fucking vegetable," Aleksei threatens Nikolai.

He trails me to the bathroom and actually follows me inside.

"Who the fuck are you?" I scoff in disbelief. "Get out of the bathroom and leave me alone."

What am I, a child?

He corners me. "I think the more appropriate question is what the fuck are you doing?"

"Well, I was planning on taking a pee. Alone, I might add," I reply as I slam the stall door in his face.

I hear the bathroom door slam, so obviously he took a hint and finally left.

I'm wrong again. He's right outside the door waiting.

Grabbing a hold of my arm, he's practically dragging me out the door. "I'm taking you up to your room. You're trashed."

We make a pit stop at the bar by Nikolai.

"We'll talk about this later. You need to keep your hands off what's mine."

So now I'm his?

They argue quietly enough that I can't hear. Not that I could comprehend much at this point.

I quickly order two more shots and drink them as quickly as possible before dickhead decides he wants to act like he's my dad.

After downing the shots, I can barely walk. I'm seeing double and I start heading toward the door to leave.

I don't protest as Aleksei picks me up and carries me to the elevator. I rest my head on his shoulder and let sleep take over.

I briefly register him placing me in bed and crawling in with me, pulling my body close to his.

Even being completely shit faced, I can still feel the electricity from his touch and I fucking hate it.

CHAPTER SEVEN

ALEKSEI

This whole night has been a total mind fuck.

I knew something was off when I found out her last name and came up with nothing when I ran a background search on Lyra Garber. But I disregarded it. My judgment was clouded.

She's a completely different person than I thought she was.

I don't know if I'm more relieved to be business associates with her or completely pissed off about this situation.

Nikolai will be getting a beat down. He thought because I walked out of the meeting, that suddenly he could move in on her, but he was wrong. She is mine.

Feelings of betrayal infiltrate my mind.

By her.

By my own brother.

I'm paranoid for no reason.

I'm the reason she got as drunk as she did and the magnetic pull between us is too much. I needed to feel her, to be close to her. So, I got in bed with her, just to hold her and wake up and see her beautiful face in the morning.

Brushing her vanilla scented hair out of her face, I study her. Her face is perfectly proportioned with soft plump lips. It's slim with high cheekbones. With such a` petite body, everything about her is proportionate.

Beautiful is an understatement.

Closing my eyes, breathing in her scent, I slip into a deep slumber. And it's the best sleep I've ever had.

Waking up, our limbs are tangled in one another. One leg in between mine, the other thrown over my hip. I don't bother moving my hand from her ass as she begins to stir.

She makes a wholehearted attempt to lift my arm from her and pull her leg from mine. I tighten my arm and thighs, not allowing her to slip from my grip.

"Shhh," I whisper into her ear. "Just lay here with me for another minute."

Reluctantly, her body relaxes into mine. She buries her face into the crook of my neck. Running her hand over my abs, her hand comes to a stop on my chest.

"Let's just stay like this. Forget we have any type of a business relationship. Can't we just pretend we're two normal people, just getting to know one another?"

"You have no idea how much I wish it could be like that."

"Let me enjoy this before I realize how pissed off I actually was last night."

So much for things being any different this morning. There's no reason for me to care.

The feelings I was developing before were clearly

false. People like me, we don't really have feelings. We do what we have to do in order to survive.

Our relationship is strictly business now. I don't do this, it's not in my makeup, but she makes me want to be different and try something I've never done before.

My mind and feelings are so conflicting and foreign right now.

It needs to stop. I need to get out of this bed immediately.

Releasing her and separating myself from her, I instantly feel the heat leaving my body and I don't like it.

I push the thought of laying back down with her from my mind. "We'll order room service and then we'll talk."

"Yeah. I'm not hungry. You go ahead. I'm going to get a shower."

She's pissed. Her body language and tone make it apparent. Controlling her emotions doesn't appear to be her strong suit.

She better not fuck this mission up or I'll have to put a bullet between her eyes myself.

Yes, those are the feelings I should have, not ones of being attached. She's merely a pawn to complete a job and if need be, I would end her without batting an eye.

Calling room service, I order some food for her as well. She's going to be hungover and she needs to eat something. We need her on top of her game.

As the shower turns on, I can't help but picture her naked. The hot water running down her tight body. The stream of water hugging her curves. What I wouldn't give to feel my cock slide inside her.

Maybe if I fucked her and got this out of my system, these strange feelings would subside.

I have a raging hard-on when room service arrives. I don't bother hiding my arousal as I open the door. Fuck it.

As I close the door, she's coming out of the bathroom with nothing but a towel on. A short towel. The bottom of it landing just below her ass.

I can't help but wince as my dick strains against my pants.

She glances down and cocks an eyebrow at me. Completely unfazed and disinterested, she motions toward the buffet of food.

"What, you order the whole damn menu?"

"I wasn't sure what you liked so I ordered a little of everything. Considering the only thing you probably put in your stomach yesterday was alcohol, you need to eat something. You're going to need your energy."

She grabs a piece of cantaloupe from the tray and walks toward the chair with her clothing, dropping the towel on her way there.

What in the ever-loving-fuck?

My feet are moving before my mind registers what the fuck I'm doing.

Coming up behind her, I grasp her shoulders. I spin her around and take a step back.

"If you're going to put it all on display, I'm going to admire it because you have a body that should be worshipped."

My eyes trail back up to her face. Her eyes are full of lust, her lips curl upwards into a smile.

She's fucking with me. Testing me.

And now she knows she has me by the balls. I'm totally fucked.

CHAPTER EIGHT

LYRA

His eyes are burning a hole into mine. His stare so intense. Lust and fire are evident in his crystal blue eyes. The coldness that was once there has been replaced with heat.

This was a test. For whatever reason, I wanted to see his reaction. This isn't what I was expecting.

But I can't help but feel some type of satisfaction, for many reasons.

The fucker acts like he's such a hard ass, but his actions are telling me something completely different.

The air between us is buzzing from the sexual tension.

The tension is real, but my words—my feelings—are all part of the game.

The feelings, they aren't real.

Closing the space between us, he brings his hand up to my cheek. He waits for me to make a move.

Fuck it, I started this and I'm already being reckless. He tells me my body should be worshipped, so I'm going to let him worship it.

· · ·

Placing my hand on his firm chest, my body leans closer to his. His mouth collides with mine as he meets me in the middle. Our lips mold to one another. Slowly and sensually, our lips move in synchrony. His hand dives into my hair as the other grips me by the back of my neck with my arms wrapped around his.

Tugging on my hair, he deepens this kiss. Our tongues are intertwined with one another, mimicking each other's actions.

My head is swarming, the heat rushing through me straight to my core. Running his hands down the sides of my naked torso, a burning sensation trails along with his movements against my skin.

Reaching for his shirt, he pulls it over his head, revealing the body I've been waiting to see. Mimicking his movements, I run my hands down his chest, his stomach and back up. He begins to trail kisses, suckling down my throat and collarbone, making his way towards my breasts.

He kisses his way across, just barely touching my nipples as a tease.

I let out a soft moan, running my hand through his soft waves.

Gently pushing me onto my back on the bed, he straddles me. He meets my eyes and they tell me all I need to know.

He slowly draws one nipple into his mouth as he rolls the other between his fingertips. Sucking on my nipple and biting it, my back arches from the pleasure.

"Oh Aleksei, fuck."

His hand trails down my body as he continues his assault on my nipples.

"You're so wet for me. That tight pussy's dripping. I

need to taste you."

Kissing and sucking his way down my torso, he meets my center.

"Smells so good, so fucking sweet"

He slowly licks through my folds, dipping his tongue inside me.

"Holy fuck," I moan. My insides are already clenching just from his tongue touching me.

He circles my clit with his tongue, nipping my sensitive bud.

I'm completely losing touch with reality, too caught up in the overwhelming pleasure he's bringing to my body. Devouring me, I yell out obscenities as everything around me fades away.

"Come for me, Lyra. Let me hear you, taste you as you come undone."

Gripping the bed sheets, my hips buck and I lose control, falling over the edge.

Coming back down from my high, he licks me clean. Placing a soft kiss on my tender skin, he slides up beside me.

His lips find mine in a slow kiss. I grab his face and intensify it. He picks up on it quickly and claims my mouth.

Rolling onto his back, he pulls me on top of him, never breaking the kiss. I reach down between my legs and begin unbuttoning his pants. The sound of his zipper mixes with the sounds of our need.

He lifts his hips as I slide his pants over his hips. Lips still connected, I grab him with my hand and guide his length into me. As I slide down his shaft, it registers how big he really is. So big that it almost hurts. With the pain comes pleasure.

We begin moving together, our movements matching one another's. He takes and I give, while I take and he gives. Time becomes lost. Our bodies are no longer separate and slowly, we drift into our sweet abyss.

Waking up, I feel hungover. Not hungover from drinking too much alcohol. Hungover from drinking too much from him. My body suffers from a pleasurable soreness and my mind is hazy from our sex induced coma.

Aleksei clings to me in his sleep as if I might vanish. His features are soft, the hardness not present as he sleeps. He looks much younger, more innocent.

He's vulnerable and he's letting me in, exactly as I planned he would.

He begins to stir, his eyes flying open as he squeezes me tightly.

He visibly relaxes as he sees me and feels me beside him.

"I don't know why I thought you'd be gone," he loosens his grip and the worry leaves his face.

"I don't usually dream. But, I know if I did, that's exactly what a dream would feel like."

"Now that I've had you, I can't let you go," he stares into my soul.

"So don't," I challenge.

Glancing over my shoulder, his eyes widen as he finds the clock.

"Fuck!" As he jumps up, his phone starts ringing.

"What?...Yeah, no shit we're running late...We will be there," he barks into the phone as he ends the call. He looks to me, "Lyra, we've got to go. We were supposed to leave twenty minutes ago."

ABIGAIL DAVIES

He paces the room in a frenzy, getting our belongings together and throwing clothes on himself.

"Aleksei, calm down. You own the plane; they're not going to leave us here."

It's evident that he's not in control. And he does not like it.

"We still have to drive to the airport. We had things scheduled accordingly as to not fuck this up."

He throws my clothes at me. Ignoring them and letting them fall to the ground, I go to him. I grab his face and kiss him. His hands reach mine in an effort to move them from his face. Instead, he responds to the kiss and matches me, working his lips against mine until we're both breathless.

Pulling away, I soften the kiss.

"Hey, it's okay. Things happen, we overslept. Just breathe. We'll hurry, we'll get there, and everything will be fine."

Running his hand through his hair, he says, "You're right, you're right. I'm sorry. I'm used to being in control. Since I've known you, everything has been thrown off. I'm late to shit all the time and all over the place. It's fucking with my head. We both need to be level headed for this. I can't have this happen."

Just like that, our walls are back in place.

Stepping away from him, I hastily get dressed and put my hair up in a bun.

I walk out the door as he grabs our bags.

There's an awkward silence the entire ride to the airport.

We board the plane and take our seats without a word or a glance in each other's direction.

· · ·

252

"It's about damn time you guys came," Nikolai smirks. "I mean that in a number of different ways," he winks at me.

Aleksei huffs and scowls as he pulls out his laptop.

"Seriously, what happened? Since she never came back to me last night, I know she was with you. Something's not right with either of you," Nikolai looks back and forth between the two of us. The tension in the air is so thick, it's suffocating, and I've never wanted to be removed from a situation so badly.

"Nikolai, mind your business."

Aleksei is extremely dismissive. The hardness is back on his face, lining his features with his eyebrows pinched together. His body language is not inviting. He sits with a straight, rigid back.

"Whatever. You guys better work your shit out before we get to New York. We need to go over the details and then you guys can get back to whatever the fuck this is," he waves his hand between Aleksei and me. "And if I find out you fucked her, we're going to be having some problems," he warns Aleksei, who ignores him.

Suddenly, I feel awkward and out of place even though everything is working out the way I need it to. Aleksei had me fooled, like he was actually feeling something for me. I can't ignore how he reacted when he woke up. He wanted me there and he let me in but just like that, his mask is back on and he's all business. He's back to his pissy self, dismissing me.

When he was pursuing me before he knew my real identity, I had never witnessed this side of him.

His loss.

Adjusting myself in my seat, I push back my shoulders with my confidence back in place. Nikolai and Aleksei both think I want them, yet neither of them know that I've had them both. They have their suspicions; they're slowly inching closer to each other's throats.

Fucking fools, thinking only with their dicks.

We discuss our plans. Aleksei talks in a very clipped tone.

"We will be staying at a new hotel. Nikolai, you will be in the room attached to mine." His brow furrows at his laptop. "Lyra, it's best if you stay with me, so I know you're protected."

"Absolutely not," Nikolai commands. "I am capable of protecting her."

Aleksei shakes his head. "Lyra and I will stay together just in case anything happens," he avoids any and all eye contact with me.

HA! I let out a harsh laugh. "No. Not happening."

Nikolai looks back and forth between us as his grin reaches for his eyes. "Exactly. Lyra should get a say in where she's going to sleep."

Aleksei glares at me. "Be professional about this Lyra. We're here to do a job. That is it."

I stare at him, not responding until he looks away.

"I'll be staying with Nikolai," I concur, winking at Nik.

Mission accomplished. He feels uncomfortable which is obviously another feeling he's not used to. He's conflicted and torn between the two of us.

Buckle up fucker, because this is going to be a bumpy ride.

. . .

As he begins to go over the details of our mission, I put in my earbuds and turn the music up as loud as it will go. I know enough that I need to know of their plans. What they don't know of is my agenda. We're all here for the same thing, the same mission, but mine is a little more intricate than they're aware of.

As much as I hate it, I begin to fall asleep. My mind as blank as my soul feels.

CHAPTER NINE

ALEKSEI

As we finish up our discussion, Nikolai directs his attention to his own laptop.

When Lyra dismissed our conversation and rudely put in her headphones, I wanted to demand this plane be turned around and for someone else to be put on this mission.

I do not tolerate disrespect. Especially from someone I am to work with and someone who I'm beginning to care for.

She had awoken feelings deep inside me. Finally finding what I'd been missing my whole life, I was overcome by many emotions and feelings. All of which I do not do.

It scared me. I don't do scared; I do the scaring.

I lost control this morning. I blamed her when it wasn't her fault.

It was easier that way. To blame it on her and be pissed off at her. It gave me something to use to disconnect myself from her. It makes it easier to push her away and this needs to end before it is too late. Before I lose myself in her completely. I could feel it happening after being with her for just one night.

Either of us could be killed during this mission and we can't have our feelings conflicting us.

In this business, it's kill or be killed. I will not allow her to kill me or have me killed.

Her soft snoring draws my attention to her. There's no denying that she's beautiful. Despite being in this business, she hasn't lost that part of herself yet. And I won't be the one to take it from her.

Nikolai clears his throat, causing me to look at him.

"Don't be such a dick to her. If you want nothing to do with her after this, cool, that's on you. At least play nice for now. If you don't, this won't work out in our favor. You can go back to your life without her in it when we get home and since we have to share her while we're here, maybe I'll officially make her mine when we get back."

"Just because I can't have her doesn't mean you can. I will not let this compromise our mission. We get in, we get out. We do what we have to do. I will do what I need to do to get this done. Keep your fucking nose out of what we do or don't do."

"Then don't put your shit out on display for anyone. What you're fucking with isn't yours and I'd tread lightly, brother. She needs someone who will give her more and I am just that someone. It wouldn't be the first time."

"Do what you want Nikolai. I couldn't care less."

Nikolai shakes his head and turns away from me.

As the hours pass on our flight, I replay what Nikolai says and what happened between Lyra and I.

Maybe he is right.

Maybe he isn't.

I study her as she sleeps, looking for some type of answer. In return, all I get is the swelling in my heart.

She's like a breath of fresh air. Something different, something good in my life. Instead of fighting it, maybe I should just go with it.

I'll play nice like Nikolai said.

"Stop watching me sleep, you creeper."

"If I want to watch you sleep, I will do as I please. Plus, I was just watching to make sure you were still breathing."

Nothing gave away that she was awake. Her eyes remained closed. Her breathing did not change. She didn't even move.

Shit, she was good.

"Maybe those were my intentions. I guess you'll never know. Don't doubt my ability to get this done the right way."

I open my mouth to speak, but she stops me.

"No. I'm not done."

I wait.

She takes a deep breath.

"I'm going to get this out. You can be as pissed off as you want. But you should be pissed with yourself, not me. You're the one who is going to fuck this is up. All of this," she waves her arms around. "Stop being a bitch about everything and get your head out of your ass. We have a job to do here."

My mouth falls open. Who the hell is this woman? She called me on my shit like she knows what she's talking about. This is not the place, nor is it the time for her to do so.

"I don't expect you to respond. I gather that you have a difficult time when someone else is right." She smirks at me.

And I still have no response.

"Finally!" Nikolai comes out of nowhere. "I might be in love with you."

She blows Nikolai a kiss and I see red, but I give her no satisfaction in her correct assumption.

Collecting myself, I say "Let's do what we came here to do and then we'll deal with this when we're done here."

"Fair enough," she says curtly.

The rest of the flight is silent. As we get ready to touch ground, I feel more unprepared than I ever have in my life.

Fuck me.

Our arrival in New York and the ride to our hotel is rather uneventful.

I remain silent as Lyra and Nikolai shoot the shit on the way to the hotel. Thankfully, the drive isn't very long, or Nikolai may have been thrown out of the car. We arrive at the hotel and quietly shuffle inside to check in and retrieve the keys to our rooms. Skirting around the two of them, I make my way to the elevators and quickly hop on one without them.

"Hey, wait!" Nikolai calls out, rushing after me as I turn to face him. "Want to go get dinner and drinks?"

"Can't," I reply as the door finally begins to close. "I have too much to do."

I catch Lyra's gaze through the crack as the elevator door closes. She glares at me from the other side.

She made her bed, so she'll lie in it... with him.

CHAPTER TEN

LYRA

For once, Nikolai is silent, leaving me in peace as we make our way to our room. The room is vast with a small sitting room and a bedroom with a master bath. Pulling in my suitcase, I stop short in the doorway glancing around with a growing annoyance.

"There's only one bed," I declare, feeling Nikolai step up behind me. He lightly brushes passed me, pushing into my shoulder as he steps into the bedroom.

"Hmm," he replies as he drops his bag onto the bed. "It's not like we haven't shared a bed before."

Shaking my head, I stand firmly in the doorway as he glances back at me with a smirk.

"No way in hell," I scoff.

"Come on, I won't bite," he winks, turning to face me. "That is unless you ask me to."

I shake off the urge to drive a knife through his throat. I'm not here for him this time—he is simply an obstacle in my way, but I can't be irrational. I'll play along and play the game.

Smiling at him sweetly, I enter the room, walking to

the opposite side of the bed and lift my suitcase in front of me. "We can sleep together, but don't you fucking touch me unless I tell you to."

"Play hard to get all you want, love," he calls out, walking into the bathroom, straightening his collar in the mirror. "We both know how tonight is going to end."

Yeah, not with your cock inside me.

Laughing lightly, I shake my head as he believes the deception that I've become. Unzipping my suitcase, I dig in and pull out my clothes, arranging them on the bed.

"I'm going to the bar," Nikolai declares, stepping out of the bathroom. "Care to join me?"

Giving him a small smile, I shake my head. "I'm going to finish unpacking and I think I might lay down for a little bit."

Nikolai shrugs and rolls his eyes as he leaves the room. "Suit yourself," he mumbles, as he closes the door.

Listening for the door to lock, I glance over at the clock, taking a mental note of the time before I finish sorting my clothes. A half an hour should be enough time to make sure I'm cleared to go. By that time, Nikolai will probably be two drinks in and too distracted chumming it up with some blonde with a cigarette dangling between his lips. I'll be nonexistent in his mind at that point.

The time passes quickly as I slide an outfit into one of the dresser drawers and shove the rest of my clothing back into my suitcase. I won't be needing half of what I packed, but I have to play along. Grabbing the ice bucket from the counter, I leave the rest of my belongings behind and slip out into the hallway. Walking down to the end of the hall, I fill the bucket with ice and head back to my room but stop in front of Aleksei's instead.

Knocking lightly, I take a step back and wait a few

moments. His strong scent of expensive leather slips out of the door as he opens it slowly, peering down at me.

"Lyra," he says slowly with his eyebrows pinched together. "What are you doing here?"

Giving him a small smile, I shrug. "I forgot my room key and Nikolai went out and isn't answering his phone," I lie.

He stares at me, his gaze hard and cold, burning holes into my eyes before closing the door in my face. I listen as he unlatches the chain and the door slowly reopens. Aleksei's back is to me as he walks back into his room, sitting down at the small table. I follow him into the room, carefully peering over his shoulder as I walk passed him, taking a seat on the couch.

Small pieces of paper are spread out around him on the table, some trapped underneath a bottle of vodka and a half-filled glass.

"You can wait here until he's back from whatever it is he's doing," Aleksei mumbles, staring down at the mess in front of him. Shuffling some of the papers together, he glances at me from the corner of his eye. "Why aren't you with him?"

Rising to my feet, I take advantage of our positions and walk over to him. Stepping behind him, I peer over his shoulder, catching sight of an address and some other random information and rest my hands on his shoulders.

"He's not who I want to be with," I reply softly. "There was nothing between us like he insinuated and there never will be anything between us. He knows where I stand and how I feel."

Walking in front of Aleksei, he looks up at me as I take his face into my hands. "He knows that you are who I want to be with." His eyes are dark, swirling with emotion as he scans my face in disbelief.

He's looking for any indication of a lie, it's a good thing I can act with a poker face to envy.

Grabbing onto my wrists, he rises to his feet and gently pushes me backward, out of his space. My arms fall heavily to my sides as he glares at me. "You need to leave," he commands in a harsh tone.

Staring up at him, I meet him head-on, challenging him. I don't hesitate as I step forward, entering his personal space again. "I'm not going anywhere," I retort, stopping short as he holds out his hand, pressing it into my chest to halt my movement. "We both know you want me as badly as I want you."

A low growl comes from deep inside his chest as he closes his eyes tightly. Reaching up, I rest my hands on his shoulders at the base of his neck as the pressure he has against mine loosens.

"Your body gives you away with every reaction you have to me," I tell him in a hushed voice, slowly stroking the pad of my thumb against the side of his neck. "Don't fight this. Don't fight us."

His hand slides up my chest, wrapping around my slender throat. He clamps down, tightening his grip and his eyes light up as a ragged breath barely slips out. A smile plays on his lips as his hand slides around the back of my neck and I'm suddenly pulled flush against him as his mouth crashes into mine.

Aleksei gives in, he stops fighting the pull between us, the pull that he feels is true. I give in to the game, letting my mind take a backseat as my body takes control, following his lead. He pushes and pulls, and I give and take.

We play a delicate, dangerous game together.

It's a race against time, against the ticking hands of the clock. Our time together will be short and as much as I plan on finishing my mission, I'm going to get my fill of him first.

We move together around the room, skin on skin with our clothes in a pile kicked across the floor. He slides in and out of me with ease as I arch into him, grinding against him. We end on the bed, a mess of limbs wrapped together in tangled sheets. Together we climb higher and higher with each thrust and every stroke until we reach the brink of ecstasy. My orgasm hits me full force in a consuming rush as he pounds into me until he tips over the edge, losing himself in me completely.

"Fuck," he mutters, collapsing onto the bed beside me. He rests his hands on his heaving chest as he struggles to catch his breath. I look over at him, smiling, as my eyes meet his. With a content look, he smiles back at me before closing his eyes, taking a deep breath. Curling onto my side, I place my hand on top of his and he wraps his around mine. I watch him as his face slowly relaxes and his breathing grows heavier. Soft snoring escapes him as he falls into a comfortable sleep.

Slowly easing my hand from his, I carefully climb out of bed, making sure not to disturb him. Searching the room, I find my clothes and quickly slip back into them before shuffling over to the table with Aleksei's notes on them. Glancing over my shoulder, I quickly check on his still sleeping form before sifting through the papers. Finding the ones I need, I slip them from the pile and fold them up before sliding them into my bra.

Giving Aleksei one last glance and scanning the room

once more, I quickly slip out of the room without a sound, leaving no trace of my visit behind.

I walk across the hall to my room just as the door is pulled open. A tall, thin woman with long blonde hair stumbles out, adjusting her boobs in the top of her dress. She knocks into me as I reach out to prop the door open.

"I'm so sorry!" she squeals as she regains her balance, leaning against the wall. Her eyes dart toward my hand propping open the door and back to my face. "Um, is this your room?"

"It is," I respond indifferently as her face turns a bright shade of red. She opens her plump lips to speak, probably to throw an explanation or apology my way before scurrying away. I hold up my hand to her. "We're not together."

She lets out a deep sigh of relief and glances back into the room, searching for Nik.

"Don't bother," I tell her, stepping into the room. "You won't hear from him again."

Her mouth hangs open as she stares at me, processing my words as I shut the door in her face. Walking over to the bed, Nikolai is lying flat on his back in the middle of the bed snoring loudly. He got wasted like he planned and fucked some random chick, so kudos to him for getting it in one last time.

My hand dives into my bra as I slip out of my coat and tuck the papers into my purse. Grabbing a pillow and a blanket from the bed, I get situated on the couch. I nestle deep into the cushions and submit to the exhaustion that consumes me, pulling me into a deep sleep.

Pulling on my coat, I grab my purse and carefully pick up

Aleksei's notes from the coffee table, tucking the papers inside. I must have woken up in the middle of the night and moved the notes from my purse. Nikolai is still lying with his back to me as I pull myself together and quietly make my way toward the door. A rustling noise sounds from behind me as I reach for the door handle.

I should have expected this.

"Where are you going?" Nikolai demands, climbing out of bed in his boxers. His eyes are cold and calculated as he assesses me with suspicion, and I can feel my heart rate spike.

He saw Aleksei's notes. That has to be it.

Looking over my shoulder, I narrow my eyes, rolling them at him. "I just have a few errands to run and I'll be back."

Nikolai glares at me as I offer him a warm smile before opening the door. The last thing I need is for him to be suspicious.

"Don't go too far," he warns as I silently slip out of the room and into the hall, running directly into Aleksei's firm body.

Fuck.

CHAPTER ELEVEN

ALEKSEI

Rolling over, I feel along the other side of the bed expecting to find her, but only find a cold, empty space. Sitting up, I look to my side before surveying the room, looking for any sign of her. Other than the rumpled sheets, you would never know she was ever in here.

Lyra must have left not long after I fell asleep since her spot in the bed is so cold. I let my guard down and let her in, which is something I never do, something I never thought I was capable of doing. I fell asleep before she did, comforted by her presence and left her free to roam about my room without a second thought. Then again, I have nothing to hide, nothing that she has access to or would be of any value to her.

I think.

Fuck, my mind is a clouded mess because of her.

Shaking off thoughts of her and my doubts, I head into the bathroom to shower and wash away my feelings of unease. Today is far too important to be feeling unsettled.

I have a job to do and I can't fuck this up.

There's no room for error.

My phone chimes as I exit the bathroom with a towel wrapped around my waist.

Nikolai: Meet me at the bar in 30 minutes, we need to talk.

Fuck. This has to be about Lyra and last night.

Aleksei: What's this about? It can't wait until later?

Nikolai: It's extremely important information and something you need to know immediately.

Scratching my head, I stare down at my phone trying to come up with any idea of what this might be about, but I come up with nothing. Nikolai is a cocky, arrogant asshole, but he wouldn't request we meet over something trivial.

Aleksei: See you then.

Setting my phone back down, I quickly slip into a pair of boxers and black dress pants and throw on a white button up shirt. After securing each button and tucking my shirt in, I pull on my jacket and adjust my collar before tucking my gun into the waistband of my pants and head out of the room.

Slipping out of the door and into the hallway, I collide with a petite framed woman. Reaching out, I grab her arms as she falls with a flash of black hair, steadying her on her feet. I cock my head to the side as my eyes meet hers.

"Hey," Lyra says breathlessly, brushing off her coat.

"Hey," I reply, hesitantly. "Where are you going?"

She quickly glances around nervously before giving me a bright smile. "I just had some errands I needed to run."

"Okay," I say, watching her carefully, not fully trusting her. "You're not supposed to be leaving here without Nikolai or myself."

"I know," she admits quietly, looking down at her feet. "It's kind of embarrassing, but I need to get some feminine products."

"Of course," I admit, acknowledging her discomfort and quickly dismissing the topic. "Go handle what you need to but be careful and don't be gone too long."

She looks up at me shyly with a small smile forming on her lips. Taking me by surprise, she steps closer to me, wrapping her arms around my midsection and presses her face against my chest. Putting my arms around her shoulders, I hold her close against me and bury my nose in her ebony hair. "I have some things I need to take care of, but we need to talk about last night."

"You'll see me sooner than you think," she murmurs, nodding against my shirt.

Pressing my lips against the top of her head, I release her, taking a step away. "Be careful and I'll see you later tonight."

"It's a date," she smiles before turning to walk toward the elevator. I let her go ahead of me, not wanting to arrive in the lobby with her. She steps on and turns around, blowing me a kiss before the doors slide shut.

I wait a few minutes before pressing the down button

for the elevator. Checking my watch, I still have about fifteen minutes until I need to meet Nikolai at the bar but knowing him, he'll be fashionably late per usual.

Taking the elevator down, I step out into the lobby and walk across to the hotel bar. The lights are dim even though it's still early in the morning, but I can see his form sitting at the bar.

He's never early unless it's important.

Fuck.

I stride across the room and slip onto the bar stool next to him. He doesn't look over at me as he slides a glass of clear liquid in my direction. Lifting his own glass to his lips, he takes a long sip from his own glass.

"Nikolai, it's the middle of the morning," I say, sliding the glass back toward him, but he holds out his hand, stopping me.

"Trust me," he replies, pulling a cigarette out of the pack beside him. "You're gonna need it."

Letting out a deep sigh, I grab the drink, holding it with both hands as he lights his cigarette.

"Lyra isn't who we think she is," he exhales, the smoke lacing with his words. "Something is off about her and I don't trust her at all."

"Tell me exactly what it is that you're talking about and what you mean by this," I reply angrily at his cryptic speaking, deciding to take a long sip of the vodka after all.

Nikolai turns his head and looks at me. "I don't think she's here for either of us, at least not in the way she's been leading us to believe."

So, this isn't about what has happened between her and I.

"I found her looking at pieces of paper this morning that was all in your handwriting. They were directions you had written down for our plans for today. Did you tell her or give them to her?" He probes with his intense stare boring holes into me.

"Of course not," I scoff. "That is information I would not share with her, but there has to be a reason for why she has them. Perhaps Arnold asked her to keep close tabs on us, just in case."

Nikolai laughs loudly. "Jesus, that pussy is turning you into a dumb-fuck."

"Watch it," I growl, cutting my eyes at him, gripping my glass tightly in my hand.

He raises his eyebrows before rolling his eyes. "I know you two are fucking, I'm not *that* stupid. You need to get your shit together though, Aleksei. What the fuck is going on here? What the fuck happened to you?"

"I'll talk to her," I concur, ignoring his questions, taking another sip of my drink. "Surely if something is going on, I'll be able to tell from talking to her and if needed, I'll press her."

Nikolai lets out a low chuckle. "You're as blind as a fucking bat when it comes to her. You've grown soft, at least toward her, so you really expect me to believe that you'll interrogate her if necessary?"

"Yes," I confirm without hesitation. "I am your brother and the last thing I will do is allow someone to come between us or fuck up a job as important as this one."

He stares at me with his cold, hard eyes that are laced with doubt. A war rages inside him, a fight between whether he believes me or not and his ability to lay all of his trust with me.

"Call me when you're leaving to go visit our father and I'll meet you there," he says in a hushed voice as he rises to his feet. He finishes off his drink, lightly setting the empty glass back on the bar before walking away, leaving me alone with my own thoughts as his words linger in the air, plaguing my mind.

He's been wrong before.

What if he isn't this time?

CHAPTER TWELVE

LYRA

Wrapping my coat tightly around my body, I stride out of the hotel and into the parking garage, occasionally glancing over my shoulder. My heels click against the concrete as I hurry down the different rows of cars.

No one can notice you; look natural or you'll fuck this all up.

When I finally reach the car that was left for Aleksei, I slide along the passenger side, looking around the garage and crouch down. Reaching into my coat pocket, I pull out a small magnet GPS sensor and slide it underneath the car until it's in the proper place. Pushing the small button to turn it on, I quickly stand up, surveying the garage once more before hurrying outside into the cold.

After hailing a cab, I take the short trip to the rental car place a few blocks away and tip the driver generously as I hop out of the taxi. The process is mindless and goes seamlessly with my fake ID, and soon after, I'm given the keys to the small sedan I'll have for the next few days.

The salesman doesn't question my intentions or anything that has to do with me renting the car. Just as long as I don't fuck it up and bring it back when I'm supposed to, then everything's good.

I leave with a friendly wave and 'thank you' before walking out to my new car parked out front. It's exactly what I need. Something that blends in with the rest of the vehicles on the road, isn't too flashy, and isn't too big. It should work perfectly for me to be able to finish my work here.

Weaving in and out of traffic, I get back to the hotel as fast as I can, making sure I won't miss Aleksei's departure. Pulling over onto the side of the street, I park a little bit away from the hotel's garage and grab my phone, checking the GPS app. The small red dot on the screen is slowly circling around the location of where Aleksei's car was parked. Waiting a few moments, I finally see the car pulling out onto the street and catch a glimpse of Aleksei's face.

Letting him pull out first, I hang back and let a few cars drive ahead of me, hopefully creating enough distance between us that he won't notice I'm following him. Looking down at my phone, I watch the red dot continue to blink as it slowly moves down the street. As long as the GPS is working, I don't need to stay too close to him.

Leaving the city, I follow him into the countryside and let him lead me to our final destination.

CHAPTER THIRTEEN

ALEKSEI

"Goddammit, Nik," I grumble, shoving my phone back into my pocket as I walk briskly to the car. I know that Arnold's reasoning for Nikolai being involved wasn't out of the kindness of his black heart. It was to make sure I did what I was supposed to do and get the job done. It was all bullshit, though. There were no ties between my father that would stop me from carrying out one of Arnold's orders.

I work for him, not my father.

After I met with Nikolai earlier this morning, he disappeared. I haven't heard from him since then and he isn't answering my phone calls. He was supposed to go along with me to do this, but I guess it will just be me now. He ought to know that this won't go unnoticed, especially after the bullshit he tried to feed me earlier about Lyra.

His negligence for being here right now proves how little his word is worth.

His word has no worth, right?

. . .

Following the mapped-out directions, I drive not too far outside of the city and onto an old dirt road leading to a small house off on the side of the road. There are no cars, the windows are boarded shut, but a small sliver of light shines through one of the cracks.

Daddy's home.

Pulling into the stone driveway, I put the car in park and kill the engine, staring at the small house in front of me. Letting out a deep sigh, I climb out of the car, carefully shutting the door behind me and make my way to the front door. He's waiting for me as I approach.

"Aleksei," Viktor greets me as he opens the door. "I've been waiting for you."

"Hello, father," I reply coolly, entering his home with my pistol in hand. He closes the door behind us and motions to the small living room as he walks inside. Following him, he takes a seat in a leather armchair situated in the middle of the room.

"Please, take a seat," he states with his thick Russian accent as he gestures to the chair across from him.

Shaking my head, I walk across the room, standing not far from him. "That won't be necessary. I won't be staying long."

"Very well then," he submits as he folds his hands across his lap. "Arnold sent you, I presume?"

"He did," I concur. The details are insignificant as to why I am here, but he already knows.

He was expecting this.

He was expecting *me*.

"How did you know Arnold would send me?" I question him out of sheer curiosity.

He smiles and chuckles lightly. "I've known him for enough years to know how he operates. Surely he would only send you as a true test of your loyalty when I took out someone valuable to his organization."

I nod slowly, assessing his position of submission. "You know why I'm here then?"

"Aleksei, please," he rolls his eyes. "I know what I've done wrong and the consequences that come with my actions."

"Very well," I concur, giving him a small smile. He knew even before he killed Rossi that this was how things would end. A sudden rush of cold air fills the room as the front door is shoved open. Looking toward the open door, a barely audible gasp escapes my lips as I stand face to face with our new visitor. The door closes softly, shutting out the cold and trapping the warm air inside.

"What are you doing here, Lyra?"

CHAPTER FOURTEEN

"You mean Nikolai didn't tell you that I was coming too?" I ask Aleksei with a confused expression. Of course, he never told him; I was never supposed to be here.

Aleksei's brow furrows as he watches me in confusion. "Why would you be coming here with him?"

Fucking question after question.

"I'm supposed to make sure that you two get the job done. I waited for Nikolai, but he told me to go ahead and he would meet me over here," I shrug, giving him a small smile.

Viktor looks up at me with careful eyes as a flash of recognition passes through his expression. I smile brighter at him as he slowly realizes who he's looking at.

That's right, motherfucker.

"Well, hello there," I say to him, looking past Aleksei. "Surprised to see me here?"

Aleksei glances between the two of us, still visibly confused and his gaze stops on me. "You two know each other?" he demands as he looks back at his father.

His father quickly shakes his head. "I don't know her," his voice is gruff. "Not personally, at least."

"What the fuck does that mean?" Aleksei probes, stepping closer to him.

"Yeah, Viktor. Why don't you go ahead and tell your son here what that means," I press him, urging him to speak up. Either he tells him, or I do. I could care less.

"Rossi," he says, hanging his head slightly. "This is Lyra, his daughter."

Aleksei glares at him. "I was sent here to kill you because you killed *HER* father?"

"Jesus fucking Christ," he mutters, running his hands through his hair. "As if this situation can't get any more fucked up."

They both start talking at once, arguing with one another with the occasional Russian word thrown in there. It's hard to follow everything they're saying, especially with Viktor's thick accent. Standing there, watching the two of them go on as if I'm not there, I eventually block out every word they say as I reach into the deep pocket of my winter coat. I quickly pull my hand back out, bringing with it my small handgun and point it at Viktor without either of them paying any attention to me.

Pointing the pistol at his stomach, I pull the trigger once.

He grunts loudly and lets out a low groan as he folds in two. Aleksei's eyes jump to me.

Now that I finally have his attention, we can actually get started here.

CHAPTER FIFTEEN

ALEKSEI

"Don't fucking move," she screams pointing her gun at me. "I know you have a gun on you, put it on the ground."

Nodding, I slowly reach behind my back. Grabbing the pistol, I crouch down, laying it on the floor. Extending my leg, I nudge it with my foot and push it farther away from me.

"Fucking idiot," Lyra cackles. "It's funny what a few words and a good fuck will do to a man's head." She drops her hands ever so slightly, pointing her pistol at my thigh and pulls the trigger. Letting out a loud groan, I feel the bullet lodge itself in my muscle, the fibers tearing around the cool metal. Grabbing my leg, I drop down to the ground, falling onto my opposite hip.

I move, trying to find some comfort, some relief as my leg throbs from where Lyra shot me. Slowly, she saunters toward me with a smile of satisfaction playing on her lips. She stops in front of me and squats down with her face in mine, resting her gun on her knee.

"Oh, my sweet Aleksei," she coos, cocking her head to

the side as I look up at her with blank eyes. "You really thought I was falling for you, didn't you?"

She's a fucking fraud.

Where the fuck is Nik?

"I didn't expect things to be so easy with you, getting inside your head and all. I was expecting more of a challenge and definitely more reluctance from you, but you made it nice and easy. It all worked out perfectly and the timing was impeccable with coming to see your father," she laughs lightly.

"And what are your plans, exactly?" I question through clenched teeth, slowly running my eyes over her.

Nikolai was right.

"Your dumbass brother was supposed to be here, but he's probably balls deep in whatever pussy he can find," she shakes her head and rolls her eyes. "You and Nikolai were supposed to die, your dad was supposed to watch before I got to have my fun with him."

Her bright smile reaches her eyes. Her beauty is undeniable, even with the lies and deceit surrounding us.

"Since Nikolai couldn't join us, I guess it's just the three of us."

She makes the mistake of taking her eyes off me, looking over at my father. Using both arms, I sweep her legs out from underneath her, sending her onto her back. She lets out a yelp as she hits the hard wood floor. Ignoring the throbbing pain in my leg, I use all my strength to lurch myself at her. She struggles to get up just as I land on her, straddling her waist. Her hand still clutches her gun and she fumbles to raise it at me. Using the palm of my hand, I smack it from her grip and tighten my grasps around her wrists.

"You were wrong to think you could double cross me," I growl at her, slamming her arms above her head. Leaning down, I bring my mouth just barely above hers. "From the moment I saw you, I knew I'd either have to fuck you or kill you." My lips lightly brush hers as I whisper against them. "Looks like I'll get to do both."

Taking me off guard, she lifts her head up slightly, pressing her lips against mine, kissing me with an urgency and coaxing my lips open with her tongue. My mind loses sight of the position I'm in, the position she has put me in. I'm wrapped up in a web of her lies, drinking her poison straight from her toxic lips.

And then she flips the script.

Drawing my lip in between her teeth, she bites down hard and draws blood as they pierce through my skin. Pleasure and pain collide, swirling together as it spreads through my body. I groan into her mouth, expecting her to let go, but she doesn't. She bites down harder, trapping me.

"What the fuck?" I mumble against her mouth as she continues to draw blood. Trying to jerk away, I raise my body from hers and she simultaneously lifts up her knee up, driving it into my balls.

"Fuck!" I yell out as she wiggles one of her hands free and grabs ahold of my thigh. Her small hand skates across my pants until she finds the bullet wound and shoves her finger deep into it. My vision blurs for a few moments as I see stars, letting all inhibitions fly out the window and I let go of her other hand. She released her grip on my lip at some point and I fall to the floor beside her as she twists her finger in my bloody wound.

Sliding her finger out, she jumps on top of me,

throwing her legs on either side and leans up past my head. Sitting back down on me, pistol in hand, she positions it directly between my eyes, pressing into my skin.

"What is it you were saying about double crossing you?"

CHAPTER SIXTEEN

LYRA

Pressing down harder, the barrel of the gun cuts into the skin on Aleksei's forehead. My finger is on the trigger, about to fire when the door flies open, slamming into the wall. Aleksei doesn't move an inch, but his eyes are diverted over toward the intruder. Keeping the gun to his head, I quickly turn toward the rush of cold air coming from open the door.

Nikolai stands just inside, his shoulders and chest heaving with every breath he takes as pure rage rolls off of him, slowly consuming the room.

"Get the fuck off him," he growls, staring me down as he strides across the room.

My lips curl upwards into a smile and he stops. "Come on, Nik. You know how all of this has to end or else you wouldn't be here," I give him a small shrug.

He narrows his eyes at me as he clenches his jaw. "You weren't as slick as you thought you were."

"Or was I?" I push back, cocking my head to the side. "I do have all three of you here right now, so who's to say that wasn't my plan all along?"

"Lyra," Nikolai grumbles. "This is done. Get your revenge, kill our father and go."

Shaking my head, I purse my lips at him. "That isn't what I came here for, your brother knows about it all. I told him everything, but I have an even better plan," I smile, winking at him. "Let me finish these two off, and we can get out of here, just the two of us."

I need to buy myself some time, to get this taken care of without him interfering and I can worry about him afterwards. I know Nikolai well enough to know how much he thinks with his dick instead of his mind or that shriveled up, barely beating heart in his chest.

A wave of doubt passes through me as I keep my eyes glued to his. That frigid, lifeless heart could be a problem, the downfall of my plan. It's dark and essentially non-existent, but it's still there and sometimes blood is thicker than water.

I need to act fast, kill them all.

"Sorry, doll, but that won't be happening," he murmurs as a dark shadow passes over his face and a sinister grin slowly forms.

It all happens so quickly, within a matter of seconds, before my mind can even process what's about to happen. Nik's fast—his movements are fluid and calculated as he swiftly reaches into the back of his pants and rips his arm back out.

My eyes follow a silver flash of metal and come face to face with the end of his pistol, staring straight into the barrel.

"See you in Hell, cunt," he sneers and pulls the trigger without another word.

CHAPTER SEVENTEEN

ALEKSEI

The soft sound of Nik's gun echoes through the room as he pulls the trigger, planting a bullet in the center of Lyra's forehead. Silently, she starts to fall forward onto me, but I shove her backwards, quickly scooting away and sitting up as she lands on her back with a thud.

Sitting on the floor, I stare in disbelief at her still warm corpse and my brother on the opposite end of the barrel. This is the way it had to end, I know that deep down, but the shock factor of everything is real.

"You good?" Nikolai asks, nodding at me.

Looking down at my thigh, my eyes find the bullet hole through the tear in my bloodstained pants. Clenching my thigh muscle, I can feel the bullet situated inside. "I gotta get this shit out," I tell Nikolai, ignoring his question.

"We'll get it," he assures me, "but first, what are we going to do with him?" I follow his gaze over to our father, still sitting on the chair awkwardly hunched over. It takes a moment for my mind to process everything and to remember that Lyra shot him in the stomach.

Fuck. Fuck. Fuck.

Roughly running my hand through my hair, I hold the top of my head and close my eyes for a moment. Caught up in how quickly everything went down, I had forgotten this was even about my father or the fact that he was sitting in this very room, still alive.

I look up at Nikolai who is watching me, his expression grim as he waits for me to respond. Shaking off the unwanted feelings of betrayal and shock, I clear my throat. "Is he still alive?"

Nikolai glances over at our father before looking back at me, giving me a swift nod, rolling his eyes.

"I'll take care of it," he stops me as I start to move to get up. Resting my back against the wall, I watch as Nikolai walks over to our father sitting in the chair. Reaching down, he taps the top of his head with the silencer attached to the barrel of his gun.

"Rise and shine, daddy," Nikolai mocks as our father looks up at him. "Damn, you don't look so good."

My father looks over at me and directs his eyes back at Nikolai before opening his mouth to speak. Nik's forefinger twitches, lightly pulling the trigger and plants a bullet right between his eyes.

"Sweet dreams, daddy," he smiles as our father bends forward with his head hanging down between his knees. Blood surfaces from the hole in his head and droplets begin to hit the wooden floor in a slow and steady pattern.

Drip.

Drip.

Drip.

Nikolai stares down at me with a frown as I watch the crimson liquid collect on the floor beneath our father's head.

Drip.

"Aleksei," he demands my attention.

Drip.

"Aleksei," Nikolai says louder.

Drip.

"Aleksei!" He barks, gaining my attention as he stands rigidly, staring at me with hardened eyes and his arms crossed over his chest. "I need to get a first aid kit and shit, so stay put."

Closing my eyes, I rest the back of my head against the wall and listen to him rushing around the house, rummaging through different cabinets until he finds what he's looking for. The faucet turns on for a moment before his footsteps grow closer, echoing throughout the silent room.

"Aleksei," he shakes my shoulder lightly as he crouches down beside me. Opening my eyes, I look down at all of the supplies he found for a makeshift bandage and am mildly impressed with everything he was able to collect.

Sitting down on the floor next to me, he tears my pant leg where the bullet hit me and opens a bottle of vodka, quickly splashing my wound with it. I inhale sharply, wincing as my flesh burns from the clear liquid. Looking down, I watch as Nikolai grabs a pair of tweezers and positions them over the open hole and glances up at me. His eyes meet mine and I give him a curt nod, giving him the 'okay' to begin.

My jaw clenches and my eyes pinch shut as a flash of white-hot piercing pain erupts from my leg, hitting every nerve ending in sight as Nikolai digs into my flesh and muscle fishing for the bullet. He moves quickly and diligently with the precision and skill of a talented surgeon.

Wiggling the tweezers back and forth, the bullet pops free from my muscle and instant relief from the decreased pressure overrides the pain.

Nikolai pulls out the tweezers and bullet, dropping them to the ground and splashes the vodka back across my leg. Air escapes my lips in a hiss as the stinging, throbbing pain hits me.

"You know who she was, right?" Nikolai looks at me as he preps the bandage.

I nod. "She explained everything; why she was here, who she was. You were right," I admit.

Taking the homemade bandage, he places it over the open hole with extra gauze from the first aid kit. "I didn't want to be right, but she was throwing out red flags left and right. I just found out everything about her right before I came here," he confesses. "I came to tell you before she got to you, and well..." His voice trails off.

Nothing else needs to be said.

The two of us know the truth and the dead bodies say the rest.

Nikolai helps me up after securing the bandage and makes sure I'm steady on my feet before releasing me. "I just need to make a phone call and then we'll get out of here and get that shit properly taken care of, okay?"

"Yeah, sure," I mumble as I test my leg, easing my weight onto that foot. A sharp pain shoots through my thigh in protest, but I start to walk, ignoring the throbbing pain. Nikolai watches me for a moment before walking over to our father as I slowly circle Lyra.

How could someone like myself be such a fool?

I always keep my guard up, yet this woman lying by

my feet in a pool of her own blood somehow got through. She penetrated the thick walls that grew around my heart and made herself at home. But my heart was never her home, it was a place for her to hide, to plot and plan the demise of my family. She decorated her hideout with lies and deceit and I believed all of the bullshit she spewed.

For once, I had felt something for someone.

For once, I had imagined a future that wasn't confined to solidarity.

She did me fucking dirty.

And I fell right into her trap.

Looking down at her, there's something beautiful, majestic even, about how good death looks on her. Her face remains flawless, like a sculpture handcrafted by a meticulous artist with her ink colored silk hair splayed around her head. Small streaks of blood run across her skin from the open hole in the center of her forehead with a bullet lodged deep within her brain.

Death was always sitting at the head of the table, waiting to sit down for dinner with each and every one of us. I was supposed to make her dinner reservation for her, but Lyra decided her own fate and made that call the moment she chose to cross us.

I understood her need for revenge and what she needed to do to accomplish that; the lies, the manipulation, I understood it all. She did everything right and everything that I would have done.

What I don't understand is me and how someone like myself could fuck up like this. She could have destroyed everything that we had built with Arnold and I might have been the one to let her.

Lyra fucked with my head.
She fucked me up.
And no one fucks me up.

My mind vaguely registers Nikolai as he paces the room, talking on the phone to the cleaning crew. Walking to the door, I don't look back at him and slip out before he notices. He can handle this and get this mess taken care of. Pulling out my phone, I look around, expecting to be on a busy street and remember I'm in the middle of fucking nowhere. Shoving my phone back into my pocket, I stride over to my car and get the hell away from this place as quickly as possible.

Speeding down the backroads, I don't stop driving until I reach the city. Pulling the car over onto the side of the street, I slam it in park and get out, leaving the keys inside since I won't be needing the car anymore. I walk down the busy sidewalk, holding my hand out until I'm finally able to hail a cab.

"Good evening, Sir. Where will you be headed to tonight?" The driver asks as I slide into the back seat.

Adjusting myself in the seat, I grab my phone and unlock it. "The airport," I reply gruffly to the man.

"Very well," he concurs, pulling back onto the New York street.

Scrolling through my contacts, I find his code name and press call. It only rings twice before he quickly answers.

"Aleksei," his deep voice comes through the speaker. "Everything has been taken care of, I presume?"

"Yes," I admit, not going into details. "Nikolai was handling the rest."

He clears his throat quietly. "I'm aware," he pauses. "I was also informed that the girl is no longer a problem."

"Did you know?" I ask him in a hushed voice.

"Of course not," he barks. "Do you think I would bring someone in that could jeopardize everything? I knew of her ties to the family, but I was not aware that she was his daughter and that she had other intentions."

He was the one who brought her in in the first place.

How can I even believe a word he says anymore?

"What is this really about Aleksei?" Arnold demands. "We discuss these situations at our meetings."

Taking a deep breath, I slowly exhale, collecting myself. "I'll be needing to take some time off."

Arnold sighs. "Take as much time as you need. I don't need any explanation, but I do need you to know that you will be coming back."

Like a goddamn puppet, I'm always under his control.

"It won't be long," I assure him. "I just need some time to clear my head."

"Like I said, take your time. You're not of value to me if you're not on top of things," Arnold reminds me. "We'll be in touch."

He ends the call before I get a chance to but grants me the solidarity that I crave and need right now. Before I realize it, we're only a few blocks away from the airport and I have nothing planned. Searching on my phone, I find a flight to St. John in the Caribbean where I own a beachfront condo and book it. It's not an ideal place for absolute seclusion. Nikolai is the only one who knows of the property, but knowing his nosy ass, he'll come looking for me.

The cab pulls up in front of the airport and I shove him a hundred-dollar bill and exit without another word.

Glancing down at my watch, I make a mental note of the short amount of time I have to make my flight. Without any luggage, I should make it in time.

Pulling my phone out of my pocket, I open it and stare blankly at the screen. Nikolai should know that I'll be back. I should give him a heads up this time.

But this isn't about him.

This is about me.

This is about her.

Locking the screen on my phone, I chuck it into the trash can by the front entrance and make my way into the airport without so much as a second glance back at everything I'm leaving behind. All that matters now is putting as much distance between myself and this place as possible.

My brother was always right and after Lyra, it was clear. I'm not like everyone else. Happiness with someone else will never be mine. For the rest of my days, the only happiness I'll ever know is the blood on my hands.

ABOUT C.M. RADCLIFF

C.M. Radcliff lives in Pennsylvania with her husband and two demon children. Known as the Psycho Queen, she speaks fluent sarcasm, dark humor, and has the mouth of a sailor. If she isn't reading or writing, she's probably on an adventure with her little family.

Sign up for her newsletter here.

SIN KEEPER

MICHELLE BROWN

BLURB

The first day at a new school should have been the worst
thing to happen to me.
It wasn't.
There I met them both.
One shouldn't have piqued my interest and the other was
perfect. One thing lead to another and now we all have
our secrets.
The thing about secrets is, like sins they never stay
hidden.
My secrets, those could destroy everything.

CHAPTER ONE

JASMINE

Secrets are a powerful thing. The ability to destroy someone lies in just a few whispered words. My secret has the power to ruin his world, mine, and theirs, all in one swift motion. So tell me, can I trust you won't tell anyone? Probably not, but I'm going to tell you anyway. To do that, I have to start at the beginning.

"Jasmine! You are going to be late if you don't get moving!" My mom shouts from the kitchen.

Pulling my hair into a high pony, I double-check that I have everything I need: pencils, pens, my phone, and my backpack, all check. I sling my backpack on my shoulder and rush to where she is standing. I take the glass of orange juice and a piece of toast from her. Thank goodness, I need something to settle the nerves in my stomach, and carbs will do the trick. "Thanks, Mom," I yell as the screen door slams behind me. It's my first day at this school. My parents' thought it would benefit us all. We didn't last two months here before we figured out why Dad wanted to be closer to the city. It was so he wouldn't be far away from his other family. His other family is his

301

mistress and their two sons. It's all kinds of complicated, but it's too expensive to move home since our old house sold. Walking the few blocks to my school, I do a sweep of my hair for flyaways and straighten my skirt. Private school means uniforms, and the starched material feels like sandpaper against my skin.

Walking into the building, I take in a calming breath, I can do this. I pull out the worn copy of my schedule and the building class-map, yes, this place is big enough for a map to show you the way. The day passes in a blur. No one acknowledged I existed, and no one bothered to take pity on the quiet girl. My last class of the day is Filmography and Photography. It seemed like a decent elective when they offered. I needed something other than Art 101 to shine on my scholarship applications. I find the classroom and walk inside just before the bell finishes sounding. I look around at the empty seats, worried that I'm in the wrong place when someone crashes into my back. I tense when I feel rough hands grasping my hips in an effort not to push me over.

"Oh, wow, I'm sorry. I haven't had any students ever make it here before me," the voice sounds from behind me. His voice warms my body, as his hands loosen from their hold on my hips, I instantly feel the loss. Clearing his throat, he's voice drops an octave, "Are you going to take a seat, or should I teach from the doorway?"

My cheeks warm as my blushing covers my body from my face down to my chest. Not answering, I rush to a seat near the middle of the room, I don't want to seem like I'm not eager to be here, however sitting at the back would make me look like a slacker. The clock ticks as time passes without anyone else coming in. It's hard to believe I'll be the one in this class, and surely they have a required quota to fill to teach. The door finally clicks as it opens to the typical teenage wet dream, broad shoulders and thick thighs tell me he has to be a football player or is it field hockey? I'm not sure what they have here. Winking at me, he hands the teacher a scrap of paper and takes a seat next to me.

"You must be new. I'm Taylor, what's your name, gorgeous?"

I've never been called gorgeous before, pretty, and hot were the extent of vocabulary used at my old school. Smiling, I whisper, "Jasmine."

Opening his mouth to speak, the teacher's voice booms across the room, "Wonderful, you two know each other now. I'm Mr. Allen. I'll be your teacher for this class, and I expect both of you to follow directions."

Mr. Allen's eyes never leave mine as he speaks, they are blue, almost the shade of the sky, and the way he commands the room with just his words makes me want to do as he instructs. Listening to him go over the syllabus and the expectations of the class, I try to pay attention as Taylor slides a note to me. I glance at the paper and notice his number written down with an invitation to grab something to eat after school. It's innocent, almost pure in the scheme of how my dating life was in the past. My throat goes dry at the thought of how unprepared I was for this. At my last school, I was deemed the school slut. I'm smiling to myself when his shadow blocks my light.

"Is there something you would like to share with me? Apparently, Mr. Walker and yourself are privy to whatever it may be," there's a hint of anger lacing his words.

"No, sir," I quietly respond, his eyes dilating at my words. My nipples pebble under his gaze. It's been far too long since I had sex, far too long since I felt the heat of another person. The bell sounds, breaking the trance he has on me. I gather my bag and follow Taylor to the door and feel his hand on my lower back as he motions me ahead of him. It ignites something in me, something I thought I had contained since moving away from our home. We sat at the local pizza place for hours talking about our lives, him mostly while I sat and daydreamed of Mr. Allen.

CHAPTER TWO

OLIVER

I shouldn't be this interested in my students. It's wrong, and I know better, but that doesn't stop me from wanting her and watching her long legs cross under the desk. I mentally give myself a shake and look away as she leans into Taylor. They would be ideal together, and maybe it would stop my lustful gaze, perhaps not since I know he won't waste time before he fucks her, and that thought would be on repeat in my mind.

I move to stand, and think better of it when I look down at my erection. It's not suitable for school, not when it's her causing it. Sliding my chair under the desk as far as I can, I tap my fingers on the wood to get their attention, "Okay your next assignment is to capture black and white images in order to tell a story. I don't care what the story is, just be sure that it can be told without words."

I hate this school, I only teach photography to a few students, and the pay is shit. I only moved here because of Julia, my fiance, who doesn't believe in sex before marriage or even living together. It's been hell, and I've been a moody fucker. The bell sounds as the class dismisses, and I watch as Taylor puts his hand on Jasmine again. A low growl escapes me before I can tame it down. His eyes meet mine at the sound. A smirk plays on his lips at my obvious jealousy, "Later teach."

Grabbing my things, I escape to my car as the students mingle in the parking lot. That's when I see *her*. She's standing just outside of the crowd, studying them while she tries to talk to the other girls. I rush to my car, sliding inside and putting the stack of papers in the seat next to me. My cock is rock hard, and it's almost painful to be this stiff. Unbuttoning my pants, I pull it free from the confines of my slacks and briefs, I lean my head back on the headrest as I stroke myself. The heat of my hand and the blood rushing to the tip cause me to hiss, gripping my cock at the base, I imagine Jasmine's lips wrapped around me as I stroke faster and faster. My mind goes crazy with thoughts of her. The vision of Jasmine's perfect face as the tears run down her cheeks while she takes all of me running through my mind. Groaning, I feel the pressure building of my release. It's cut short when I hear voices near my car. Other teachers are leaving now, and any of them could see what's going on. Shoving myself into my pants, I look across the parking lot to where she was, now Jasmine's eyes seem as if she's watching me. Grinning, I wink as I pass by where she is.

Driving home, I call Julia and listen to her go on and on about the wedding plans. Anything to distract me from what I want to do to a teenager. "Babe! Did you hear me?" comes across the speaker, and I'm ashamed to say I didn't. "Sorry, Julia. What was it again?" I ask, hoping she won't ask why I didn't hear the first time.

"I asked if you were free Sunday for brunch with my

new boss and his family," she repeats. I hate brunch, and she knows this since I've told her before. Honestly, I don't see why someone can't decide if they want breakfast or lunch by eleven in the morning. "Sure," I answer, already knowing I would rather be anywhere else.

CHAPTER THREE

JASMINE

Days went by, routines were made by both my mom and me, and soon I was left alone in the tiny house she bought after the divorce. Flicking through the movie selection on tv, I tossed my hair into a bun and picked up my phone. I scrolled until I found my best friend's social media page, it was filled with experiences I didn't have since she cut me out of her life when she found out about her dad and me.

Taking a chance, I search for Mr. Allen's profile and find him quickly enough when I finally figure out his first name is Oliver. He's engaged, and she's gorgeous. I picture myself in her spot, slowly falling into a daydream of what it would be like to be with him. He doesn't know me, not outside of class; however, I feel like if we were to have met years in the future, we would share something. My fingers toy with the hem of my crop top as I think of a future with the man I don't know. I listen for sounds to be sure I'm alone before I open my favorite porn site on my phone, the first video is one of a schoolgirl and her teacher. She's in a cheap plaid outfit while he's sitting at his desk, pretending he's not going to spank her. Touching myself over the jeans I'm wearing, I grind against the friction it's causing. I could come like this, it's been so long since I've had an orgasm. I watch as the storyline progresses, applying more and more pressure against the stiff fabric as he swats her with the ruler. Unzipping my jeans, I moan when she wraps his dick with her lips. This girl is a pro, and she barely gags as he shoves it down her throat. Pushing my fingers inside when Mr. Teacher drives into her, I keep his tempo while imaging them as Mr. Allen and me while Taylor watches us. Crying out, I cover my mouth with my hand as I hear the front door slam closed.

"Jas! I'm home, and I have dinner." Leave it to my mom to ruin my orgasm high. I grab my jeans and run to the bathroom to clean up before she comes in. The fabric caresses my clit through my underwear, causing me to shiver. Opening the bathroom door, I'm met with my mom's face looking into my room at the laptop and ruffed bedding. She doesn't say anything, but I can tell she's not pleased that I'm "sinning" again. Following her to the kitchen, I grab plates and utensils for us. Holding the dishes, I don't notice I grabbed three out of habit until she walks out. Even when dad isn't here, he's still here the way a ghost would be. Sitting at the small table, I let her cool off alone. She's like me that way. If she walks away, it's for the best; otherwise, she could go off like a bomb and take everyone down with her.

When she comes back in, I can see the glassiness of her eyes, letting me know she was crying. I pretend I don't notice, I said something the first time, and she was mad about it then. We eat in silence; both of us lost in our own thoughts. "How is school?" she finally questions, as if she has a real interest and not just for conversation's sake.

Pulling my backpack closer, I reach in for my camera, "Well, we have an assignment to do. I started mine, but I'm not sure it's what Mr. Allen wants." Clicking through the memory, I find the pictures of the old part of town. The buildings and train station that no one uses anymore. Smiling, mom listens as I ramble about how I've started to fit in with some of the girls. It's all a lie, none of them speak to me. Taylor might be my only friend out there, and he wants to get in my pants.

Finishing dinner, I retreat to my room to work on my other homework, but the camera keeps calling my name. Adjusting the settings, I accidentally click the button and capture an image of my thighs. I grab my camera tripod and set it up near the edge of my bed. I've seen boudoir sessions online before, and I was always interested in how sensual they seemed. Click, I give my best sexy look as the camera clicks again. Lying back, I spread my legs as it clicks again. I look over to be sure my door is locked before I start to undress. Click, another shot of me in less clothing than before, I slide my shorts down my legs and turn over, giving the lens a chance to capture an image of my bare ass. Wrapping my arms around my chest, I look at the camera as it clicks, and then I move my hands lower. I finger my clit as the camera continues to sound with each captured moment. It feels freeing to let go and be watched at the same time. I just need to be sure I remove the memory card before I turn in my assignment.

CHAPTER FOUR

TAYLOR

It's odd how often Mr. Allen looks at Jasmine. It causes my blood to heat, but not from anger as much as it is lust. Watching her work silently on her classwork, I reach for her camera to see what she takes pictures of. Jasmine's hand reaches out and stops me from pulling it back. Worry flashes across her face, biting her lip she shakes her head in order to tell me not to.

"Is there a problem here?" comes his voice. He's nearly in front of us when I look up. Shaking her head, Jasmine looks to me as if she needs someone to step in. "Not at all, Teach. We were just comparing notes on our assignments so far."

Nodding, he comes closer, "Turn in your cameras. I want to see what you've got so far." He waits as I pull it from my bag, and Jasmine holds hers close. I don't understand why she's worried, I've seen her work before, and it's great. Pausing, he reaches out his hand for the strap, his fingers coming close to touching her. All of us hold our breath, the classroom dead silent as she finally gives in. Her face turns pink from her blushing as he sits on the edge of the desk in front of us. Turning my camera on, he quickly flicks through the pictures. He doesn't offer feedback as he moves on to hers. I watch her as he powers it on; her body is shaking as she watches him. His sudden intake of breath causes her to whimper. Looking at him, I wonder what is going on.

"Excuse me a moment," he croaks all but running towards the supply closet door at the back of the room. I catch a glimpse of the tiny screen as he passes, the picture is of Jasmine masturbating, her mouth open and her eyes squeezed shut in ecstasy. My eyes find hers. Jasmine offers me a forced smile, her voice barely above a whisper, "Do you think I'll be forced to leave the school?"

Her question confuses me. The door opens, and Mr. Allen walks back in with the camera in his hand. His earlier composure back, he's back to himself no longer the man he was when he saw the picture. Placing the camera on her desk harder than he should have, Mr. Allen doesn't look at us as he says, "Class is over. Go home."

I glance at my watch and see that we should still have over an hour in our day, but I don't bother to ask why. Jasmine nearly runs out of the door without another word to either of us. Pausing by the door, I turn to where he is sitting with his head in his hands, "Teach, you didn't have to embarrass her that way."

Nodding, he opens his mouth, but I don't expect him to agree so easily, "I know. Now leave."

I grip the shoulder strap of my backpack and look for Jasmine. I make it outside before I see her, she's sitting on the front steps. Tears brimming in her eyes, she smiles at me, trying her best to push past what happened. I don't think twice about grabbing her hand and pulling her up from the concrete step, "Ice cream?"

It's innocent and normal, which causes her to burst out laughing. Jasmine nods and starts for my car. She doesn't pull her hand away until she's sliding in the passenger seat. I close the door behind her and look at the school. There I see Mr. Allen watching from his classroom window, I can't tell if it's her or me that he's studying. I offer a salute and get a head nod in return. It's like an unspoken conversation, one where he knows I'll take care of her because he can't, even if he wants to.

CHAPTER FIVE

JASMINE

I can't believe that happened, I don't know if Taylor saw the photos, but even if he didn't, they have been seen by my teacher. It's only a matter of time before I'm made to leave this place before someone finds out about my past, or I ruin everything. I can fake a smile all day, eating ice cream with Taylor is a way to be normal, and right now it's exactly what I need in order to cope with what Mr. Allen saw. I didn't intend to leave the memory card in, but I fell asleep after my self-induced orgasm before I could. I was even late this morning because I didn't set my alarm before sleep overtook me.

The ice cream shop that Taylor takes me to is one I know, it's on the outskirts of town, and it's one I went to with my friends when we lived on the other side of it. Hesitating, I tell myself that I have nothing to fear, none of my old friends should be here at this time of day. I was wrong. We hadn't been there long before the door opened to a group of girls walked in, my best friend at the front.

"Can we leave?" I question quietly.

Gripping my hand in his, Taylor pulls me into him as we begin to leave. Without words, he understands my body language. He knows how to read the things I don't say. "Jasmine!" I hear her call out just before the door closes, and I know I'll have to explain my reluctance to stop later, but I don't care. I need for her to stay in my past, I don't want Taylor to know the person I was, the one I think I still am. When the car door closes, I reach for my phone needing to set up an appointment with my therapist. I send the email as Taylor drives us away from the ice cream shop back towards our side of town. He doesn't ask questions like I thought he would; instead, he rubs small circles on the soft flesh between my thumb and finger. It's soothing, comforting in a simple way; it makes staying away from him harder than ever. My phone chirps and I check to see when my appointment will be, but it's Rachel asking if we can meet up on Saturday. It's odd, yet I don't think twice. She's just trying to mend things, I tell myself.

My phone sounds breaking the quiet, answering the call, I wait as she rattles off dates and times. "Now?" I ask my voice hopeful that she can see me. Turning to Taylor, I try to figure out how to ask him without giving away where I'm going. "Can you take me to the pharmacy? I need to meet someone there, but don't worry. You don't have to wait for me."

I know he's confused about me, yet he agrees as he parks the car. I'm out of the vehicle before he can ask who or why I'm here. I go inside and wait for him to leave before I walk out and into another building, the one that holds my therapist's office. She meets me at her door with a kind smile, "Jasmine, what's going on? Are you having impulses again?" My therapist isn't a normal one, or at least that's not why I come to her. She's a sex therapist for sex addicted people like me, even though she listens to me talk about everything else too.

It's over an hour later when I leave her office, I don't own a car, and asking my mom to pick me up is out of the question. She likes to believe I don't still have impulses, and it's better this way, this way she can still pretend I'm her innocent daughter. The innocent one that didn't fuck a man twice her age. Making my way down the road towards home, I palm the can of mase on my keychain. It was a gift from Charles. He didn't like it when I would walk home after our fuck-fest late at night. I thought it meant he cared. He didn't, though. He only wanted me until he got caught. It was his wife or me, and I was left in the cold.

A car horn blares behind me, and I freeze, waiting for them to go around, yet they don't. I turn around and am met with an angry face, Mr. Allen staring back at me. He shifts it into park and climbs out, saying something I can't hear. My focus is only on his face and the fury I see. I should be scared, and any sane person would be. But I never claimed to be that. Mr. Allen is inches away from my face when I finally hear him calling my name, "Jasmine!"

Licking my own lips, I stare at his, watching the way his mouth moves, "Yes?" It comes out softer than I wanted, so I try again, "Yes, sir?" A low growl is his response. It makes my legs shake, and my breath catch. Shaking his head, Mr. Allen backs away from me, and I feel the loss of his body heat. "Why are you walking alone? I thought Taylor was taking you home?" I shake my head, not trusting myself to speak. "Do you need a ride home, Jasmine?" It's a simple question and offer, anyone else would do the same, but coming from him, it feels as if it means more. "Yes, please."

CHAPTER SIX

OLIVER

I let out the breath I didn't realize I was holding as I shut the door for her. Fuck, I shouldn't be driving her home. I don't trust myself. I couldn't let her walk home alone though, that's what I tell myself as I walk around the back of the car and adjust my dick. Jasmine looking at me that way, and calling me sir had my cock at attention.

I allow my fingers to graze her leg on my way to the gear shift. It's obvious I went out of the way to do it, yet she doesn't call me out on the slight touch. Driving towards the way she was heading, I wait for her to give me directions. Her voice is soft and stirs something in my blood. Clearing my throat, I try for small talk, anything to break the awkward silence that falls, "So tell me about yourself? What made you want to take my class?"

Jasmine folds her hands together and places them in her lap before she answers, "Umm, well, my mom and I moved here to be closer to my dad. He owns a business here. I honestly have always loved photographs because they tell you about what matters to the person taking the picture." She laughs at something, and when I catch on to what matters to her, I can't help but grin.

"Your what seventeen, or eighteen? What do you plan to pursue as an adult?" I question, curious at what her dreams are, and wanting to be sure I wasn't lusting after someone younger than eighteen.

Pausing, Jasmine looks away, and when I begin to think she's done talking, she answers. "Eighteen, and I don't know yet, I just don't want to be stuck in one place. I just want to be happy and have a family of my own. I'm not sure if that makes sense." She gets quiet again, lost in her own thoughts. I understand her dream, and if it weren't for Julia and her new job, I wouldn't be in this town. Reaching over, I take her hand in mine and give it a squeeze; it's meant to be comforting. However, it only makes me want to continue touching her more. Jasmine doesn't pull away from me; instead, she moves my hand to her thigh, holding it in place with her hand.

Parking in front of the small house, I don't move from my seat when I see her mom standing at the door. "I'll see you tomorrow, Mr. Allen," she says, pulling my attention back to her thigh beneath my palm. "Oliver. When we aren't in school, you can call me Oliver," I offer. Smiling at me, she looks over to her mom and sighs, "Well, I should go, my mom is already going to fuss that I'm late for dinner."

Just before she closes the door, I reach for her hand, "Next time you think of walking home alone, call me." I wait for her to pull her phone from her pocket to rattle off my number. The idea of her walking alone worries me. Not far from here, a young girl was taken. Her name was Emily, I think. I watch her until I can't see her anymore, the wooden door blocking Jasmine from the harsh world. I back out and make my way home, not expecting Julia to be waiting for me there.

Julia's glare from the couch stops me in my tracks the moment I walk into the living room. "Oliver, where were you?" she questions, her words sharp. Sighing, I sit down across from her, taking the glass of wine from her hands. "I saw a student walking home and offered to drive her home," I wait for her to ask who it was, yet she doesn't. Her face relaxes; all her anger is gone at my explanation. Jumping up from her spot, I notice her clothes. She's wearing a tight dress and heels, nothing like Jasmine would ever wear. "Where are you going?" I ask, taking a sip of her wine, even though I'm not a fan of drinking. It hinders your actions and lowers your inhibitions.

"Where we are going, and out with a few friends," she corrects me. I glance at the time and my own clothes, "I'm not up for it. How about we stay in for the night? I'll cook, or we can order in," I counter. Putting her hands on her hips, Julia sighs, "Oliver, I'm going out. Stay here if you want, but this is our time to have fun."

Grabbing the wine glass, I walk to the sink and pour it out, "I don't want to party. You know that, in fact, I thought we were on the same page about wanting to settle and have a family in five years."

I almost don't hear her, but I can just barely make out her words, "Maybe I don't want to do that anymore. I don't think I still want the same things you do. Actually, I know I don't. " I listen as the door shuts behind her, and her car outside cranks. Turning around, I spot her engagement ring on the counter.

CHAPTER SEVEN

TAYLOR

I watched her leave the pharmacy and walk into another building. I knew she was trying to hide something or someone, I just wanted to be sure she was safe. Jasmine was seeing a therapist if the internet was correct. Driving away, I sighed in relief that she didn't meet up with a boyfriend. Therapy, I could handle but not someone else. I couldn't fathom her not being mine in the end.

I reach into my backpack and pull out the memory card I pulled from Jasmine's camera at the ice cream place and swap it for mine. I need to see just what those pictures held earlier. It's completely blank. Grinning, I chuckle when I realize what Mr. Allen did. He kept the card for himself. Apparently, he doesn't like to share. Lying back on my bed, I fantasize about how Jasmine's tongue lapped at the ice cream. Sliding my boxers down, I wrap my cock with my hand and stroke. One stroke for each thought I have of her. She consumes me without even trying. It doesn't take long before I'm coming, Jasmine has that power over me. I clean the come from my stomach, and lie down, ready for the next day to come.

Mr. Allen and I have a conversation coming. It doesn't take me long to fall asleep.

I walk into his classroom a bit earlier than necessary, a wicked grin on my face, "Tell me Teach, how many times did you come while you looked at her pictures?" Mr. Allen doesn't answer. Instead, he begins to gulp like a fish. "You want Jasmine, I want her too, and if she wants us both, then why couldn't we make that work?" I can see the wheels turning in his mind when the classroom door opens, and she walks in. Smirking, I back away from where he is and sit next to her. I reach out and touch her, I can see the jealousy in his eyes at how often and where I'm able to without consequence.

Leaning closer to Jasmine, I press my luck, 'What are you doing this weekend? Would you maybe want to get dinner?"

"I'm actually going out with my friend Rachel, she knows of some club in the city that's suppose to be fun," Jasmine replies, as she doodles on the corner of her notebook. I don't know of anyone named Rachel at our school, and then I remember the girl from the diner. Something about her was off, almost as if she was oozing hate. "Listen, I don't know her, but maybe just send me the club name and where it is, that way, if you get stuck, I can pick you up," I offer, unease settling in my stomach.

CHAPTER EIGHT

JASMINE

I pack my bag for the weekend and explain to my mom, again, where I'll be. She isn't pleased that Rachel is back in my life, but she understands that I've moved past my infatuation with Charles. "We won't even be at her house. We are doing a spa weekend in the city," I lie.

My mom gets to the door before she turns around, "Since you will be in the city anyway, your dad is having a business brunch tomorrow. He wanted you there to show off, be nice." I hang my head in defeat, mom knew I wouldn't agree to brunch but now that I'll be close, I don't have a reason not to go. I'm personally not a fan of brunch, I don't see the point in mixing good ol' OJ with champagne and calling it a drink. Besides, I can't drink with the medication I take. It causes me to be sick, among other things.

A car horn sounds outside, letting me know Rachel and the girls are here. I slip on my flats and run out the door. The front seat is empty, taking that as where I'm supposed to sit, I slide inside. "Oh, before I forget, what's the name of the club? I need to tell my friend," I question, already typing out a message to Taylor. Rachel rattles off the name, and a quick search finds me the address. I send both to him and turn my phone on silent. The ride into the city doesn't take long, and before I know it, we are walking into a hotel to check-in. It's part of our thing. We don't bring people back to our home, so we get rooms and hook up here. This way, there's a camera and witnesses. I'm not sure who thought of this, but it's always been this way for us.

I take my key card from my pocket and walk into my suite. I put the room on my dad's card, buying myself the biggest suit they have. It's the least he could do for all the pain he caused mom. I run and jump onto the bed; it's big enough for four people. Spying the bathroom, I take in my bag and spread the few products I have on the counter. Stripping, I step into the shower and get ready for the night. I don't plan on hooking up with anyone, not since Taylor and Oliver occupy my mind completely, but I shave everything anyway. When I turn the water off, I hear a faint giggle come from in the other room. It must be the others, I think to myself as I wrap the towel around my still naked body. Peeking into the room, I see all of them are already drinking. I'm not sure which has the second key to my room, I only know I have Gina's. It's going to be a wild night if the way they are throwing them back is any indication. Spotting me, Rachel walks over, holding out a cup of purple drink, "Grape juice and vodka, I know you love it."

Not wanting to explain why I don't drink anymore, I take a sip and notice that the vodka is strong. If Rachel wanted me drunk, this would be the way to do it. I decide that one drink won't hurt and swallow the rest down. Finding my outfit, I slink back into the bathroom to change and fix my hair into a fancy looking ponytail. I don't bother to put in curls or anything extravagant. The mix of body heat and sweat would only ruin it later.

"Seriously? You are going to wear that?" comes from across the room when I step out. I look at my jeans and top, shrugging as I slip on my sliver flats. "I like comfort. Plus, I'm not looking for a hookup, just wanting to have fun."

I feel dizziness take over for a moment and wonder how strong that drink was to be affecting me this way. Hopefully, a glass of water and food will help. Rachel glances at her watch and deems it late enough to leave for the club. None of us drive; instead, we get a cab since most of them will be too drunk to drive later.

The cab drops us off at the entrance, and we skip the line, I think Gina is sleeping with the bouncer based on the way he grabs a handful of her ass on our way in. It doesn't take long for the girls to find their way to the bar, as I make my way to the dance area. I need to burn off all the pent up energy and tension I've built us since the last time I saw Rachel. A wave of dizziness courses over me, causing me to step wrong, and pain shoots up my leg.

A man's voice comes from behind me as his hands steady me, "Woah, I've got you. Do you need to sit?" Nodding, I allow him to help me to the edge of the bar. I can't see my ankle to see if it's sprained, but I can tell it is. Sliding down from the stool, I hobble to the restroom and sit on the edge of the counter as he walks in behind me. I can't tell if its that he's kind or if he's a creep. Hoping for the first, I let him inspect the slight swelling. "Let's get you out of here. Are you staying nearby?"

I pull my phone from my pocket and hit Taylor's name. I shouldn't call him, but he's the first name I get to.

"It's okay. I'll have someone pick me up. No need to ruin your night." A flash of irritation flashes across his face at my words.

"Hey, Taylor, can you pick me up? I'm at the club I told you about," I say into the phone, keeping the guy in my line of sight. "I'll be in the bathroom, I sprained my ankle."

Chuckling from his spot near the door, he turns to me, "You know, Rachel said you were this huge slut. Said she needed to teach you a lesson. I was promised sex, and I'm going to get it." Flipping the lock on the door, he turns back to me. Nausea builds in my stomach. The way I've felt since the drink earlier reminding me how Rachel handed it to me already poured and made just for me. Surely, I'm just being paranoid, but mixed with his words, I look for anything to use against him.

CHAPTER NINE

OLIVER

I was irritated when I saw Jasmine's name flash across his screen, why she was calling him didn't matter. That quickly changed from jealousy to concern when he answered. I could hear the panic in her words, even if no one else could. Something was wrong, and she needed help. "Get in and tell me where," I call out, already starting the engine. It was a chance meeting with Taylor, both of us picking up food at the same place at the same time. Not that there are more than three places to eat in this town.

Punching the gas harder, I drive the thirty minutes in far less. Thankfully we don't get stopped by the police, or in an accident. I don't even waste time looking for a place to park. Instead, I stop directly in front of the door. The bouncer yells at us to stop, but Taylor pushes him out of our way. Glancing around, I look for the bathroom sign, once I find it I head there. A group of girls is standing around the door, waiting for someone to come out. Taylor doesn't waste time as he throws his shoulder into it repeatedly. "Just a minute!" I hear called out from the other side, a man's voice. I know Jasmine was there and she was scared when she called, putting it all together I rush the door with him. I don't waste any time when I see her. Pushing Jasmine into Taylor's arms, I swing at the man. My fist connects with his jaw over and over again. It's Taylor who pulls me away.

Gasps and screams sound from behind us. The girls who were there when we came in are long gone. I suppose those were her *friends*. I reach for Jasmine, needing to be sure she is fine in order to calm my racing heart. The security guards come in to take him outside, hopefully into a waiting cop car.

"I'll need her statement," comes from the uniformed officer at the door. "Yours too."

Fuck. I needed to be in the city anyway, I remind myself, Julia texted me earlier to beg me to go to brunch even though she ended our relationship. "Let's get a room. We can go there in the morning." Taking her hand in mine, I walk Jasmine out to my car. I wait for Taylor to slide in the back with her before I shut them inside. He can comfort her on the way, but once I'm locked away with them for the night, I'll need to see her for myself. Jasmine names the hotel, and I drive us there. When we walk in, I watch the desk clerk staring at us. It's obvious we are all here together, considering neither Taylor or myself have let her hands go.

Stopping Jasmine from climbing on the bed, I pull her to the bathroom. While she stares at me, I begin to fill the bath for her. "Let me wash him away." Nodding, Jasmine strips out of the silver top and jeans. She's gorgeous. The tiny scrap of fabric underneath does little to hide her body. I feel Taylor's eyes burning holes into us from the door. I didn't bring more clothes with me, I wasn't planning to be here when I left earlier. Pulling my shirt over my head, I quirk an eyebrow at Taylor, "Like what you see, Mr. Walker?"

Fire dances in his eyes, his playful words causing Jasmine to giggle, "Just wondering if I'll need to do CPR later. You know, Teach, when you have a heart attack from seeing my dick."

A low growl sounds, and it takes me a moment to realize it was me. Reaching out for my hand, Jasmine pulls me to her and motions for me to join in the bath. Running the washcloth down her bare breasts, I stop at the apex of her thighs. I shouldn't, but I do anyway when she spreads her legs wider. Resting her head on my shoulder, she gasps when I replace the cloth with my fingers. Teasing her soft flesh, I watch as Taylor strokes himself in rhythm with my pace. Pinching her nipple with my other hand, I bite down on her neck as she clenches around my fingers. Whispering in her ear, I add another finger, "That's it. Show him how much you want this. How much you want him, how much you want me."

Jasmine's moans and whimpers fill the air, watching them both is ecstasy. Taylor's deep groans mixed with her harsh breathing have me ready to explode. "Come here," she calls to him, as she reaches behind her to palm my cock. Jasmine waits for Taylor to be closer to us before she wraps her other hand around his cock. Stroking us both, our combined groans match as I continue to fuck her pussy with my fingers.

CHAPTER TEN

JASMINE

All of us reach our orgasm one after the other, each release spurring on the next. I lie back against Oliver's chest, the worries from earlier forgotten. Sighing, I try my best to stand and would have fallen over if not for Taylor catching me. Whatever was in my drink was strong. "Here, baby, let me help you to the shower," he offers, already carrying me.

I'm glad I used my dad's card for the biggest room, the shower is big enough for an orgy, and I laugh at my thoughts when Oliver slides in behind us. Even with the water raining down on us, nothing was going to wash away our sins. "I'm surprised you can keep up, Teach," Taylor quips as Oliver sets about washing our bodies. Grinning wickedly, he looks from Taylor to me and back, "Keep on, and I'll have to find something to fill that smart mouth."

It's as if a fire was lit under us all, quickly rising off and climbing out, none of us bother to dry completely. Crashing his lips to Taylor's, Oliver pushes him towards the bedroom as I follow. Their tongues are at war for dominance, each one biting and devouring the other. Sitting on the bed, I watch as Oliver pushes Taylor to his knees, "Open." Taylor doesn't stop there. He looks over to me as if he needs permission. I nod at him, eager to watch them. Wrapping his lips around Oliver's dick, he sucks and laps at him until Oliver moans the words, "Fuck. Just like that." Gasping, I push two fingers inside of my wet pussy as Taylor presses against Oliver's taint. They notice what I'm doing and stalk over to me. "Teach, I think our girl needs another orgasm," Taylor says as he drops to his knees in front of me. I can't hear what Oliver says. The only thing I can hear is the beating of my heart as Taylor laps at my juices and plunges his fingers inside of my pussy.

I lie back on the bed, I can feel every swipe of his tongue, and every thrust of his fingers. It's more than I can take, knowing that Oliver is watching us. I ride my orgasm until the end, sleep threatening to pull me under. I feel the bed shift as they climb in on either side of me. Their bodies close enough to touch. I listen to the sounds of their collective breathing as I fall asleep. I have to meet my dad in the hotel lobby in order to get brunch. It's not something I look forward to. His new wife is barely a few years older than I am, and her judgment is harsh on how I should act. It's as if she wasn't a homewrecker herself.

The shrill sound of Oliver's phone wakes us up, the morning shining through the curtains blinding us in the process. "I'm on the way," he answers, looking for his clothes. I turn over and look at the clock to see how much time I have before I need to leave when I notice I'm late. "Oh, shit," I screech as I pull on my yoga pants and a teeshirt that says, fuck 'em. My dad is going to be pissed, but I don't dress up unless it's required. Laying in bed,

Taylor looks at us, running around while he makes no effort to get up. Throwing a pillow at him, I smile, "Come on. You can come with me to this breakfast thing."

Groaning, he rolls out of bed and pulls on his clothes from the night before. It reminds me of how willing he was to come to get me and how they showed up together. They'll have to explain that one to me later. Oliver is near the door when he explains, "I have a thing to get to. I'll be back in a couple of hours." Shooing him out, I grab my bag, and we follow him out.

CHAPTER ELEVEN

TAYLOR

I wish I had known where we were going now, I think to myself as the cab driver parks in front of a luxury hotel and country club. I look at Jasmine's shirt and laugh at the expression on the valet's face. He isn't used to a girl like her, and truthfully I'm not either. There's a woman making her way over to us before we even walk in. Jasmine isn't pleased to see her that much is obvious.

"Jasmine! What in the world are you wearing?" the woman whisper yells, trying her best to keep a smile on her face as older couples watch us. Grabbing my hand, Jasmine looks back at her with confusion, "Pretty sure it's called clothes. I could be wrong, though." Trying no to laugh, I squeeze her hand.

Rolling her eyes, the woman practically drags Jasmine towards the back of the room, "We don't have time for you to change, let's hope they understand your humor. Let's go. Your dad is waiting for you."

We follow her towards the patio, and I can see a group of men and women in their best while we are in casual clothes. My eyes nearly pop from their sockets when I see Oliver sitting next to a woman who introduces herself as his fiance. Jasmine doesn't say a word, and she doesn't have to, her disapproval written on her face. Oliver can explain later, right now wasn't the time. I'm not sure why Jasmine needed to be here, considering her dad never even told her hello. As soon as the last plate is cleared, both of us stand ready to leave.

"Jas," her dad calls, "I would like for you to meet Julia. She's one of our newest receptionists at the office."

Jasmine takes a moment to size her up before she speaks, "Funny, the last person in that position that I was introduced to, you were fucking." Julia doesn't speak as the woman from earlier screeches, "You little whore! How dare you say such a thing? Unlike you, not everyone sleeps with married men." Oliver is staring at his fiance, and I'm trying to figure out what's going on. Grabbing a drink from the man walking by, I down the glass of water watching everything unfold. I have no reason to step in unless someone messes with Jasmine, but I have a feeling she can hold her own. "Julia?" Oliver questions, his face not showing any emotion. The woman named Julia looks from Oliver to Jasmine's dad, answering more without words than if she had come clean. I'm more concerned about the married man that our girl slept with than anything else, however. I know she has a past, all of us do, I just wonder if hers is going to interfere with us.

Jasmine's dad turns to his daughter, disapproval on his face, "I think it's time for you to go. Take your *friend* with you." He doesn't tell her he loves her or to be safe, none of the things my parents would. Instead, he chooses to leave with his wife and her constant yelling. I wait as Oliver finishes his whispered conversation with Julia and turns to us, "Taylor, you can drive. Let's go, and I'll fill you in on a few things."

Placing the empty glass on the table behind me, I grab Jasmine's hand and follow behind them. She's pissed, and rightfully so if Oliver is engaged, but I think we are missing part of the picture. Closing the door, I watch them in the rearview mirror, Jasmine is tucked into Oliver's arms. Her eyes filled with unshed tears, she speaks just above a whisper, "You need to explain now because I won't be the other woman again. I won't be the second choice for someone else."

Someone else, she won't be the other woman, again. Fuck. I can hear Oliver reassuring her, explaining how he and Julia weren't together anymore. They hadn't been happy for a while. Pulling into the hotel parking lot, I toss the keys to the valet as I follow them inside. I watch as Oliver slowly wraps her in his arms, showing our girl that she's just that *ours,* she isn't second anything. Sitting on the chair in the corner of the room, I watch them undress as I pull my cock out of my jeans. Blood rushes to my dick with each kiss, each fucking content sigh coming from her gorgeous lips. Oliver turns her head to the side to look at me, "Watch him, baby, look at what you turn us into."

I'm mesmerized by the way their bodies work together to reach their orgasm, chuckling to myself when Oliver shudders, "What's wrong, Teach? Is that heart giving out on you?" Standing up, I shed my clothes and join them. I drop to my knees behind Oliver and palm his ass as he thrusts into her, biting his cheek, I push against his taint with my finger, "Tell me Teach, have you ever been fucked here?" The way his ass tightens tells me he hasn't, and that's okay. We can save that for another day. "Roll over, Teach. Let our girl get on top for a bit, I need her too." Oliver understands what I mean and does as I ask, spreading her ass cheeks for me once shes seated on him. "Suck on them," I command her, placing my fingers at her mouth. Wrapping my fingers with her lips, she massages them with her tongue, an action I'll want on my cock later. Pushing against her taint with my fingers, I slowly fuck her ass with them as she chases her orgasm. Our girl is loud, barely able to stop herself from screaming at the pleasure. "Tell me, Jasmine, do you like when he fucks you? Do you like it when he fucks what's mine?" I question as I add another digit, stretching her for my cock.

Stepping to the side of the bed, I shove my dick into Oliver's waiting mouth needing the lubrication his saliva gives. I take my place behind her on the mattress and gently stroke her back as I begin to push inside of her tight hole. Oliver reaches around and holds her cheeks as wide as he can to make room for me as Jasmine rubs at her clit. Once I'm entirely inside of her, I feel him move against the thin barrier of flesh. We slowly rock back and forth, finding our rhythm. It's euphoric, and it feels as if it should have always been the three of us. Groaning, Oliver releases inside of her, causing me to fill her ass with my come. Jasmine rides the high of our joint release and chants our names. My cock softens, and I slowly pull out, not wanting to hurt her. I grab a washcloth and clean our mess. Jasmine chooses that moment to laugh hysterically. Confusion at her laughter, both Oliver and I look at her until she stops. "Oh god, did I really just out my dad as a cheater, again?" Shrugging, I lay on the bed next to her, "I guess so." Lying on the other side, Oliver reaches over and takes her hand in his, "What now? I mean, I obviously can't be your teacher anymore, either of yours, not now that I've had my dick in some part of you both."

Thinking, I say what we all want to hear, "We have a month left of school. After that, then what does it matter? We'll still be together." Nodding, Jasmine agrees as Oliver reaches for his phone and sends an email. It's odd, but at least it's not post-sex social media. Throwing his phone on the floor, Oliver reaches for my hand too, "I just quit. Now, one of you suck my dick."

Grinning at me, Jasmine climbs on top of me and places my hardening cock at her entrance as she leans over to wrap her lips around his cock. This girl is perfect.

CHAPTER TWELVE

JASMINE

My mom doesn't ask questions when she sees me with both Oliver and Taylor at my side on graduation day. Thankfully she's more accepting of our relationship than I thought she would be. As long as I'm happy, she said. It probably helps that neither of them is married.

The three of us fuck like rabbits, but our relationship is more than that. It's thrilling and loving without the jealousy one would expect. I'm glad my therapist recommended the IUD for me; otherwise, there would be a little version of one of us running around. I smile at the thought of us having children later in life. It's one thing I've always wanted, a happy family. The school didn't take Oliver's resignation well, and they didn't understand why it was so sudden, none of us explained why to them. I think he's happier without it though, he didn't want to teach anyway from what he said. Oliver is starting his own photography business, and we will all three be traveling across the world for a year.

Leaning closer to Taylor's ear, I whisper, "You know, everything I tried to wear with this was showing through.

I couldn't even wear panties with it." Groaning, he grinds his cock into my ass as our eyes search for Oliver. Winking at him, I motion for him to check his pocket. Pulling the tiny scrap of fabric from her pocket, he looks from it to us. He wastes no time pulling his phone out and sending a message to Taylor. Laughing, he shows me what was said, "I'm fucking your ass tonight. Taylor can have your pussy." Our names are called from the stage, our diplomas ready to be handed over. Oliver and my mom cheer the loudest when we walk off the stage, now not tied to anything that could land Oliver in jail.

EPILOGUE

OLIVER

We have been together for five years now, the three of us, now soon to be four. Jasmine told us last week that she is pregnant, something we have been trying to achieve for months. Neither Taylor or I want to know the biological father; instead, we agreed that we are both equal parts of our child. Walking up and down the beach, I wait for them to get here. It's a special night for us, and tonight I plan to propose to both of them. I looked up the laws on polygamy, and in certain states and countries, it's okay.

Running my fingers through my hair, I watch as the two figures come closer. I don't waste time. Instead, I drop to my knee the moment the step in front of me, "Jasmine, Taylor, marry me." It's not a question. I'm not asking for them to say yes, I'm telling them. Crashing her lips to mine, Jasmine knocks me over, and Taylor settles on top of her. I don't need to hear them say yes, I already know they're mine. "Come on, Jasmine, let him up. We aren't fucking him in the sand," Taylor jokes when she reaches for my belt. Our girl is horny all the time, and I'd say it

340

was the pregnancy, but that's a lie. She told us about her sex addiction years ago, and we try to keep up with her, but even we have to rest sometimes. Pulling me to my feet, Taylor leans close to me, "Tonight, I'm taking your ass. It's about time I owned that too."

ACKNOWLEDGMENTS

To my husband, thank you for understanding all the things I needed to do just to get back here today. It's been a long year, but I'm finally where I want to be as an author.

To Cassie, my milkshake, you have quickly become one of my best friends. I don't think there's anything you don't know about me, and yet you stick around. In my yard. Thank you for listening to me rant, offer advice, and be there when I needed you.

To Megan, thank you for sprinting with me, even though most days we failed. It was the push I needed to write.

To my betas, Ari, Tania, and Faith, I would say thanks to you all, but it wouldn't be enough. You three are everything. Thank you for letting me tease you as I wrote this story.

To Brittany, my Hufflepuff, I don't know why you put up with me. I really don't. Just know I won't ever let you leave me.

ABOUT MICHELLE BROWN

Michelle writes in multiple genres such as Mafia Romance, Dark Romance, Horror Fiction, and many more. She lives in a small town located in North Carolina, USA. A wife and mother, she writes stories that will break your heart only to put it back together again, just a bit bloodier. Michelle also co-writes with a close friend under the pen name Ally Michelle.

Website: http://bit.ly/MBrownWebsite
Author Page: http://bit.ly/MBrownFB
Newsletter: http://bit.ly/MBrownNewsletter

ALL WE KNOW

J. M. WALKER

BLURB

She's older, beautiful, and perfect on her knees...
Every time my best friend invites me over, I can't resist.
Because then I get to see *her*.
Lynne is a walking wet dream.
Curves, long legs, and a smile that would bring the most
dominating man to his knees.
Even though she's much older than I am, there's
something about her that I crave.
Her innocence, her strength but most of all, her
submission.
The only problem is, she's my best friend's mom.

CHAPTER ONE

LYNNE

Having a kid at the age of fifteen years old was frowned upon. In most countries anyway. And especially in the United States of America. But when the cute boy next door asks you out on a date, you say yes. One thing led to another and the next thing I knew, that tiny little stick came back positive. It might as well have screamed at me, saying, *You. Are. Pregnant! And you're only fifteen years old! How could you?*

But it takes two. Right? Or that was what I was told anyway. My boyfriend at the time, had other ideas.

We used protection. It's not foolproof.

Did you poke holes in the condom? Yeah, because that was my thing.

You trapped me. That's why you did this. Isn't it? Yup, you caught me.

But even after all of those hateful words, Randy Lindt was still the one. Even after I heard that he was sleeping with everyone. Including my best friend at the time. Although, I wasn't sure much sleeping was involved.

Bottom line was, he broke my heart, but I did get a

beautiful baby boy out of it. As painful as it was at the time, I wouldn't change it for anything.

"Mom."

I looked up from my spot at the kitchen table, finding my son, James, and his best friend, Gabe, standing at the entranceway to the dining room.

I smiled, leaning back in the chair. My heart stuttered at seeing Gabe. It had been ongoing for the past few months. These new feelings. The stares that lingered a little longer than what was deemed necessary or the light flirting between us. But it had never amounted to more. For whatever reason, my body reacted to him in ways that were frowned upon. He *was* thirteen years younger than me.

Clearing my throat, my smile widened. "Hey guys."

James came over to me and wrapped his arms around my shoulders and kissed my cheek. "You were daydreaming again."

A laugh escaped me. "Hardly." I tapped his hand. "What are you guys up to?"

James released me and sat at the chair beside me.

Gabe took that moment to join us, sitting on the other side of the table. I noticed how his dark eyes lingered on me. They slid over my skin, sending a wave of heat rushing through me. It was as if they were touching me themselves. The tiny hairs on my body tingled under his scrutiny.

I shifted in my seat, the back of my neck heating under his intense stare.

The corner of his mouth twitched. "I told him to get some studying in, but he wants to wait until right before school starts."

James rolled his eyes. "Thanks for ratting me out, fucker."

"Language," I scolded my son.

"Sorry," he muttered.

"But some studying wouldn't hurt," I added. He had barely made it out of this year of college without having to take some summer courses. My son was the type to party his way through school. Couldn't say I blamed him too much though. His dad and I had put him through hell over the years.

James's face softened. He reached up, rubbing his thumb along the crease between my brows. "Stop worrying so much. I'll be okay."

"I'm fine." I rose from the table and went to the fridge to grab a bottle of wine. It had been an anniversary gift from my parents when they came back from South Africa a year ago. A month later Randy handed me divorce papers. I really should have divorced him long ago but stayed with him for our son instead. Little did I know that my son had wanted me to leave him ever since he was a kid. For someone who was only twenty-one, he was highly intuitive. And he knew me well. He knew I wasn't happy with his dad, but I wanted to try everything I could to make it right with him.

"He's right."

I turned, my gaze landing on Gabe. He had been my son's best friend since they were kids. Living across the street from us, the two boys had been inseparable ever since. Even though he was two years older than James, he was still young at the age of twenty-three.

I looked around the room, noticing that James was no longer with us. "Where's James?"

"He got a call." Gabe stood from the table. "Something about setting up a date."

"Oh." A tremor of unease twisted my stomach. Would Gabe be joining him on that date with his own girl on his arm? I swallowed hard, forcing those thoughts to the back of my head. Why would I care? I shouldn't care. I was thirty-six. Even though I was still young, I was far older than him. Whatever these feelings were, I wasn't used to them, but I chalked it up to being alone for the past several months.

My son had some good-looking friends. Friends that I noticed if I was younger, I would have been attracted to. These new feelings were not the norm. Especially not for someone like me. I had played it safe ever since I found out I was pregnant. I never went to parties. I didn't do drugs or have sex with random people or drank. I didn't have my first sip of wine until I was well into my twenties. Maybe I had played it safe for far too long and I was finally coming to terms with the fact that maybe I needed to live a little. I wasn't sure but at the moment, all I could focus on was how Gabe continued to stare at me.

He came toward me and leaned against the kitchen counter. He stood so close, I could smell the mint on his breath and the spicy cologne on his skin.

The hairs in my nose tingled, my fingers itching to run along the hard lines of his tall, lean body.

My eyes widened at that unexpected thought. Had it been that long since I felt the touch of a man? Of someone making me feel good. Of someone not so damn selfish that he only chose to give me pleasure once he was satisfied. And most times, that was only if he was in a good mood.

I stepped away from Gabe, needing to put some distance between us when a firm hand grabbed my upper arm. My breath caught in my throat, but I refused to look up at him. I couldn't for fear that his eyes would tell me everything I was dying to know.

But before he could say anything, James's voice carried into the kitchen.

I pulled away from Gabe, grabbed the bottle of wine off the counter and sat back at the dining room table.

"Gabe, Taylor and Raven are up for drinks tonight," James said, coming around the corner and into the kitchen. "You cool with that, Mom?"

I nodded. "Sure." I gave him a smile of reassurance. Truth was, I wanted him home with me, but I refused to be that kind of mother. I didn't want to smother him. And he was at that age where he was experiencing life. He was almost done school and as much as Gabe was right, James needed a break. Maybe that was my issue. Maybe I was too nice and lenient. I sighed, running a hand over the back of my neck.

"Mom." James sat beside me, taking my hand in his. "Did you want me to stay home with you instead?"

A lump formed in my throat. "No. You guys go have fun."

His light blue eyes that mirrored my own, searched my face. "You sure?"

I nodded, pulling my hand from his and cupped his cheek. "Thank you but yes, I'm sure. You need to have a life, James. Go, have fun." I reached for my purse and pulled out my wallet before handing him a couple twenties. "Use that for a cab and drinks." I put my wallet away before he could argue.

"Are you sure?" he asked again, looking at Gabe before meeting my gaze once again. "I can cancel."

"No." I shook my head and reached for the bottle of

wine. "I'm going to spend the evening watching movies and I have to call your father anyway."

James rolled his eyes. "He called me. Just a moment ago."

I frowned. "Really?"

He nodded.

I sighed. "What did he want?"

"He wants me to go there for the rest of the summer. I don't want to though," he added quickly.

"Whatever you do, I'll support you." As much as I didn't want James to spend the summer away from me, I would understand if he wanted to be with his father. "I'll talk to him."

James stood, gave me a quick hug and went up to Gabe. Clapping his shoulder, he looked back at me. "I'm going to go get ready." He muttered something to Gabe that I didn't hear.

Once we were alone, I filled up my glass.

Gabe's eyes burned into the side of my head. I wasn't sure what was up with him this evening. He had always just been my son's best friend. But now, with the scrutiny, the air became thick between us.

"Lynne."

My gaze snapped up, finding Gabe leaning with his shoulder against the wall. His arms were crossed over his chest, his dark eyes peering into mine.

"Shouldn't you be getting ready?" I asked, my voice coming out rough.

"I *am* ready. Besides, this is more for James. Not me."

"What do you mean?" I asked, frowning.

"I mean." He pushed away from the wall and came around the table to my side. He sat before continuing, "That I don't really want to go."

"Then why are you?" My body became hyperaware at how close he was sitting to me.

"Because James is my best friend and I'd do anything for him. I want him happy." Gabe's eyes dropped to my mouth. "But for some reason, there's something that I really want to do that I'm not too sure he'd be happy about. Not at first anyway."

I swallowed hard, heat creeping up the back of my neck. "What would that be?"

Gabe smirked, his tongue peeking out to lick along his bottom lip. "I want to kiss you, Lynne."

A breathless gasp escaped me. "Y-You what?"

"I want to kiss you." He cocked his head to the side. "I know it's been awhile for you."

I snorted. "And how could you know that?" It wasn't like I brought a guy home every night, but I tended to keep my personal life to myself. I also didn't want to subject James to a new man when I knew that it would only end up being a fling. It wasn't like I was ready to get married again anytime soon.

"I know because I watch you, Lynne." Gabe inched the chair closer, his knee brushing against mine. "I watch you drink a bottle of wine and then stumble up the stairs to your room. Maybe you play with your pussy. You know...to try and take the edge off."

My mouth fell open at what he had just said to me. "I have no idea what you're talking about."

His smirk grew. "No? How long has it been since you tasted a man's lips, Lynne?"

Six months.

"That's none of your business," I grumbled, bringing the glass of wine to my mouth. I took a sip and then another before placing it back on the table.

Much to my surprise, Gabe cupped my knee. Even though I was wearing jeans, his touch burned through the fabric and down to the marrow of my bones.

"I think I should make it my business," he murmured.

I jumped to my feet, needing to put some distance between us. Was I that desperate for physical contact that I craved his touch? No. It wasn't possible. He was my son's best friend and hell, he was thirteen years younger than me. It wasn't normal. It would never be normal. But if it wasn't normal, then why did it feel so damn right at the same time?

Gabe smirked, sitting back in the chair and crossed his arms under his chest. "How long has it been since you felt a man between your thighs?"

I swallowed hard, my mouth going dry. Randy had never talked to me this way. It was one of the things, even though small, that tore us apart. I wanted to be ravished, used, completely consumed. But my ex-husband was only into sex to procreate. Or so I thought. Truth was, I never did it for him. Why we got married in the first place, was beyond me.

"Why?" I leaned against the counter. Gabe had always been nothing but nice. Sure, we flirted every now and again, but it had been nothing more than that. I wasn't sure why the sudden change but a part of me was excited just the same for it.

Gabe leaned forward, placing his elbows on the table. He scratched his jaw, his dark eyes roaming down the length of me. "Do you forget how it feels to have a cock inside of you?"

My cheeks heated. "Why are you asking me these questions? Have you never heard of the whole saying, respect your elders and...so on?"

His smirk grew. "Oh, I do respect my elders. And I respect the hell out of you."

"Then why are you saying these things to me?" I wasn't new to dirty talk. Hell, I watched PornHub. I had seen every James Deen video out there. But hearing it come from Gabe, my son's best friend, a guy who was much younger than me, wasn't normal. Was it?

Before Gabe could give me any sort of an answer, James took that moment to join us in the dining room.

"Ready?" he asked Gabe, smoothing his hands down his navy-blue dress shirt. It was tucked into black pants. His deep brown hair was slicked back.

"You look handsome," I told him. "You must really like this girl."

His cheeks reddened. "I like one of them, yes."

I laughed, going up to him. I fixed his collar before cupping his cheek. "You have fun. Alright?"

He gave me a small smile. "You too. Don't get too wild tonight."

My laugh deepened. "Oh yeah. That bottle of wine and I are going to have such a wild night together."

His smile grew. "You never know." He pulled me into his arms, wrapping me up in a hard hug. "I love you, Mama."

My heart swelled, returning the embrace. "I love you too, baby boy. You have fun. Lots of fun. And if you can't catch a cab, you call me. Okay?" It wasn't like I was going to get very far into the bottle of wine. I never did when he went out, but he just didn't know that. I always waited up for him. My parents did the same whenever I went out in my younger days. Even though I was never a drinker at that time, they still waited up for me. It was a trait they passed down to me and I appreciated it just the same.

The guys left after that, leaving me alone to my own thoughts. My gaze landed on the bottle of wine.

I sighed again and put the bottle back in the fridge. No point diving that deep into the pits of alcohol. It didn't help anyway.

As much as I didn't want to, I called my ex-husband.

"Hey," he answered.

"What's this I hear that you want James to spend the rest of the summer with you?" I asked, getting right to the point.

Randy grunted. "He needs to be with his father."

"Yeah, and he needs to also be with his mother. You know that he won't get any schoolwork done if he goes to your place." I had loved Randy at one point but another thing that split us apart was his constant drinking and partying. He still did it, even though he was pushing forty. James didn't need to be subjected to that. I didn't care that he was of legal drinking age. His father was a bad influence.

"Lynne, we keep having this same conversation—"

"No." I was not taking this shit anymore. "You agreed that I would have him for the summer and you would get him for his birthday and all of the holidays. That's what we both agreed to." Even though James was no longer a kid, he still went to see his father during the holidays just to save face. Randy was a good dad at times. When he wasn't drinking anyway.

"How about we let him decide if he wants to come see me or not?" Randy said, his voice taking on that tone I had come to know meant he was finished with the conversation.

"Fine." I hung up. Knowing James would stay with

me, set some ease on the anxiety rushing through me but his father still pissed me off.

I spent the rest of the evening watching TV and reading. But I was distracted and kept reading the same page over and over again.

Was Gabe having fun?

Did he like the girl who would have been his date while James focused on the other one?

Lost in my own thoughts, I didn't realize the door had opened until Gabe came into the living room with an arm wrapped around James. He wobbled on his feet, pinching the bridge of his nose and muttered something about how he was never drinking again.

"He had too much I imagine?" I asked, placing the book I had been trying to read on the coffee table.

"Yeah." Gabe helped him to the recliner. "A guy we went to school with was there. Hadn't seen him in a while. So James decided to go shot for shot with him. It didn't last long." He shook his head.

James started snoring as soon as he laid his head back.

I grabbed the blanket from the back of the couch and placed it on his lap. "He'll be out for a while."

"Maybe I should put him to bed." Gabe stared down at him.

"He's fine here." I lightly touched his arm.

Gabe met my gaze, something flashing behind his eyes.

Clearing my throat, I headed back to the couch.

Gabe sat beside me. He was closer than what was deemed appropriate. But I found that I didn't care.

"What are you watching?" he asked, nodding toward the TV.

"Some old movie. I was reading but turned on the TV

just for background noise." I curled into the corner of the couch. "Did you have fun tonight?"

Gabe shrugged. "James did. That's all that matters to me."

My heart swelled. "You deserve to be happy too."

"I am now." Gabe winked.

I laughed, shaking my head. "Did you not have fun tonight?"

"I'm not really into the drinking thing. And the girls we met up with were a little too immature for me. James likes the one. But all they talked about was partying and shopping." Gabe rubbed his jaw. "Not my thing."

"I can understand that." Gabe had grown up with an alcoholic father. It only made sense that he wasn't a drinker. "I never did the whole partying thing. Even when James was old enough to take care of himself. It wasn't my thing either."

"Randy was a drinker," Gabe added.

"He was. Still is. I don't mind if people drink and party but when that takes priority over taking care of your kids, that's where I draw the line."

"Understandable. He's a dick."

I laughed. "He is but I won't bad talk him in front of James." As much as Randy and I didn't get along, he was still my son's father.

"That's because you're a decent human being."

I smiled. "Well thank you. I try. We all have our moments though."

"We do."

Silence fell between us until the movie ended and another one started. I rolled onto my side, suddenly aware that I was in just shorts and a tank top.

Gabe inched closer to me.

"What are you doing?" I asked, my eyes wide.

He pulled the blanket off the back of the couch and spread it over both of our laps, shielding us from James if he so happened to wake up from his drunken stupor.

"I think you know what I'm doing, Lynne. It's quite obvious, isn't it?" His hand inched beneath the blanket. When his fingers came into contact with the back of my bare leg, I jumped.

"Gabe," I whispered.

"Shhh...James is drunk, but we don't want to wake him up, now do we?" Gabe's voice was low, his fingers brushing back and forth over my skin.

I should have pushed him away. I should have jumped from the couch and screamed for him to stop touching me, knowing it wasn't right. I should have done a lot of things in life but for once, I found myself wanting to live on the edge. Hell, forget the edge, I wanted to jump off of it and right into my son's best friend's arms.

My gaze landed on my sleeping son. He was passed out in the recliner only a few feet away from us. The movie was playing, the sound loud enough that he wouldn't hear Gabe's and my conversation from where he sat.

I took a deep breath, rolling further onto my side. I knew I should have worn pajama pants instead of the shorts I had on, but I never thought that Gabe would be touching me like this.

We continued watching the movie. I wasn't even sure what was playing anymore. All I could focus on was the fact that my son's best friend was touching me.

His fingers slid up the back of my thigh, reaching the crease beneath my ass.

My breath caught. My skin vibrated over my bones.

My gaze flicked to James. He was still sound asleep in the recliner across the living room. His chest rose and fell, soft snores leaving him.

"Focus on me, Lynne."

I swallowed hard, Gabe's deep voice travelling over every inch of me.

His fingers inched beneath the fabric of my shorts, his knuckles running over my bare skin. A low grunt left him. I wasn't sure if it meant he was satisfied with what he felt or if it meant something else, but either way, it gave me some sort of power. I felt in control for just a moment.

Rolling over onto my back, I met his gaze.

He gave me a small smirk. His fingers slipped between the folds of my center, the tips running over my clit.

My heart pounded in my ears, my chest rising and falling with ragged breath.

Keeping his gaze locked on mine, he slowly inserted a finger inside of me.

A soft sigh left me.

His smile grew. His eyes twinkled, desire and heat burning in the dark irises.

His finger pumped slowly in and out of me. As much as I wanted to demand for him to do more, I reveled in the way he was making me feel. For someone so young, his touch made my thighs tremble.

He pulled his finger out of me, replacing it with two.

I bit my lip to keep from crying out.

Gabe wouldn't look away from me, his touch singeing into my skin.

Getting a moment of clarity, I reached beneath the blanket. "Gabe." I grabbed his hand that was between my legs. "I..." Should we stop? Was that what I wanted?

He turned his full body toward me, a dark shadow passing over his face. He pulled his hand from between my legs. In a rough move, he ripped my shorts down my legs.

"What are you doing?" I demanded as loud as I could without waking up James.

"First, I am going to finger fuck you." He pulled the blanket off of my lap, his eyes dropping to my waist before meeting my gaze. "Then I'm either going to shove my cock down your throat or just fuck your pussy. Not sure yet. Depends on how much sass you give me."

I sat up. "Is that so? You can't do any of that if I say no."

A wicked grin formed on his face. "You can't tell me you don't want more. You can't tell me that you're not curious. You also can't tell me that your cunt isn't soaked right now."

Before I could protest, his hand was back between my legs. "Tell me you don't want me."

I glared at him, the passion igniting between us. "I don't want you."

He leaned forward, cupping my cheek with his free hand while keeping the other between my thighs. "Tell me to stop and we'll go back to watching the movie."

I searched his face for a sign that he was kidding. That he didn't actually want to do this and mess around with someone who was thirteen years older than him.

"Tell me," he grit out through clenched teeth. Slipping a finger back inside of me, he pumped his hand hard and deep against me.

My eyes rolled into the back of my head.

A deep chuckle sounded in my ear.

My eyes popped open.

Gabe was leaning over me, his gaze hard and determined.

Pushing him away, I pulled up my shorts and left the couch. As much as I wanted to continue, I wasn't doing this in front of my son. I didn't want to take the chance that he would wake up.

As soon as I reached the hallway, the hair on the back of my neck tingled. I looked over my shoulder, finding Gabe following me. From this spot, James couldn't see us unless he actually woke up and came down the hall.

I backed up until I hit the wall.

Gabe closed the distance between us, placing his hands against the wall on either side of my head. "I'm going to fuck the innocence out of you."

CHAPTER TWO

LYNNE

A breathless laugh left me. "I had James when I was fifteen. I'm not that innocent."

Gabe smirked. "Turn around."

I swallowed hard, doing as I was told.

He brushed his fingers along the back of my neck, pushing my hair out of the way. His fingers were soon replaced with his mouth.

I sighed, leaning into him.

"Tell me how long it's been," he murmured, his lips never leaving my neck.

"Too long."

"Tell me." His hands roamed down my sides before dipping beneath the hem of my shorts.

"Six months," I answered, rocking into him.

"Random fuck?" Gabe cupped my jaw, while diving his other hand into my shorts.

I almost wished they would have been tighter. So it would make him work harder for it.

"Yeah." It had been the only one night stand I had

ever experienced. And it was something I would never do again. No matter how much I wanted to be used for the night, I would rather my hands than to have to deal with the awkwardness the next morning.

"You won't need random fucks anymore, Lynne." Gabe hooked his fingers into the waistband of my shorts and pulled them low enough until they sat just below my ass. "I'll be the only thing you need. The only thing you crave." He sunk his teeth into my shoulder. "You got me?"

I let out a slow breath.

A heavy hand cracked against my ass.

I yelped, trying to jump away from him but was stuck against the wall and his hard body.

"I asked you a question." His fingers dipped between my thighs, running over my hot flesh.

"Yes, I got you," I panted, pushing back into him.

I was still very much aware that James was passed out on the recliner. But no matter how much I knew this shouldn't be happening, especially not out in the hall for him to see, I couldn't stop Gabe.

A tinfoil wrapper sounded, followed by a zipper lowering. I shivered, knowing what was about to happen.

Gabe lowered my shorts a bit more. "Stick your ass out for me," he demanded, his voice low and guttural.

I did as I was told at the same time he thrust into me. I gasped, my eyes going wide at the unexpected invasion on my body. His thrusts were deep and hard, his pelvis slamming into me each time. He grunted, digging his fingers into the cheeks of my ass and spread me open.

I pushed back against him, meeting him thrust for every delicious thrust. "Please."

He held the back of my head, pushing me face-first into the wall and picked up speed with his hips.

My thighs trembled, a fast release rushing through me.

He grunted his approval but never let up. With his other hand, he slipped it to my center and slipped two fingers into me while he kept fucking me with his cock.

I whimpered, arching into him and taking him even deeper.

His hips slowed, his mouth finding the back of my neck. When his teeth sunk into my skin, another orgasm rocked through me.

I sighed, my knees shaking at how quick he could make me come.

Much to my surprise, he released me and spun me around.

Without him having to ask, I dropped to my knees and removed the condom from him before taking him into my mouth.

He groaned, his hands latching onto my hair. He guided me up and down the length of him. The tip of his cock bumped the back of my throat, forcing tears to my eyes and making me gag.

He smirked, thrusting even harder between my lips. A few more pumps and his release shot down the back of my throat.

I moaned, licking up every drop and swallowing his orgasm.

He shivered, pulling from my lips once he calmed down.

Gabe helped me to my feet and righted his pants.

I pulled up my shorts and reached out for his hand.

His eyebrow rose.

He no doubt wondered what I was doing. I wasn't sure myself, but I knew that I wanted more. I started walking to my bedroom, pulling him along with me. Once we stood outside my door, he leaned down and brushed his mouth along the shell of my ear. "You sure?"

I opened the door, backed up a step and started stripping.

His dark eyes watched me the whole time. He came toward me and kicked the door closed. Once he had the lock in place, he was on me.

———

GABE

I had a crush on Lynne for as long as I could remember. She was beautiful, smart, and perfect. I didn't give a shit about the age difference. She could have been twenty years older than me and I still would have wanted her.

But now, with her laying on the bed and her feet by her ears, she was in the perfect position.

"Gabe," she whispered, staring up at me with wide eyes.

I ran my hand back and forth over her dripping center. Gave it a few light taps and watched her tremble and squirm.

When I had hinted for more in the first place, I almost expected for her to turn me down. But when she didn't, I took advantage of it.

"Please."

Lynne's pleas pulled me from my thoughts.

"Did his father ever make you feel this good?"

She chewed her bottom lip, shaking her head quickly. "He wasn't a fan of sex. I found out it was because he was fucking everyone else but me."

"Fucking bastard," I growled and lowered my mouth to her pussy.

She sighed.

Pushing against her thighs, I opened her even more for me. She was completely exposed, showing me every inch of her. I ran my tongue from her tight little asshole, up to her clit before giving it a gentle bite.

She yelped.

"You're fucking delicious."

She gave me a big smile. The biggest I had seen on her face in a long time.

Slipping two fingers inside her, I sucked her clit between my lips.

Her thighs trembled and shook, soft sounds of pleasure leaving her mouth.

"So fucking delicious." Running my thumb over the tight little rim, I licked up the cream dripping from her center. "Have you ever been fucked in the ass?"

A hard laugh left her. "No."

"Good." I wanted to experience firsts with her. I wanted to show her that not all men were like her ex. Truth was, I had been in love with her for as long as I could remember. But there was no way I could tell her that. Not now. Maybe not for a while. But it would happen. I would prove to her that age was only a number and that we were good for each other.

I pulled a condom from my back pocket and brought it to her mouth.

She ripped it open with her teeth and sheathed me.

I shivered when her hands came into contact with my cock. Beating the head against her pussy, I rubbed it over her clit.

She moaned.

Covering her mouth with mine, I slid into her in one smooth move. I swallowed her cries, drank in her pleasure and let the passion completely take over.

CHAPTER THREE

LYNNE

I woke the next morning to a hard body wrapped around me. Gabe cupped my breast, his heavy cock resting against the seat of my rear. His leg was curled over mine and he was breathing deep and even.

I hadn't woken up next to a man in a long time. It was nice and scary all at the same time. I wasn't sure what Gabe wanted out of this, but I knew that eventually, we would have to come clean to James.

I played out the scenarios in my head. How would he react? Would he be pissed, or would he approve? I wasn't sure. I liked to think that I knew my son but at the same time, I had never slept with his best friend until now.

I sighed, rolling onto my side.

Gabe groaned, pushing his waist into me. "Too early, babe."

"It's almost nine," I told him, glancing at the clock.

He pulled me further beneath him. "Don't care."

A husky laugh left me. "I forgot that you're not a morning person."

"Nope." He kissed my shoulder, rolling my nipple between his fingers.

"I should get up." It wasn't unheard of for Gabe to spend the night. But he usually stayed in James's room. Hopefully James wouldn't ask too many questions.

"Not yet." Gabe ran his hand down my spine before delving between my thighs.

I jumped when he came into contact with my swollen center.

I turned my head toward him, spreading my legs.

He kissed my nose. "Come for me, baby." He ran his fingers over my clit, rubbing back and forth until I was trembling.

I bit the pillow to keep from crying out when a fast orgasm hit me.

Gabe wrapped his arm around me and pulled me against him. He lined the tip of his cock up with my center.

"Please," I whispered.

"I want you bare." He licked up the side of my neck. "Let me fuck you with no condom."

I shivered at the desperation in his voice. "Yes. Now. Please."

He cupped the back of my thigh and thrust into me.

I gasped.

"Fucking hell." He stopped, letting me get used to the size of him in this position.

"Move, please move."

He pushed me onto my stomach and towered over me. Cupping the back of my neck, he shoved me face-first into the pillow before pulling from my body. "Ready?"

I shivered at the growl in his deep voice. "Yes."

He thrust into me so damn hard, a fast release rocked through me.

He grunted, proud of himself at how quick he could get me off. "Keep coming for me, baby."

I bit the pillow, my thighs shaking as he pounded into me with a brutal force I felt right down to the marrow of my bones.

"God, Gabe."

He chuckled, leaning over me and kissed the spot behind my ear. "Your pussy feels so fucking good. Nice way to wake up."

A breathless laugh left me. "Your cock is nice and hard."

"Hmmm...for you."

Gabe used me for the next hour, taking everything he wanted and gave it back to me tenfold.

After a couple more orgasms and a bite here and there, we took a shower and got ready for the day.

It was still early so I didn't think James would be up yet but when I left my room, he was coming down the hallway. I quickly shut the door before Gabe and I got caught.

"Morning, sweetheart."

James smiled down at me and gave me a quick hug. "Morning, Mama."

"Sleep well?"

He nodded. "Did Gabe go home last night?"

"He did. He was going to come over for breakfast. I'm just going to get ready." I was shocked at how quickly the lie rolled off of my tongue. But before James could ask any more questions, I slipped back into my room.

Gabe was sitting on the edge of my bed, a deep frown settled between his brows.

"We can't do this again," I blurted, leaning against the door.

"Lynne."

I couldn't meet his gaze for fear that I would fall back into the depths of his dark eyes.

"This was a mistake," I said more to myself than to Gabe. I wasn't sure who I was trying to convince. Probably myself.

But it didn't matter. "We can't do this again," I repeated.

"Are you sure about that?" Gabe slid off the bed and came toward me. Once he reached me, he placed a hand on the wall beside my head. He ran his fingers down my arm before linking them with mine. "Did you not enjoy yourself? I seem to recall the many times you screamed out my name."

My cheeks burned. "As amazing as it was." And it was truly amazing. Randy had never made me feel the way Gabe had. Hell, none of the guys I had been with, were as good as him. "We shouldn't do this again."

"Tell me why not." Gabe pinched my chin, tilting my head to meet his gaze.

I licked my lips, my eyes dropping to his mouth. A mouth that had been on every inch of my body. "You're my son's best friend."

"I am." Gabe's voice was low as he continued to stare at me. "But I also know that he loves you and he would want his mom to be happy. He would want me to be happy as well."

"Are you happy?"

He cocked his head to the side. "Last night was the best night I have ever had. I don't care about the age difference between us. I like you. I have always liked you."

"But you deserve someone your own age."

"Age is only a number, baby." He kissed the corner of my mouth.

I shivered at the term of endearment. That had never been Randy's thing. He called me by my name and my name only. No pet names.

I pushed Gabe back a step and slipped out of my pajamas, no longer shielding him from my nudity. It wasn't like it mattered anymore since he had seen and been in every part of my body. My throat still burned from the way he had shoved his cock into my mouth.

"We can take this one day at a time." His eyes roamed over every inch of me. "We don't have to tell James anything yet. But I know last night wasn't a onetime thing for me."

I let out a breath of relief. "It wasn't for me either."

He gave me a cocky grin. "Good. Cause I wasn't taking no for an answer anyway."

I laughed. "So...now what?"

In a quick move, he pulled me back into his arms. "We fuck. And we fuck some more." His hands slid up and down my back.

His cock twitched against my lower abdomen.

Wrapping my arms around his neck, I ground against him.

He shivered, a low groan leaving him.

"I like that idea." I covered his mouth with mine, letting him use me like I knew I deserved.

Like we both deserved.

CHAPTER FOUR

LYNNE

It had been a month since Gabe and I slept together for the first time. James was none the wiser. Although we were discreet, every time he came over, he would touch me whenever he could. Even if it was just his fingers grazing my rear. Or a light kiss to the back of the neck. He was constantly touching me, letting me know that he was actually in this. For the long run? I wasn't sure. But I did know that it was fun. Maybe I was going through a mid-life crisis.

Every time Gabe spent the night, he would join me after I went to bed. He would wake me up by kissing down the length of my body. My eyes would open as soon as his mouth ended up between my legs.

He would wink at me and have me coming undone in a matter of minutes.

It had been our routine ever since that first night together. I wasn't sure if James caught onto anything. Gabe and I talked more now than before we started sleeping together. So maybe he did. But he never hinted.

One night, the three of us were watching a movie. I

had cooked us homemade lasagna that I spent all day preparing while the guys were out.

They started the movie while I cleaned the kitchen and did the dishes. With my back to the entranceway, the hairs on the back of my neck tingled.

A warm body came up behind me. Fingers pushed the hair off my nape, followed by a soft bite to the back of my neck.

I shivered, a slow smile spreading on my face. "Miss me?"

"Always." Gabe gripped my hips, pushing his pelvis into my rear.

"You should stop," I said, keeping my voice low. "James could walk in."

Gabe's hands went around to my front. "Let him."

"Gabe." But I couldn't push him away. His hands felt so damn good on my body. It had never been like this with James's father. There was never any passion. That specific need and hunger for each other.

Gabe popped open the button of my jeans, lowered the zipper and moved to my side.

"Gabe," I whispered.

"Shhh..." He lowered my jeans to just below my ass.

Thankfully my sweater was long enough that if James did happen to walk in, he wouldn't see anything.

Gabe ran his finger over my clit.

I jumped, wanting to spread my legs but was confined by my jeans.

He continued watching me, running his finger back and forth over the swollen nub. Slipping his fingers lower, he thrust two inside me.

I sighed, reveling in the control he had on my body.

"You're fucking incredible." Gabe kissed my cheek.

As soon as he leaned back, James walked into the kitchen.

"I thought you were coming back with beer."

"I was but thought I'd keep your mom company while she did the dishes," he told my son while keeping his fingers deep inside me.

My cheeks heated, unable to focus on their words. My body vibrated, my hands stumbled over the dishes I was trying to wash. This was something I had never done before. Not even with James's father. This was far from the norm for me. This was...this was taboo.

Gabe pushed his thumb against my clit, rubbing it back and forth over the hard bundle of nerves.

I chewed my bottom lip, forcing myself to keep from crying out for him to bend me over the counter and just fuck me already.

"Mom, you talk to dad today?"

I nodded. "Yeah. He said he's good with you just going up to see him for a few weekends here and there."

"Okay, good. Listen, I'm heading to my room. I'm going to try and look for a job tomorrow."

"Okay, good luck."

He came up to me and kissed my cheek.

I jumped, almost expecting him to find his best friend's hand between my legs.

When James left the kitchen, Gabe's hand sped up.

"God," I whimpered.

He smirked, leaning down to my ear. "You're nice and soaked for me. Isn't that right?"

I nodded. "Yes. God, harder, Gabe, please."

"You're fucking perfect." He slammed his hand against my center, shoving his fingers harder and faster inside of me. The pleasure was almost too much. My knees shook.

"Come for me," he growled, kissing my cheek. "Let me hear my name leave your lips."

I looked down, watching his fingers disappear into my body. "So good."

He chuckled. "Come for me, baby."

Two more pumps and I broke.

My thighs shook, a soft cry leaving me. His name left my mouth, sliding between us and made me realize that I could get used to this.

Gabe wrapped an arm around my shoulders, placing a soft peck on my cheek. "I like this. With you." He pulled his hand from between my legs, sticking his fingers between his lips.

"I like this too." I pulled up my jeans and did them up.

"Was it ever like this with him?" He meant my ex.

"No." I finished up the dishes and dried my hands before turning toward him. "He used the excuse that going down on me was gross."

Gabe scowled. "Fucking please. It's one of my favorite things. Probably more than sex."

"Oh I figured that." I laughed.

He grinned, leaning against the counter across from me.

"Are you spending the night again?" Please say yes.

"Do you want me to?"

I closed the distance between us. Placing my hand on his chest, I felt the thump thump of his heart beneath my palm.

"I won't hurt you," he murmured, grabbing my hand.

"I know." I looked up at him. Even though he was

younger than me, he was far more mature than most of the guys I knew who were my own age. He was good for my son. He helped him keep a good head on his shoulders. He was the best influence for him when his father and I were going through our hard times.

Gabe leaned his forehead against mine.

I let out a soft sigh, breathing in the scent of his cologne.

"I want you, Lynne." Gabe gripped my hip, pulling me closer. "Not just for sex. I want a relationship with you."

I leaned back, staring up at his handsome face. "You don't think it's weird?"

"Why would I?" He kissed the corner of my mouth. "I don't give a shit about the age difference. We're good together."

I took a chance and wrapped my arms around his shoulders, holding him tight.

"I want to date you." He kissed the side of my neck. "I want to go to bed with you every night and wake up beside you every morning."

"Really?" I shivered against him. I wasn't used to this kind of treatment. I had settled for Randy, not knowing the difference between being treated just okay and being treated phenomenal.

"Yes, baby." Gabe hugged me, holding me against him like his life depended on it.

"I haven't dated since James's father and I split up." I leaned back and cupped his face. "I also can't have anymore kids." We had almost lost James due to some complications with my pregnancy. I had to have a hysterectomy right after he was born. "Are you okay with that?"

"If I'm with you, I'm okay with anything." He brushed his thumb along my bottom lip. "I don't want kids anyway. And even if I did, we could always adopt."

"I've thought of adopting but I'm happy with just having James being my only child."

Gabe lowered his mouth to mine. "I'm happy with you," he murmured against my lips.

I deepened the kiss, sliding my tongue against his.

"Hmmm..." He cupped my ass, lifted me into his arms and placed me on top of the counter.

"James could come out of his room," I said, pushing my hands beneath his shirt. "He could find us."

"He could." Gabe ran his mouth down the length of my jaw. "He could come in and see me kissing his mama." He lifted my shirt, sliding his hands over my skin. "He could see me touching her. Holding her." His hands slid up my torso to my chest. He pushed his fingers beneath my bra, cupping me.

"God." I shivered. I loved the way his hands felt on my body. He made me feel owned but cared for. His touch completely consumed me.

Gabe pulled a hand from beneath my bra and wrapped his fingers around my throat. "You're mine. Aren't you?"

"Yes." I stared up at him. "And you're mine."

———

GABE

Stepping between Lynne's legs, I cupped her head and deepened the kiss.

She sighed, inviting me in.

Slipping my tongue against hers, I ground into her.

"What the fuck are you doing to my mom!"

I jumped away from Lynne.

James stood at the entranceway to the kitchen. His face was red, his hands clenched into fists at his sides.

As much as I knew I should explain, the words wouldn't form on my tongue.

Lynne jumped down from the counter. "James, I can explain."

"Explain what? How I walked in and found my best friend with his tongue down my mother's throat?"

She stepped in front of me, no doubt shielding me from the wrath of her son.

James and I had been through a lot together. We had our good days and our bad ones. Just like most friendships. But I wasn't sure how this one would turn out. And I feared that this would break us.

"How long has this been going on?" James demanded, pulling me from my thoughts.

"James," Lynne said gently.

"Tell me."

"Over a month," she murmured.

"Fucking hell." He stepped around her and shoved me back. "Out of all the women in the world, why my fucking mother?"

"James, watch your mouth," Lynne scolded, trying to step between us.

James ignored her and got in my face. He was so close, I could see the specs of brown in his deep blue eyes.

"You know I've always had a crush on her," I told him.

His grows narrowed. "That was when we were kids. Hell, all of my friends had a crush on her at one point or another." He pushed me. "But I don't give a shit about them. You are my best friend. I know your reputation."

I rolled my eyes. "That is old and done. I'm not like that anymore and you know that."

"James, please." Lynne pushed her way between us. "This isn't just a fling."

James looked between us. "I can't with this shit right now. Maybe I should have gone to dad's after all."

"Baby, please." Her eyes shone. "I'm happy. I'm really happy."

James shoved away from her and headed into the living room.

"I'll give you two some time alone." I kissed her head and left the kitchen.

"Gabe."

I stopped.

Lynne stood a few feet away. "Give him time."

I wanted to go to her. To pull her into my arms and keep her safe from her son's rage. But I knew they needed to talk.

"Please don't leave," she added.

"I'll be in the backyard."

She nodded, her shoulders slumping with relief.

I walked by her, letting my fingers graze hers.

James was in the kitchen. I could feel his eyes burning into me. He probably thought I wanted to just fuck his mom and be done with it. But it was more than that. He was right though. I did have a reputation but then I got bored and calmed down. I had an itch, and no one came close to scratching it until Lynne. I finally had the balls to move things forward. I was going to confess how I felt until James walked in.

"Gabe."

I stopped at the patio door.

"This better be worth it."

Of course it was worth it.

But instead of saying anything, I ignored James and headed outside.

———

LYNNE

"Mom."

I sighed, turning toward my son. I looked at him then. Really looked at him. He was a younger version of his father. With light brown hair and freckles on his cheeks from the sun kissing his skin, he was my ex-husband's twin. But his personality was nothing like him. He was kinder. Gentler. His heart was big. He would give the shirt off his back with no questions asked.

"I'm sorry if I hurt you." I looked down at my feet. I had never felt ashamed before. Not where my son was concerned. But now I did, and I prayed that he could find it in his heart to forgive me.

"Mom."

I looked up at the gentle but firm command.

"You have nothing to be sorry for." He rubbed the back of his neck. "Am I a little surprised? Yes. But I want you happy. I want Gabe happy too."

"This came as a surprise to me too. I wasn't looking for a relationship at all. Your dad hurt me. So I guess it..."

"Ruined you for other men?"

I nodded. "I've had a hard time trusting men but with Gabe, I feel like a completely different person. But I will stop this if you want us to."

James closed the distance between us and wrapped me in his arms. "Are you happy?"

I returned the embrace. "Yes. I am. Gabe treats me well. And I know there's an age difference between us but he's more mature than most of the guys I've met who are my own age."

"I know." James leaned back, cupping my face. "I love you, Mama."

"I love you too." I gave him a small smile. "Are you good with this? With us?"

"I..." He sighed. "I had every intention of yelling and demanding for you to stop seeing each other but then I noticed the way you looked at him and he at you. You love him." He raised his hand when I opened my mouth to argue. "You don't have to tell me. But I see it."

He grabbed my hand and led me to the backyard.

Gabe was sitting on the patio set off to the left. He was on his phone, but his head snapped up when he saw us approach.

James led me toward him. "Stand up."

Gabe looked between us but did as he was told.

James pulled me in front of him and cupped my shoulders. "I want you both to be happy. That's all I've ever wanted. So, while this did come as a bit of a shock, I give you both my approval."

My heart leapt to my throat. "You do?"

"I do." James smiled down at me. "I just want you happy. Like I said, I was going to throw a tantrum just for shits and giggles but decided against it."

"Aren't we lucky," Gabe murmured.

James raised an eyebrow. "I can still do that."

Gabe scoffed. "You're not five."

"Asshole," James threw at him.

"Fucker," Gabe retorted.

James pulled Gabe in for a hug, muttering quietly to him.

"I know." James clapped his upper back before releasing him and pushed me into his arms. "If you hurt her, I don't give a shit how close we are, I will kill you."

Gabe wrapped his arm around my shoulders. "I wouldn't expect any less from you."

"Are you sure you're okay with this?" I asked James, needing reassurance that he did actually approve and not just say he did to make me happy.

"I am." James sat on the patio couch.

I joined him, with Gabe sitting on the other side of me.

"I think if it was anyone else, I wouldn't be." James covered my hands that were in my lap. "You weren't happy with dad. I knew that. But I also know that you deserve more. Both of you do."

My eyes welled. "Thank you."

"Just don't hurt her," he said, looking over my head.

Gabe brushed his finger down my arm before linking our hands. "I don't plan on it."

I gave him a small smile.

The guys started talking about sports and what they had planned for the rest of the summer. I sat back and listened, soaking it all up.

I was thankful James reacted the way he had. It could have been worse. I could have lived out my worst fear. It was one reason why I hadn't actively searched for a partner.

Listening to the guys talk, laughing every now and again, made my heart soar. I could get used to this feeling. Happy and elated that things were finally moving forward. As Gabe and James poked fun at each other, the talk of our relationship no more, I realized something. James was right. I was falling in love with Gabe. But it was a love I had never experienced. Not even with Randy. There was no passion with him. He never put me first. It was his way or no way. I understood now what love was and I couldn't ask for a better man to grow with.

CHAPTER FIVE

LYNNE

A warm body came up behind me. I smiled, leaning against Gabe. He wrapped his arm around my shoulders and placed a soft peck on my cheek.

"Happy, baby?" he asked, nuzzling into me.

"I am. Are you?"

"Definitely."

Gabe and I had been dating for six months and he was finally moving in with James and I.

After James found out about us, Gabe had confessed his love for me later that evening. He also never spent the night again until a month ago. He wanted James to get used to the idea of us as a couple. I fell in love with him even more at that point.

"I love you, Lynne." He pulled me tighter against him. "So fucking much."

I grinned. "I love you too."

His mouth brushed along the shell of my ear, sending a hot shiver racing down my spine.

"I'm nervous."

He turned me in his arms. "Why?" he asked, cupping my face and tilting my head back.

"It's been a long time since I've been in a relationship. I don't want to screw this up." I had thought that Randy and I had divorced because of me. Maybe something was wrong with me that I couldn't keep the father of my son happy.

"Lynne." Gabe brushed his thumb down the length of my jaw. "You could never screw this up. I have a history. So if anyone is going to make a mistake, it'll be me. But that won't happen either. I love you."

"I love you too." I cupped his nape, pulling him down to meet my mouth.

"We will make this work." He kissed my forehead and then my nose before wrapping his arms around me.

For the rest of the night, James and I helped Gabe unpack. When he was finally settled, we were lying in bed later that evening, holding and touching each other. No words fell between us as we laid there in silence.

"I love you, baby," Gabe whispered, brushing his mouth along my ear.

For the rest of the night, we laid like that. Whispering our feelings for each other over and over. We made love two times before passing out in each other's arms.

I never knew that it could be like this.

Happiness.

Passion.

Lust.

All consuming desire.

It was everything I wanted and more.

THE END

ABOUT J. M. WALKER

J.M. Walker is an Amazon bestselling author who hit USA Today with Wanted: An Outlaw Anthology. She loves all things books, pigs and lip gloss. She is happily married to the man who inspires all of her Heroes and continues to make her weak in the knees every single day.

"Above all, be the HEROINE of your own life..." ~ Nora Ephron

www.aboutjmwalker.com
Reader Group

DECIEVER

ALEXANDRA SILVA

BLURB

Damon Coldwell is the richest a-hole in Manhattan.
I wish I knew that before we hooked up...the night before
I started my new job.
Now, Mr. Dark and Handsome isn't only Manhattan's
problem—he's my boss.
And I'm possibly the best game he's ever played.

CHAPTER ONE

AVA

The bar is buzzing. The dimness is sliced through with colored rays of light that punctuate the fast-paced beat of the music. Pinnacle is one of the most popular bars with the affluent Manhattanites.

"I still can't believe you're going rogue. Are you sure you want to walk out on your dad?" Lacie asks, looking around the bar for any of her clients. She likes to keep a close eye on them during season. Who knew ballers were such hard-core partiers?

"He didn't give me much choice."

"I know you wanted that promotion, but going to his competitor seems extreme." Taking a sip of her old-fashioned, she pins me with the kind of sorry smile that makes me certain I'm making the best decision for me.

"Dad picked Marsh over me. He picked my fiancé over me—his daughter. His flesh and blood."

"I know that sucks, babe. And believe me, I'm fucking livid for you, but it all feels like so much. You're walking away from Monroe Pub and Marsh..."

The espresso martini I'm sucking down burns a little

more with the anger blazing in the pit of my stomach. "I'm not walking away from Monroe. I *am* a Monroe—it's impossible to walk away from my name. I have a plan, and in the end, I'll be sitting right where I should be...heading my family's company."

"And Marsh?"

"Marsh can go to hell. He should never have accepted that promotion. He knew what it meant to me...what it means...and he still took it." Yeah, the asshole can rot when I'm done. "He betrayed me."

Raising her hand at one of the waiters, she indicates for him to bring us another round of drinks. "Is CPM going to make you happy again?"

I think of my new job at Coldwell Press & Media, and I smile. "Yes, it's going to make me happier because in spite of all this, I am happy."

"You're always happy."

"Silver linings, Lace," I remind her with a chuckle.

The waiter returns with his shirt half-unbuttoned so that his washboard abs are on show, and damn, he's hot. The kind of hot that's pleasant to look at but that invariably makes you feel self-conscious.

"Thanks," she croons at the besotted guy, batting her golden eyes while she brushes through her copper curls.

"Can I get you anything else?"

"No, this will be all...for now."

After the waiter walks away, she holds up her drink and sings, "Here's to kicking ass and getting laid."

"Getting laid?" I almost spit my martini.

It's only been a few weeks since I threw my thirty-three-carat engagement ring at my fiancé's smug face, and even if he is an asshole, I haven't thought about moving on.

"Babe, this is the best time to get out there and make the most out of life. You're twenty-nine, Ava, have some fun. Fuck and live a little."

"Fuck and live a little?"

"Cheers to that!" Lacie touches her glass to mine and without ceremony finishes her drink.

We chat about everything and nothing while she keeps a lookout. The waiter comes back a few times with fresh drinks. We're finishing up the last round when her phone starts going crazy.

"I'll go get another round," I tell her as she answers it.

"I won't be long."

"It's okay," I assure her while I readjust my dress. It's a pointless task because as I stand, the low back cowls lower, and I feel the AC flutter the golden ivory silk over my ass.

It's one of Lacie's good-time dresses—the ones she wears after a breakup and she wants to forget the asshole.

Shouldering my miniature Chanel purse, I head for the bar, trying not to flash my goods. This dress is indecently short and barely covers my boobs.

"Don't forget the shooters," she calls behind me.

Pulling up to the bar behind a group of women, I check my own phone. There's nothing. No surprise given I've upset my family. It's the only remorse I hold over my decision.

It takes the group a while to decide on what they're drinking. The straight vodka shots they shoot back have them making a choky, giggling scene.

Who even shoots vodka outside of college?

"God help us all." I look up toward the low, rumbling voice and pause.

Dark eyes peer down on me with a chiseled, dark

stubble-framed pout. Heat flares high on my cheeks, and all I can hear over the heavy suggestive beat of the music is my speeding heart.

"Yeah," I manage to croak with a shake of my head.

What is wrong with me?

The party girls move along with their fruity concoctions waving in the air. I'm not sure what to do. Do I let him go ahead of me? Do I push forward?

Before I can decide, a large, warm hand hovers over the base of my spine. The radiating heat causes goose bumps to prickle up my back, setting the roots of my hair ablaze with awareness.

Without touching me the handsome stranger guides me forward. There's enough space for him to stand beside me at the bar, but he stays angled behind me so his elbow perches on the bar as he leans forward, his shoulder touching my shoulder blade.

At five foot nine, I'm tall, but he is taller. And when he crouches to my level, his thigh tucks to the back of mine, below my ass, like he's ready to catch me if my legs give.

"What are you drinking?" Fire licks at my insides at the cool gravel of his voice.

I'm in a mute stupor when a bartender stops in front of us. "Same again?" he asks, looking between the two of us before he settles on the man beside me.

Readjusting himself, Mr. Dark and Handsome skims his body across mine so that he's leaning on the bar sideways. Taller and broader, he looks down on me.

"Uhhh, yes—" I take a deep breath. "—please. Umm... an espresso martini, an old-fashioned and..." I sigh, embarrassed after his remark at the other women. "And six tequilas. Orange instead of lime, please."

I don't even have to look to know that Mr. D and H is assessing my order.

"Celebrating?"

Turning to him, I stagger back a little, bumping into the guy on my other side.

"Sorry," I apologize over my shoulder before stepping forward again. My cheeks are burning so red that my vision is blurred around the edges.

Dark eyes crinkle at the corners which is odd because he doesn't look much older than me. But yet, there's something about him that makes me feel small and young and like he could wolf me down without even having to chew.

With his eyes smoldering into mine, I'm entirely transfixed. I have to force myself to look the other way. Lacie's pacing with her phone to her ear, her free hand waving about like she's schooling some poor bastard. When she finds me, she nods at the stranger beside me and wiggles on the spot.

I can't ask him to dance.

"Do it!" she mouths before carrying on with her phone call.

A low, rumbling laugh has me turning back to the man giving me his attention.

"We'll have an espresso martini." Mr. D and H gestures at the bartender, who's only just pouring the tequilas. "Glenfiddich 50—no ice—and two tequilas: one orange and one lime."

Gaze narrowing on mine, he comes closer and asks, "Would you like anything else? Water maybe?"

With his proximity all I can see is his mouth. My fingers itch to scratch at his thick stubble, and when he breathes out, I devour his expelled breath greedily— almost choking on the smoked oaky air.

"That's all."

A moment goes by where I take him in. I roam my sight over the sharp contours of his face, sculpted lips, and perfect Roman nose. There's a kind of familiar kindling in my mind, but I don't know if it's the alcohol or the dim lights...I can't put my finger what it is.

"Have we met before?"

Chuckling, he hands me one of the tequila shooters. The orange slice sits on the thickly salt-crusted rim.

"It's New York—there's no such thing as strangers. You've either been face-to-face or in the same room as a person a handful of times before you actually meet them." Raising his own shot, he chinks it to mine, watching while I lick across the rim of my glass. He does the same, and we both shoot the warming tart liquid.

Sucking the remainder of the salt and lime from his lips, he hums before he says, "Nice to meet you..."

"Lacie," I blurt.

I'm not sure why I lie, but I do, and I don't feel in the least terrible about it. In fact, the thought of spending time with this man without him knowing who I am thrills me. Maybe it's the aftereffect of the tequila, but my insides fizz and my core pulses with the quirk of his brow.

Reaching across the narrowing space between us, he swipes his thumb down the fullest part of my lip to my chin. Without removing his heated gaze from mine, he takes it to his mouth and sucks the side of it.

"Henry." Handing me the espresso martini, he takes his own drink, and then just as he guided me to the bar before, he sweeps me across the busy bar to a glass-ensconced corner.

The view is spectacular. Overlooking a dark Central Park, the lights on the other side appear like fairy lights suspended from the black sky. And still, it's not enough to hold my attention. I just want to look at Henry.

Henry.

Something about the name doesn't seem right. Like it doesn't fit him. Wrong almost, but then the old regality of it makes sense. Everything about him is majestic—even the prurient actions. Like licking his thumb after touching me. Or the way his body molds mine without physically touching me.

"What's your story, Lacie?" The lull of my friend's name on his lips makes me regret not giving him mine. I'm jealous of the way the two syllables drip with sex and seduction.

I'm not sure whether he truly is trying to seduce me, but if he is, it's working. I'm primed and ready.

Ask him to dance.

Blinking back at him, I swallow down the request for a dance, and instead I ask, "My story?"

"Why is a woman like you drinking in a bar filled with girls chasing fame and money?" The luring depth of his onyx stare traps me in a speechless second.

"Celebrating."

"Let me guess..." he breathes, coming closer. "A promotion?"

There's a cryptic tilt to his crooked grin that's wicked. Almost like he already knows all the shit that's happened the last month and his question is but a way to keep me talking.

"Actually, no. Not a promotion. My asshole fiancé stole that from me."

Henry takes my drink and sits it on the high table along with his. "He's a sack of shit, and you probably deserve better."

"Probably?" Pressing closer to him, I rock back on my heels so I can see his full face. And again, that bolt of familiarity shoots straight through me. Twisting my insides, lighting my senses until every single one of my pores burns and the urge to touch him is impossible to resist.

I push my bloodred manicured finger into his chest, swallowing down the gasp that bubbles up my throat from the smallest of touches.

"If I knew you better, I would say he's not only an asshole—"

"And a sack of shit." I sway a little with the way my legs turn to Jell-O when his hands bracket my hips.

"And a sack of shit, but he's clearly stupid. Now, Lacie." He licks his lips like the name on them makes him hungry. "You don't strike me as a stupid woman, or a woman who humors stupidity. So, I'd say he did you a favor."

"He did," I utter when he pulls me flush to him.

Beneath his black shirt and jeans, his body is hard, and I really want to become acquainted with it in a way that I have never really wanted before. Not even with Marsh.

Our chests press together with every breath, rubbing and squeezing until my nipples are furled so tight that the friction between us aches.

"You can have better," he says, looking down on me, his focus sweeping from my face to my boobs. The shadows of his face darken, and at the same time as his hands round to the top my ass, I roll onto my toes.

"Are you better, Henry?" Tilting my face to within a breath from his, I melt into him.

Henry swipes his tongue along his bottom lip with a

smirk, and the humid heat of it clings to the contours of my mouth like static pulling us together.

"Are you going to ask me to dance?"

"You look like the kind of man that likes to control the situation."

"Actually, I couldn't give a fuck about control." I'm momentarily thrown back by his remark, and my stare darts from his glistening lips to his eyes. Maybe he's telling the truth, but the way his eyes bore into mine...it doesn't add up.

I'd ask, but the thrill is in the mystery and the knowledge that after tonight and whatever this is, I may never see him again. He'll never know who I am. This will be a fun blip in my otherwise tame life.

Turning in his arms, I press my back to his front, tilting my head on his shoulder so that my lips graze the line of his jaw as I tell him, "Let's dance."

CHAPTER TWO

AVA

The traffic is a disaster. It's my first day, and I can't be tardy.

"This cannot be happening," I grit out, taking out enough cash to cover the cab fare and tip. I can see the office tower a couple of blocks away, and it would take me less time to rush in my heels than sit here agonizing over my first impression.

"I'll walk from here," I tell the driver, handing him the money before I get out.

It takes all of seven minutes, groaning lungs and a sore shoulder from running into every possible person. Pulling my security card out, I freeze as a familiar scent throws me back to last night. Amber and freshly chopped wood. Like sap, the scent sticks to my senses. I'm looking around, but apart from the throbbing ache between my thighs...there's nothing.

Get your shit together! I tell myself as I go through the barriers and straight to the elevators. I keep telling it to myself in the one of the elevator's packed corners. Just when I think we're done and the doors are about to close, two guys press inside. Everyone shuffles closer together as one walks in backward, laughing at whatever the other has said.

That deep laugh...

"I hope you know what you're doing." The one facing me looks up, and his eyes narrow before he smiles.

"Sometimes if you want the job done right, you got to do it yourself."

That voice...

"I bet it was a hardship." The guy smiling at me cocks his head to the side like he's trying to see me through the crowd or over them. "A real hardship."

The elevator fails to stop at all the floors people have requested, shooting right to the top where the two men get out. Luckily, I'm only two floors down and next to get out.

Claude, the HR woman I've been dealing with since signing my contract, is waiting for me at the front desk. With the exception of the glass walls and floor-to-ceiling windows, the place is a polished concrete box. Hard and cold with the letters *CPM* frosted over most of the partitioning glass and Coldwell Press emblazoned across the front desk in a luminous orange hue that is the only focus of the large space.

"Miss Monroe!" The older woman holds out her hand, already walking ahead before I shake it.

"Please, call me Ava."

"We're running a little behind this morning. We had an issue with the servers, and it caused havoc. I wanted to show you around properly, but I won't have time. So, it will be this floor for now, and when we have the weekly meeting later, I'll show you around the meeting rooms and executive floor."

I keep following and absorbing the things she points out around the floor.

"Don't worry, it's a debrief of what's on the agenda. The management like to know the pipeline."

I'm not worried. I'm more than prepared.

"Makes sense."

Claude introduces me to the other editors—all men, of course—and to the team of assistants that keep this floor running. Before I know it, the entire day has flown by with IT taking up a good portion of my morning and lunch.

It's so quiet here compared to the bustle at Monroe where the editors aren't on a floor of their own.

Shuffling the papers and files around my desk, I try to ignore the tight squeeze of my heart. Leaving Monroe wasn't easy. I miss it terribly, but I needed to make this move. Even if to merely prove to myself that in spite of what happened, I'm as good as I believe myself to be.

"Knock, knock!" I look up to find one of the other editors leaning into my open doorway. "Owen...in case you've forgotten."

"Hi, Owen."

"So, you ready for the meeting?" He leans on the edge of the glass wall. "Even if you have shit, you always take something, or Coldwell will chew your ass."

"I have something." I gather the files I worked on over the last couple of weeks. I knew I wouldn't be able to walk through the door empty-handed.

"Ooooh," he croons with a high-pitched whistle as I round my desk and start for the elevators. "And here I thought you were the token female of the floor." Owen shoulders me. His hand wraps around me, and oddly I don't find it too much too soon.

"Token female?"

"Yeah, they have me—the token queer—and they used to have Marcella—the token female slash exec slut."

We head up to the top floor.

"Rumor has it she was banging one of the gods and it went sour." Shrugging, he exits the elevator, and I follow him past the front desk of this floor. It's identical to ours, except all the glass is frosted with the company logo etched in orange.

"Rumor has..." He nods me forward with him as he walks through the floor like it's ours. "Rumor has it that you jumped ship because Monroe is sinking."

What?

"I'm not judging," he adds. "I would too."

"I didn't jump ship; I made a career decision...for me." I add that last bit because rumors are worse than boils on the ass...or herpes. "And Monroe is doing fine."

"Transparency is the foundation here, Ava."

"You realize I've had my interview and got the job, right?"

"Yeah, but I don't get why you'd leave your house for ours if it is *fine*."

"I left because I'd capped out and I want more."

We sit on one side of the long boardroom. While Owen goes about spreading his stack of manuscripts and files, I leave mine closed in front of me with my sheet of notes sitting on top.

Claude enters followed by a petite brunette who sits on the other side, opposite Owen. The two other editors walk in; one is on the phone talking loudly to a client. The other carries his laptop in, still opened as he one-handed types away.

"Ava," Claude calls from where she's sitting beside the other woman. "This is Francesca Wilson, the CFO."

"Hello." I smile.

"Good to meet you. I wasn't sure what Damon was thinking, but I see that maybe he was right." Nodding at the table, she adds, "You've come prepared."

Damon Coldwell—New York's most elusive bachelor. Apparently, he's an asshole too, or so I've heard.

The man from this morning walks in with the same smirky smile on his face. Something about him sets me on edge.

"This is—" Claude begins her introduction when a deep gravelly voice cuts in from behind me. "Miss Monroe."

Heart dropping to my stomach I feel as though the ground has disappeared from beneath me and I'm plummeting through all forty-eight floors.

It can't be, I tell myself as I search the reflection in the glass for him, and when I find the same dark stare I lusted over last night, I know it is.

His scent envelops me as he meanders around the boardroom table to stand in front of me.

"Ava." He says my name like it's always been on the tip of his tongue, and all the regret from not giving it to him last night consumes me until I'm having to exert myself to hold in my shock. "Good to see you again."

Did he know who I was the whole time? Maybe he's put two and two together...

The bolt of familiarity from last night strikes with a vengeance, lighting me on fire.

I'm lost in my thoughts and wonderings when a sharp stab gets me right in the ankles. I shake myself loose from the grip of my spinning mind to find a large, tanned hand extended my way. A hand that knows more of my body than it should.

Shit.

Fuck.

What the hell?

All I can picture as I look into his eyes, placing my hand in his, is the way his body pinned me against the wall. The way his stubble felt over my sensitive skin.

The squeeze of his hand around mine draws me back to the here and now. I don't need a mirror to know that I'm beet red, and I certainly don't need to look around to know that every person in this room is thinking of me in the exact same way they thought of my predecessor.

Exec slut.

I feel as though I'm about to implode with my nails digging into his flesh. I hope it hurts even if the grin on his face hitches higher and wider.

"Damon Coldwell," he rumbles with a harder squeeze that has me retracting my hand. "Should we get down to business?"

Damon or Henry or whatever the fuck his name is doesn't bat an eyelid throughout the entire meeting. There are no signs that he's surprised at my presence. There's no look or lingering stare that says he's thinking of the way his hands cupped my ass while we fucked in a dark corner of some upscale bar. There's nothing but a stone-clad front that is all business.

The boardroom empties. While everyone else filters out, Owen sits looking at me with that gossip-hungry ogle that nails in the fact that this is a disaster. This is a horrific mistake, and I screwed up.

I'm mortified, and the longer I try to work the situation out in my head, the more the realization sets in.

He knew who I was last night. He had to, or he would've been as thrown back as me.

"What just happened?" Owen asks as I stand.

"Nothing."

"Didn't look like nothing."

"I guess not everything always appears as it is." Leaving him gawking in my wake, I storm out of the room.

With no clue as to where I'm going, I head for the front desk. I'm about to leave when I see him enter the office at the very end of the hall. There's no second thought or pause when I stalk past his assistant into the office.

Holy shit.

There's another assistant and solid walls and heavy wood doors. No glass and transparency. And I know without a doubt that I've entered the Devil's lair. I feel it in my bones and my pulsing flesh.

"How can I help you?" The middle-aged man stands from behind his desk. "If you have any issues, I would be happy to point you to the right person or—"

"Come in, Miss Monroe," the Devil speaks from the intercom on the desk.

Standing in debate of which door to go into, I'm trembling. My nerves fray a little more, and following the direction his assistant points me in, I spit out my thanks.

"How can I help you, *Lacie*?" he has the audacity to chuckle as he pours himself a drink.

It's all the confirmation I needed to know he's playing

some kind of game. Why else would he pretend he didn't know me?

"Cut the shit, *Henry!*"

My thoughts are screaming, my brain racing a hundred miles a second making it impossible for me to voice any of the things running through my mind. The longer I stand here, the more my tongue swells and curls in my mouth, threatening to choke me.

"My contract has a three-month trial clause. I'm taking it."

Ire stains his laugh as he sits on the edge of his desk, sipping his drink while assessing me from head to toe.

"Are you sure?"

"Yes."

"Take a moment, think it through..."

"There's nothing to think about. You knew who I was last night."

"If I remember correctly, you chose to withhold your identity." With a sigh, he stands and rounds his desk, pulling his chair out. "Come."

There's no way I'm getting any closer to him. I might hate him, but my stomach is still flipping and twisting like it did last night. Even if I want to tear him to shreds, my body is throbbing for him.

"I'd like to show you something that might change your mind." He waits beside his chair, his charcoal suit tailored to his impeccable body with the cuffs of his white shirt peeking slightly. He truly is a sinful sight, just like he fucks.

"Come, Ava," he orders in his deep gravel. "Sit. I'd hate for you to make the wrong decision."

Approaching with caution, I do all I can to avoid contact, but he doesn't need to lay a single finger on me for me to feel him as though he is draped all over me and my senses.

The moment I take a seat, he sits on his desk. His pants strain around his thick thighs as he watches me like he's appreciating the sight, and for a second I'm lost to him. A shallow insignificant flash because when he taps a key on his keyboard, my attention goes to the screen.

Blood congealing in my veins, I feel the world tilt and fall off its axis for the second time today.

The black-and-white footage isn't all that clear, but it's enough that I can see the scene we made together. My face is recognizable, and the rake of his stubble on my neck that I've been fantasizing over is clearly a ploy to keep his identity hidden.

I'm sick to my stomach. Ice pounds in my veins, and the whooshing in my ears drums daggers into my head.

"You son of a—"

"Be very careful, Miss Monroe," Damon cuts me off.

Looking up at the smug bastard, all the things that made him irresistible make him just as repugnant to me.

"What do you want?"

"You." His stare bores into mine with no quibble. "Until I no longer require you, or that video will be the next big thing. It would be a shame for your career to be lost to scandal."

"Why are you..."

"Insurance."

"For what?"

"For one, I wouldn't want you jeopardizing my company, and we don't want you running back to daddy either."

I desperately blink back the burning tears stabbing at my eyes.

"Go home, Ava. Think long and hard about your future and make the right decision. For you and for Monroe, I'd hate to destroy what's left of it. And I will."

Putting his drink in my hand, he leaves me staring at the screen as he disappears out of his office.

This can't be happening. It can't be.

But as the video restarts, there's no doubt that it is.

CHAPTER THREE

AVA

Two weeks later

Lacie and I sit in the corner of a little café opposite Central Park. The small space is decorated in a New England style with a menu that brings summer to life in the city all year round. It's one of our favorite spots. Many a shit day at work and bad breakup has been commiserated here. And since I called her the afternoon Damon blindsided me with...everything, we've come here almost every other day.

Although she's claiming to be cool about my decision to stay on, it's obvious she's biting her tongue. Not very Lacie-like, but I appreciate it. The last thing I need right now is my best friend's judgment.

"And he still hasn't spoken to you?" she asks with her forkful of salad suspended by her mouth.

"Nope. Nada."

I push my plate away because every time I think of Damon-*fucking*-Coldwell, my appetite disappears. And it's happening a lot lately. I can't stop thinking about him for all the wrong reasons. It's bordering on obsession.

I want to tear his hair out strand by strand, while at the same time, I ache over his godlike fucking. He's as repugnant as he is irresistible. And I'm that stupid mouse that sees the death trap and still goes for the cheese.

Fucking idiot.

"At least the prick knows to keep his distance." Sighing, she reaches for my hand. "Silver lining?"

My eyes line with tears through my smile. "The whole world hasn't seen me fuck my boss in public?"

"I got a better one."

"You do?"

"Yeah." Her grin is rueful. "You're going to kick major ass, and when all is said and done, your dad will beg you to go back and you'll destroy that lying sleaze."

"Until then, I better get back to the office."

"Ugh, I don't want to go back to work. I want wine and Netflix," she whines, following me out of the café.

"Is everything okay?"

"Yeah, playoffs are around the corner, and every fucker wants something."

"Isn't that good?"

"For business? Yes. For me? No. Good news is that after this season, I'll be the highest-grossing agent. The man children will all have to give me the credit I deserve."

We pause by a stopping cab. The passenger gets out, and as I'm about to get in, a hand grasps my arm. "Ava?"

"Hi," I say before I turn around, spinning on the spot to find one of my clients from Monroe. "Robert. How are you?"

"All the better for seeing you."

"How's the book coming along?" Being one of the

longest-serving news anchors on American television, this man knows more about everything than a person should. The first part of his memoir is one of the most anticipated biographies, and the fact I landed him is the remedy I needed to perk me up.

"It's coming...slower without you. I keep telling your father that Mar—"

"Miss! Are you in or out?" the cab driver yells out of the window.

"Anyway, I better let you go." His wrinkled hand squeezes my shoulder, and I know I shouldn't do it, but with me being a Monroe and all, I wasn't made to sign a noncompete. It wasn't written into my contract. Besides, I'm not poaching Robert, I'm just making sure that all the work he's put into his manuscript doesn't go to waste.

"Here." I extend one of my new business cards. Concrete gray with the orange CPM logo foiled across it. "Friend to friend, if you ever need anything, call me. Okay?"

He holds it up, looking it over with a squint. "You're a good girl, Ava Monroe." He sounds like my gramps, and it's another thing that makes me smile.

"Miss!"

"I better go," I tell him, sliding into the taxi. "Remember, you can call me anytime."

"Take care, Ava." He wanders into the café we just left, and right as the driver is pulling away, I see them—Damon's right-hand man and Marsh.

What the hell are they doing together?

With Lacie on a call, I pull up Marsh's social media accounts and search for Dexter Thorpe and their connection.

"Eww, what the fuck are you doing?" Lacie snatches

my phone out of my hand. "Babe, you don't *ever* stalk your slimy ex on social media. Unfriend and unfollow right the fuck now, Ava!"

"I'm not stalking." I try to grab my phone back, but she scoots to the other side of the car.

"Who's Dexter Thorpe? And why are we searching for him?"

"*I'm* searching for him; *you're* invading my privacy."

"It's my job as best-bitch-friend. But seriously, who is he? He's got entitled douche-canoe stamped all over him."

"He's the VP of CPM."

"And?"

"And he and Marsh just walked into the café together...after Robert."

"So..."

"Nothing, I guess. It just seems odd."

"They went to college together." She shrugs, passing me my phone with Dexter's profile open.

They both attended Stanford at the same time. I scroll down, but the rest of his profile is set to private. *Damn!*

Maybe it's coincidence. Robert lives close by, and the café is popular enough that you have to make a reservation.

"Unfriend."

"What?"

"Unfriend Marsh. I'm not letting you get out until you've done it and I've seen it." Her brow quirks as she watches me follow her orders.

"Just so you know, this isn't exactly mature behavior."

"Petty is my middle name." She sticks her tongue out at me as I slip my phone back into my purse and get out of the car.

"Try bitch too," I spit at her with a wave, and because

she always has to have the last word she yells, "I don't need to try, I own that shit."

———

Robert has called me almost every day the past week. While I have no intention of taking him from Monroe, I also have no wish to give Damon the impression that I'm helping the competition on his time.

In order to avoid any issues, I've met Robert during my lunch and a few days after work. With my schedule filling up, I've had to arrange to meet him at a coffee shop on the same block as CPM. I really don't have the time to be going a lot farther from the office. And the less time spent in a taxi, the more time I have to help Robert.

He's one of the most interesting people I know, and the more I read of his life, the more in awe I am of him.

"This is great," I laugh at one of the more humorous memories he's shared. "Casanova Robert is funny and charming."

"I had my moments." Looking up at me from his MacBook, his stare stills on mine for a second too long for it to be acknowledgement or conversational politeness. "Ava," he murmurs before clearing his throat.

My heartbeat increases because that's how my dad sounded when he told me he was giving Marsh the VP position. "Is everything okay?"

"You have worked so hard with me."

"It's really not that arduous when the content is this brilliant."

"I can't let Monroe take credit for your work." He smiles.

A nervous laugh bubbles from my mouth. "I'm a Monroe, so it's okay."

"No, it isn't."

I open my mouth to argue, but I'm not really sure what to say.

"I agree." A deep rumble fires my heart into full gallop.

Shit.

Turning, I prepare myself to be berated, but it seems that Damon Coldwell's nice front is in place. He holds my gaze, dark eyes narrowed in a way that makes my stomach flip even with the certainty that he's going to rip me apart later. And not in the way that my pussy is clenching for.

"Coffee?" Damon asks.

When I shake my head, lowering my stare, he moves on to Robert. "Mr. Rhodes, would you like a drink?"

So cordial and pleasant.

"Ava and I are done for today. I'll be coming to the office at her next available appointment to discuss how we will proceed."

My heart splits in two at the notion of robbing my family. I swore to myself that I wouldn't touch any of their clients. Hurting my father isn't what my move was about.

"Robert, honestly..."

"We look forward to seeing you soon." Damon sits beside me at the table, watching me while Robert packs away his belongings.

"I'll call you, Miss Monroe." Robert leans down, and without warning he presses a kiss to my cheek before he whispers, "Don't let anyone steal your thunder."

He's never done anything like this before. He's all handshakes and shoulder taps and squeezes.

"Mr. Coldwell, I will see you in the near future."

With a wink in my direction, he leaves.

Grabbing my jacket and my purse, I follow suit, hoping that Damon will somehow be happy with the fact Robert wants to come to the office.

Boy, is my hope a letdown.

I feel him stalk me to his building, following me past the security barriers to the elevator. Much like on my first day, everyone makes way for him, and when the doors ding open and he walks in, no one makes a move to follow him.

"Miss Monroe." My name on his lips is sinful even with the angry edge.

The eyes of the world feel trained on me as I remain rooted to the concrete floor. Neither one of us makes a move in our battle of wills. The other elevator announces its arrival, and like they don't want to be present for what's about to happen, everyone around me squeezes into the box like they're sardines.

"Do not make me come get you."

"Or what?"

"It's quite simple, Ava," he bites out as he lunges toward me and drags me with him. His grasp of my arm is hard, and although I try to shake him off, the heat of his touch is like a sedative. "You don't fuck with me."

A low, maniacal laugh escapes me.

His pissed-off stare narrows on mine. "You will not help the competition on my time."

"I was on my lunch break."

"Until you are no longer employed by me. Until I let you go..." Damon comes closer, and although I step back, there's nowhere for me to go. I'm boxed in and surrounded by him and his scent. "You will be on my time."

The doors open with a high-pitched ring that reverberates through me. He's so close that his hot breath soaks into my hair and the angry thrum of his pulse is visible on his neck.

Without warning he breaks away from me, walking past the wide-eyed floor receptionist to the door that leads to the offices.

"Come," he orders, looking back at me. When I don't follow, he adds, "Now."

Saving myself a scene, I follow his command until we're closed off in his office.

I didn't pay much mind to it when I was here last. A wall of artfully stacked bookshelves with works from this house runs along one side, while the other two floor-to-ceiling glass walls overlook Bryant Park and Little Brazil. The dark wood desk almost feels too traditional for the space, but the brushed steel legs give just enough quirk that it fits perfectly.

"You're going to call Robert Rhodes back, and you are going to make sure he is here tomorrow."

"I can't do that."

"Yes, you can," he states, taking off his suit jacket and throwing it onto the coffee table. "And before you lie to me, note that I am fully aware of the contract you had."

"What?"

A devious grin cuts his face, and while I search it for any hint of the man who seduced me at the bar, he comes flush to me, his hand hooking into the pocket of my jacket.

"They didn't deserve you." His murmur is so low that it's almost inaudible, but the hardness in his eyes softens to a silken chocolate. Bittersweet and intense. Over-whelming.

Our breaths break the silence, permeating the air until the electricity between us zaps and zings. Focus unwavering, Damon grasps my hand, bringing it up between us. He holds it open in his palm as he places my phone in it and says, "Robert's right—you shouldn't let them rob you of your merit."

Tears fill my eyes with guilt and great sadness of what I'm about to do. The betrayal I'm about to commit against my own future.

"Call him," Damon whispers softly, his dark hair falling into his rounded eyes.

Twisting away from him, I do as he instructs. Robert picks up almost immediately, and it takes seconds to arrange for him to come see me. And even when he ends the call, I keep the phone glued to my ear, buying myself a waif of time to pull myself together.

"You're doing the right thing." Damon's softened gravel coats the shell of my ear.

His hands surround my waist as his front molds to my back. Like when we danced, my head lolls onto his shoulder. Damon is so tall, but with heels, my lips manage to rake along the underside of his jaw.

"For you and your company."

Spinning me to face him, he grasps my face in his hands. "It's your company too. Whilst you are here, this is your house. Until I no longer require it, your time is mine, Ava. You are mine until I let you go."

Lowering his face to mine, he presses his lips to my cheek. Every part of me is trembling. I'm choking on my unshed tears and my thumping heartbeats.

"He doesn't ever put his lips on you again. Do you understand?"

I have no idea what's happening right now, because he's being every bit the man I wanted in that bar and every bit the man I loathe.

"Answer me."

Shaking my head, I push away from him, only to be pulled tighter to him. As much as I try to fight him off, he's solid and stronger than me. His shirt strains over his shoulder as he holds on to me.

"I hate you."

"You were never meant to like me." With an acid chuckle, he lets me go. "Now, be a good little mouse and show the world who you belong to."

CHAPTER FOUR

AVA

Robert looks around the meeting room while he takes a gulp of his black coffee. I had his favorite bakery drop off some pastries, but he's barely touched the one on his plate.

"The contract is iron-clad," he finally says. "I'd be lying if I said I didn't expect it. I know the kind of man Damon Coldwell is."

The door opens and like his name summoned him, Damon walks in with Francesca in tow. The atmosphere cools, and the air thickens around us.

"Mr. Rhodes, it's good to see you again so soon." His eyes flicker to me and then back to Robert as he introduces Francesca. "She's the CFO. We sat together for a while last night and put together a forecast on how we expect the book to do based on interest and demand."

Robert laughs dryly, and all the while I'm taking the other woman in. Her gold-tipped brown hair dazzles under the lights like it's glitter dusted, and her blue jeweled eyes sparkle. She's an average height, but her build is petite and toned beneath the clingy shift she's wearing.

From nowhere, the thought strikes me: *Has Damon fucked her too?*

Like he can read my thoughts, a hand brushes her shoulder while he pulls out one of the chairs for her to sit.

Falling to the pit of my stomach with a wringing ache, my heart wilts.

"Is that why you're asking for more?" Robert sits straighter, all easiness evaporating from him.

"You stand to make a lot more, and you'll have a team of copy editors and publicists at your disposal. While Miss Monroe will still be on hand to help you, you will have other resources too."

The way he says it doesn't sound like I'll be working with Robert at all. Glancing over the spreadsheet with figures that Francesca puts in front of me, I'm impressed. I always thought that the value of his work was being underestimated, but seeing it like this...

"You stand to make forty percent more than what Monroe forecasted." I turn to face him. I refuse to let Damon walk into my meeting and undermine me.

He can keep his games the hell away from my clients. I might not be happy about taking Robert from Monroe, but I'm not letting anyone else have him.

"Money isn't everything." Robert faces me. "I didn't leave Monroe because of the money."

No, neither did I. But yet, currency is the gospel we all live by.

"The success of *Behind the Headlines* will be measured in sales and how it grosses. Your work deserves the credit."

His booming laugh fills the room. "Sounds like you're using my own words against me."

"I'm learning," I chuckle back at him, while meeting Damon's gaze.

I won't lose to you.

"Robert." Damon levels me with a rueful smirk before focusing back on the client. "When you sign, we'll have a team of people who will work to get you on the cover of every magazine and on every relevant show. We don't just want to sell your book to the obvious market; we'll put it on coffee tables and bedside tables across the world. We'll put *you* center stage in front of the world."

Had anybody else made the statement, I would've said it was bold. But knowing what I know of him...I'm sure Damon has it all figured out with a contingency for every potential eventuality.

"It's afternoon somewhere in the world, so why don't we go grab a drink and I can clear up any issues you might have. I know Miss Monroe has a meeting after this, but I've had my schedule cleared for the rest of the day."

Son of a bitch!

Robert looks to me in question like he's asking my approval on what to respond.

"I'm sorry I can't join you today. But I promise to catch up with you first thing tomorrow." And with a scowl at Damon, I stand at the same time as Robert. With slow intent, I step closer to him, and holding his shoulders, I press a kiss to his cheek. "Call me whenever," I murmur. "I'm always here to help you," I add, lingering in Damon's blind spot.

"Shall we go discuss the contract?" Damon grits out with enough saccharine in his voice to make it sound pleasant.

When we walk out of the meeting room, he hands Francesca the papers he brought down with him, swapping them for a copy of the contract. His hands linger a little too long over hers as they exchange a silent conversation that ends with them both snickering.

Without my consent, jealousy sets in, burning through my veins like poison. There's no sense to it, but I can't help it. I can't help wanting Damon as much as I hate him.

I bite down on my lip as we get in the elevator, and during the short ride to my floor, all I can do is watch the way they look standing beside each other. Francesca's so delicate and pretty next to his tall, broad body and his dark features.

"Talk soon?" Robert nudges me as the doors ping open for me.

"Anytime you need me." With a squeeze of his arm I leave them, rushing to my office in search of refuge, but the dang glass offers me no shelter to fall apart and piece myself back together.

———

"Hey stranger!" Owen pops his head into my office in the devious way he has almost every day since I started working here. "You look like you need a taco and margarita stat."

I do, but I can't. For one my head just isn't in the right place for alcohol, and I want to finish the manuscripts I inherited from my predecessor so I can focus on Robert and the other three projects I brought to CPM with me.

"If you rain check on me again, I'm likely to bitch out. The testosterone on this floor is too much for me. Ellis and Morgan are pushing my limits with their two-horse race shit."

"I need to finish up with Marcella's load. The publicist team is hounding me for live dates." Pulling my glasses off, I throw them onto the stack of paper in front of me tagged with Post-it notes for rewrites.

"Looks like you're about to go cross-eyed. Come on, Avie..." He whines the ridiculous nickname he's given me as he settles himself into the armchair of the small sitting area to the corner. "I can even order in. We can sit right here where you can death stare at work. Just have lunch with me. I need girl time."

"Fine, but you call me Avie again and my taco will go so far up your ass you'll have a whole new meaning to ring sting." Dragging my heels across the concrete floor, I check my phone for a reply from Lacie about dinner tonight.

BBF: Charlie Hunnam and a dirty burger is exactly what I need. XoX

I'm not sure about the dirty burger after Mexican. I don't think I can take it.

"Food is on its way!" Owen croons, kicking off his shoes before resting his feet on the arm of the small sofa beside his seat. "Heard you landed Robert Rhodes."

What?

"How...?"

"My dear, news travels faster than you know in this place. Besides, I told you...transparency is a thing here."

"Who else knows?"

"Who doesn't?" he counters. "I didn't think you had it in you, Ava girl."

"He hasn't signed yet, and fuck you!"

"Hasn't he? Because the press release has just gone out. Robert Rhodes is all over CPM's website."

It's not possible. It can't be.

Picking up my phone from the coffee table, I find another message from Lacie and a string of them Marsh.

BBF: This is not what I had in mind with kicking major ass. WTF???

Ava: I can explain. X

I ignore the trail of abuse from Marsh, blocking his number before deleting his contact. Then without hesitation I check CPM's website. It's all there. Publicity that takes weeks, if not months, to hammer out.

An avalanche of hurt and guilt smothers me until I honestly think I'm about to wither into nothing. How must my father be feeling? How disappointed is he? How relieved must he be that he didn't give me the job?

"You okay?" Owen's question echoes in the distance, behind the chaos of my thoughts.

Without reply, I stand, grabbing my jacket and purse from the rack by the door before I walk out of my office. I don't look back even as Owen calls me.

I can't be here anymore. I don't belong here. This isn't me.

Staring at the floor buttons in the elevator, I press the one I know I shouldn't after a while. The hum of the doors as they close slashes through me, turning the dirt inside me until I'm vibrating with so much anger, I can't fist my hands or clench my teeth tight enough to get to grips with it.

I'm a trembling shell of fury as I walk through the top floor. My designer heels clack behind me as I ignore the first assistant and launch into the inner circle of what has become my hell.

The other assistant isn't present, and without pause, I walk into Damon's office. I have no fucking clue what I'm doing, but I dump my shit on his coffee table before I pour myself a long drink of the whiskey I know to be the most expensive.

I don't even like the liquor, but hey, it's at least a hundred dollars or so I'm taking from him. It's nothing compared to what he took from me today.

Kicking my shoes off, I drop to my ass in front of the window overlooking the city. My heart in my throat burns as I sip at my drink, not able to taste it through the storm inside me.

Looking across the city, loneliness blankets me, and I realize that I have no idea what I'm doing anymore. I'm lost.

CHAPTER FIVE

DAMON

"I'm sorry, Mr. Coldwell, I tried to remove her, but..." William doesn't have to finish for me to know what awaits me in my office.

"Go home, William." I sigh with exhaustion.

Today can go fuck itself already. The office is darkening when I walk in, early evening setting across the city. Ava's sitting on the floor hiccupping like she's been crying for fucking hours.

I don't need this shit.

Before I deal with her, I head to the drinks cart. I need something to tame the shitstorm inside me.

I need something to sedate the fucking need to break something or someone. Taking a glass from the bottom shelf, I reach for the Glenfiddich, but it's gone. And there's only one person stupid enough to touch my shit in my space without my say-so.

Here goes... Grabbing my glass, I go sit beside her, hoping she doesn't fucking start bitching at me the moment she's aware of my presence.

I pour myself a drink, gritting my teeth at the lightness of the bottle. How much has she had? I don't recall the bottle being this empty.

"I really wanted to shout at you," she hiccups, looking up at me with sloping eyes. Surprisingly there aren't any tears, and although her speech is a little slurred, she looks like she's holding the booze all right. "But—" Another hiccup. "—I don't want to give you the satisfaction."

Drinking the measure I poured myself all in one go, I chuckle as I pour myself a full glass to match the one she's got in her hand.

"This is a twenty-five-thousand-dollar bottle of whiskey, and I'm pretty sure you've managed to drink at least a couple months' salary of it."

She laughs, and like at the bar, it makes me like her more than I should. Ava has the kind of warm and inviting laugh that makes you forget yourself. It's a fatal attraction. Like her anger and her sass.

"Dock it." Chinking her glass to mine, she hiccups again. "I'm a terrible drunk."

I've seen worse.

"Water?" Although I ask, the idea of getting up isn't pleasant.

"Do you want water, Mr. Fuck Control?"

"No." I sip some more of my drink, and with certainty that I'm going to regret it, I ask, "Why did you want to shout at me today?"

"Because." She hiccups again, and I have to hold in my chuckle because she's not even finished and she's already gulping down some more liquor. "Because you're an asshole who's ruining my—" Hiccup. "—life."

"And how am I—" I feign a hiccup. "—ruining your life?"

"See? Asshole."

"I'm sure there are better adjectives to describe me."

"No, it sums you up nicely." Her mouth quirks to one side, and in an impeccably coordinated move for her inebriated state, she turns to lean her back on the glass, her legs spread alongside mine. All of a sudden, New York gets a little prettier. "You're tall, dark, and handsome. Hot actually, and you're not so bad down there." She gestures at my cock with her glass, dark manicured toes nudging my thigh. "But then you do shitty things, like film us fucking and then blackmailing me... You made me do shitty things too. So, yeah...asshole."

There's nothing I can say in my defense because it's all true. Instead, I finish my drink, and when I reach forward to pour myself another at the same time as she goes to hand me the bottle, our gazes catch. Close. Wide. And Ava really is beautiful.

She's tall, slender, and tanned. Her thick hair is so dark that it makes her eyes a bright cerulean even in the dark. Hypnotizing with the pink blushing her high cheekbones.

"Truce?" she murmurs with the faintest hitch.

Fuck.

"For now." Ava barely waits until I've finished before her lips press to mine. Plump and pretty even in feeling.

"I still hate you."

"I still own you." Licking across her lips, I cup her face with both hands, pulling her up onto her knees.

Kneeling on the ground beside me, she's a contained ball of fire, and fuck if I don't want to break her open until she's an out-of-control, blazing inferno.

My heart drums along to her breathy groan as her mouth opens for me. She's all aged oak and smoked wood with the most delicate hint of her. Sweet and sassy and soft.

The urge to devour her is irresistible as I taste and breathe her in. With her nails raking across my jaw, I could be putty in her hands.

Ava's all breathless and shaky when I pull away. Glittering eyes widen on mine, and when I lick the residue of her from my lips, her thumb sweeps across them, parking itself right in the middle.

We sit in the silence with the city twinkling around us for longer than I can bear. The need to fuck and the urge to soothe is too much. And truce or not, emotions and feelings are further than we can go.

Grabbing the bottle, I stand, the loss far too palpable.

"He won't answer my calls."

The waver in her voice makes me pause, and the sight of her at my feet is more satisfying than any liquor or workout or...

Stop, I tell myself before things get more complicated than they need to be.

Reaching down, I grasp Ava's hand and pull her to her feet. Before the silence engulfs us again, I say the one thing that will douse whatever this is. "I'm an asshole. He's an asshole. We're all assholes."

As I predicted, she pulls back with a snarl. "My father is not an asshole."

"Yeah, he is." Heading back to the drink cart by my desk, I place the bottle of whiskey back. When I turn, she's right there, so close that I can feel her potent heat.

"No."

"Yes," I snap at her.

Ava takes a step back. My desk at her ass blocks her escape.

"It's what it takes to be who we are. Mice can't fight lions."

"Sometimes they do," she retorts with a growl.

"In fairy tales perhaps. But not in boardrooms. You ever think that's why he picked Marsh over you?" Her hand flies through the air, and I only just manage to catch it in mine before it greets my face. "You're soft, Ava. You believe in peace and harmony and kumbayas. But that's not how this world works."

"I hate you so much."

"Because I'm right."

"You ruined everything." She fists the unbuttoned collar of my shirt.

"You came to me. You left your family and came here. Did you think that you were going to get special treatment?" Her audible swallow is all the answer I get. "I'm not that guy, and you're not that woman. You're better. You deserve to be at the top, but you need to wise up on what that entails."

Pulling away from her, I give her space to walk away. There's no hesitation. She slips her heels back on and grabs her things from the coffee table. And although the place feels like it magnifies with every step she takes away from me, I hold my ground.

Before she makes it out of the door, I tell her, "Truce is over."

There's no place for feelings in business. After all, isn't that what I just preached to her?

CHAPTER SIX

DAMON

The sun rises high above the cityscape. Grayson from legal sits opposite me with a scowl on his face. We'd agreed to give the transition a cooling period before we announced Robert Rhodes as one of ours. We should've had enough time to produce a real fanfare that would've been the focus of the media this morning. Instead, people are talking about publishing wars, broken families, and sordid affairs.

"Fix this." I slam my hands down on my desk in frustration. I've never made headlines; I've made darn sure that the only headlines I'm a part of are the ones reported by the media umbrella of CPM.

"Damon, the media is the least of your concerns. This suit..." He gestures down at the paperwork on the desk with both hands. "You didn't even give Monroe twenty-four hours before you made the announcement."

"Somebody leaked the news. I wasn't going to let it become worthless gossip. This needed a bang." Standing, I toy with the different bottles of whiskey on the cart beside my desk. "We've been sued before."

"Not like this, and certainly not this publicly."

I check my watch. It's barely past seven in the morning, but... *Fuck it.*

I pick a twelve-year-old Japanese single malt. The honeyed color and sweetness bring out Ava's delicate scent still trapped between these walls. My mouth waters as I pour and then inhale the warm liquor.

Dex saunters in unannounced with Fran hot on his heels. It feels like my office has become a revolving door for everyone. No one bothers to fucking knock anymore.

Taking the whiskey from me, Fran hands me a cup of coffee. "Let's stick to the soft stuff this morning." She smiles, sitting on the edge of my desk. When I sit back into my chair, she leans forward, smoothing over the creased shirt I've had on my back for almost twenty-four hours.

"What do you want to do?" Fran asks, sniffing the whiskey she's still holding. "Fuck, I miss this so much."

Her hand falls from my shoulder to then settle on her stomach like she needs a reminder of why she can't have a hard drink. "I've gone through the figures, and you have options, but as CFO, I have to remind you that a loss like this will affect our turnover dramatically."

"The only option here is to cut the Monroe girl loose." Dex leans over the side of my desk. "It's not about options or what you want to do. It's about what needs to be done. This whole thing has gone far enough, Damon. Monroe isn't worth it."

"God, you're a pussy," Fran spits at him. "The whole point was to weaken them. Take away their most valuable assets to bring their market value down."

"You're all fucking crazy." Grayson blows out a long breath. "But a lawsuit of this magnitude puts them in an awkward position, and it could be beneficial in terms of a buyout."

"See?" Fran sticks her tongue out at Dex. "Options, dickhead."

"So mature, Franny. My faith in your mothering abilities just rocketed."

"More than I can say for my faith in your dick ability." Rolling her eyes, she focuses back on me, putting the whiskey down before she reaches for her large purse and takes out her MacBook. "I looked into the baller biography you mentioned yesterday. I'm not into basketball, but from my googling, I got the impression Callum Warner is king of the court right now."

"Callum Warner is writing a book?" Dex pulls up a chair from the small meeting table. "Can he even read?"

"God, you're an entitled prick, you know that?" Fran grits out. "Anyway, he's set to earn over three hundred million this season on endorsements alone. That's impressive and it tells me that whatever he puts out will bring in enough to swallow any loss." She laughs, and jumping from my desk she adds, "Now tell me my game is off!"

The look she gives me is identical to yesterday's outside the boardroom.

"This isn't college. Stop using me to make her jealous."

"Getting knocked up has cost you your game."

Looking up at me, she laughs. "Careful, Damon, you might actually care about this one."

Fran isn't wrong, but she's not right either. I care about Ava. I care about her assets and what she can bring to my company. It's why I wanted her here in the first place.

"She's an asset," I grumble at her.

"Oh, gathered that when I looked up Warner's agent."

"What the fuck are the two of you talking about?" Dexter groans, echoing Grayson.

"I'm going to go over this again. Find a loophole or make one that will stand up. Just don't fuck any more shit up, all right?" Grayson collects his things, and before he leaves, he presses a kiss to the top of Fran's head. "I love you. Stay out of trouble."

"Aww," Dexter teases her when Grayson disappears out of the door. "Pity you won't agree to marry him."

"Shut up, asshole!" she smarts back at him. "Anyway, I need to talk to my boss alone."

"Technically I'm your boss too."

"Technically you can go fuck yourself. Now, seriously...I have womb talk to tend to."

Ugh, I knew this was coming. I've tried to put it off as much as I can because I don't want to think about Fran leaving CPM, even if it is just for a year or so, until the baby is old enough to be left with childcare. I've tried to talk to her about options, but a wet nurse is too medieval, and the idea of breastfeeding at work isn't appealing to her either. *Ugh!*

When Dex leaves us, she takes his chair and sits there looking at me with narrowed eyes.

"Go on, tell me the bad news." I twist to face her. "I'm still all for a wet nurse or opening a company crèche."

"You're a bad, bad man, Damon Coldwell."

"The crèche would benefit the staff..."

"I'm not talking about maternity leave. We've settled that. Come end of June I'm officially out of here, and I won't be coming back for a year—we discussed this—we agreed." She rolls her eyes as she twists her MacBook to me. "If this was the real reason for bringing Ava here, why bother with Rhodes?"

I look over the photo of Ava and her friend. She's perfection; thick pink lips, neat straight nose, and piercing eyes that feel like they see right into your soul, even in the picture.

"Why not?"

"I'm a pregnant woman. Don't make me exert myself."

"Business, that's why. Monroe were meant to be too busy licking their wounds to make a move for Callum Warner."

"But not only have they made a play for him, they're suing the shit out of our asses!"

"Like you said, Warner will more than swallow any losses."

"And Ava?" Fran scoots her chair closer until her knees touch mine. "Are you prepared to lose her?"

"Once Warner is in..."

"I'm going to stop you right there before you become a liar to everyone around you." Cupping my jaw, she leans closer. "I've always loved you, Damon. You're the brother I never had. I've held my tongue and waited for you to realize that this..." She looks around us. "This place isn't everything. I mean, you've had everything all your life. Your parents loved you beyond reason. They gave you the best life possible with all the things a person could ever want or need. You have no reason to be this man. You might think you don't care if she leaves, but that's because she's here now. Don't spite your heart for the sake of your wallet and your pride."

She stares me out with soft glittering eyes. And while

her hands smooth down my face, I hold in all the things I want to retort.

Standing, she sighs as she packs her laptop back into her purse. I walk her toward my office door, pausing halfway to adjust my shirt.

"Listen," she breathes, stepping to me. Her hands busy themselves righting me before they land on my chest. "It doesn't matter what Grayson and Dex say. At the end of the day, this is your company and you can do whatever you want."

"I'm glad you think so."

"I've told you a thousand times before, I'll always have your back. But please, make sure Warner happens. As the CFO, I'd like to leave with fireworks and champagne popping."

"You can't even drink." A laugh finally leaves my lips, and she wraps her arms tightly around me.

"I'll get drunk off the smell."

I hug her back, and in the middle of our snickers, a soft "Oh" breaks us apart.

CHAPTER SEVEN

DAMON

Ava stands frozen in the open doorway, eyes flitting between Fran and me.

"I'm sorry," she finally speaks. "I can come back later."

Licking her red painted lips, she looks at me with disappointment furrowing her brows.

I hate it. I hate that all I can think about is how I want to devour her mouth. How much I want to push Fran out of the door so I can have her.

"We're done here," Fran says, walking past her. When she's out of Ava's sight, she looks back at me and winks while closing the door.

God, she's such a girl sometimes.

I head back to my messy desk, and before I sit down, a white envelope lands in front of me.

"I saw the headlines," Ava murmurs. "You got what you wanted. I can't go back to Monroe after this and..." She pauses when I rise and round the desk. "And I can't stay here."

Fran's words swirl around my head—*Are you prepared to lose her?*

I fucking hate her sometimes. She's always getting into my business.

Picking the envelope up, I put it in Ava's hand.

"Rip it." I level her soft gaze with my pissed-off one.

I knew she'd bolt first chance she got. I just didn't think she'd pick a shitstorm of a day.

Maybe she's more lion than I thought.

"Damon..." She holds it out to me.

"I said rip it up." Grabbing her other hand, I close it around the envelope. "I told you, you only leave when I say. Until then I own you."

"You don't own shit," she laughs with tears flooding her eyes. "Blackmail doesn't give you ownership of me."

"Then walk out, Ava." In spite of my anger, I step closer. "Leave. After all, the press will want something new to expose of you."

"What is wrong with you?" Her growl vibrates through me with a fire so strong that all I can do is grab her and throw her on the desk. Leaning over her, I brace myself on the cluttered tabletop with my dick hardening in my pants. "I'm trying to help you!" she spits breathlessly.

The only thing she's doing is driving me insane. Her shimmering eyes soften as I lower myself on her. My erection presses to the bottom of her stomach and throbs to my hammering pulse as I breathe her in greedily.

"You don't need me anymore."

I need her more now than I did before, because I won't take a hit lying down, and I certainly won't lose to anyone. Especially not a blind old man.

Ava looks perplexed as I stand and pull her up to a sitting position.

"You're not going anywhere."

Surprisingly there's no argument, only scrutiny and deep consideration while she silently studies me. Eyes roaming up and down my chest, they settle blankly on the open collar.

"You didn't go home." She drops the envelope scrunched up in her hand and presses her manicured finger to the first done-up button.

I bark a curt laugh, and when she looks up at me with those ocean eyes brimming with pity, my clenched mouth loosens.

"I have one thousand four hundred and thirty-three people on my payroll that I can't let down. So no, I didn't go home."

Her eyes soften, dropping down my front to where her legs are spread around me.

I hate her so much. I hate that she can so easily unravel me. I hate that she has the audacity to pity me. And most of all I hate that even hating Ava, all I can think about right now is fucking her. All I want is to bury myself in her and punish her flesh for all the ways she's got me all fucked up.

"What do you want from me, Damon?" she asks, her finger raking down my front to the top of my belt.

Her chest is heaving. Her voice is raspy. Her cheeks are warmed crimson.

"You," I state.

"You can't have me." She's wrong. I can have her, and the way her body opens up a little more for me, coming closer so that her cunt hovers over my hard-on...it's all the proof I need.

Lowering myself into Grayson's vacated chair, I bring myself flush to her, my chest bracketed by her thighs as I breathe into her chest, "I already have."

Ava tries to push away, but in her efforts, she lands in my lap, and when she tries to stand, I hold her down.

"You can't have me!"

"But I can smell how much you want it."

"I meant professionally." She pushes the heels of her hands into my chest and launches herself off me. She stumbles a little in her high heels, but when she finds her balance, she perches on the edge of the desk. "What do you want, Damon?"

I can tell she'll give whatever I ask for, so long as I don't make her accept the fact that she wants me more than she can bear. It's an affliction we share.

"Callum Warner."

She levels me with a heated glare and her cute little nose flaring. She's angry. I like angry Ava.

"No, I'm not—"

"You are because there's no one else that can land him as easily as you."

"If that's what you wanted to begin with, you got the wrong woman," she snarks. When she tries to stand, I rise and block her. "You must really think very little of me."

"On the contrary, if I did, I wouldn't want you here, and I certainly wouldn't have fucked you."

"Stop!" Her hand pushes to the base of my neck. "I won't play your game anymore."

"Yeah, you will." I lean over her even as her hand tightens around my throat. "Because you want to. You want to take as much from Marsh as he took from you. It's why you're here. To prove you're better."

"I know I'm better, just as I know you're trying to play me again."

"I'm giving you the opportunity to break him."

Ava swallows. She can pretend she's holier than me, but we're exactly the same. She only needs to accept it and embrace it.

"Take what you want, Ava," I whisper into her ear.

"You don't know what I want."

"Yes, I do." I nudge her legs open wider, lodging myself flush to her. "I know exactly what you want." Closing my hand around her slender throat, I press my thumb to the bottom of her jaw.

I want it too.

With her head tipped back, her hair cascading around her, it's impossible not to undress her with my eyes. It's impossible for me to contain any of my need to take what I want right now.

I lick up her neck to her ear. "You want it as much as I do."

There's no argument. Her pulse pounds in my hand, the skin beneath my lips prickling with her desire.

Hands flattened to my stomach, she gasps, "Where's the camera? I'd like to know where to look this time."

It's cute she's still sassing me, but it's pointless.

I run the tip of my nose over the side of her face before touching our foreheads so that our eyes are boring into each other. "Cheese, little mouse."

Standing, I bring her up with me, and when she's on her feet, I spin her to face the city below us.

Without my aid Ava sheds the black leather jacket she's wearing over her clingy, black wool dress. Peering over her shoulder at me, she twists her hair over the other suggestively. In a bid for control, she folds her body over my desk, her gaze unwavering from mine while she hitches her dress up her legs and over her ass.

Fuck, it's so perfect with the tail of her nude lacy thong accentuating its roundness.

I would truce this shit, but we both know this is just a part of our war. I'll fuck her and she'll stay because she doesn't have any other real choice.

Squeezing the tops of her thighs, I lift her legs, tucking them beneath her body so she's on full display to me with only the skimpy underwear covering her asshole and her cunt.

Breathless moans fill the air as I trail my finger over the tail of her thong, through her crease to the wet lace over her pussy. Her front flat to the cluttered wood, she curls her hands around the edge of the desk by her feet.

I lower myself and take a bite of her ass cheek, licking and sucking down to her pussy as I free my cock. Ava's writhing on my tongue before I've even tasted her bare flesh. But even like this, she tastes so fucking good. Too good.

Hitching her thong to the side, over her butt cheek, I lick around her swollen entrance. She's so fucking wet that her juices drip down my chin and her thighs before I have a chance to drink them all in.

We may never admit it out loud, but whatever this is between us, it's obliterating. It cuts through all the shit: hate, attraction, lust...this surpasses it all. It's a primal need, always simmering in the background, and now we've reached boiling point. The only way to sate the craving is to let it overflow and spill. Let it burn through us.

"Oh, fuck. Fuck. Fuck. Fuck!" Ava cries huskily as I press my tongue into her tight cunt, my teeth grazing her folds the deeper I bury my face in her. And with the press and sweep of my thumb over her clit, she comes apart, her walls clenching and her heels pressing into my shoulders with the sweetest bite.

Fisting my dick, I stand over her, taking in the marled blush of her orgasm on her exposed skin.

So fucking beautiful. It's all I can think as her thick hair splays around her. The higher I drag her dress, the more I get of the faint trail of miniscule stars and planets that wind up her spine. Delicate and elegant, just like her.

Releasing my cock, I bracket her waist and pull her up until her back is to my front and I'm nudging at her wet heat. I could fuck her like this. I could squeeze her cries into silence with my bare hands as she begs me to go easy on her, but then I wouldn't kill the curiosity that niggles at me every time I see her face with my eyes and in my thoughts. I want to see what she looks like when I fuck the pleasure right out of her.

A low groan hums through her as I sit her on the desk, facing me. And grabbing her ass, I impale her on my dick to a raspy, garbled cry she buries in my chest. Her hands sweep up my shoulders with every hard, blunt thrust and slap of our flesh that has her legs tightening around me for purchase.

Hands cupping my jaw, she looks up at me with heavy-lidded and trembling eyes. Her blazing blues melt through me with a force that is beyond anything I've ever felt.

"Cheese, little mouse."

Ava's stare doesn't waver once. No matter how deep I drive or how hard I punish her cunt.

She takes everything I give her with her pants and her gasps and moans and choked cries. She doesn't let go or relax her hold on me as I fuck her, pounding and pounding and pounding until we're a wreck. Breaking and shattering. Crashing.

And while my cock is still pulsing inside her clenching cunt, her thumb trapped between my teeth, she still holds me with those eyes. It's like she's stealing everything with her soulful depths. And in this moment, I know that I would break every fucking rule for her...even my own.

I can't let that happen. She can have all the control she wants, but the power has to stay mine.

CHAPTER EIGHT

AVA

One month later

Lacie's pissed. We've never done each other professional favors. It's not how we operate, and until now, there hasn't been any crossover in our fields and clients. The last month has been hell without her to talk to, so much so that Owen has become the only person I talk to outside work.

Dad is ignoring me, Mom pretty much told me she needed time to forgive me, and Lacie *hmms* and *ahs* during our conversations. I'm on my own, and surprisingly, I'm surviving. No thanks to Damon and his constant demand to know where I am on Callum Warner.

The answer: right where I was when Lacie told me that if I wanted to be considered I'd have to work like every other literary agent and editor approaching them. Again, no thanks to Damon. Her hate of him and his guts is feral. And completely warranted.

Lacie's become a stumbling block as far as Warner is concerned, but I've found a possible resolution.

It's taken me long enough.

"Do you ever use the door?" Damon calls from my open doorway.

He's standing tall and broad, his black tailored suit and light blue shirt molded to his chiseled body. The shirt is so light that it's more like a blue-tinged white. It brings out the golden undertone of his skin and the pink in his lips.

My mouth waters as I take him in. My stomach swoops. Like I'm physically hungry for him.

"I open and close it occasionally," I tell him, slipping my white suit jacket over my nude lace camisole. "Typically, I open it in the mornings and close it when I leave. Does that answer your question, Mr. Coldwell?"

We're treading a thin line since fuck-gate or fuck-gate-the-second. Or rather since I walked out of his office trying not to look like I'd had seven shades of Wednesday fucked out of me.

Damon is like a car wreck. I don't want to look at him. I don't want to acknowledge him. I don't want to want him. But I can't help myself on any of those fronts.

My world would be better off without him. And yet, I can't imagine it without him. There's something about this man that brings out the parts of me that aren't the prettiest but make me stronger nonetheless.

Still, I'll never admit that, not in a million years.

My nude stilettos hammer on the concrete floor as we walk side by side to the elevator. Damon has his typical "I own everything" swagger on—hands in his pockets, straight face, eyes taking everything in. A king looking over his kingdom.

"You don't have to come," I tell him as we wait for the elevator.

I don't know why he's insisting on coming to my lunch meeting with Robert, but it's annoying the crap out of me.

He turns his face to look at me, eyes raking over me from head to toe. "But I do."

"Oh my God!" *He's jealous.* "Robert is old enough to be my father." I turn to face him, and his eyes go to the low V of my top that peeks from the blazer. "Scratch that, he's old enough to be my grandfather."

"Your point?"

"My point is..." How do I say this without sounding like an idiot?

He takes a step back and waits for me to finish with an amused quirk of his lips. "Well?"

"You and I...we're not a thing, and you have no right to be jealous...or whatever."

The doors ding, and the drop of his grin is followed by a stern "Shut up, get in."

I do as he says because I don't have another option if I'm getting to my meeting on time. Once the doors close, I stand as far from him and his brooding as possible.

"If the only reason you're coming is becau—"

"I'm coming because if you're incapable of landing Warner, I want to make sure you don't fuck things up with Rhodes." His offhanded cutoff lands in the pit of my stomach with a sickening crash.

I bite my tongue because I'm the reason Robert is with CPM, not because of any of the other shit Damon threw at him during the contract meeting. And after today, Warner should happen a lot quicker.

We're fifty-six floors above New York City. The music is getting louder as the lights get dimmer, and we're finally done going over the publishing schedule that I've worked on with the production and publicist departments. Right on time for summer break.

"Is everything okay?" Robert asks while Damon is taking a call.

Right on time, Lacie walks in with Callum Warner at her side. Thank God for social media.

"Everything is perfect," I tell him, kind of ogling the basketball player heading our way. Damn, he's so tall that the urge to crane my neck is overwhelming even at a distance. But so I don't make my ruse obvious, I focus on Robert. He'll do exactly what I need him to without any prompting from me.

"You're awfully quiet."

"Sometimes it's nice sitting back."

Callum walks past our table, and as I'd fucking prayed, Robert lights up. He's naturally a Mallards fan, being a Manhattanite all his life. Something I found out in the last part of his book I read through.

"Callum Warner?" he croons, sitting back in his chair and picking up his drink like he's king of the castle.

"Robert Rhodes," Warner sings back. I feel him pause behind me, his long shadow cast over me like the most blessed shade.

They banter back and forth, Warner coming closer with his soft booming voice. And behind him stands Lacie. She's got her eyes narrowed on me like she's got me all worked out. Which she probably has, but in my defense, she told me to work like all the other agents and editors, and a staged encounter like this...is exactly what they would do.

I smile at her, ignoring the fact that we're in this awkward place, and with a sigh and roll of her eyes, she smiles back. She's pissed, but she misses me more. And it's really taking everything in me not to jump her with a hard hug.

"Here, let me introduce you two." Robert takes my hand across the table, holding it up to Warner like I'm some kind of offering. "This is Ava Monroe. Miss Monroe is one of the editors over at Coldwell Press."

I offer him the broadest smile I can muster, and with a wave of my fingers, I say, "Hi."

Robert tells him all about the wonders I'm working on his book. At one point he calls me an angel, something I'm really not. At least not anymore. I don't have to say anything; I sit contentedly quiet while he sells me.

"You have to join us." Robert waves over at a passing waiter and asks him to join the table beside us to ours.

It all happens very quickly, escalating beyond my intention or prediction.

"Don't look so pleased with yourself," Lacie grumbles, but there's a pursed smile on her lips. "How did you know we were coming here?"

Side-glancing at her, I shrug with a proud grin. "You told me to work for it like everyone else...right?"

"Smart-ass." She palms my face with a shoulder bump.

"Wait." Warner breaks away from his conversation with Robert and asks, "Do you know each other?"

I look at Lacie, and when she rolls her eyes, I tell him, "Since kindergarten."

"That's cool. I don't I have any friends that go that far back."

"Ava is a boil on my ass."

"Lacie is..." I pause, trying to come up with something witty, but Damon's stare from across the room scrambles me, and all I can come up with is "Lacie."

"She is kinda special," he chortles, hanging his forearm on the back of her chair.

"That's one way to put it."

"Shut up!" Lacie kicks me under the table with a genuine laugh.

It's sort of a pity that when Damon returns, she becomes a bit snarky even through her professionalism.

It's a wonder that by the time we leave we have a personal invite from Callum to watch their next home game, because the vibes Lacie puts out are anything but inviting.

Lacie makes her excuses to leave soon after Warner, and once we've put Robert in a cab, Damon walks with me the few blocks to Central Park.

We're both quiet; I'm not really sure what to say after his remark when we left the office. And as always, Lacie saves me from the awkwardness.

BBF: I miss you. xox

I smile at her contact photo. She's changed it back to one of us.

Ava: I miss you more. X

Damon comes to a stop at one of the park gates. Turning to me, he studies me.

"Good job," he finally says, his voice serious and deep.

"Thanks." Clutching my purse in my hands, I look up at him.

"Want to grab some ice cream?" he asks from nowhere, and while my heart is thudding relentlessly and everything in me is screaming yes, I can't.

"Actually, I want to go home." I sense his disappointment. Although I'm disappointed too, it's for the best. "Good night, Damon."

I turn and walk away, my heart hammering in my throat and my stomach twisting until I'm so nauseous, I'm clammy.

A hand grabs me by my elbow. I almost go flying off the edge of the pavement onto the road.

Damon pulls me back, turning me to face him. "Wait..."

"Don't, okay?" I shake my head at his drawn face. "I'm not that woman, and you're not that man. Let's not pretend we're something more than this."

Shaking him off, I manage to cross the road and hail a cab before either one of us presses for more. For something we're never going to be.

CHAPTER NINE

AVA

The next couple of days at the office are a blur. I'm rushing from meeting to meeting, trying to keep myself stupidly busy so that I have an excuse to miss the weekly forecast meeting with management. Every moment of quiet I find myself in is tinged with words and whispers of what might have happened if I hadn't walked away the other night.

"This all looks great." Francesca sits back in the chair opposite my desk. Her hair tumbles past her petite shoulders while she takes a sip of the ginger tea that's scented the air around us. "The numbers are incredible, and Damon believes you have Warner in the bag."

"Nothing's concrete." I shuffle the papers in front of me with Damon's words ringing in my ears. *You're incapable of landing Warner...don't fuck things up with Rhodes...*

"That's not what he believes."

There's no point in arguing with her over it; we both know what he believes doesn't mean anything until

Callum is fully on board and a contract is signed. We're both quiet, me waiting for her to leave so I can continue with work, but she has other ideas.

Sitting up, she folds her arms over the edge of the desk and leans over them, leveling me with her bright gaze. "He's stubborn and cantankerous."

"Excuse me?"

"Damon."

"Oh." I hope my indifferent reply doesn't betray my hammering heart at the sound of his name from her lips.

Perhaps her impromptu drop-in to go through figures is a ploy to deliver some kind of warning to stay away from him. Regardless, it's unneeded. She can have him and his pissy attitude and ruthless antics.

My stomach twists at that, making my heart stutter with the sharp groaning ache.

He's a bastard! Complete jerk, I remind myself, but it does nothing to quell the burn in my chest.

"He's incredibly smart, and the problem with being that and stubborn is that he acts like an asshat. Especially when he cares about something...or someone." She pauses, brushing her coiffed hair back like it was messy. "The thing is, he's a spoilt rich brat that feels the need to make more of what was passed to him because this company was the sibling he never had. He loves this place, and when Damon loves something...he will do whatever it takes for it. *Nothing* will stand in his way."

"Francesca—"

"Fran."

"Fran, I'm not sure why you're telling me all this, but there is nothing between Mr. Coldwell and me. He's my boss, and that is all."

She laughs, shaking her head. "He's my boss too."

Okay...

My phone rings and before I pick it up, she grabs the headset, holding it to her chest even though she's placed the call on hold.

"We're friends. That's all." She stands, shaking out her loose dress. It's different from the bodycon outfits she used to wear when I started here almost two months ago. "And beneath the mercurial veneer, he's a good guy."

"I'm sure," I tell her simply as I take the phone from her and hold it to my ear. "Thank you for stopping by." I take the call off hold and answer it.

Walking out of my office, Fran looks back with a soft smile. It's like she's trying to impart some kind of feeling to me. It's a pointless task because I refuse to be the stupid mouse any longer.

———

Three weeks later

The game is on the last quarter. Lacie is practically falling off the edge of her seat on one side of me, as is Damon on the other. I'm not one hundred percent sure what is going on, but the place keeps going crazy every time a player gets close to the semicircle by the hoop.

The atmosphere is electric, and with seats being so close together, I feel Damon's energy pulsing through him. Every time he moves, his body touches mine. Our thighs graze or our arms press together and my heart races like I've been running up and down the court.

I take a sip of my soda to stop myself obsessing over

the way his skin stretches over his muscular forearms when he clenches his hands around his water bottle.

"God, look at those arms..." Lacie groans. "I love a man with strong, ripped arms."

Shit. I look away from Damon and over at her, but she's engrossed on the court. Seems as though my gawking hasn't been caught.

"It's like their muscles have muscles..."

"Yeah." I clear my throat, leaning forward to put my soda down on the floor. And when I sit up, my hand catches on Damon's thigh. I pull away instantly, but it does nothing to diminish the shock from the contact.

Our eyes lock and it doesn't matter how much I try to distance myself because there's a pull that draws me back to him. We're a breath away from touching, and that wisp of space is more painful than anything I've ever felt.

I hate it, and I hate it even more that when his hand falls down to my calf, I feel the touch rushing through my veins like it's giving me life. I detest that all I can think about are all the other times he's touched me and kissed me. My body aches like it's still raw from him.

I'm a fluttering butterfly caught up in his net, and the bizarre thing is that I don't want to be set free.

My throat swells with the trail of his fingers to the crook of my knee. And just as I'm about to self-destruct, the place goes up in roars. Lacie's hands grasp my arm as she pulls me up to her. I'm not really sure what's happening until I glimpse the scoreboard.

"We won! We fucking won!" she screams right in my face. I can't seem to shake her up, and her happiness is infectious in a way that I can't help but celebrate with her.

It takes a while longer for her to come back down to earth, and by the time I manage to break free to find Damon, he's gone. Something inside withers with disappointment. Was he as happy as she was? Did I miss my chance to see him without his carefully controlled front?

CHAPTER TEN

DAMON

It's impossible to ignore Ava across the room. She's probably the most casual woman in here with her loose-fitting jeans and low-cut Henley. And still, she manages to look better than all the other women in their designer clothes and high heels. She and her friend look like the only two normal people here.

"Hey, man." Warner bumps my shoulder as he walks into the room. "Good to see you again."

"You too." I take his proffered hand, and he pulls me into a preppy handshake. "Nice game."

"It went all right. We should've done better." He scouts the room, and when he finds Lacie and Ava, he makes a start for them. "Has Lacie spoken to you yet? After what Robert said about what you guys are doing for his book, I wanted to set up a meeting with you."

I pause within safe distance from the two women so I can speak without being overheard. I don't want Ava to create some false illusion from what I'm about to tell him. Whatever's happening between us is getting complicated and messy. We're pushing and pulling, and I cannot allow myself to care beyond what she can bring to CPM. I can't...no matter how blurred our lines become.

"We can arrange a meeting with me, but if you want the best—" I look to where Ava's standing by the viewing area with Lacie. The two of them are laughing as they clink to whatever Lacie has raised her champagne glass to. "She's it."

I want to wipe the smile off his face as he stares at her with his gray eyes. The way he's studying her puts me on edge, making me regret the moment of candidness, because I've just fed Ava to a wolf. I know what these sports heroes are like: they create an image of wholesomeness that hides a multitude of sins. Maybe not all, but I see the way Warner is looking at the two of them—like they're his next supper. I wonder what his pop star wife would think.

"Word of warning," I tell him as we start in their direction again. "The only relationships at CPM are professional. I don't tolerate scandal."

A low rumble vibrates out of him. "Gotcha!"

"Hey!" Lacie spins to us with a wide grin. "Great game!"

'He's about to say something when she adds, "Yeah, I know, it could've been better." The roll of her eyes is an obvious admonishment of his modesty. "We won again. It's what matters. Nobody wants to play us, not with the streak you're on."

"I'm going to start thinking I'm your favorite client." He looks down on her. Lacie isn't a small woman; she's tall and voluptuous in the way lingerie models are.

"You wish!"

"You disappeared after the game." Ava looks up at me with confusion softening her stare.

"I had to make a call," I lie.

"Oh." One of her hands grazes my arm, and when I tense, she licks her lips. Eyes darting to my forearm, she takes a deep breath as a blush tinges her cheeks. "Nothing serious, I hope."

"No, noth—"

"Oh my God, baby, there you are!" America's newest hit machine pushes between Ava and Lacie, a little unsteady on her feet as she holds her glass of champagne upright. She stands in the middle of us all like an attraction, and I don't miss the way Warner moves her to stand between us.

"This meeting," he sighs, pushing her out of our circle a little more. "I've got three days before we're back so—"

"Wait." His wife pushes in front of him again, her hand twisting in his T-shirt, the other barely saving the drink she clearly doesn't need. "We're meant to be going home tonight."

"You go on without me. I can join you once we're done."

I'm about to tell him we can figure something out when he's back in town, when she turns to Lacie and spits, "You're his agent, right?"

"Holly." Warner tries to grab her, but she smacks his hand away. "Stop."

"She's your fucking agent, so maybe she should do her fucking job!" She reaches for Lacie, but before she gets closer, Callum stops her. Wrapping his arm around her waist, he pulls her back. The jolt sends her champagne glass flying...drenching Ava's bright white top with its contents.

"Oh my God," Holly shrieks like she's in shock. "I'm so sorry."

"It's okay..." Ava breathes. "It's okay."

I can tell she's being polite because the corners of her eyes are creased, and the tip of her nose is twitching.

Fuck, I'm not meant to know those things. Although, she's been pissed at me enough that it's not all that surprising I've memorized them. *Right?*

Her Henley is clinging to her tits like cellophane, and like it, it's gone translucent enough that you can see through the thin cotton and her lace bra.

Shit, I don't even have a jacket to give her. Instead, I hover my hands over her like that's meant to help the situation.

"Excuse me." She hands me her own glass, and crossing her arms over chest she moves briskly for the restrooms.

I feel her mortification, and I have no idea what comes over me, but I thrust the glass in my hand at Warner's wife's chest. "Enjoy," I spit at her when she grasps it, and as I turn to follow Ava, I make sure Warner understands I won't tolerate this kind of crap. "No scandal. No public spectacles. She doesn't go near my staff."

The woman's a fucking mess for someone who's become the darling of the media.

"Damon." Callum chases after me. "I'm sorry, Holly's exhausted—she's not normally like this."

"Your wife isn't my problem." I walk through the female restroom doors to a few gasps.

"What are you doing here?" Ava snaps at me when I pause beside her in front of the mirror. "It's called the female washroom for a reason. Can't you do the math?"

Her pride is visibly hurt, and as I turn her to face me, she covers herself up. There's no one left in here but us,

469

and it bothers me that she's embarrassed in front of me when I've fucked her in a public place and at the office.

"Here—" I take a step back. "—have mine."

"Wha-what the hell are you doing?"

"Giving you the shirt off my back."

Her already flushed complexion reddens a little more.

"Come on, little mouse..." I pull my long-sleeved T-shirt off and hold it up to her. "I've seen your cunt; I don't think your tits are going to make a difference now."

Ava practically chokes at my words, but when the door opens, she takes my offering and runs into one of the cubicles.

Lacie walks in with a green and blue sports top dangling in her hand.

"Holy shit!" she blurts, freezing in her tracks. Her eyes roam up and down my body. "Jesus fucking Christ."

"Feel free to keep going. I can take it."

"Lace?" Ava calls from the stall. "What the fuck just happened?"

"Holly Warner happened," Lacie replies acidly, finding the cubicle and letting herself in. "I'm sorry."

"It's not your fault."

"She's Callum's wife. Of course it's my fault." There's a heavy sigh, and then the shirt she took in comes flying through the gap over the door. "Feel free to leave it off!"

"Lacie!" Ava's bitten whisper is audible through her friend's laughter.

"What? He's got a hot bod..."

"Bad, *bad*, Lacie!"

"Excuse me, I'm not the one that fucked it in public."

"Oh my God, shut the fuck up!"

I pull the top on, trying not to laugh at their conversation. The damn thing is so tight that the seams are pretty much cutting into me. I message my driver to let him know we're leaving, and before Ava dies of embarrassment, I walk out of the restroom.

Warner is waiting outside, his wife nowhere in sight.

"Listen, I want to have the meeting with you before I have to get back. I have a few other editors and agents booked in, but I'd like to hear your pitch. I'm heading home, and if you and Ava would like to join us in the Hamptons, Holly and I would love to have you stay for a couple of days."

"How far are you into the book?"

"It's done. I didn't write it. Words aren't my thing."

"Yeah?"

"Dyslexia." He shrugs. "Lacie got me a ghostwriter, and we worked on it together."

"Look, I was going to visit my parents—they're up in East Hampton. Maybe we can do lunch one of the days?"

"Thanks." He nods. "Also, you might want this." He takes his hoodie off and hands it to me. "Preserve your dignity."

Without another word he saunters away, leaving me to wait for Ava. And the idiot that I am, I text Mom to let her know I'm coming to visit her...with Ava.

I know it's a bad idea, but I like it.

CHAPTER ELEVEN

AVA

The radio murmurs quietly in the background as we navigate through Manhattan, toward my apartment. Damon's been on his phone for most of the journey, and although the atmosphere isn't awkward, it feels strange to be sitting beside him in silence. We've never done silence. We've filled all our moments with flirting and fucking and fighting and fucking and...

"It wasn't that bad."

I look up to find him closer. There's this look on his face that's not the man from the bar, but not the Damon I've come to know either. He almost looks a little uncertain compared to his usual surety.

"Except it was." I comb my poker-straight hair to one side so it curtains my mortification from him. "Note to self: don't wear white around sports wives."

I'm still slowly dying inside over the fact my potential client has gotten an eyeful of my goods.

"Either way," he exhales. His fingertips run through my shield of hair, sweeping it away from my face. An observant pout puckers his lips as his eyes rove over me.

"It doesn't matter," he states, softer than I've ever heard him.

And I'm left wondering if I'm something he cares about. Whether I'm someone to him, rather than a means to an end.

With those thoughts and the way he's still looking at me, it's easy to forget to hate him. I could almost believe I like him. That I admire his lack of scruples and how far he's willing to go for what he loves.

How far is too far?

How far am I willing to go?

Damon sucks all the breath out of me, filling his lungs as his hand cups my face. Thumb smoothing over my hot, pulsing cheek. Lips ghosting mine. Overgrown stubble bristling over my jaw.

I want him to kiss me. And not with ignorance of who he is—I'm fully aware of it. And still, I want it. I want Damon Coldwell. In spite of all his lies and wrong-doings. I want him like I've never wanted anything before. Like he could make losing myself worth it, because he's shown me a stronger side of me. A better side.

"I'm going to kiss you, little mouse," he murmurs over my lips, like he's giving me a real choice. A chance to push him away. To stop.

It's the one choice I want him to keep. I want him to take, and I never want him to stop.

I nod, and he doesn't waste a second. His mouth comes down on mine, hard and commanding as the man I know so well. But his tongue licks into my mouth, slow and savoring. The hand cupping my face slips to my hair as his other rounds my waist and pulls me onto his thighs.

Sitting on his lap with him caressing me with his

strong hands and devouring me with his luscious lips...my heart hasn't beat this fast or this hard in all my life. Ever.

The car jolts to a stop, and the driver's door slams shut. I expect Damon to stop, but if anything, his kiss deepens. We're hot and breathless. My body is begging for more, and I feel his solid need pressed to the side of my thigh.

"Truce," he rumbles when he pulls away.

"Truce."

Opening the car door, he shuffles to the edge of the seat without letting me go. Carefully, he gets out of the car with me still in his arms. He only puts me down when we're on the stoop of my front door. I let us in to the building, and before the door shuts behind us, he's turning me back to him, kissing me all the way to the elevator.

Damon doesn't stop, and the minute the doors roll shut, he hoists me up between his body and the wall. His hands knead my ass with his thick erection grinding into me and his teeth biting at my lips in between licks and sucks.

He walks me to my door with my guidance when we get to my floor. And I don't know how long he continues kissing me up against my apartment door, but eventually he reluctantly puts me down so I can open it.

I grab his hand and start inside but get pulled backward when he doesn't follow. I try to tug him in again, but he remains glued to the spot.

"What? Are you a vampire or something? Do I have to invite you in?"

He pulls me back to him, spinning me like we're in a dance. My back crashes to his front at the same time as his teeth sink into my neck.

Holy fuck.

My knees are ready to cave with him licking at the spot he bit down on. "You need to pack."

"What for?" I turn to face him again, enjoying the way his hands grasp my hips.

"We're going on a field trip." I laugh because he's got that uncertain haze in his eyes, and it's making me nervous. "I'll pick you up at eight tomorrow morning."

"Where are we going?"

Damon visibly takes a moment, like he's trying to get his fill or memorize my face, before he kisses me again. It's a short, firm press of our lips.

Taking a step back, he hooks his thumbs into his jean pockets. "We're having lunch with Warner. He can't wait to sit down with you."

He's chewing on his lip, but his stance is all business. And I'm so fucking stupid. I'm not anything to him—I'm business.

"See you tomorrow." I walk inside and am about to close the door when he holds it open.

"Ava..."

I wait for him to say something. Anything. But Damon stands there looking at me like I'm a problem he needs to solve. Like I mean something, but maybe too much has happened and it's too late for any of it to be more than what it is.

"Good night, little mouse." He grins, but it doesn't have its usual mean glint. And while I watch him walk away, I pull the neckline of his top over my nose and mouth, breathing in his scent.

Good night, Damon.

CHAPTER TWELVE

AVA

Damon comes to a stop in front of the sprawling home. The sun is shining down over a large oak on the front lawn. It's beautiful, and nothing like what I expected from Callum Warner and his wife. They seem like the super-modern show home type.

This house is cute with its off-white cladding and worn gray shingle roof. The weathervane topping one of the dormer windows spins with the spring bluster. It's perfectly picturesque with the way it sits amongst the verdant trees and lawn.

"We're here," Damon announces, ducking to look across me to the property.

"It's not what I expected."

He chews on his lip as he glances at me with raised brows. "Well, it's home."

It takes a second for the penny to drop. "Excuse me?"

Without answering my question, he gets out of the car, standing at the front trunk, like he's admiring the place. I should climb across the center console and run the shit out of him.

But of course, he grins at me with his stupid charismatic grin, and everything sets on fire inside me.

Fuck, I hate him!

Getting out of the car, I slam the door to his McLaren as hard as I can before I stand gawking at the house like he is.

Damon comes to stand beside me after a moment. His shoulder nudges me like it's meant to make me stop freaking the hell out.

"What am I doing here?"

"Working." He shrugs.

"Meeting your family isn't working. Do you bring your other employees here too?"

Fate must be having a great laugh at my expense because Francesca comes barreling out of the quaint, red front door. "Thank fuck you're here! I'm starving!"

When she pauses in front of us, she looks between me and Damon. "You didn't tell her, did you?"

"No, he didn't."

"You're an asshole." She scowls at him with a tap to his cheek.

"Harder would be better," I tell her.

Fran laughs, threading her arm through mine, and leads me toward the house. "Get the bags, Coldwell."

I can't help but laugh with her, however, I'm still very aware that I'm on my own, navigating a situation I can't read. We're not friends...fuck, we're not even fuckbuddies.

I freeze as Fran tries to take me inside. My heart is hammering in my throat, my vision is clouding over...I'm not okay with this.

"Excuse me." I pull away from her, taking the few steps down the porch as fast as I can. It's a wonder I don't fall over myself. I'm no Forrest Gump, but the farther I run, the more impossible it is to stop.

"Ava," Damon calls behind me, each echo of my name getting louder as he catches up to me. "Ava!"

I feel his proximity, and as magnetic as it is, I keep running until I'm at the edge of his parents' manicured drive and he's holding me prisoner in his viselike arms.

"Stop." He turns me to face him, and when he tries to press me to him, I hold my arms out, pushing against his chest. "What happened?"

What happened?

My stomach twists, with my lungs wrung out.

What happened?

My heart is in overdrive, and I have no idea if it's anger or frustration or whether I am just frayed to the core.

What happened?

"Did it ever occur to you that I've already done this shit before?" I snap. The tears that I've held back so many times finally fall. "With a man I was supposed to marry. Not my boss. Not some guy I fucked in a bar."

His arms drop to his sides, setting me free. Only I've lost the power to run. It's all coming out in treacherous tears, making me hate him even more for reducing me to this. My pride is gone. Broken. Something I've held together for so long. After everything with my father at Monroe. After Marsh...Damon was the one to burn it to the ground.

"I can get you a hotel," he says, voice more gravelly than usual. Dry almost.

"Please." It's all I can manage.

DAMON

I guess she loved him after all.

Does she still love him?

Loosening my arms around her, I step back.

For all the shit that's happened, *this is what breaks her?*

Maybe it's time I cut my losses and let her go. I should let her go back to the people who have no appreciation for her capabilities.

Maybe that's what she's wanted all along—to go back to him.

I try to swallow down the bile the thought of her with him pulls from my stomach, but the longer I stand looking at her, the more impossible it becomes.

"I can get you a hotel." I don't recognize the sound of my own voice, and I hate her for it.

"Please." Red-rimmed, teary eyes widen on mine. She really does look like a lost little mouse. And I'm the idiot who thought he could change that.

CHAPTER THIRTEEN

AVA

The hotel is an old colonial farmhouse, white clad with black shutters. The receptionist is nice, young, and I'm sure she believes we're having some sort of sordid rendezvous. I'm not sure how because the atmosphere between Damon and me is glacial at this point.

"I'll pick you up for the meeting tomorrow," he says, looking at the ground between us.

I didn't know that you can miss someone looking you in the eye until now. He's always looked at me, even when I wished he didn't. And now I wish he would, and he won't.

"Damon..." I move a little closer, breathing in his warm ambery scent. "I'm sorry."

"Stop apologizing." His hand grazes my shoulder, and I swear that it tries to hold on, but it drops to his side as he turns to leave.

Watching him walk away feels like a sledgehammer to my heart. It doesn't make sense for me to feel this way, not when he's deceived me at every turn. Damon is always one step ahead and ready to pounce with his games. First the bar, then the blackmail...Robert and this whole thing with Warner. The only reason he wanted me for that is Lacie, or my friendship with her.

Damon is like some kind of omniscient and omnipresent being. Every time I think we're on the same page, another surprise pops up.

He acts like an asshat, especially when he cares about something...someone.

Fran's words echo around my thoughts, getting louder and louder and louder until my feet are moving of their own accord, tracing Damon's steps back to his car.

The sky is clouding over like it's about to pour down. The salt in the air coats my lungs as I suck as much of the cool air into them as possible.

And as his car rumbles to life, I pull the door open.

"Why did you bring me here?" The question bursts from me. "I'm not Fran. I'm not your friend."

"I'll call you back. Okay, Mom?"

"Of course, darling."

Shit. I can't fucking win today. If I ever meet this woman, she's going to hate me.

I hope she doesn't. The thought makes my heart stumble in its erratic pace.

Standing from his car, he shuts the door and perches on the hood. The wind is picking up a little like it's brewing a storm. And the way he's watching me, it's like I'm it. The storm.

"Truce?" he asks.

"No. No more truces, Damon. Just be straight with me...no more games and surprises." I edge closer to him, not enough to touch, but enough that when the wind whirls around us, his scent wraps itself around me. "Why didn't you tell me? Give me some warning? I don't even know what we are..."

"Can't we just be me and you?"

"We are, Damon. I'm me and you're you." The air around us begins to mist as the sky darkens to a deep violet, shadowed with the grayest clouds I've ever seen. "You're my boss, and I'm your employee. You're the man that lied to me and then blackmailed me into staying. The guy that had me steal from my own family." There's a low rumble above us, the mist becoming thicker until it's a hardening drizzle. "You kiss me like you care, but in the end, when you're done, you'll discard me."

Damon nods, his head falling back as he looks up to the sky. He's the most captivating person I've ever known. The rain trails over his face, rivering down his neck in glistening streams that soak through his shirt.

It's cold and windy and I'm rattling in my skin, but I can't bear the thought of walking away without an answer from him. The freezing rain heavies, and it doesn't matter how tight I wrap my arms around myself, I can't stop my shivers.

Glancing back to me, he leans forward, hooking his arm around my waist and pulling me to him. His eyes are darker than I've ever seen, and the pull between us is more powerful than I've ever felt it. I could try to fight it, but I don't want to. I'm done fighting him and whatever this is.

Damon's hand flattens on my back; the other smooths my wet hair from my face. This is my kryptonite. Moments like these where there are no words, only touches and breaths and stares.

"I wasn't meant to like you," he whispers, tipping my

face up to his so his eyes bore into mine. "I wasn't meant to care."

With the way he leans over me, my blood rushes through me like hot oil, waiting for his kiss. Waiting for him to devour me with the hungry, feral look in his eyes. But his forehead touches mine, his gaze stamped on mine...and all there is, is me and him.

None of the past. Not even the future. It's just him and me. Both lost in a moment where nothing else matters.

I have to ask myself if this is it. Love. Because I've never felt it before. I've never felt my soul belong like this. And so, there is a reason for everything. A journey to this perfectly imperfect, rainy, cold, and consuming moment.

"Would you have dinner with me? Only me and you..." The tip of his nose trails up the bridge of mine until his lips press to my forehead.

Nuzzling into the crook of his neck as he wraps his arms around me, I nod. "Yes."

His chin dips down until his warm lips touch my cool neck. His teeth graze the same spot he bit down on last night. And all the air pushes right out of my lungs.

"Cheese, little mouse," he murmurs, a hand pulling me flush to him as the other caresses my face, bringing it up so we're eye to eye once again. Except he doesn't hold my stare; his mouth finds mine, and all the wild hunger in his dark depths pours from him. And I take it. I drink every bit of it and let it fill me up until I'm certain I have no room left for anything else, barring him.

Damon wraps his arms around me, walking me around the front of the car to the passenger side as thunder starts to grumble loudly around us. Pulling away from me, he nips at my lower lip a couple of times before he focuses on getting me in the car.

"Don't I need to get changed?" I ask as he finds the seat belt and buckles me in.

"Trust me?" He tugs at it.

"Okay."

He chuckles, ducking back out into the rain and jogging around to his side. His normally neat hair is a wet mess, the short lengths sticking to his forehead. He looks almost a little childish with the content grin on his face. I can't help the urge to trace his jaw, and when I meander over his stubbled beard, he sighs like this too is a perfect moment for him.

"I like it when you kiss me in the rain." I like all his kisses, but I loved this one. I can still feel it everywhere. It's like a living thing inside me like the thunderstorm building around us. Powerful and enthralling.

My fingertips tangle in the short lengths of his hair while I watch him drive. The quiet feels peaceful with the hum of the heating, the thrum of the rain, and occasional crack of lightning along the shore. I could live with him in this warm cocoon forever.

CHAPTER FOURTEEN

AVA

Oh my God.

"You told me to trust you." I stare out at the lobster shack that's all lit up in the storm.

"I did."

"Are you trying to get us killed?"

Damon doesn't answer my question, of course. He gets out and comes to my side to get me out too. I'm only just beginning to dry out thanks to the half-hour drive. I press the central lock as he gets to my side, already dripping.

"Open the door, Ava!" he yells over the rain.

"No. Na-ah!" I'm a mouse, not a fucking drowning rat.

We have a glaring competition through the misting glass, and then he does the most logical thing—he unlocks the car.

"You're being sorely melodramatic about this," he chuckles as he pulls me out of the car.

"This place looks ready to blow away."

"It's been here over thirty years; it'll survive this storm

just as it's survived all the others." We jog up the short steps to the wide surrounding porch. We're barely out of the rain when he kisses me. It's soft and quick, but it still makes me giddy, and I can't hide my smile. "I thought you liked rain kisses."

Rain kisses. I love them actually.

"You can't use my words against me."

"I just did." He's laughing as he pulls the door open, and the heat from inside blasts us. It's like being back in his warm car, only it smells delicious and my mouth is watering for food and not the sight of Damon handling the steering wheel.

A few bistro tables line the wall opposite the food counter, but he takes me all the way to the back and through a curtained doorway that leads to the porch. Heavy clear plastic sheets are pulled taught over the open intervals, and it feels like we're hanging off the edge of a cliff or something because there's only sea ahead of us.

"You actually have a death wish."

"Trust me, you're safe. You'll live to see another day and with a belly full of food."

"Well, look what the cat dragged in!" We both turn to the opening we came through. A tall, older woman is standing there, wiping her hands on her apron with a big grin on her face. "Damon Coldwell, are you sure you're in the right place?"

"I'm always in the right place," he replies, his voice light and cheery. "Where's Jo?"

"Right here." She points at herself as she comes closer and whips him with a dishcloth from her apron pocket before she starts cleaning a table in the corner.

"I meant the other Jo."

"He's in the kitchen. Always in the kitchen, that

man." She shrugs. "Sit down. I'll go grab a menu, give you and your lady friend a minute to get settled."

"Ava, Jo-Anne. Jo-Anne, Ava," he introduces us.

"Aren't you pretty," she coos.

"I guess so." Damon pulls out the chair for me at the same time as I thank her.

"Pretty?" Scowling up at him, I trail my finger from the middle of his chest, down to the top of his jeans. "You should think I'm the most goddamn beautiful thing you've ever laid your eyes on if you're going to save this date."

"Don't you worry, the food will do that." He pulls the chair opposite mine across and sits beside me. "What would you like to drink? They have one beer, one white, one red, and one rosé. Oh, and vodka. That's it. Nothing else. Except water and soda."

"I'll have whatever is good."

Smiling, he takes my hand. Twisting the slim band on my middle finger, he asks, "Do you love him?"

The serious expression on his face deepens when I don't reply straightaway, and his fingers thread through mine. I look at the plain ring on my finger, trying to figure out why it triggered such a question, but it's only when he traces the white line from my engagement ring that I understand.

"I don't know. I mean, I don't even know if I did really." I feel embarrassed admitting it, but it seems to relax him again.

"Why would you marry him, then?"

"I thought I did. Things between us were easy. We enjoyed some of the same things. My parents loved him, and he had all the credentials and potential... I...I don't know. Why are you asking?"

Looking up at me, with the outdoor heater light

reflecting in his eyes, he looks devilish. "Because I want to know if he's competition."

His seriousness is kind of sinister, and given how he handles things...

"Damon, I was more upset at the fact he stole my promotion than I was over breaking our engagement. I suppose that means I didn't love Marsh. I don't know, but if I wanted him back, I would never have let anything happen between us."

Jo-Anne comes back with a menu, but he orders everything off the top of his head, without a second thought. And although it's not the fanciest of places for a date, I love that it means something to him. That he loves it here.

When she leaves, he continues. "I don't do competition."

"Because you're a brat?"

"I'm not a brat!"

"Really? Fran seems to think you're a spoilt rich brat who won't let anything stand in his way. Basically, boundary issues."

We get our beers with red plastic cups and paper plates with cute tiny lobsters wearing chef hats.

"Fran's a pain in my ass." Sucking a long gulp of his beer, he takes in the view, darkness lined with breaking waves. "And besides, since she got knocked up, she's all weird."

"What?" I'm not sure how she's kept that so quiet and hidden so well. But I am grateful she had the friends talk with me. After today, the last thing I'd want is to freak out about something I don't need to.

"Don't worry," Damon laughs. "It's not mine," he adds with an exaggerated wink.

I take a pull of my beer, not bothering with the plastic cup. I'm in complete awe as the sky lights up a bright violet, the clouds a deep indigo as a lightning bolt strikes the sea. The thunder that follows it is so loud and surrounding that my heart feels like it's being shocked to life. And as the wind sucks at the plastic holding the storm out, I squeeze his hand.

"Isn't it amazing?" he breathes, lacing our hands together.

"Yes, it's incredible."

We watch every encore and new strike like we're front row at our very own private show. Chef Jo brings our lobster roll and fries dinner out. He's much like his wife—friendly and happy. And after Damon's introduction, he disappears again.

"So, the trick is to just get as much in your mouth as possible." He throws a fry into his mouth and eats it while he arranges the filling in his roll. "Come on, you've got to spread the filling evenly so that you don't lose any of it. Don't be shy, your mouth is big enough to run itself, so…"

"My mouth is big enough to run itself?"

"You and Fran have that down." Putting down his roll, he chuckles. It's playful and light…and I love it. He picks up mine and arranges the filling like his.

"Didn't your mother ever teach you not to touch other people's food?" I smack his hand away and carry on with what he was doing.

"My mom taught me a lot of things, but there are no rules here." There's so much fondness in the way he speaks of his mom that it gets me all anxious over the prospect of meeting her in the future.

"Is she going to hate me? I hope she doesn't feel I was

rude or...or...oh God, she's going to think I'm an awful person."

"It's not a big deal. She's got Fran there with her unborn grandbaby."

"I didn't mean to be rude, it's just you blindsided me, and the only other guy that's ever introduced me to their parents like that...I freaked out. My parents aren't even talking to me."

"Ava, it doesn't matter, and if you really want to know, Mom was pissed at me."

"She was? Why?"

"Fran couldn't keep her mouth shut as per usual. I feel sorry for Grayson."

Grayson. The name is familiar. "Hold on, she's with the legal guy?"

"Yeah, he's decent, and she deserves someone that will really look after her." He shrugs, sucking the dressing from his fingers before he picks up a quarter-sized token. "So, every customer gets a song." He nods at the corner. There's an old jukebox plastered with stickers and surrounded by lobster memorabilia. "Go on."

I take the token from him and wander over to the jukebox. The oldest disc on there is from the eighties. My favorite disc is from the seventies though.

The sound crackles once I select the song, and vocals fill the air soon after.

"No. No fucking way," Damon calls from his seat, looking all affronted by the opening to ABBA's "Take a Chance on Me." "Of all the songs on there."

"My song, my choice." I dance along to the music as I mimic the lyrics. It's one of mine and Lacie's favorite.

"You wasted a song; I can't believe that." He picks up

both of our rolls and hands me mine. "Now eat. Remember, as much as you can. The more the better."

"Got it."

"Right. Okay. One, tw—"

"Wait, why are you counting us in? It's not a competition."

"It's part of the experience. Now hush and eat."

I do as he tells me, getting as much in my mouth as I possibly can. It tastes divine, and I can't wait to finish the rest.

"That's potential right there," he laughs, still holding his food. Leisurely, he takes a normal bite.

I'm still chewing and swallowing through my first bite when he takes his second. Once I'm done, I wash it down with a mouthful of beer.

"You're an asshole."

"Maybe, but that was impressive." He offers me a fry from the shared basket.

"Whatever." I stick my tongue out at him before I take it from him.

My song ends, and he's up and at the jukebox quickly. "Because the Night" comes on, and I really can't believe that it's his pick.

"What?" Sitting down beside me, he shovels in the rest of his roll.

"Nothing." It takes me all of two normal bites to finish mine.

Jo-Anne brings us another couple of beers, and we sit and talk. We continue taking in the sporadic thunder and lightning. I haven't had this much fun in forever. And honestly, I never in a million years thought that this would be us.

CHAPTER FIFTEEN

AVA

Damon walks me to my room. We're both silent watching the door swing open. Pulling me into his arms, he puckers his mouth on the tip of my nose in a chaste kiss. But his hands skim the hem of my shirt, his thumb slipping beneath it, stroking across my stomach. I love the feel of his skin on mine, how warm his touch always is.

"I'll see you tomorrow," he groans over my lips as I press myself to him, my arms locking around his neck.

In spite of all the calm, my heart is thundering in my chest. My blood is burning through my veins. I don't want tonight to end. Ever.

"Don't go." I skim a kiss over his plump lower lip. "Stay with me."

Grasping his hand, I tug him with me through the door, but before we get farther into the room, he pulls me back to him, not dissimilar to the way he did last night.

"What's wrong?"

Warm brown eyes trace my face as his large hands comb through my knotted lengths. "Nothing," Damon replies with a low chuckle.

Nothing feels wrong, but he's not exactly ripping my clothes off and fucking me senseless. He's so good at that.

Like he can read my mind, he draws me flush to his body, every chiseled line molding to my soft curves. Spinning us around, he walks me into the wall beside the open doorway. The bulge in his pants hardens at the base of my belly.

Hands roving up my sides, he skims my silhouette up to my shoulders. "I'm going to kiss you good night," he breathes over my jaw. His stubble grazes my skin in that way that has my stomach twisting with need. "And then I'm going to leave."

What? Why?

Slowly he drops kisses over one side of my face before he repeats on the other.

"I don't fuck on a first date."

I almost choke on the laugh that bubbles up my throat, but before it can escape, he kisses me. Hard. Deep. Slow. It's the kind of kiss that has every inch of me ready for more. My toes are curling in my sneakers. My fingers coil in his hair. My skin erupts with a million goose bumps that make every touch, graze, and skim of our bodies feel like the best foreplay.

I can barely breathe when he pulls away with his chest heaving like mine and his hands clenched like he's using up all his control.

"Good night, my beautiful Ava," he rumbles, pressing a kiss to the corner of my mouth before he leaves.

My knees cave, my body slipping down the wall until I'm sitting on the ground, tracing all his kisses with my fingertips.

DAMON

The porch light is on, like Mom always used to leave it when I used to stay out late. It's not even that late, but with the storm it got dark earlier than usual, and Mom is a stickler for the safety of her only child. Her favorite line to drive home—*"You're my only child, Damon. There's no replacement for you."*

I was so happy when Fran came along and became the daughter she never had. It was a relief.

"There you are," Mom sighs halfway down the stairs. "You didn't call me back. I was worried. With the storm and that car...why can't you drive something that's sturdier."

"Mom." I meet her at the bottom step. "I'm home. I'm fine. Pretty great actually. Stop worrying."

"Darling, you're my only child." She links her arm through mine as I usher her into the kitchen.

"I know."

The place looks like a bomb hit it. There's enough food to feed a small army. I don't think she's ever cooked this much for Thanksgiving or Christmas.

"Jesus, did you want to cook any more food?"

"Well, I thought I was going to have a girl to impress and..."

"It's probably a good thing Ava didn't stay. She would've had a meltdown." Taking a plate down, I walk around the kitchen island, eyeing up all the trays covered in foil and plastic wrap. "Come on, I think I might need your help making a plate."

"You don't have to do that."

"Yeah, I do."

"He really does," Fran sings from the kitchen doorway, holding up a plate of her own. She's changed from her loose dress into leggings and Grayson's Yale sweater. "It's what he gets for being an asshat."

"Don't you have a home of your own?"

"Not with this much food. And besides, since I'm on a sex ban, I need to live vicariously through you." She sits herself at the kitchen table with a grimace on her face. I'm not really sure what to reply to that. After a moment of silence, she perks up again. "I can't stop eating the cornbread and the ham. It's so good."

Mom serves me some of her baked ham and cornbread.

"Where's Grayson?"

"In a food coma."

Mom hands me my loaded plate. I'm really not hungry, but I feel bad that she went to so much trouble and I fucked it up.

"And Dad?"

"He's gone to bed. He needs rest, and after the stroke he's slower." Mom's smile is weak which makes her look sadder. "But he's okay."

She pours me a water and follows me to the table where we sit with Fran. They're both looking at me quietly, in the way they do when they're either fishing for information or have to give me bad news.

"What?" I take a sip of my water, washing down the mouthful of cornbread.

"What happened? Is Ava mad at you?" Fran moves her food around her plate. "Was it something I said? I can't even remember what we were saying when she freaked out. My head is all over the place, and I feel terrible."

"I'd love to blame you and your big mouth, but it was me."

"And?" Mom leans closer, eyes wide. "What happened?"

"We went to Jo's for dinner and we talked."

"That's nice." Mom sighs at the same time as Fran asks, "And?"

"And mind your own fucking business."

"I am minding my fucking business!" she snaps, and Mom jumps right in to pacify the situation. "No fighting. Civilized conversation at the table."

Fran puts her fork down, pushing her plate away. Her face is all kinds of twisted and sorry-looking, and I know there's something wrong before she even says anything.

"I need to make sure you have someone to watch your back when I'm gone." Her eyes are all wide and waterlogged.

"What are you talking about?" My heart is racing, and I don't mean to snap, but Fran doesn't cry unless it's something serious. Like her parents dying. That's the only time she's ever really cried.

"Can we all calm down?" Mom stands to rummage in the kitchen. When she returns, she has a bottle of scotch in her hand and three glasses. She pours one and hands it to Fran. "Sniff." Then another for me and one for herself. "There's no use stressing," she tells Fran. "Your ob-gyn has a plan. Everything is going to be okay."

"Can someone tell me what's going on? Are you okay? Is the baby okay?"

Fran takes a long inhale over the rim of her glass. I still think it's fucking weird, but whatever makes her happy and keeps her ticking.

"I'm okay, it's just that my placenta is in the wrong place, and I'm going to have to leave early because my doctor's put me on bed rest."

"And?"

"And I'm not ready to leave!" she grits out, her frustration evident even through her tears. "I can't just leave you."

Taking her hand, I link her fingers with mine. "Yeah, you can. I'm a grown-ass man; I don't need you to put yourself or your baby in danger for me."

"But I haven't finished organizing everything, and there's no one to have your back."

"Dex will be there."

"Dex cares about the business. He's all about the business and the money..." She sniffs, squeezing my hand tighter.

"It's why I made him VP." My laugh doesn't have the soothing effect I'd hoped for. If anything, it gets her even more worked up.

"But you need someone to be about you and what you want. You need someone to have your back and your vision...and Ava cares. I know she does, and if she loves you, then she'll make sure you are happy and not just doing shit for the sake of success or the money. She'll have your back, and you care enough about her that you'll listen to her. I know you care. I do."

"This is what you've been stewing over all day?" Mom asks her crossly.

"You don't understand, Elizab—"

"Fran!"

"Damon, Ava's going to find out you construed everything, and she's going to hate you. And there'll be no going back because she won't trust you ever again, and you can't love someone you don't trust. So, you have to fix everything. You have to give her Monroe, and you have to walk away from it completely. It's not worth it. You know that, don't you?"

I pull my vibrating phone from my pocket, and as I'm about to check it, Fran places her hand over it, peering up at me.

"If you let her go, she'll come back to you."

She lifts her hand, and my screen instantly lights up.

Ava: I wish you were here.

Damon: Me too.

Ava: Maybe next time...

Damon: Are you asking me out?

Ava: Goodnight, Damon. x

Fuck. I know Fran's right, I do, but I can't let Ava go. I just can't.

"Damon." Fran scoots her chair closer, resting her head on my shoulder. "You know it's the right thing to do."

"You're right, Monroe should be hers, but it won't be unless I stick to the plan."

"What on earth is going on?" Mom levels us both with a glare. Of course, it's all Fran needs to tell her everything, and as much as I love Fran, I need to walk away before I end up losing my shit.

"Where are you going?" Mom calls as I leave them, and I don't bother replying. Instead, I go find Grayson. He and I have a lot to discuss.

CHAPTER SIXTEEN

DAMON

Ava's got all the effortless charm down to perfection. I picked her up in another pair of dark blue jeans that make her long, slender legs look lithe with the nude heels she's wearing. The oversized blue shirt is tucked into her pants, making her waist look small. Her hair is up in a casual knot with wisps framing her face. She's so laid-back as we talk to Warner that you would believe she's the boss.

"Those are some of the things we'll do, but once I've read your book and have a feel for it, we can put together a plan that's personable to you. The important thing is that you're comfortable with the direction we're going. At the end of the day it's your story and your life, and whatever approach we take it has to reflect that." She takes a sip of her wine spritzer and actually listens to him and all the things he wants to achieve.

And the whole time I'm sitting here thinking about last night and the conversations I had with Mom, Fran, and Grayson.

For the first time, I'm uncertain of what I'm doing because I don't want to lose Ava, but it feels like it's an eventuality. Regardless of what I do, it will happen because she's not like me or the industry we're in. She's soft. So fucking soft and caring, and she would rather let someone take from her than cut their throat.

"Thanks for meeting up today, I'm sure you have other clients..." Warner stands, drinking the rest of his pressed juice. Turning to me, he offers me his hand, and when I shake it, he says, "You're right, she's the best."

"Ava certainly is."

"I'll talk to you guys soon. I have a couple of meetings in the next few days, but playoffs are here and..."

"You should focus on your game." Ava shakes his hand, and with the loose collar of her shirt shifting with the motion, I smile at the glimpse of her tattoo fading into her hairline. "We're here whenever you're ready."

It feels like Warner doesn't want to leave her presence because he keeps finding something to say or ask. To the point that I want to tell him to get on his way and leave us to the evening I have planned.

"Why are you scowling?" she laughs as he walks away.

"I thought he'd never fucking leave."

"Well, you know, he wanted to stay with the best." Falling onto my lap when I sit, she strokes my jaw with her nails. "I thought you said Warner asked for me."

"He did."

"Once you nudged him in my direction."

"He wanted the best."

"Damon." She sits straighter, looking me in the eyes. "I don't want special favors. Whatever we're doing. Whatever we are..."

"Have I ever given you preferential treatment?"

"No."

"You don't need it. And you're not that kind of woman, and I'm sure as fuck not that kind of guy. You get what you work for."

"Okay." She smiles wide, her forehead touching to mine.

"You hungry?"

"Are you a feeder or something?"

That would be Mom, but... "I thought you wanted a second date badly enough to ask me out?"

"Whatever." She glares at me, getting to her feet.

"I accept, and I've made a reservation."

"How forward of you. What if I wanted to take you to my death trap?" She pulls her oversized jacket on and grabs her purse.

"Maybe next time," I tease as I walk us to my car.

I thought I had Ava all figured out. More so than I should, given I wasn't meant to care. But she's got these little endearing traits—like the way she fusses with tendrils behind her ear, curling them as she gets lost in her thoughts. Her expression matches whatever's going through her mind. If it's pleasant, she smiles, like she's doing now. Like she did the entire drive on the way here.

The tavern is busy, but it has a hotel right across the street that means we can both enjoy the meal and our drinks without having to drive anywhere afterward.

"I've never really been to the Hamptons." She looks around the modestly decorated interior. It's got a cozy farmhouse feel with nautical décor. "I always thought it'd be uppity, but so far it's so calm and relaxed. I like it."

"It a little different in the summer when all the rich folk come in, but this is it."

The waitress brings our drinks with the dinner menu, and we're about to order when Fran starts blowing my phone up. I'm instantly on edge given our conversation yesterday, and the worst-case scenarios are going through my head even though I have no idea what they are. I just see blood and tears because it's what I remember from when Mom had her last miscarriage. I was fourteen and it was terrifying. I thought she was going to die.

"Everything okay?" Ava asks, eyes furrowing at my phone.

Fran: PICK UP.

Fran: CALL ME.

I do. It doesn't ring once before she answers, "Oh my God, Damon. Oh my God...he fell. Just fell. He was fine and then he fell, and the ambulance is here. The paramedics... Oh my God."

"Dad?" I'm standing and dropping some cash on the table. I can hear the clack of Ava's heels behind me. "Is he okay? Is Mom?"

"I don't know." She's in tears, and I can't be an asshole and tell her to get her shit together because of everything that went down with her parents. "I'm on my way to the house. Let me know what happens and where they take him, okay?"

"Okay."

"It's going to be okay, all right?"

"Yeah."

"Grayson's there, right?"

"Right." She's on autopilot. It's her thing when something goes seriously wrong.

"I'll be there in no time."

Hanging up, I turn to Ava. She looks as worried as I

feel—something Fran would be. It's a stupid moment to wonder, but... *Would she really have my back? Would she love me?*

"Can I do anything?" She doesn't even know what's happened and she wants to help.

Because she's a good person.

"I've booked a room in the hotel. If you give them my name..."

She takes my hand as I search for my keys. "I can come with you."

"You don't have to do that."

"I'd like to. I mean, I can't drive your car or anything because it scares the shit out of me, but I can hold your hand or...I don't know." She's oozing compassion and tenderness, and I can't help but take it.

The car journey is quiet for the most part. I get a call from Grayson telling me Dad's been taken to the hospital.

The perpetual silence that follows is more burdening than anything I've ever felt. It allows fear to sink right in and wreak havoc with all my foundations. But she's there with me, and it's impossible not to let her into all the places I've tried to keep her out of.

The hospital is quiet, it's nothing like the New York modern giant Dad was taken to when he had the stroke. But the staff are kind and quick to point us in the right direction.

Grayson's pacing up and down the long white and gray hall as we walk in, and Fran is sitting on a chair that's clearly been put outside Dad's hospital room for her. Eyes red and face tear-streaked, she's impassive.

"You can wait with me," Grayson tells Ava. Reluctantly, she releases my hand with one of her lip-biting smiles.

504

All I want is to bring her with me. I just want to hold on to her. Instead, I hold on to Fran. We stand outside Dad's room and watch as the doctors talk to him and Mom.

The only relief is that Dad is awake and he's talking. He's okay, and the world finally stops spinning too fast for me to gather myself. I can breathe.

"See?" I draw Fran into my side. "I told you, it's okay."

She nods, pushing away from me. "You didn't see it. You didn't see him."

"Francesca..."

Walking back the way I just came, she looks exhausted. I don't bother arguing with her over her pessimism. I let her go, because she will come back. Like Fran always does.

The doctors leave, and Mom settles Dad. I sit with them for while listening to what happened and why.

"So, it's just low blood pressure?"

"Yes." Mom pats my knee. "The meds he's taking were too strong, but the specialist is coming to see your father tomorrow morning to review everything."

"Honestly, I'm fine. I'm just sorry I scared Francesca." He winks at the door.

"You're not funny!" she growls from the doorway.

"Bring it in, kid." He pats the bed beside me, and with a sulk she ambles over, sitting next to him.

He wraps his arm around her shoulders, and in spite of looking frail, he comforts her. Like he would Mom and me.

"You're really okay?"

"Yes," he tells her.

"You scared the shit out of me," I grumble, my heart still trying to slow to its normal rhythm.

"Yeah," Mom sighs, standing. "Apparently assholism runs in the family."

"That's not a word," I tell her as she shoos us off the bed and pulls the covers over Dad.

"Out with both of you." Mom walks us out of the room. "You—" She points at Fran. "—go home and put those feet up. Stooge one—" Pinching my chin, she winks. "—you make sure she does as she's told, and stop worrying. Okay?"

"Mom…"

"He's fine. It was a dizzy spell." She takes a deep breath. "We're staying so the specialist can see him first thing. Now go on, get out of here."

"I can't leave you here on your own."

"I'm with your father."

"And you've got your hands full." He nods at the open double doorway.

Ava's standing behind Grayson with a tray of drinks in her hand. Her mouth tips up softly, and my world pauses, tilting on its axis.

"Go on…" Mom presses a kiss to my cheek. "I'll call you if anything changes. But we're good here."

Fran and I trudge out of the room, and as we're about to disappear, Mom calls, "I love you. Both of you."

"Love you too." Fran blows her a kiss.

Always the kiss-ass.

Grayson takes the drinks from Ava, taking them to Mom, and a quiet second with her is all I need to relax.

"He's okay," I breathe the minute Ava wraps her arms around my waist.

"Good." She presses a kiss to the top of my chest. "Are you okay?"

"I think so." My heart finally begins to settle, but I keep holding on to her. "Thank you for being here."

She smiles in response, looking up at me with heavy-lidded doe eyes that are all affection and speak of so many feelings. Too many feelings that are impossible to hide.

And I could love her. *Maybe. Probably...*

"You want to show me your room?" she trills, her head tipped back, and azure eyes creased with affection.

...Definitely.

CHAPTER SEVENTEEN

AVA

Damon drops our bags on the floor by his bedroom door. Taking my heels from me, he throws them beside our things, followed by his jacket and then mine. His boots join the pile, and before I get a good look around the moonlit room, his hands are cupping my jaw, drawing me into his body.

"My beautiful Ava..." I swallow at the low rumble of my name from his lips. "Little mouse..."

The pounding of my heart blurs my vision, and my breathless pants burn my lungs.

"Thank you," he whispers into my slightly gaping mouth.

I touch my fingertip to the light freckle just visible above the stubble running along his top lip. "Stop thanking me."

I didn't do anything except accompany him. There wasn't anything for me to do, so I don't get why he's so thankful. I did nothing.

Damon lowers himself to my height, his eyes meeting mine. In the silver light of the moon, they look a relucent charcoal gray. So intense and magnetic. In spite of all he does, I don't think he knows how powerful he is. Because with one look he can change everything I've ever wanted.

His mouth lowers to my lips, skimming over them until they trail up my jaw, depositing kiss after kiss after kiss punctuated by his hums and groans and sharp inhales. The higher his lips roam—over my ear to my temple, tracing my hairline until they stop with a hard press to my forehead—the taller he stands over me.

With my head tilted back, he pulls my messy knot loose, running his fingers through it and working out the tangles with gentle tugs that send frissons of need to my core, until I'm molten desire in his hands.

Grabbing my ass, he hoists me up his body until my feet are hooked over his butt. My hands fist the open collar of his shirt, pulling him to me as I take his lips with mine. His tongue pushes into my mouth, and God, he tastes so damn good. He's all sensual masculinity and overwhelming need. Strong and overpowering, gentle and caring all the same.

Trailing kisses down my neck, he sits me on the edge of the bed, slipping to the plush carpet on his knees. Kneeling between my legs, he unbuttons my shirt—button by button, slow and quiet. My every pore is aching and every limb so heavy with want for him that I can barely sit upright.

My hands coil around the comforter as Damon slips the shirt over my shoulders. His face nuzzles into the crease of my breasts, and he pulls at the cups, his tongue traces the engorged curves, thumbs rounding my tightly furled nipples until I'm squirming on the bed, incapable of catching my breath.

Oh Lord.

Every moan is cut short by his purposeful touches. Every pull of air into my lungs is stilted by the lust swelling in my throat.

Holy shit.

My hand winds into his hair, holding him to me as he pulls my nipple into his mouth, his tongue laving around the turgid point in between grazes of his teeth. And when I think I might just explode from Damon's attention to my breasts and the way his hands roam the curve of my waist to the heavy swell of my chest and down to the tops of my thighs, he stops.

Standing, he removes his shirt without ceremony. Every chiseled line of his body is shadowed, making him look lethal in every possible way. He pulls my shirt from me, discarding it with his. Then his hand is coiling into my loose lengths, tugging my face up to his. And while he cups the side of my face with his other hand, skimming his thumb over my lips again and again, I trace the light trail of hair from his navel, to the top of his jeans.

"I could look at you all day," he rumbles, with blazing eyes raking over me. "And I would never tire."

I work his belt and pants open, leaving the top of his thick bulge exposed with his underwear barely containing it. As I begin to tug everything down at once, he pushes me onto my back, bracing himself over me on one hand as the other works the buttons on my jeans open. Slipping his hand under my butt, he grasps my pants and under-wear, and in one swift motion he yanks them down my thighs to my knees, leaving me exposed when he stands to fully discard them.

Dear God.

Impossibly, my body heats further. Every part of me is pulsing and clenching. And as I watch him strip off his pants, it hits me that we've never been intimate like this. He's seeing all of me and I'm seeing all of him and somehow it doesn't seem enough. I want to feel all of him. I want to be besieged by all his virility and completely overtaken by everything that makes him.

Straddling my thighs, he rids me of my bra, his weeping dick trailing over the base of my belly. And I really can't take any more, not with how fucking hot I am and with the way my pussy is so wet that my arousal is coating the swell of my thighs and spreading down the crease of my ass with every grind of my hips on the bed.

Cupping the belly of my tits, he shifts me up the bed, and lifting my legs, he spreads me open with a groan.

"I fucking love the sight of your cunt all wet for me," he growls, fisting his cock as he strokes it up and down my folds, barely dipping it into my pussy. With my ass resting on his thighs, he hooks my leg over his shoulder while pushing the other up to my chest.

And without another word he slams into me, so deep, so big, so hard, and I'm left so full and yet with my moans and through my cries, I beg for more. Faster. Deeper. Harder.

"Fuck, little mouse, I might break you."

"Please," I rasp, my hands clawing at his sides and the hand pushing my thigh as high as my body will allow.

With every blunt thrust, my body coils tighter. With every stroke that bottoms out inside me, I want more of him. I want everything he has, the parts he wants to part with, the depths he wants to share, and all the secrets he keeps. I want them all. I want all of him.

———

DAMON

"Oh God, Damon...oh fuck," she chants hoarsely.

With her body bowing off the bed and the sound of our flesh slapping together surrounding us, I can't think of a more perfect moment. And her hair is all tangled around her like a thorny halo. And her tits are bouncing. And God, I can't get enough of her.

I've never wanted to live in something so much as I want to be a part of her. And I want her to be a part of me. I want her to be mine because it's the only possible ending. Call it fate, call it love, call it whatever the fuck it is...so long as she's mine, I don't care.

Lowering her legs to the side, I sink over her. "Who do you belong to, little mouse?"

A muffled reply is distorted by her cry as I push deeper, her pussy clenching tightly around me.

"Who do you belong to, Ava?" I pull her legs wider, my chest bearing down on hers until she's visibly unable to draw air into her lungs. And I'm so deep that her eyes water with her cries. "You. Damon. You."

"Why are you mine?" I give her room to drag in her breath, and her arms wrap around my shoulders as I lick into her mouth. She's all ragged pants and breathless moans as I brace myself over her. "Why, my beautiful Ava?"

"Because," she whines with my throbbing cock stroking up and down her walls.

"Because?" I pull out and her eyes flit from where we're joined to my eyes.

"Just *because.*" Her eyes round in the way they do when she's overwhelmed and still trying to work shit out in her head. But she knows just as I do why she's mine.

Because I love you, I tell her silently as I thrust back into her.

I love that she fights the urge to close her eyes. That she loves watching the way our bodies meld together. That she's so fucking desperate for me that she can't get enough. No matter how deep I go, it's not deep enough. Not even when her groans are pained and her temples are tracked with tears. She wants more, and she isn't afraid to ask or take it.

With her body trembling beneath me, I lower myself over her, bracing on my forearms. "Fuck, baby, you feel so fucking good."

"Yeah?" she pants.

"Yeah, and I'm going to fill you up until you can't take any more. Until there's no part of you I haven't marked as mine."

"Yours." Ava lifts her arms over her head, finding my hands, and she pushes hers beneath them until our fingers are laced together.

"Mine."

She nods frantically, her heels pressing to my ass as I fuck her without pause, driving into her until she's gasping for her release and the need isn't physical anymore. Her nails are clawing at the back of my hands, and she's kissing and holding like she wants me inside all the places no one's been, the ones where you can't be erased from, not even in death.

And when I think I can't get any deeper, any more inside her if I tried, she shatters beneath me. Her body pulls me in until I bottom out, and my hot cum spurts inside her tight cunt. We're both a sweaty, breathless, clenching and pulsing and throbbing mess.

Her hold doesn't lax on my hands as she gasps into

my chest in between kisses and soft bites. "Oh God. Oh God. Oh God..."

When she stills beneath me, her body soft and her breaths a low murmur, I roll onto my side, tucking her into my chest as I tell her, "All mine."

CHAPTER EIGHTEEN

AVA

Three weeks later

I'm getting too used to these late nights and Damon's warm bed. I hate leaving him, especially when it's obvious he's frustrated. Which in Damon land means he's pissed. But I did things wrong with Marsh; I let him blind me, and in the end it was meaningless.

"I should go," I sigh, disappointment tightening my chest as his trailing fingers over my naked body halt and his hand drops to the mattress between us. "Damon..."

"What?" Rolling onto his back, he tucks his hands under his head. His body coils tight with everything he's holding in, which for him is hard work.

I hate that I'm the one causing him grief, because with everything with the lawsuit and how he's handled it all so coolly—maybe I am being unreasonable. But I don't want to be let down again. Damon has the potential to obliterate me, and I can't lose sight of that.

Straddling his hips, I trace the grooves of his chest, enjoying the way the muscles flex beneath my touch.

"My clothes are at my apartment." I peer up at him. "And I have a meeting with Lacie tomorrow about Warner. I know she's going to be difficult and grill me about every little thing, and I need to be prepared because she's tricky. And if she knew about us...it would be another thing for her to hold against me and to get in the way of things. You want Warner, don't you?"

Damon nods almost unnoticeably and without warning flips me onto my back. His arms braced either side of my head as his hips settle between my thighs.

He doesn't answer the question, but it's why he wanted me in the first place. Because my friendship with Lacie should've made Warner a sure thing. And I don't want to disappoint him.

Skimming the side of my face with the tip of his nose, he asks, "Who do you belong to?"

"You." I grin back at him because I know what follows this question, and it always makes heart swell.

"And why are you mine, Ava?"

"Because," I reply in lieu of telling him that I'm his because...well, *because*.

He skims the other side of my face, his nose rounding my brow before stroking down the bridge of mine. "Because?"

God, there's so much in his eyes right now that my heart races at all the possibilities.

"Just because."

The corner of his mouth tips up wonkily, and I hold on to his strong arms as he kisses me. And every one of his kisses is better than the last, better than anything I've ever had.

"You better bring Warner in stat," he quips when he pulls away, his hand brushing down my side to my thigh.

He hooks it over his hip, and with a teasing scowl he tickles me right behind the knee. I don't even know how he found that out, but it's become his thing now, and in spite of hating it...I love it too.

"Stop it!"

"Are you going to bring Warner in?" He continues his playful torture.

"Yes!"

"You better do because if you don't, I might have to show up at that meeting and who knows what I'll do..."

"You wouldn't."

"Wouldn't I?"

"You promised..."

"I promised I wouldn't go easy on you." His laugh is too light for him to be serious. It's something I've learned about him. His laugh fades, and with the friction of our bodies, he's more than ready for another round of a different kind of fun.

———

Of course, just as Damon said, his driver is waiting for me outside my building. He's pushing. It's what he does when things aren't exactly how he wants them: he nudges them in his direction. It honestly doesn't bother me anywhere near as much as it should.

"Good morning, Miss Monroe." The driver opens the door for me, and before I get in, I pause. "I'm sorry, I feel so rude...I don't know your name."

"Gerry, ma'am."

"Good morning, Gerry." I lower into the car, pushing my shades up onto my head.

"Morning, little mouse." A steaming cup of coffee

appears right under my nose. "Figured you could use the extra caffeine this morning."

"And whose fault is that?" Taking the coffee, I turn to face him. His starched white shirt is stretched taut across his chest. The top two buttons are undone, and he looks so fresh and inviting that I can't help but scoot closer to him and breathe in his cologne mixed with the soapy scent of his clothes and body wash.

Oh man, and this is why spending the night would be bad. We'd never leave his place.

"What are you doing here?" I ask, barely resisting the urge to jump his bones.

"Coffee." He nods at the cup in my hand, from my favorite coffee shop close to the office. When I've had a sip, he takes it from me and places it in the cupholder. Cupping my nape, he pulls me to him, so that our mouths are almost touching. "And coffee," he murmurs before pressing his lips to mine, kissing me like I didn't only leave his place at the ass crack of dawn.

"So, my mom is in town today. She's organizing a baby shower for Fran. Obviously, it's got to be pretty low-key given the situation, but she's going to be around for lunch, and I thought that..."

"Sure."

"You don't have to. But she wanted me to ask and—"

"I know I don't have to, but seeing as I've slept under her roof and all..." My heart races frantically in my chest, the voice in my head warning me to slow down, but I guess after seeing her at the hospital and their interactions...I'm curious.

"I'll have William make a reservation somewhere. Any suggestions?" He sounds as nervous as I am.

"Umm...I'm sure your PA knows better than me."

The car stops about a block from the café where I'm meeting Lacie. Gerry opens my door, and I'm a little confused.

"I figured you wouldn't want Lacie seeing you arrive in my car."

I'm tempted to throw caution to the wind. "How much do you want Warner?"

"You better land that fucking baller fast." He nips at my lips, before I get out of the car.

"See you at lunch, boss man."

"See you later, little mouse." He hands me my bright red purse that matches my heels. His eyes meander down my bare legs to my feet, and a devious grin cuts his face. "Nice shoes."

"I'll keep them on." I head toward the little New England haven with the car trailing after me. As I walk in, I wink at him over my shoulder because two can play at the same game, right?

I've only just found Lacie when my phone chirps.

Damon: Only the heels.

A schoolgirl giggle escapes me, my cheeks flushing with warmth. And my body is already on timer for its next fix of him.

"Oh my God." Lacie practically jumps out of her seat. Her arms engulf me in a tight hug. "It feels like I haven't seen you in forever."

"You're a busy lady." I take her in. She's all tanned from her week on the East Coast seeing clients. "So, business first, catch-up after?"

Shaking out her copper waves over her shoulder, she

rolls her eyes. "Honestly, I'm not sure what you expect me to tell you."

She sits, opening up her monogrammed leather document folder. She takes out a couple of papers with handwritten notes.

"Here's the thing, Monroe wants less. Schultz wants less too. Coldwell is taking a big cut..." She shrugs like it's a no-brainer.

"We're taking a bigger slice from a bigger pie, Lacie. And it's so we can put more into it. You can't compare what we've presented to anything Monroe or Schultz or any other publisher out there has."

"Ava..."

"No. I know Monroe. I know their projections are nowhere close to ours, because they're not willing to put everything into this, but the reality is that you can't expect a lion to take the same bite as a mouse."

I pause as my analogy sinks in. I'm starting to sound like Damon. Mice and lions. Bites and cuts...

"It's my job as Callum's agent to make sure that every risk pays off, that every investment has a return. It's my job to be the bad guy so my client can be the great guy. And Callum...he's not about the money or any of that superficial shit. He's a normal guy that had to graft to get to where he is, even with his talent. He invests in people..."

"Lace, you can't look at any of this as my friend. As someone who knows how Damon and I started out..."

"What?" she blurts, eyes narrowed on me as she sits straight in her seat.

Shit.

I take a deep breath and continue. "This is business, and we both know that Coldwell is the only publisher with the resources it will take to keep up with Callum's profile...to expand it even."

She glares at me, tapping her pen on her pad. She's playing hardball, like I knew she would.

Eventually she pulls out the contract I sent her earlier in the week. Placing it on the table in front of me, she spins it to face me.

"He would've signed it without even reading it, that's how much he's bought into you."

"What?"

"It's yours, and not because you're my best brat friend." She rolls her eyes again. "Because you deserve it. You worked the hardest, and giving it to Marsh would've made me twitch into a seizure or something."

I look through the document, page by page, still in disbelief that it's signed because it's the biggest deal I've ever made.

"Business over, now time for catch-up!" she announces, signaling the waitress for a top-up of our coffees. "What's going on between you and asshat?"

Of course, my face glows and my excitement turns into nerves. "I'm meeting his mom today. Like really meeting her and not running from her home."

"Well, I guess I already knew you were fucking, so it doesn't matter that you skipped over that part."

"You knew?"

"Babe, he pretty much told Callum to keep Holly away from you."

"He did?"

"Not in so many words, but the message was clear with the way he barely kept himself from pouring your drink over her..." She pauses. "That was my fault, because Holly hates me and...anyway, the point is that for jerk, he totally didn't care whether or not Callum would be pissed. He cared more about you, ergo, he's either getting pussy or he wants to get pussy."

"Really?"

"I wasn't wrong, was I?" She marks me with a challenging grin. "I don't hate him, and I don't like him. My opinion of him doesn't fucking matter so long as he doesn't fuck you over again. But if he does, I'll cut his balls off and feed them to him...in front of a camera so he has that treasure for the rest of his life."

I'm not sure if I find it funny or petrifying, but regardless, I nod. "Okay."

She goes on to ask me all about my freak-out in the Hamptons, and by the time we leave, I'm actually looking forward to meeting Elizabeth properly. Especially with how much Fran talked about her.

CHAPTER NINETEEN

AVA

Elizabeth Coldwell is beautiful. Brown eyes as dark as her son's and the same golden complexion. She's a smiler, and I like that her smile brings out his. Her long silver hair is up in a neat ponytail, her lips are glossed over a light mauve, and although she has an air about her that screams money, she's in a simple black sweater with slightly puffy cap sleeves and black jeans. She's only a tad shorter than me, even in my stilettos.

"I'll see you soon." Palming Damon's face, she smiles around his shoulder at me. And as he helps her into a cab, they share a short conversation filled with sharp whispers and a definitive huff from Damon at the end. Still, they part with a kiss that leaves me feeling homesick for my own mother.

"Okay," Damon sighs, standing back to watch the taxi drive off. "Time to celebrate."

He steps back, eyes roaming down my light blue-and-white pinstriped shirt, lingering on the few open buttons and the flesh they expose. As they meander over the high cummerbund waist of my navy skater skirt, he takes a half step back and follows my bare legs down to my bright red shoes.

"See something you like?"

"Not yet." His finger hooks into the top of my skirt, pulling me to him. "But you can rectify that."

My stomach dips and twists at his devious smirk. Just like that, I'm primed and ready for anything he wants to do to me. And when he kisses me, everything around us disappears. It's like we're standing on the surface of the sun, and God, I'm burning up.

His driver arrives and rather than heading to the office, he takes us straight to Damon's place. His apartment is everything you'd expect from a rich, single guy who likes his privacy. The walls are thick concrete with floor-to-ceiling windows. The floors are polished stone, and everything is so utilitarian, but there are odd bits, like these huge canvases boasting blue open waters and gold sand and large driftwood sculptures...all things that remind me of the warmth of his parents' home.

"This is beautiful." I pause in front of a long panoramic painting of a beach going through all the seasons. It starts off faint and light with the depth of colors darkening the farther down the corridor we go. The last quarter is my favorite. The blue and gray hues become purples and black with crackles of gold and silver-speckled white.

It takes me back to the lobster shack. Our first date. It's sort of crazy that it was almost a month ago, and somehow it feels like it's been longer.

"My mom painted it." He traces a lightning bolt with fond contentment.

I can only watch him with how my heart swells,

making it feel like it's lodged in my throat. There are all these sides to this man, and some are dark and ruthless like the storm in the painting, and then there are others that are so light they make you feel as though you are on a constant high.

Damon is so capricious in his temperament, but it's all driven by his intense care and love.

He turns to me, his brown eyes rich, molten chocolate, holding so much promise and so much affection that I can't deny it anymore. I can't pretend that I don't feel it. My heart has never felt so full and achy and happy... because he owns me. Because...

"Shit," he curses, reaching for his ringing phone. "I need to take this."

"That's okay." I watch him walk toward his office.

"Grayson..." he answers it, looking back at me as he closes the door.

———

DAMON

Dex leaves the call. I know he's pissed that I'm changing the plan. But Fran is right—it's not up to him. This is my call. My decision. He may be VP, but I'm the boss, and he needs to remember that.

"Are you sure about this?" Worry tinges Grayson's question. "Dex is worried you're making a mistake."

Chuckling, I brush off his question as I open the office door. "Dex is always worried."

The apartment smells of burnt sugar and cinnamon, and there's a deliciously nutty undertone that makes my mouth water. I'm not sure how long I've been on the phone, but it's getting dark and Ava's in the kitchen. Her long hair is piled messily on her head. She's got her thick framed glasses on as she fawns over the skillet.

My kitchen has only ever been that messy when Mom and Fran have used it. There are jars of things I didn't even know were in my cupboards. She's made herself right at home, and I like it.

"I'm sure," I tell Grayson, leaning over the breakfast bar.

Ava turns toward me with a soft grin on her face as I take in the chocolate spread and the peanut butter jars.

"Hey," she mouths, opening the oven and sliding the skillet in before she grabs another jar and comes to lean over the counter in front of me so that we're face-to-face. Removing her glasses, she drops them on the counter between us.

"All right, I'll send the paperwork over." Grayson blows out a long breath while I watch Ava sweep her little finger into the jar and suck the fluff clean off it.

She knows what she's doing with her lusty smirk and gleaming eyes.

"This doesn't get out. Understood?"

"Yup." He hangs up and I drop my phone on the counter between Ava and me.

"Sounds ominous." Her remark is throaty and all kinds of sultry. It's got a real fuck-me edge to it that with her finger licking, it's got my dick bulging in my pants.

"Business always is."

"Because you're underhanded and you do what it takes to get your way." Coming closer, her nose touches mine, and when she licks her lips, the tip of her tongue skims the seam of my mouth.

"What's the point of going into something if I'm not prepared to do what it takes to get what I want out of it?"

"So competitive, Mr. Coldwell." Teasing, she sweeps a fluff-covered finger over my lips.

I resist the urge to lick it off, rounding the breakfast bar to stand in front of her. I notice she's still wearing her heels. Her long sleeves are rolled all the way up to her elbows with her bangles pushed as far up as they'll go too.

Rocking up onto her toes with her finger in her mouth, she presses her body to mine. Her breath shallows and her eyes widen, and when her hips touch mine, an almost silent groan vibrates from her lips as she licks mine clean.

"It's not a competition if I always win."

A low laugh bubbles up her throat as she steps away and turns the oven off. Before she has a chance to get away, I pull her back to me.

"What are you making?"

"Dinner." She shrugs.

"Doesn't smell like dinner."

"We're celebrating, right? We can have fluffernutters for dinner. They're my favorite."

Her fingers trail my lips, and when I suck one into my mouth, she practically disintegrates in my arms.

"You're going to ruin dinner, boss man." Not that she gives an actual fuck about it with the way she's grinding her groin onto my throbbing erection.

"I going to ruin your cunt."

Her cheeks flush, but in complete contrast her hands scramble to unbutton my shirt. She manages the first couple of buttons, but when my hand slips beneath her skirt and my fingers fill her tight pussy, she yanks the last two.

Her body writhes on my hand with the most beautiful moans. I can't rein myself in as I pull out of her clenching cunt and grasp her throat, pulling at her shirt with my other hand as I walk us to the couch.

Her hands hold tight to my wrist until I drop her on the back of the seat. Her face is flushed a dark crimson from my hold, her chest mottled with need and her perfect tits practically bursting from her bra.

Fuck.

"Take it all off," I demand, trying to control my breath-robbed voice.

Ava does as she's told without getting up. Her shirt, skirt, and bra pile on the floor. When it comes to her panties, she slips them down her thighs to her knees, letting them fall to her ankles, over those fucking shoes I haven't stopped thinking about all day.

"Leave them." Her hands rest on her thighs as she squirms on the black leather. "What are you waiting for?" She looks at me confused. "Undress me."

Again, she does it without question. Dragging my shirt down my arms, she removes my monogrammed cufflinks with curiosity pinching her brow before moving on to my pants.

Startled eyes flash to mine. I guess she's worked out what the *H* in my initials stands for. *Henry.*

Slipping off the back of the couch, she works my underwear down until I shuck it off with my slacks. Her hands push on my thighs as she stands, her wet lips grazing the head of my cock.

When she's standing in front of me, I sit her back in her place. Swiveling her away from me, I nudge her off the back of the couch until she's on her knees on the cushion. Her head falls back onto the leather still wet from her pussy. And her slim throat tightens with her swallow as my heavy erection bobs over her face.

"Open." She does.

Ava's mouth gapes open in a perfectly shaped O. Her tongue licks at her lips as I press it farther open with my thumb, her pretty neck straining as she cranes back. Her tits push up to the ceiling...

Fuck, she's a sight unlike any other I've seen. And when I guide my cock into her mouth there isn't the slightest protest, not even as I press past her gag reflex. Her hands claw at her thighs, and her nipples harden further. Her skin prickles with a million goose bumps.

"You think you can take it all?" I thrust all the way in, watching my length stretch her throat, inch by inch, until it bottoms out. If I don't pull out, she might pass out.

A loud gasp echoes around us as she devours air back into her lungs. My cock glistens with her spit. Her lips are a raw red from being stretched so wide, and her fucking eyes are a wild shade of lilac where the choked pink of the whites has stained the vibrant blue of her irises.

"Good little mouse," I tease, tapping her cheek until her mouth falls open again, and as I thrust deep into her clenching throat, I lean over her, stroking through her dripping cunt until I find her clit.

I work her hard nub until her moans choke around my cock and she's pushing at my hand.

"Behave." I push deeper before I pull out.

Her tits tremble with her endless gasps, and her black-stained tears run into her dark hair.

Ava's the hottest thing I've ever had, and I will do whatever it takes to make sure I'll always have her.

"Fuck me," she grunts, looking up at me. "Now."

She sounds so hoarse, so fucking breathless, and so

fucking mine that I can't deny her. Lifting her from the couch, I help her stand in front of me. I take in her reddened eyes and her swollen lips, her lust-stained skin and her needy gasps.

So fucking perfect.

"I want you to fuck my pussy like you fucked my mouth," she commands breathlessly.

I turn her round, bending her over the back of the seat. Her pert ass is at attention, her engorged lips glistening through her pressed thighs.

"Who says I want your cunt?" I run the tip of my cock through her folds to her crease, thrusting between the round globes of her ass.

Her panty-tied ankles cross as she folds completely over, her hands clenching at the edge of the seat cushion as her cheeks spread. Her asshole is so fucking tight as it clenches at the feel of my cock rounding it. She's got no idea what I'd do to her.

My hands squeeze her flesh over my thrusting dick to her throaty mewls and shaking legs.

"You want to get fucked in the ass, dirty girl?" I slap down on her flesh. The sight of it imprinted with my hand is divine. The sting that ricochets through my arm is fucking addictive.

Her reply is garbled through her moans and her cries as I tease and mark her flesh. My cock aches, throbbing with the need to take every inch of her.

Trailing down to her pussy, I spread her ass, and as she drags in a deep breath, I plunge inside her without warning. A hoarse scream pushes from her, her wet cunt pulsing around me, her ass clenching at the merciless intrusion.

"So deep...so fucking deep," she chants, a hand

reaching back to try and ease my assault. "Oh my God, Damon...fuck..."

"If your cunt can't handle my cock, how's your ass meant to take it?" I spit on her hole and spread it with my thumb, rounding and probing as I fuck her pussy to her obliterated moans and groans.

My thumb inches in as I edge my cock out of her pussy. Her hand grabs at me, and releasing her ass cheek, I hold her arm to the curve of her star-dusted spine as I slam home.

And fuck what a picture it is with her loud moans and hoarse cries. Her pleas for more and overwhelmed groans. Her body trembles as I remove my thumb, releasing her arm and pulling her flush to my chest by the knot of her messy hair.

"Who do you belong to, little mouse?" I yank her hair, tilting her face up to mine. It's tear tracked and fucking glorious.

"You." A long, languid sob escapes her lips as I flex deeper into her.

"You want to know why, Ava?"

Smoothing her sweat- and tear-drenched hair from her face, I kiss the moans right out of her mouth.

"Because I love you." Her eyes widen on mine. Terrified. Overwhelmed. "You should be scared, because once you're mine...once I love you...there's nothing I won't do to keep you. Nothing. All bets are off."

I pull out hastily, turning her to face me. Grabbing her arm, I throw it over my shoulder before I hoist her up my body and bury myself inside her again. Perching her ass on the back of the sofa, I grasp her throat, squeezing and stroking as I fuck her in earnest.

I fuck her until she's boneless in my hands and her

body is shaking so violently with the spurts of my cock, that I'm not sure whether I've broken her or not...but either way...she had it coming. Because if she's going to rob me of my power, I'll rob her of everything. Her body. Her heart. Her soul.

CHAPTER TWENTY

DAMON

"Have you lost your fucking mind?" Dex slams his drink down on my desk. "This wasn't the plan."

"The plan's changed. If you can't handle it..." I clear the drive with the surveillance clip from the bar and sign the paperwork Grayson drew up last week.

"If I can't handle it? You're thinking with your goddamn dick, Damon!" He falls silent, clearly waiting for me to say something. When I don't, he leans over my desk, grabbing my attention. "Is her pussy really that good?"

"It's better actually." Resisting the urge to ram my fist through his fucking teeth, I sit back in my chair. I lace my hands together, resting my elbows on the arms of my seat. "Dex." I call his full attention to me. "Don't forget—I made you VP, but this is my company. It's my money, and I'll do whatever the fuck I want with it all."

"You're going to regret it."

"Get the fuck out, before I fire your ass." I grab my drink and finish it as he leaves my office.

Before he walks out of the door, he turns back to me. "Bros before hoes, right? Isn't that what you always said?"

"Get out." It's the last warning.

I'm glad he listens; I'd hate for our years of friendship to be obliterated by his loose tongue.

Once I've finished signing the contract, I hand the documents to William. "Grayson needs these today."

"Yes, sir." He pauses and then asks, "The awards. Will you be taking a plus-one?"

He knows the answer of course, but he wants confirmation.

"Yes," I tell him just as Ava comes through the door in time for lunch.

"Hey." She grins at me, standing in the doorway. When William looks at her, she waves and says a soft "Hi."

"Good afternoon, Miss Monroe."

"Are you ready?" she asks me. She's wearing a tight pencil skirt that cuts off below her calves, but the slit to the middle of her thigh shows enough of her long legs to make my dick twitch. The thin, string-like straps of the top she's wearing expose the crystal-embellished straps of her bra and the strings crossing over chest. I'm not sure whether it's even a bra because her nipples are too obvious for there to be a barrier between her skin and the shirt. "Damon!"

"Yeah?"

"I have a meeting with Robert this afternoon and—"

"You're going to see Robert today?"

"Yeah."

"Wearing that?"

"What's wrong with it?"

Is she serious right now?

"What isn't?"

"You didn't take issue when I put it on this morning." She shrugs. "Come on, Damon, I don't have time to argue over this. I have a jacket. You know I do."

I do, but still, the thought of Robert ogling what's mine doesn't sit right.

"Fine."

"So, lunch?"

"Let's go." I grab my jacket from William and head out with her.

We settle on the small Mexican cantina a block from the office. Ava barely touches her food though. She's moving it around the cardboard dish, and her margarita is untouched.

"What's wrong, beautiful?" Grabbing her fork, I put it down and tip her face to mine.

She looks a little bit peaky. Her blue eyes are darker than usual, and her skin is a little pale.

"Nothing," she murmurs. "All the late nights we keep having. Robert and Lacie on my back to get things with Callum rolling...I guess I'm tired."

I'd noticed she was working late; even after we're in bed she's reading through Robert's manuscript or writing emails. I just didn't realize it was all piling up on her because she makes a point of not being given favor. But if it's making her sick...

"Get an assistant. I'll email HR and tell them they need to find someone."

Ava sits up in a flash, affronted. "No way. We have assistants."

"They're clearly not enough."

"Or maybe we need to slow down."

"That's not going to happen."

"So what, Damon? You give me my own assistant while the other editors share...and I'll be exactly what everyone is already calling me."

I know people are talking. I'm not stupid, and I'm not exactly hiding our relationship, but I haven't heard anything bad.

"What are they calling you?" I ask her. She's clearly upset even though she's trying to hide.

"It doesn't matter. I just need to be more efficient." Ava picks up her jacket and throws it on. "I'm going to be late for my appointment."

"Ava!" I follow her out, grabbing her before she gets away. "What are they saying?"

"It's silly, and I'm an idiot for letting it get to me. It doesn't matter."

"It matters to me," I snap. Her eyes round, and with the bright sun, I see the dark circles around her eyes. And I notice how her hair isn't as bouncy and full as usual.

Fuck.

"You matter to me, and we'll slow down if that's what you need, but you need to tell me what the fuck people are saying. If you don't, I'm going to go back to my office and issuing a memo to the entire—"

Tensing, she looks up at me. "I'm not a gold digger. I'm not a slut. And...and..." She swallows. "I work hard, Damon."

"You don't have to tell me, I see it."

"If you give me an assistant, people will just see it as—"

"I don't care what people think. You're getting an assistant because you work hard and have a shit ton of things pilling up on you. It's in the company's best interest."

"It's not how it will be seen."

"Fine." I stroke my thumb down her nose. Her skin feels different. And the longer I cup her cheek, the more evident it becomes that it's lost some of its plumpness. "I'll get HR to find personal assistants for all the editors. I'm sure we can then allocate the extra work to the current team. That way everyone wins...and you're not killing yourself."

"That's insane. That's four extra salaries you'll take on. Fran wouldn't agree on this."

"Fran would have your back like she's always had mine." I press a kiss to her head. "I told you: there's nothing I won't do for you, little mouse."

"Some things are too much."

"Not when it comes to you."

She collapses into me, her arms wrapping around my waist. After a while she looks up with a long drawn-out breath. "I need to go. I can't be late for my appointment. I'll see you later, okay?"

I don't bother telling her to move her meeting with Robert to another day. She won't, and it'll be another thing that she'll fret over. Instead, I make a mental note to book some time off with her. Maybe take her somewhere nice where she won't be working at all.

———

I call Ava one more time, but she doesn't pick up. My worry amps up. I should have taken her home. I shouldn't have let her carry on like she was all right when she very clearly wasn't. I send her a quick message, while Robert goes on about everything they've been doing.

Damon: Are you okay?

"Is everything all right?" he asks, taking his coffee from the server.

"Yes." My sighed reply comes out terse. "It's that time of year where we're full steam ahead."

He laughs. "I can't believe the book will be done in the next couple of weeks. After the last twelve months of writing and reading and rewriting... Of course, Ava is already onto the next part. I sent her the first few chapters, and she said it was good, so..."

"I thought she was meeting with you today?" I grab my own coffee.

"We were, but she asked to reschedule. She had a clash in her schedule." He shrugs as we leave the coffee shop. "Anyway, it was good to see you."

Fuck. I call her again as I part with Robert. And again, her call goes to voicemail. I'm about to message her when she texts:

Ava: Call you after my meeting.

Huh?

Every possible scenario is going through my head, but I resist the urge to track her down. She's probably with Lacie going over Warner's shit.

Still, a lump forms in my throat, and my chest tightens in that way it always does when I can feel something's off.

Not bothering to go back to the office, I call Gerry to pick me up. Once he arrives, I head straight to Fran's. She's good at talking sense, and I don't want to be a dick when Ava's clearly not feeling great.

Fran opens to the door to her and Grayson's Chelsea red-brick town house. "What are you doing here?"

I walk in, taking my shoes off—like she always gripes at me to—before I head into her kitchen. It's all mismatched wood and exposed bricks painted a bright white with beams and wide windows.

"I need you to talk me off a ledge." Dumping my cold coffee in her sink, I dispose of the cup before I sit at the kitchen table. She has the back door opened out into the small walled patio garden and a chaise in front of it with a stack of books beside it.

Sitting, she hugs her belly. It's swelled enough that even in a loose dress it's impossible to hide.

"I'm listening." She lies back, looking at me like this is some kind of counseling session.

"Ava lied to me."

"Okay. What about and why do you think she lied?"

"She said she had a meeting with Robert this after-noon, but I bumped into him at the coffee shop close to the office and he said she'd rescheduled."

"That doesn't mean she's lying."

"I was worried because she wasn't herself at lunch, and people have been talking... I think she's overworking herself and..."

"Get her an assistant," she says like that's the fucking issue I'm trying to work out.

"Yes, I know. I'm on that already."

"Good."

"I tried to call her and it went to her voicemail."

"Right..." She's already looking at me like I'm being an unreasonable asshole, and I haven't finished.

"I sent her a text, and she didn't reply."

"So you called her again?"

"Yeah, and she text me telling me she was in her meeting." I sit, going over everything I've just told her, feeling like a whiny adolescent.

"Damon, it sounds like she wanted you stop calling. Maybe she wanted some space...especially if she's not feeling herself. Being a woman is fucking hard, okay?" Fran rolls her eyes with a *give me patience* laugh. "Besides, Robert isn't her only client. Not to mention that she could've rescheduled the meeting after she left you and again, didn't want you all up in her space and making her feel worse. You guys can be so overbearing at times. You make shit harder than it has to be."

"Don't preach to me about how Grayson takes care of you. That's not what I was doing at all. I was just making sure Ava was okay."

"So, she answers and tells you she's had to reschedule because she's that sick. What would you have done?"

I have a feeling this is a trick question that's only going to make me look like an even bigger ass. But I answer it honestly anyway because Fran lives to point that shit out.

"I would've gone to her. Made sure she was okay. Taken care of her."

"Is she an invalid?"

"No."

"Is she dying?"

"No."

"Is she incapable of looking after herself?"

"I guess not." She gives me that *be real* look. "No."

"So, we agree that your little freak-out is completely blown out of proportion and you're being a tad melo-dramatic."

"When you put it that way..." I bury my face in my hands.

"Damon..." The chair beside me scrapes on the floor before Fran sits with me. "You love Ava, and I know that it's hard for you see the people you love hurt or feel shitty. But sometimes, the best way to love someone is to give them space. Especially if they're feeling crappy or over-whelmed. Fuck, sometimes we just want space for the sake of it."

"I know. And I'm a jerk. And I'm sorry I came to whine about it to you."

"Are you kidding me? This is great. I love that you're on your toes with her." Nudging me with her shoulder, she asks, "Is she going with you to the awards next weekend?"

"Yeah."

"And you actually asked? You're not assuming?"

"What do you take me for?"

"Do you want me to answer that for real?"

"It was one of the easiest conversations we've had, actually." Not that she was exactly with it after I fucked her so hard, she could barely move.

I can't help but grin at that, because we had to take it easy the next day.

"Oh Jesus, you fucked her into it, didn't you?"

I smile wide at her.

"Oh man..." Getting up, she puts the kettle on her stove and goes about making us a drink. All the while I keep trying to reason with my worry.

CHAPTER TWENTY-ONE

DAMON

Ava leaves my office a little drawn and sad. She seems better in herself; her color has come back some, but there are times where she's distracted. I know she's desperately trying to mend things with her mother, but the woman won't even give her shit.

Maybe I should've written that into the contract with her father. Forced them to be better parents. Forced them to care. To love her like she needs them to. Even if they don't deserve her. Maybe I don't deserve her after the way I reacted last week...doubting her even though she's never given me reason to.

Still, it's water under the bridge, and I've had her new assistant send me her schedule so I can plan something for us, away from the city and all our responsibilities.

"Is there trouble in paradise?" Dex saunters in, a grin cutting his face like he's about to win a bet or something. "Why else would Miss Monroe be looking for a job elsewhere? On a different continent...that bad, huh?"

"What are you talking about?"

He sits in the chair Ava just vacated. It's probably still warm.

"Did you know Beckett are looking for an editor?" he asks simply. "I thought they were going broke, but it seems they have one last hurrah up their sleeve."

The fucking nervous habit I've had since I was fourteen comes back. Frantically tapping my thumbs on my desk, I wait for him to get on with whatever he's about to tell me.

"Hayden's in town for the awards."

"Hayden Hearst? Since when is he in publishing?"

"Since Beckett restructured and merged the management for press and media. They cut management costs to invest in a new editor. Someone that could bring *big* business their way."

My chest tightens with the way he's so fucking jolly over whatever is coming.

"Word is they were seen together last week." His smarmy grin finally fades, and he straightens in his seat. "Beckett were one of houses she approached when she left Monroe. So why the fuck is your girlfriend entertaining them now?"

Shit. All the fucking worry and suspicion from last week blast me, and all I can do not to lose my shit in front of him is swallow it down. Push it right down until I've had a chance to clear it up with Ava. Because she wouldn't go behind my back like that.

Would she?

But then she's been distracted and distant...what if there's more to it than her relationship with her mother? What if it's something other than her workload?

Fuck.

Why was she even talking to Hayden fucking Hearst?

"Get the fuck out, Dexter."

He doesn't say anything else, but the shake of his head and his bitter laugh is enough to tell me he thinks I'm a fool.

And I'm not anybody's fool. Ever.

———

AVA

Damon's quiet the entire drive home. It's been one of those days where everything that could go wrong, goes wrong. Mom still isn't talking to me despite my best efforts to reach out to her. But Damon's here, and he makes everything better.

It seems crazy that I can't imagine not having him with me. Seems crazy that a few months ago we were at each other's throats. I guess not everything happens the way you think it will.

We walk into the apartment, and unlike he usually does, he heads straight to the kitchen. Normally he gets changed into sweats and then we figure dinner out together, but today he's gone straight to the kitchen and poured himself a drink.

I guess his afternoon wasn't any better than my morning.

Dropping my purse by the breakfast bar, I head toward the bedroom. I need to change out these clothes.

"Where were you last week?" he asks dryly.

I freeze, my heart hammering in my chest because I know exactly what he's asking, and I've been dreading this conversation. Especially after he was given access to my schedule.

I turn, trying to figure out the best way to tell him where I was, because I don't want him to freak out. And I know he's going to lose his shit.

"Dammit, Ava!" His voice booms around me, making me shudder. "Where the fuck were you?"

He seems so angry. Maybe he already knows.

Of course he doesn't.

It's impossible. The only person that knows is Lacie because I had to talk to someone. I had to know that I wasn't being stupid or...I don't know. Things with Damon have moved so fast. And I wouldn't have it any other way, but...

"Start fucking talking," he bites out before he throws what's left of his red wine down his throat. "Now!"

I take a moment to gather myself, stupidly, because it only makes him angrier. Refilling his glass, Damon looks up at me. There's so much hurt and indignation on his face that I can't hold his stare.

"Did you think I wouldn't find out about Hayden and Beckett?" He takes another measured gulp of his wine. "What? You were going to leave me like you left Monroe? High and dry?"

"What are you talking about?"

"I gave you everything you wanted. Everything you never had at Monroe...wasn't it enough? You had to go behind my back..."

"I didn't...I..."

"Then why were you meeting with Hayden fucking Hearst instead of Robert Rhodes?"

All the blood drains from my head to my feet. And I curse this day for ever happening because it just keeps getting shittier.

I wander over to the breakfast bar, standing opposite

him with the counter between us.

"I bumped into Hayden at the bar I was meeting Lacie at. He came over and we spoke briefly. He asked if I was happy at CPM, and I told him I was where I belonged. It wasn't a meeting. It lasted all of two minutes."

He remains quiet, nursing his wineglass. I'm about to walk away again when he asks, "Then why did you lie?"

"Because I was freaking out about you freaking out. When you called me, I was at the doctor because... because I was late. Like really fucking late, and I'm never late."

He looks at me blankly, like I'm talking out of my ass. He's so fucking clueless.

"God, Damon, I thought I was pregnant. Is that clear enough?"

"You thought?" he breathes, looking overwhelmed.

"Yes, I thought I was pregnant because why else would I be late, right? And we fuck a lot. Like a lot. And... and then I took a test, but it was all funny. It wasn't negative or positive, so I called Lacie and she said that I needed to go to the doctor. Of course, I did, because that's what any grown-ass woman would do if the home test was all weird and shit. But I was freaking out because it's too soon and...God, you don't even trust me."

"How am I meant to trust you if you can't be up-front with me about things," he murmurs, looking into his glass.

"I was feeling awful and I panicked. And I didn't lie— I rescheduled my meeting with Robert after I left you because you looked worried, and I didn't want to put another thing on you." It's the truth. After I left him, I couldn't bear the thought of having to sit with Robert and try to pretend that I was okay when I was anything but.

Damon reaches for my hand, but I'm just so tired of today and the way he was so quick to jump to conclusions without talking to me first.

My Damon bubble is popped, and I'm feeling a million things because I've trusted him in spite of everything he did to me. The blackmail. The bullying. The coercion.

I trusted him in spite of it all.

"I already had an appointment booked with my doctor for after the meeting with Robert, so I met with Lacie earlier and she went with me. It just happened that I got to the bar first and Hayden was there. He saw me and he came and talked to me. Did he try to sound me out? Absolutely, but I told him I wasn't interested."

"Ava..." He tries to reach out again, but instead I grab my purse from the floor.

"Maybe if you weren't so ruthless and conniving, then maybe you wouldn't have trust issues. You know? If you didn't go around fucking people over, you wouldn't be so damn paranoid about being fucked over."

"Maybe if you weren't so damn afraid of stating your feelings, then I wouldn't have to wonder what the fuck we're doing here!"

I don't bother replying. Instead, I walk away, leaving him with his wine and his distrust. I can't deal with this right now. I can't even think straight anymore.

"Go on, run away, Ava. Go! It's what you do, isn't it? You fuck off when things don't go your way."

"Fuck you, Damon. And fuck your love. And all your shit!"

I slam the door to his apartment and get in the elevator as soon as it arrives.

I'm done.

CHAPTER TWENTY-TWO

AVA

I don't bother going into the office for the rest of the week. For two days I hide in my apartment and pretend the last few months haven't all come crashing down like my four years with Marsh.

Go on, run away, Ava!

I'm not running away, and I don't have issues with my feelings. Being careful isn't a crime. Maybe I should've been more careful.

Definitely should've been more careful, I sigh, throwing the negative test in the bin.

There's still no show from Aunt Flow, and I'm waiting to get the blood test result from my doctor. She said she would call, but I've heard nothing from her yet.

Maybe it's a good sign?

I'm not sure how I feel about either outcome. Baby or no baby. Pregnant or not. It all seems unimportant when Damon isn't here. I'm trying not to make myself sick with anxiety while at the same time I'm trying to convince myself that the breather between us is a good thing.

Clarity. Space. And loneliness.

I feel so terribly lonely without him that all I can do is crash back into bed.

It's the middle of a Saturday afternoon, and all I can think about is what he's doing. If he's as torn up over our argument as I am.

It's award day and it was meant to be our first public event together. Instead, I'm lying in my bed trying to force myself to sleep so that I can escape this horrible feeling in my chest, my bones, and my stomach.

I flit through my phone, staring at his number, willing him to call me because it feels like an entire part of me is missing. The happy part that believes in silver linings.

He doesn't call, and with the slew of my lonely tears, I drift off. It's all black like endless night until warmth envelopes me and there's a crackle of light. And my dreams are haunted by his scent and his strength. They're an inescapable reminder of everything I'm missing.

"Ava."

I whine at my bleary consciousness. Wishing it away.

"Baby."

No. Go away.

"Ava!"

My eyes flutter open to my bright sunshine-filled bedroom and the pounding at my door that may as well be in my skull.

Pound, pound, pound!

"Ava, open the damn door. I know you're in there."

Bang, bang, bang!

"Do not make me break this door down!"

Fuck.

My body is achy as I trudge through my apartment.

God, this is not what I had in mind when I willed him

back to me. Why does he have to be a bull in a china shop with everything?

I take a deep breath before I open my door. I don't have it in me to argue if that's what he came here for.

I hope it isn't.

Damon stands there looking at me, his wallet between his teeth as he holds his bank card aloft like he was about to break in.

Jesus, he's fucking crazy,

"You realize you can't break in with that, right?" I point to the metal guard that overlaps the seam of the lock.

Shrugging, he puts his card and wallet away. It's only then I notice he's all dressed up in his tux. He looks so good that it takes everything in me not to throw myself at him.

"What are you doing here?" I block him when he tries to walk into my space, and he sighs a long, drawn-out, and tired breath.

"You didn't tell me what the doctor said. And I've given you space, but it's enough now." He unhooks a dress bag from the picture rail outside my door and drapes it over the small chair by the sideboard in my hall.

Taking my hand, he guides me to my couch, sitting me before he perches on my coffee table. The thing is a rickety antique that could collapse at any moment, but he leans over his knees, looking at me like everything else can just fucking disappear.

"I was a jerk."

"Jackass."

"Fine. I was a jackass the other da—"

"Actually, asshole's better."

"Ava," he growls. "I was a huge jerky asshole, and I'm sorry."

His apology is straightforward, but it's sincere. He's not here with his cocky attitude or mightier-than-thou smirk.

"I should've handled things differently. Given you the chance you deserved to talk to me without accusations looming over us. I just..." He pauses, looking at me, his dark eyes sloping like all the happiness has been sucked out of him too. "I...I just..."

His stuttering over his words has my heart squeezing in my chest and tears flooding my eyes because Damon's not a wordless person. He's lost his words as I've lost the silver linings. And it only serves to make the sadness greater.

"There's no excuse or justification for my actions, except that I'm an asshole and you deserve better."

The conversation we had that first night at the bar about Marsh flits into my head, and I blurt, "And a sack of shit."

He chuckles at that, adding, "An incredibly stupid shack of shit."

I nod, waiting for him to continue.

"I brought your dress."

"For what?" Of course, now I'm being a bitch, but with all the fretting going on inside me, I don't want to be weak right now.

"For tonight." Damon stands and heads back to my front door, coming back with the designer garment bag in his hand. "Every couple fights and argues..."

"We didn't just argue, Damon. You accused me of going behind your back because you heard I spoke to Hayden. So, what? Next time someone tells you they saw me talk to another guy, are you going to accuse me of cheating on you?"

"You're being ridiculous."

"Am I? Because it felt like you did just that. You accused me of cheating your trust. And furthermore, you haven't given me shit. I've worked hard. I've done things that quite frankly I'm not even proud of. I did every fucking thing I swore I would never do. I let you railroad me and coerce me...and in spite of it all, I trusted you enough to let you in. To love you."

He looks at me like his whole world has been made right. And I realize too late that I let him have the only thing that I was holding on to.

My love.

The one thing I've given him in the guise of lust and trust and kindness...I've handed it to him on a platter when he least deserves it. And it's odd how comforting it feels to do it.

A tear escapes me and rolls down my cheek, the go-ahead all the others need to follow. "All you had to do was trust me too."

"And I do."

"Not enough to know that I would never hurt you intentionally."

"You can't love someone you don't trust, Ava, and I love you more than everything." He sits beside me, pulling me onto his lap. "I can apologize again and again, but unless you're willing to accept it...it's pointless."

My finger finds the freckle by his lip, tracing from it to his jaw. Damon is so damn gorgeous, everything about him makes me want to lose myself to him, but what turns my want into a need is the heart I know he guards so closely.

I know he's let me in there because he's not an apologetic man. He's not someone that lives on his feelings; he's ruthless and conniving and brilliant, but he feels when it comes to me...and I can't hold that against him.

"I should've told you about my appointment. I was too chicken because I told you I was covered and now..."

"I don't care." He pauses, shaking his head. "That came out wrong. I do care but not in a bad way. And besides, it's not only your responsibility."

Lowering his forehead onto mine, he nudges his nose over mine.

"What are you doing?"

"They're called Eskimo kisses. Mom used to say they make everything better when I was little."

I'm inclined to agree with Elizabeth. They're the best thing I've felt in days.

"You still haven't told me what the outcome was." Damon searches my eyes, the hand on my legging-covered thigh rising to hold my waist.

"I don't think I am. I took another test this morning, and it was negative. I'm waiting on my blood test result. Apparently, it could be too early to tell with the usual home tests, or it could be that my body has fallen out of sync. I hope it has because I'm not ready for a baby. And I'm scared...look at Fran."

"Yeah, the whole baby thing is petrifying." He says that like he's had firsthand experience, and it leaves me curious. "Oh?"

"Mom really wanted another child, but...it never worked out. I was a fluke."

"A good one." I'm looking at him, and all I think of are the baby photos Elizabeth had around their home.

I'm kind of thawed by the picture of a little boy just

like him: thick, dark hair, deep chocolate eyes and beautiful golden skin. Maybe he'd have a freckle just like his daddy's... I love that freckle. And I love his lips. And his eyes.

"I love you, little mouse." His hand cups my face before he kisses me softly, and before he can pull away, I kiss back. Harder.

I suck his lip into my mouth, and I don't let it free until Damon opens his. His tongue licks over mine with a groan, and he takes his time savoring me, just as I take my time relishing in his hold and touch.

We only stop to come up for air, and as he smiles at me, I tell him, "I love you too."

"Enough to go with me tonight?"

"More."

CHAPTER TWENTY-THREE

AVA

The awards were great. The long night was exhausting, and although my parents were there with Marsh, I tried not to let it sour things for Damon and me. But it's hard to be indifferent when the people who raised you can't even afford you a smile.

Thank God for Damon, that's all I can say. He's the best distraction, and the worst because the rest of the weekend was spent wrapped up in him rather than Warner. Now that Robert's book is done, I'm focusing on Callum's. I'm more excited to learn more about him than I thought I'd be. Especially with the way Lacie has spoken of him.

"Knock, knock!" Owen pokes his head into my office. "Look who's home!"

"Hey, stranger!"

"I should be calling you stranger. You're never in this office anymore." He sits in the chair across from me. "But then, you've been a busy girl..."

"Don't you start with your gossip." I ball up a Post-it note and throw it at his head. "How's your Oscar winner?" I ask him about his client to deviate him from my business. Not that I don't like Owen, it's more that I don't want to talk to anyone in this place about me and Damon. It makes for awkward gossip, and I'm not into it.

"Nice try." He flicks the note back at me and sits up straight. "Is it true we bought Monroe?"

I actually laugh at his question, because that's definitely something Damon would never do, especially not without talking to me first.

"That's not an answer, Avie."

"Of course not."

"That's not what all the little birdies are saying," he sings with mock innocence.

"I'm sure we don't pay you to gossip on company time, Mr. Clay." My gaze flicks to my open door to find Dex standing there.

"I was just asking Ava about Monroe." Owen stands, shrugging at Dex as he makes to leave.

"Oh. I'm pretty sure no one's meant to know about that yet, seeing it only completed this morning."

It's impossible. My heart falls to my stomach, a cold sweat chilling me.

"That's not true."

Owen's gone when Dex saunters in, smiling. "You better believe it. Monroe is officially a part of the family."

"My father would never sell..."

He looks around my office, chuckling like I'm a naïve little girl he's got to school. "He didn't have a choice. Damon made damn sure of it. Why did you think he practically handed you this job without an interview?"

Because I'm the best, I reply to myself in the same words Damon's spoken to me.

"How well do actually know him?" The sorry way

company and everything to do with the man I let take over my heart.

Is it really true?

It all makes sense...it all fits so well with everything that's happened...

"Hello? Miss Monroe?" I come back to the call. "Hello?"

"H-h-hi."

"I hope this isn't a bad time?" she asks, and tears start pouring from my eyes. They pour and pour and pour as I listen to her tell me about my results, and my world completely plummets.

CHAPTER TWENTY-FOUR

AVA

I'm spiraling down a rabbit hole, as Dr. Cruz talks me through all my options. All the while I'm still in the office with Dexter looking down on me. Breaking my heart. Obliterating my world. It's like Groundhog Day except it revolves around the last two hours of my life.

"You don't have to make a decision today. If I were to make an estimation after the internal ultrasound, I'd say you're about five weeks along. In this state you have till twenty-four weeks to terminate the pregnancy." She smiles when I look at her startled because I never imagined myself in this situation. Having to make a decision.

"Does it have a heart?" It's a fucking stupid question, and I have no idea why I'm asking it.

"At this point?" Dr. Cruz clasps her hands over her notes. "Yes."

I nod, silencing my phone. No doubt Fran has alerted Damon to my call. It was her stuttering silence that sold them out in the end.

I look up at the doctor, trying my best to smile through the soul-splitting pain in my chest.

"Thank you," I tell her when she hands me the information on my options and all the things we've discussed.

I'm relieved I can leave when she walks me out telling her secretary when to arrange my next appointment.

I stand outside thinking of where to go. I consider my apartment, but Damon will be there, and I don't want to see him right now. Fuck, I don't want to see him ever again if not for the fact that I don't want him to see what he's done to me.

He did you well.

Fresh tears sluice down my face as I try to figure out where to go. I try calling Mom, but she doesn't even let it ring out anymore. She's declining my calls.

Was it his plan all along to isolate me?

If so, why would he introduce me to his family? I don't understand why all of a sudden nothing makes sense, and I need to make sense because there's a baby inside me and fuuuuck! I can't do this shit on my own.

I manage to hail a taxi after a while, and whilst I have no idea where I'm going, I tell the driver to take me to the park. The fucking park.

What is wrong with me?

"Ma'am?" The driver pushes a wad of tissues through the cash tray. "Is everything okay? Do you need help?"

"I'm fine."

"Oh man," she grates. "Look, I can't drop you off like this."

"I'm fine."

"You don't look fine, and you were outside that doctor's office... You're not sick, are you? You're okay, right?"

"I'm fine."

"It's just that you hear about healthy young women getting real sick now with cancer and—"

"I'm. Fine," I tell her, and because I can't bear to listen to her analyze my situation, I give her Lacie's address. It's a Monday; she'll probably be at the office, but her doorman knows me well enough to let me up.

And he does. In fact, he calls the elevator and takes me all the way up to her floor. Sitting on the floor outside her door, I look through the information the doctor gave me. I'm pretty sure I'm ready to collapse from sheer exhaustion when she arrives.

"Oh fuck." She pauses in front of me. "What's happened?"

Hoisting me up from the ground, she lets us into her home. It's not over-the-top, but impressive enough that you know she makes very good money.

Once she's got me on her couch, she starts to go through all the shit in my hands. "Oh fuck."

At this point I have no tears left to cry. I'm empty in feeling and being. I remember thinking Damon had broken me before, but that was nothing compared to this.

"What am I going to do?"

"Wash," she says, grabbing her phone and texting away as she paces in front of me. "You're going to wash this day away, and then we're going to order pizza and dirty burgers and all the shit we can get here tonight. And we're going to pig the fuck out. Besides, you have the best excuse, right?"

"I can't have his baby."

Lacie stops, turning to face me with narrowed eyes, "Did he tell you that? Is that why you're upset? Because he was a dick about it?"

I laugh because I actually wish that were the reason.

"You're laughing at least." Helping me up, she guides me into her bathroom. "I don't know what's happened, but I promise we'll work it out together. You know I'm good at working shit out."

She pushes me into the walk-in shower, and as I undress, she brings me a bath sheet and some of her bad-day fluffy pajamas.

"I'm going to order food. You take your time."

———

DAMON

Thank God!

I answer the call before she has a chance to change her mind. "Ava?"

The voice on the other end laughs sourly. "I don't know what you've said or done, but I'm going to enjoy hurting you. Every tear you've made her cry. Every piece of her you've broken...I'm going to hurt you for it. You just had to be a decent guy. Take responsibility."

She puts the phone down without finishing, and I'm left going over everything.

Take responsibility?

I keep going over her words as I leave Ava's door and get back in the car. It takes me no time to get Lacie's address from Warner. When I get there, however, the doorman turns out to be a problem. He's an old boy, but fuck, he's not having any of my shit.

In the end he calls Lacie so many times that she comes downstairs, rage coloring her face a deep crimson.

"You!" She practically runs at me. Her hands land on my chest with a hard shove. I'm taken back by how strong she is. "You need to fuck off. Haven't you done enough? Haven't you hurt her enough?"

"Miss Taylor, is this man bothering you?" The old boy tries to get in between us.

"It's okay, Sam, I've handled bigger bastards."

"I don't know what the fuck you think you know, but I need to talk to Ava." I hold her at arm's length by her shoulders.

"No, you don't. You've done enough damage. How could you turn your back on her...on your child?"

My already twisted stomach tightens around my heart. "What? What are you talking about?"

Laughing, she pushes away from me. "You're something else, you know that? To come here and pretend you're fucking clueless. Meanwhile, your pregnant girlfriend is falling to pieces upstairs. What is wrong with you?"

I'm immobile as her statement sinks in and echoes around my head.

My pregnant girlfriend?

My pregnant girlfriend.

Ava's pregnant?

Lacie heads back toward the elevators, pressing the button like it's personally offended her. The doors ding open, but instead of going in, she turns back to me. "I can't believe I actually admired you for what you did at the game. I can't believe I was beginning to think you were a decent person..."

"Is she okay?" I ignore her rant. "Is the baby okay?"

"Why do you care now?" she asks venomously, and I really can't hold back anymore.

"I don't give a fuck what you know or what you think you know," I start for her, my long strides knocking her doorman out of the way. "But I would never turn my back on her or our child."

"So why the fuck is she in pieces?" Lacie shouts right in my face.

"I did something, and I need to explain to her why. I need her to know that it's for her. It's all for her…"

"What?" She looks at me utterly confused.

"Ava wanted Monroe, so I bought it for her."

CHAPTER TWENTY-FIVE

AVA

"Damon's downstairs." Lacie sits on the edge of her bed, watching me as I stand in front of the long mirror on her wardrobe.

It's no surprise—I knew he'd eventually come here. I thought it would take him longer, but then what do I know, right? At this point I'm asking myself if I know anything about Damon. The only thing I'm sure of is that I have his baby inside me.

It's weird because I don't feel different. I don't look different. I just know that there's another human growing inside me. And it's got a heart. Too small to hear or see, but it's got one. It's alive.

I pull the pajama top down and turn to her. "Okay."

"He wants to see you." Standing, she wanders to me. Her eyes flit everywhere like she's hiding something. "You need to hear him out."

"No. I don't."

"You do, Ava. You really do." I can tell from the way she's looking at me that she's already spoken to him. She has that piteous pout to her lips she gets when she feels sorry for you. "Call him or talk to him through the door...I don't know...just listen to what he says, and then you can make a decision you are less likely to regret."

"The only thing I regret is..." *Loving him.* I can't actually bring myself to say the words out loud. The thought is another dagger through my already bleeding heart. "The only thing I regret is letting him near me."

"Babe..." Her arms wrap around me. Lacie is the closest thing to family I have left. Everyone else is gone. "Sometimes we have to do things that hurt us. But they're the right thing because in the long haul..."

I look up at her, and she looks so sad, so very sad, and it's got nothing to do with me.

"I'll tell him to go away." She smiles weakly at me before walking away. "Food will be here soon."

I follow her out, listening to her tell Damon that I'm too tired to talk today. That it's been a long day for everyone, and the best thing is to sleep on things. She fields him as though she's protecting one of her clients.

Not long after she's gone into the shower, the food arrives and with it, a note.

The blocky all-uppercase scrawl is somewhat messy, like it's been rushed. The paper has that faint woody amber scent that makes my pores come to life, and every part of me craves Damon's warmth. And all I can do is stare and stare at my name written boldly and underlined like it's the most important thing on that page.

"You're not feeling sick, are you?" Lacie asks, taking the food from me, and I follow her into her kitchen. Her eyes flicker to the hand on my chest. "Are you going to read it?" She nods at the note I'm holding to my heart like it's a salve to my pain. "You should."

"He lied to me."

"But you knew he was a liar when you let him in."

"I thought..."

"You didn't think—you wanted what Damon could give you, and you took it. You didn't do anything wrong." She sighs, handing me a plate with a slice of pizza, fries, and a burger. "Eat what you can."

She grabs her own plate and heads for the couch. We sit in silence, neither one of us eating or really watching the show.

"I fucked Callum."

Wait. "What?"

"I fucked Callum Warner."

"Shit." It's all I can say to that without sounding judgmental.

"Yeah."

"Are you okay?"

"No." Putting her plate down on the coffee table, she then grabs mine. "Read the note." She pulls it out of the pouch at the front of the sweater and hands it to me before sitting back and hugging me to her.

I stare at my name some more before I unfold the paper. I take a deep breath, but it does nothing to stop the tears from flooding my eyes. I blink and blink them away, but there's too many. I thought I was all cried out, but his scent and the familiarity of his handwriting...

My beautiful Ava.

My heart stutters at those words, before it tightens somewhere in the pit of my stomach.

"You want me to read it to you?"

I shake my head, wiping my eyes dry before I start

again, this time breathing through the onslaught of emotions and feelings.

My beautiful Ava,
I don't know where to start. Maybe I should start
by saying how sorry I am that I've hurt you. But
I'm not the good guy. I'm not a hero. I'm the villain.
And I warned you—I would do anything for you.
Once you're mine there's nothing I won't do to
keep you. To make you happy. There's nothing I
won't do to look after you and what's yours.
It just didn't start off that way.
I gave your father the chance to save Monroe from
the very beginning. But he was too proud, and
when he finally had to ask for help, he still
wouldn't concede that his ship was sinking. So, I
put as many holes in it as I could to make it sink
faster.
And when the other houses started sniffing around,
I had to make sure that I took his best asset. You.
You were the ultimate bargaining chip. Your father
was always so careful at keeping you away from
things—I thought he was protecting you. I thought
he would do anything for you.
He didn't, and it's why I made sure you took from
him everything he was willing to take from you. I
wanted him to see everything he'd underestimated.
I wanted him to fear you, like he feared me.
I wanted him to see everything I saw.
The passion. The fight. The care. The love.
Everything I had come to love and admire.
But he reduced it all to petty crumbs to dust his

*pockets, and even when he handed me Monroe on
a platter, I couldn't take it from you.
I couldn't betray you. I couldn't fathom letting
you go.
That was the first time I ever feared losing some-
thing—you.
It meant working out a different way of saving
Monroe. So that in the end, no matter what, it's
yours. Like it should always have been.
You are the only loss I fear, Ava. The only loss I
could never survive.
You are my one and greatest fall.
You.
Always, always yours,
DHC*

Incapable of staunching my tears, I hold the note to my chest, trying to process all that's happened. Trying to find my feet and a clear head because even hurt, I can't bring myself to hate him. Even when it's all I want to do.

CHAPTER TWENTY-SIX

DAMON

Grayson follows me into Dexter's office, and he looks as exhausted as I feel.

"Don't lose your shit," he warns as I walk around the desk and pull out the drawers, emptying them into a cardboard box. "You have to be smart about this. You don't have grounds to fire him."

"The fuck I don't." My fist lands on the desktop with a splintering crunch.

"Damon!"

"What, Grayson?" I spin to face him. "What? He knew what he was doing. It wasn't an accident...it wasn't a mistake."

"I know," he sighs, sitting in one of the desk chairs.

"He hurt Ava." I pick up one of the photos and throw it into the box. "If it were Fran?"

"I would kill him," he says harshly. Standing, he picks up the other empty box and sweeps all the shit that's left on the desk into it. "The best I can do is staff harassment. Ava's assistant is willing to go with it."

"Fine." I go through all the cabinets around the room,

emptying them of anything that's not related to the company.

"Have you heard from her?" Grayson asks when I sit in the other desk chair, beside him.

"No."

My already racing heart starts to thunder through my veins until I'm practically breathless, and all I can hear is the whooshing of my red-hot blood in my ears along with the echo of Lacie's words—*your pregnant girlfriend is falling to pieces.*

This shouldn't be happening. I should be with her. I should be making sure she's all right.

I'm not ready. I'm scared. It's all I've heard on repeat. All night. I'm scared too. I'm fucking afraid she won't come back.

"She needs time," Grayson offers. "She's smart—she'll see the position you've put yourself in for her."

"It's just money."

"Yeah, but the lawsuit and now the share conversion... it's a lot of money. More money than some will see in their lifetime."

"Ava's worth it."

"You love her." He chuckles, looking impressed with himself. "Fran said you would, and I laughed at her."

The office door opens, and Dexter stands there looking between Grayson and me in our casual clothes. "What? Did I miss a memo or something? I'm pretty sure we don't do dress-down Fridays."

"It's not Friday," Grayson spits at him, pulling a letter-sized envelope from his back pocket. "Get your shit and get the fuck out."

I can't believe I ever called him a friend. That I trusted him to help me run my company.

What the fuck was I even thinking?

Dexter looks around the room, and I see it all dawn on his face.

"Really? You're picking a two-bit fuc—" My fist slams to his mouth before he has a chance to finish, and because once wasn't enough, I do it again, and again, until Grayson has me pinned to the wall.

Everything is so fucking blurry. It's all a fucking red haze.

"You're going to regret that," Dexter spits at my feet. The bloody sight of it does nothing to calm my anger as I try to shove Grayson off me.

"Get the fuck out, Dex. You're done here." Grayson finally lets me go, following me as I step to Dexter.

"If you so much as yawn in your fucking dark hole, I'll crush you. You will never see an office in this city again."

Security shows up—I'm guessing Grayson must have called them. I don't know. My fucking head is a mess, my hand is throbbing, and all I can think about is the fact I still haven't heard anything from Ava.

"Right." Grayson throws me his handkerchief. "Let's go."

"Where?"

"You want to win Ava back, don't you?"

"Yes." I wrap the white cotton around my fist.

"What're you waiting for, then?"

CHAPTER TWENTY-SEVEN

AVA

Lacie stumbles in from work. I've managed to make dinner rather than driving myself insane reading all the notes Damon's sent me the last week. Yesterday he told me about his day—it was just another way of telling me he misses me.

I miss him too.

But every time I think I've made sense of everything, that it's not that bad...I remember that he had so many chances to tell me what he was doing. Yet he chose not to. He chose to deceive me, and then he was too much of a coward to face up to the consequences.

"This is crazy. My apartment is becoming a shrine to you." Lacie drops another hatbox of bloodred, velvety roses on the kitchen counter.

"I'm sorry." I grimace as I take the small envelope slotted in the arrangement.

"Are you going to forgive him yet?"

"It's not about forgiveness." I begin to pocket the card, but she grabs it off me, and before I can get it back, she's opened it.

"He found your favorite nail polish." She throws the card at me as she heads toward her room.

"So what?" My yell reverberates through the apartment.

"Many women have taken back bigger, badder bastards for a lot less." Tears fill her eyes. "Do you even realize how lucky you are?"

"I thought you hated him?"

"I do! I hate him and I want to hurt him for all the shit he did." She takes a long breath. "But, look around you. All of this is for you."

Of course, I can't hold up the floodgates. At this point I'm not sure if some of it is hormones or if I'm really just that pitiful.

"You have a man that's desperately fighting for you. Don't be too proud to concede." Lacie disappears into her room.

I go through Damon's notes as I wait for her to emerge. When she doesn't, I go to her. She's curled up on her bed, her phone in her hand.

When I sit beside her, she holds it to her chest.

"Look at the two of us," she sobs. "I'm pining after a man I can't have, and you're pushing the one that cares away."

When she puts it like that, it sounds tragic.

"Do you love Callum?" I hug her to me like she's done to me so many times.

"God, Ava..." Her golden eyes hold mine. "I'm here, but my heart feels like it's all the way across the country beating in someone else's chest. Giving my love to another woman."

"Lace..."

"I can't even be angry because she's his wife, and

what we had—I should never have given in. Or let it happen..."

I brush her copper tresses from her face. "I know that feeling."

"Damon's many things, but you can't deny he cares."

"He bought Monroe behind my back."

The roll of her eyes is sour. "He bought you a company your father was going to sell. Read into the situation however you want, but you were never going to get Monroe. Your father was never going to give it to you."

"But..."

Lacie sits up, wiping her tears. "Get over it or be done. Don't drag it out, okay? You might not want to believe it, but your father is no better than Damon. He's only better at hiding it."

"Why didn't he tell me though? Why?"

"Because he knew you'd see the worst and run. And what's more? He was right."

"I didn't—"

"Don't. Lie. To. Yourself. It's why you won't let him see you. You won't talk to him...because you know that if you really listen to him, you'll want to take him back." She lies back down.

I lie beside her. "I don't want to be bought. I don't want to be that woman. He bought Monroe, and now he's buying me all these things..."

"He's not buying those notes. He's sending you a piece of him."

"I know." I turn to her. "It's what makes it so difficult to keep him away."

"Do you love him? Like really love him? To the point that you want to have that baby and watch him be a father to it every day for the rest of your life? Fuck Monroe.

Fuck CPM. Fuck every other fucking excuse you can come up with. Do you love Damon?"

"My heart is somewhere in this city, beating in someone else's chest, and I don't think he knows it."

"Only you can fix that."

"I know."

"Good," she sings nasally as she gets up from the bed. Her eyes are still red, but there's a smile on her face. "What're you waiting for?"

"What?" I sputter as she pulls me to my feet and starts pulling me along behind her.

"No time like the present, babe. Let's get you to your baby daddy."

"Do you want me out that bad?" I jerk out of her hold.

"Babe, I love ABBA as much as the next person, but you have taken it to another level. And if he's going to send you a mixtape of the same couple of songs...he can put up with your ass."

"I haven't played it that much."

"My head is so fucked with it, that I'm mixing the ABBA lyrics with Patti Smith's. And also, FYI, did you know she's got hairy armpits on the cover of the album?"

"Eww!"

"Exactly. Thanks to you and asshat, all I'm going to think about when I listen to the damn song is hairy armpits." She's about to walk us out of the door, when I pull back.

"Lace, I need to wash, and I need to sleep because I am exhausted. Not to mention I'm so hungry he'd probably freak out that I'm starving his child."

She grins wide, pushing me back into her apartment. "I can't believe you're actually pregnant."

"Yeah, me either." I head into the kitchen with her. "Do you know what sucks?"

"We can't drink anymore?"

Ugh, I'm beginning to understand Fran's weird thing about sniffing alcohol. But... "No. Sore boobs. What if I have to go braless for like the next nine months. Because pregnancy actually lasts for ten months. Biggest fucking lie the world has ever told."

"Babe, you got yourself a sugar daddy...he bought you a company, and he's sending you two-hundred-dollar hatboxes of roses..."

"Aren't sugar daddies old men?"

"Are they?"

We side-glance at each other. *How do we not know this?*

"Google?" we blurt at the same time, bursting into a fit of laughter.

CHAPTER TWENTY-EIGHT

DAMON

William is standing at his desk with a weird-ass expression on his face. When I put his coffee down on his desk, he looks up at me with a nod of thanks.

"I need you to courier this to Ava this afternoon." I put the package on his desk.

I'm hoping it doesn't backfire, because I think Lacie might actually follow through on her promise to castrate me.

"Umm, Mr. Coldwell..."

My phone chirps with a message from Grayson just as I'm about to head into my office.

Gray: Complication. They're taking the baby out.

My heart stops for a moment while I reread his message. Fran seemed fine last night.

Damon: Keep me updated.

"William, can you arrange for a driver to pick up my mom and bring her into the city, please?" I ask him as I walk into my office.

Now I'm fucking on edge. Or more on edge, especially given I haven't seen Ava in almost two weeks. I'm not even meant to know she's pregnant, but...fuck it.

Damon: Let me know you're okay.

There's a low trill, and as I look up from my phone, I swear I could cry.

"I'm okay," she says with a long breath.

"You're here." I'm certain I sound like an idiot, but I'm in disbelief that she's in my office. And she looks so fucking beautiful it's a sin.

Her long, raven hair is tousled into relaxed waves, and a patterned scarf is tied around her head, keeping it all from her face. Her eyes are so blue and her lips so lusciously peachy that I have no idea how she's real.

Standing from the chair in front of my desk, her short red dress falls to the middle of her thighs. With legs for days and supple glowing skin, I'm using every ounce of my control not to descend on her like the predator inside me is desperate to do.

"I wanted to give you this...in person." She extends an envelope my way.

I recognize the damn thing, and I wish I'd burnt it the first time.

"I'm not letting you leave," I tell her, taking the thing from her. I'm about to rip it when her hand holds mine. "Open it."

"Only if you sit."

Smiling, she sits back in her seat. I don't bother

rounding to my own chair; I perch myself on the desk, in front of her.

Her legs cross and her hands lace over her belly, and my heart starts beating so fast in my chest at the knowledge that there's a piece of me growing inside her.

"I won't accept it, so...I'm not letting you go."

"Damon! Open the damn thing!"

"Fine." I open the envelope and take out the letter.

Ava's looking at me intently as I turn it in my hand. She seems as nervous as I am.

"Open it," she whispers. Her voice is a little wet like she's close to tears.

"Okay."

I hold her stare for a second longer, wondering how the hell I'm meant to let her go, if that's what she wants.

"Damon."

I unfold it, turning the page over and over in my hand. "It's blank."

"It's clean," she corrects. "A clean page for a fresh start."

Ava stands, taking the paper from me and putting it on the table.

"I don't want Monroe."

"Ava..."

"I want you and only you. None of the bullshit. None of the lies." Hands falling to my knees, she steps between my thighs. "I want the ruthless man that will protect me and our family at any cost, but I want to be a part of it. Do you understand?"

"Yes." My hands band her waist, and with a sigh, she comes closer, her front flush to mine as she takes one of my hands and brings it to her belly. "Good, because I have no idea how I'm going to do this mom thing."

I'm not sure if she's aware I know or whether she's nervous to tell me. Regardless, it feels so surreal knowing that we've made something so monumental together. That beneath my hand, inside her belly, there's a part of us that will forever be entwinned in one perfect being.

It's fucking mind-blowing.

"We'll figure it out."

She pauses, looking up at me with big rounded eyes full of wariness. "You already know."

"Lacie might have let it slip when she was threatening to cut my balls and feed them to me?"

"Oh God." She cringes, pressing my hand a little tighter to her belly. "I'm sorry."

"Yeah, well...I guess someone has to keep me in line."

There's a moment of silence where Ava just stares at me, like she's trying to make sense of everything in her head. And it reminds me of Fran, the way she agonized over what to do and how to tell Grayson. How afraid she was of all the things that could go wrong, and now...

My phone becomes weightier in my pocket. Maybe I should've asked more questions? May I should've called her? But the logical part of me knows that they need to focus on whatever's happening, not on my worry. Just as I know that Ava needs me to tell her that "Everything will okay. We'll figure it all out."

"Together?" Her question is tentative.

"Together," I assure her. My hands sweep down to her hips as I stand and then perch her in my place.

"How are you so calm?" Nuzzling into my chest, she tucks her hands into the top of my slacks, at the top of my ass. "I'm freaking out."

"Makes a change, huh?"

She peers up at me from my chest. "Seriously?"

"You're here, Ava, that's all that matters. You're here and you're mine." Cupping her face, I thumb over her cheeks.

"I'm yours..." she murmurs. "Because..."

"Because."

"Because." Her full lips stretch into a teary smile. "I love you, Damon. Beyond reason and right or wrong. I love every part of you, even the ones I hate. I think I might love those more..." She swallows and then adds, "Asshole."

A chuckle vibrates through me, and for the first time since she left, my heart relaxes, skipping and stuttering over its slowing beats. And it's all because of her. My beautiful Ava.

"You can't call me that forever." I tip her face up to mine, taking my fill of her. I'm completely lost in her silver-speckled cerulean eyes.

"Ass. Hole." She cranes her neck, bringing her lips closer to mine.

"That sounds like an invitation."

"God, just shut up and kiss me already." Her mouth presses to mine with the plush lower lip pushing past the seam of my lips. Teeth grazing my flesh, she sighs in that way you do when you're home after a shit day.

With her hands clambering up my chest, to my shoulders, she moans as I lick into her mouth, sating my overwhelming thirst for her.

"I love you, little mouse," I murmur over her lips, pressing another kiss.

"Why do you call me that?"

"Sounds better than Reepicheep." Tracing her jaw with the tip of my nose, I breathe her in. I fill my lungs with her scent like it's the only thing I'll ever need to keep me alive.

"What the hell is Reepicheep?"

"The mouse leader from Narnia. You know, passionate, gentle, fearless, and honorable." Planting a kiss behind her ear, I suck at the sensitive spot, laving and nipping until she's a trembling, breathless mess. "They're all the things I love about you, little mouse."

Her arms wrap around my neck, meshing her body to mine. "Take me home?"

"Every fucking day, baby."

"Forever?" Her legs wrap around my hips, pulling herself up from my desk until she's latched onto me completely.

"And ever." I walk her to my open door, William is nowhere in sight. So, I take a moment to let my hands wander over the curve of her ass and her thighs. I take my time tracing the contours of her body pressed to mine.

Opening the door to the floor, I stand her on her feet. There's a moment of bashfulness when she sees William's assistant staring up at us. But before she can get weird about it, I walk her down the corridor.

"This is not the way out." She looks up at me confused.

"Well observed." I stop her in front of the freshly scraped door before I take her in.

"Why are we in Dexter's office?" Turning to me, she tries to push us out.

"He's gone."

"What do you mean he's gone?"

I walk her to the new desk that Fran and Mom picked out to go with the new interior design. Something to keep them both from getting involved in my efforts to win Ava back.

"He's no longer an employee." Pulling her chair out, I sit her in it, crouching in front of her. "He hurt you, so I hurt him. It's how it's always going to be. No one hurts you, and if they do, I hurt them. You understand?"

She nods with a swallow.

"This is for you." I turn her to the desk, where the contract between us and her father sits. "The share breakdown is on the back."

She flits to it, and I give her a moment to take it in. "You broke it down to shares?"

"It was the right thing to do. You have fifty-one, your father has twenty-nine, and I have twenty. I don't own Monroe; we all do. And one day, your father's share will be yours."

"I don't want it, Damon." She looks at me with tear-lined eyes. "I can't let you take that loss for me."

"It's your legacy, Ava, and you can make it great. But more importantly, I want our child to have that." Perching on the edge of the desk, I take the contract from her. "Don't let anyone steal your thunder. Ever."

She tenses at the knock on the open door, and when she finds the person there, a smile softens her face.

"Good morning, Miss Monroe." Bianca walks in with the package I gave William earlier. "This just came for you."

William stands at Bianca's desk with a grin on his face.

"Thank you." Ava takes the box and sits it in front of her, staring up at me with a bashful tip of her lips while her assistant leaves us again, closing the door. "It's from you."

"Open it."

"Stop with the gifts, okay?"

"Just open the damn thing, Ava."

She does, reticently, and then she stares at the contents.

"I should've told you earlier." Pulling out the lobster plush pacifier, she cringes, holding it to her chest. "I'm sorry."

"It's okay."

"No, it's not. I was angry and upset and...I did something I knew was wrong." One of her hands reaches up, holding my jaw. "You should've been the first person to know. I should've told you."

Yeah, I wish I'd heard it from her, but at the end of the day, we're both to blame for everything that happened.

"If I'd been honest and open with you, you would've been the same with me. I can't hold it against you. Not with how it all happened. I'm just glad you had someone there with you. Even if it wasn't me. And I really fucking wish it had been me."

Dropping her hand to mine, she brings it to her cheek and nuzzles into it. "No more secrets."

"No more." I pull the photo frame from the box, standing it on her desk.

A photo Fran snuck of us in the Hamptons. It's not all that clear because she took it at a distance and in dim light, like the crazy stalker she is. But Ava's obviously smiling up at me in Mom's kitchen. Her arms are wrapped around my bare chest, and she looks as happy as I remember feeling in that moment.

"Do you have some kind of obsession with crustaceans?" She fingers the hand-painted lobsters Mom painted onto the plain white frame, to match the ones on Jo's paper plates.

"I do now. The way you ate that lobster roll...holy fuck, baby."

"Oh my God! Stop!" Her face flushes a bright crimson that makes me laugh.

"What? I'm just saying...it left an impression." Standing, I take her up with me. She's still clutching the pacifier to her chest. "You like it, huh?"

"It's the cutest thing. It's almost got me all excited."

"Almost excited?" I walk us back to my office to collect our things. "We're going to have a baby. It's fucking terrifying."

"What?"

"Babies are the ultimate cockblockers."

"You're an asshole." She slaps my chest, and grabbing her arm, I pull her to me.

Her body melts into mine. Soft and warm. Everything a home should be.

"I love you," I tell her, crushing my mouth to hers.

And I kiss her until she's trembling and breathless. Until my lungs burn for air and my heart feels so full, it might burst in my chest.

EPILOGUE

AVA

I'm nervous. Anxious as hell after all that happened with Fran. I've got every freaking thing crossed that everything is normal. Dr. Cruz walks in with her usual smile, and Damon's standing beside me, drumming his thumb on my shoulder because we're both shitting ourselves.

"Are you ready to see your baby?" She squirts some jelly on my already exposed stomach. It's cold and it sends a shudder through me as she starts to spread it with the ultrasound probe.

Damon lowers himself to perch his chin on my shoulder as she continues going over my barely noticeable bump.

"You doing okay?" he murmurs into my ear, taking one of my hands laced over my chest.

I manage to smile through my racing heart and constricted chest. It's fallen so quiet in here; all I can hear are the air particles vibrating around us.

"Okay!" Dr. Cruz turns the screen to face us. "Everything looks great."

"So, everything is in the right place?" Damon asks her.

"Everything is as it should be, yes. Perfectly normal. Baby is a nice size at this point. Placenta has good blood flow."

"Two hands?" I can't help but burst out laughing at his question.

"Two good hands and two dancing feet." Moving the probe around, she points out all the vital organs and limbs to back up her statement. Looking at me with a knowing smile, she says, "A good heart too."

The galloping thrum surrounds us, and all the worry and anxiety I've managed to push down over the last few months loosens its vise around me, and relief floods me. My eyes cloud over, and the most overpowering awe fills me.

"How's that for a strong heartbeat?"

That's what undoes me, because I can't stop the sobs that escape me with the way Damon's looking at me, eyes glassed over and a half-bitten grin cutting his face.

"Wow," he mouths, wiping away the tears tracking down my temples.

And this is by far the most incredible moment of my life. The happiness is overwhelming, like it might be too much for us to contain. I'm not even sure there's such a thing as too much happiness, but if there is...this is it. Right here, right now. Me and him...and our baby.

The promise of an eternity together. No matter what the future brings us.

THE END

ABOUT THE AUTHOR

Alexandra Silva is a tequila loving book hoarder living in London. She writes about real people who have to fight for their happy endings. Her stories are raw, heartfelt and sexy. With heroes that are flawed, dirty and sweet, and feisty heroines who give them a run for their money. Contemporary and Dark romance are her jam with some suspense to keep you on the edge of your seat.

You can connect with Alex here:
Reader Group

Printed in Poland
by Amazon Fulfillment
Poland Sp. z o.o., Wrocław

57021896R00333